good deed rain

THE SYLVAN MOORE SHOW

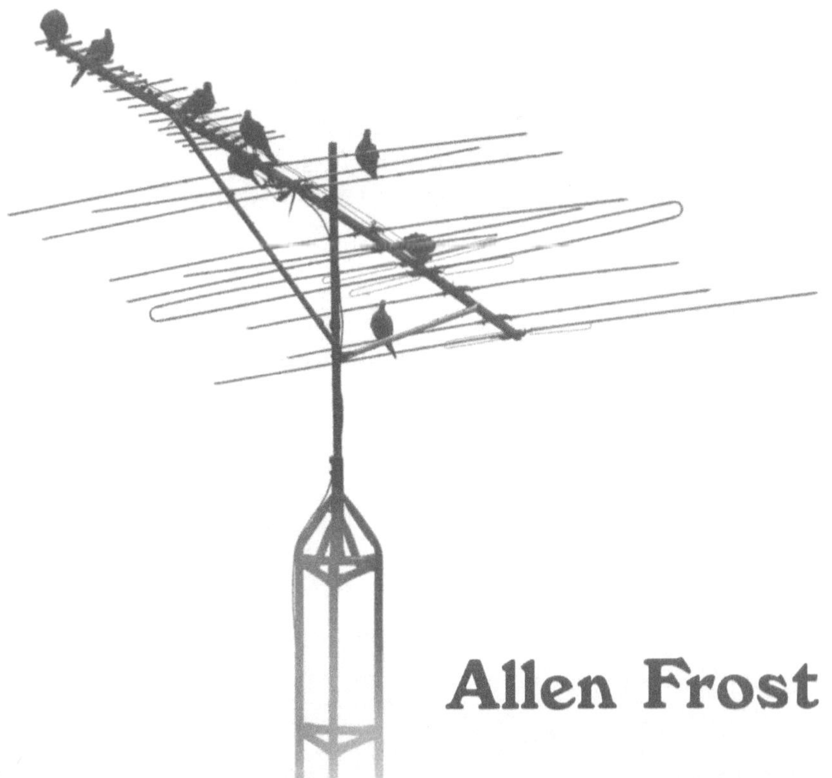

Allen Frost

Credits:
Production and Layout: Fred Sodt
Covers Design and Title Page: Michael Paulus
Writing: Allen Frost. Stories: 1982-2015
Cover Photo and Drawings: Allen Frost
Back Cover Photo: Brian Smith
Apple by TFK!
Thank you to Larry Smith for continuing support

If you have enjoyed this book
please share it with someone

INTRODUCTION

WHILE THIS IS MY SECOND collection of short stories and may seem to be a sequel to *The Wonderful Stupid Man*, it's really more of a double feature to be read with that previous book. And whereas *T.W.S.M* is an old movie house, red curtains rattling aside for those stories to glow, this new collection is a bit different.

These stories still seem written for a *Twilight Zone* or *Outer Limits* TV program that no longer exists. So this time I made my own show, hosted by the ghostly presence of Sylvan Moore. Sylvan Moore nearly made an appearance in *T.W.S.M.* but at the last second I cut his story "Now You Got Me Lost." It shows up in this book instead. A sort of Johnny Carson/Rod Serling, he has starred in a few of my stories and even a novel or two.

You will also notice the appearance of several stories about Richard throughout the collection. They sort of hold the book together like seams. Richard used to visit me at work and he inspired me with his stories; adventures from Hollywood to homeless, they remind me of F. Scott Fitzgerald's *Pat Hobby Stories*.

This book began as a compilation of just longer, mostly recent stories, but then I thought it would be more entertaining to add shorter works too, some of them like little commercials placed between the longer shows. And that decision was all it took. It was like I opened a door to another floor. All of a sudden I was drawn back in time—thirty three years!—this book really got me thinking about where I had been, to stories I had nearly forgotten.

This collection is pretty much ordered chronologically, the majority of stories coming from the Golden Age of my *Pie in the Sky* magazine in the early 1990s. This was a time when adventurous imagination was the main ingredient. There are recurring characters you'll meet like the stars of old B-movies:

Jack Shellac, The Flammable Man, Posie Crutchfield, and there are also more recent ones like Jakob Kale and Delory Martel. I hope you greet them all like old friends.

And of course there's the infamous Dr. Biocal…He's quite the sight. His name came from a mailing label I misread at a job I once had. But how much of a B-movie villain is he anyway? What does he do that's so diabolical, with his failed experiments, his machineries of joy, lust, loneliness and love, birds and botany? Always reaching out for Susan Fenton, I guess he was nothing more than the phantom of a lonely writer.

Which brings up another point of interest—who was that writer anyway? The memory returns. I can recall what I went through, though sometimes I wish I couldn't. Forget is a button you can press or suppress or put into stories. Stories become powerful little secrets, captured emotions labeled in jars. There may be some stories that seem a bit goofy in today's light, but at the time they were part of my world, as anyone who remembers that age, or is still there, will know.

It's a strange journey, retracing my steps as a writer. Just like a short story, as the author travels back in time to rediscover and shepherd stories from out of the past (some of them have been hiding in boxes and yellow envelopes for years) he also finds that much younger self. It's been a long, long time, but I still remember how it felt. I know the heart was first, expected to lead all forward. And I know you were waiting, always waiting for these stories to be gathered into a book even if it didn't seem like it would ever happen.

There were a lot of rejection letters too. Sending out stories was always the hardest part for me. Still is. My first rejection in 1983 advised: "I can only remind you that almost all good writers experience rejection slip after rejection slip, sometimes with manuscripts which eventually are accepted and become widely read. Richard Brautigan submitted *Trout Fishing in America* to 25 publishers before it was accepted." For me, this was the first mention of Brautigan, who would soon become a very big influence.

And that's part of the story too. Along the way other books appear like spirits on a totem pole. For instance, while editing this book, I discovered Jack Finney's wonderful story collection, *The Third Level*. It's a great comfort and inspiration knowing there are authors out there traveling the same path.

It's got to be one of the lonelier things to devote your life to. It doesn't seem possible to make a living by writing anymore, although for a long time I had a lot of different jobs and a lot of them became stories. I don't even know how many people read books anymore. It seems rare these days to see someone holding one. Which just makes them all the more magical, doesn't it?

For this book I have dipped way down in the well. I'm including what I consider my first professional story, "The Hangman Calls Paris," written in high school and modified only slightly. I remember how excited I was when I wrote this and how it made me feel like T.S. Garp (from the John Irving movie that came out that year) and I was a writer at the start of my career.

One of the miracles of reading this is seeing where that journey took me.

An entire parade of characters and adventures awaited that door in Paris and that little flake of paint.

With that in mind, for what it's worth, allow my advice through an old tin can string telephone because this collection is also meant for other young writers. Go into those mysterious rooms of your imagination, fear not, have faith in your creation, and if all you get are rejections, make your own magazine, make your own books. We can do that now!

Even back in the days of PIE, when I was making only a couple copies of each magazine, I always had faith that the writing would be seen and enjoyed. I knew it would just take a while. Time would prepare it for you. That is, if you are holding it now, tuned in and ready for the adventure, my wish was granted and it's happening.

Wandering around backstage at *The Sylvan Moore Show*, the lights are out, the cameras off, the studio building is huge and all the sets and stages go on and on into the dark. It's alright though: you've been given an exclusive pass. You can walk past the facades of buildings, backlots and fields, there's a section of moon, white and dusty, supermarkets and little stores, apartments, parking lots, boats and bathtubs, airplanes and trees. Walking around in this place, you can see where every story happened. You can pull up a chair and find yourself there, where it begins nine pages from here.

It is a starry night in the 20th Century.

Allen Frost
Bellingham, Washington
July 4, 2015

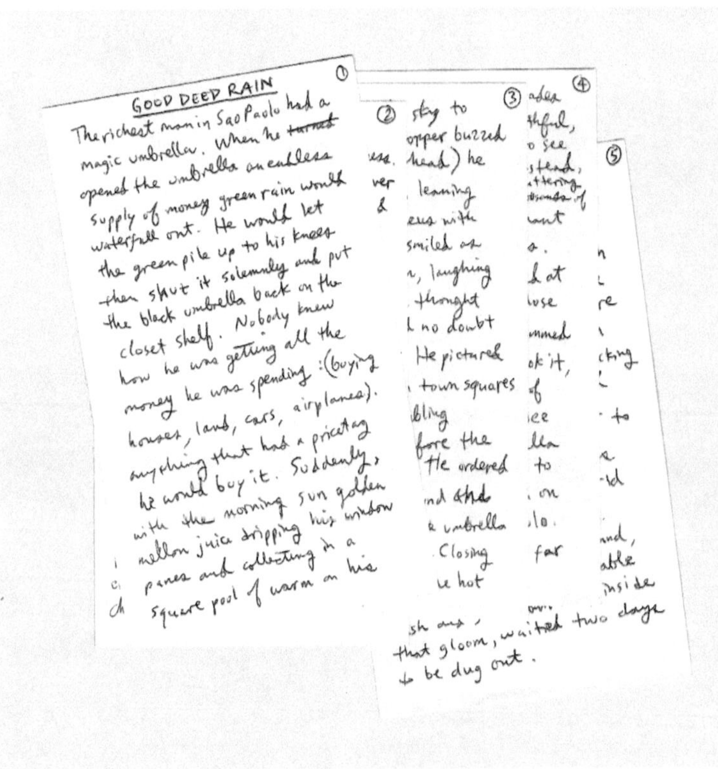

Notecards I made for "Good Deed Rain" story, possibly for radio reading in 1989.

CONTENTS

The Mae West Test   17
The Creep at Midnight   25
Mars Needs Women   30
Remember With Television   32
Drive Slowly and Carefully   35
Good Deed Rain   36
Custer's Last, Last Stand   38
Buckethead   40
Mammud, Muhammad and Mike   42
Invest in Phil Donahue   45
No, Clarence Is Not Here   47
Ant Attraction   48
Wallflower   49
Magnets and Invisible Threads   50
The Case of the Insomniac Vacuum Cleaners   52
Agricultural Revolution   54
The Flammable Man   56
B. Franklin's Discovery of Electricity   57
Gravity Lighthouse   58
OK, I'll Never See You Again   59
William Carlos Williams for Beginners   60
Wishing   61
Tying the Sheets Together To Make a Ladder   64
Decoys   66
The Cartoon Man   68
Jack Shellac's Art Shack   69
Mickey Gillay!   70
The Shakespeare Reader   73
Saint George and the Dragon   85
Mexican Dog Biscuits   90
The Sidekick   91
The Shuffler   95

Instant Cash for Guns and Flowers   97
Monster Night   98
In the Circus   99
The Hot Water Prayer   102
Dream with Mexicans and Floating Lions   103
Moving Cactus   104
Les Falls Out of a Tree   106
Something Bright Was Supposed To Be Waiting   107
Stella Winks   108
The Beautiful Trapeze   121
Posie Crutchfield at the Seashore   122
Earth's Hero and the Sunny American Town   123
Listening to the Flammable Man   124
The Mystery of the Flammable Woman   125
The Moon Was All the Mouse Could Think About   126
Dewie the Dormouse and Toad Ricky   127
The Flammable Man Somewhere   128
Dr. Biocal's New Terror   129
Posie Crutchfield and the Bee Tree   132
Jack Shellac's Back   133
Imitating the Call of Birds   134
Dr. Biocal, At It Again   135
It's Fes Smurlo and Milo T. Smiley   138
A Bargain with Emily Dickinson   140
Turning a City into a Garden   141
A Blue Ocean Voyage   143
The Green Pool   145
My Brush with the Belateds   150
A Pair of Clouds   158
Things of the Morning   160
Imagine the Things I Will See and Know   161
In This Night of Grasshopper Swinging Stars   162
The Underwater World   163
Jack Shellac's Bric-A-Brac   164
The Poor Turnip   167

Snappy Pete's Ankle Complete   168
The Rain   169
The Flammable Man Remembers   170
Bird on a Branch   173
She Spins the Round   176
An Ordinary Man   178
Jack Shellac on a Railroad Track   180
Guarantee   182
Turkey Legs   183
Now You Got Me Lost   187
Black Space Orbit   191
Ukrop's Artificial Orange   200
Wyzzler's Mother   202
Rat Trapped   205
The Phone Rings like a Woman   210
The Hangman Calls Paris   215
One of Them   224
The Man with 6 Fingers   226
The Curse of Holler Farm   229
The Small House   232
Rebicycle   234
Sapped   237
Recalled   239
The Alligator   243
Loretta's Bicycle   245
The Astronaut's Mother   248
The Urge to Laugh   249
A Photo with Sylvan Moore   252
The Great Mysterio   255
Another Land   256
Snappy Pete's Thrones of Many Feet   257
Dr. Biocal and the Element of Joy   259
Posie Crutchfield in the Apple Tree   262
Toad Ricky Returns for a Waterfall   264
Posie Crutchfield in Butterflied   265

Herman Snock Steals the Sun   267
The Tuesday Morning Girl   268
Jack Shellac, the Favorite Snack   269
Snappy Pete's Life in Montana   273
Tree Shadow   274
Rabbit   276
Dr. Biocal and the Voice of Love   277
The Pollywog Dog   279
Moth and Child   280
The Wooden Man, Her Rocking Chair   281
Backtrack to the Art Shack with Jack Shellac   282
Dr. Biocal's Surprise   284
The Village Idiot and the Town Crier   286
The Little Blue Sad Man   287
A Slice of Air of Billboard Size   288
Pauline Clock Landed Today   290
Posie Crutchfield in the Land of Sand   292
Invisibly Finding the Honey of Bees   294
I Give the Air a Flying Fish   295
She and He See the Sea Differently   296
Susan Fenton Misses the Birds   298
Falling Off Ground   300
The Japanese Sparrow   302
Made in China   306
Sidney Leaves, Your Ego Has Arrived   309
See Sidney Leaves' Life   311
Return of the Paperboy   314
Hubcaps of Detroit   315
Why the Stars Are Not Ours Anymore   316
Beedler's Welcome   317
The President's Tailor   319
One Way Suit   321
The Teether   322
The Silver Dollar Man   323
Dust and Feathers: The Television Series   324

Lou Jersey Excused Himself   325

Humpty Dumpty in the Haunted House   326

Three Masquerades   328

The Horse   332

American Stars at Night   337

The Boy Who Spoke Robot   339

Ronald Orkinson   340

More Experiments with Radio   343

1959   344

The Not-Doing Detective   345

Richard's Mouse   346

Delory Martel   347

A Television Movie   349

North   350

The Blue Parrot   351

Old Flowers   352

Martian Tigers   353

The Sound of Birds   354

Half-White Speckled Bird   355

Nameless Trees   358

The Wishing Well Walrus   359

Once Upon a Time, Mr. Tim   360

Son of a Beehive   361

What the Man on the Moon Brought Home   362

The Darkness of Another World   363

Peso VS El Condor   366

Joliet   368

Local Man Captures Alligator   372

Two Paper Birds   375

The Centaur in the Park   378

The Timesaver   381

A Morning in November   383

In the Cover of Clouds   385

They Don't Last Long   389

The Pearl Collector   391

Cars and Radios   393
Ice Cream Every Day   394
Starring Lillian Gish   396
Dream Job   398
A Pocket Problem   401
Dr. Biocal Steals the Spring   403
The Airplane Man   408
Out of One World into Another   411
Abandoned Television Stars   413
Delory Martel's History of Monsters   415
When I'm a Deer   427
Thanksgiving Street   428
The Three Hearted Saint   430
Jack's Cow   432
Ed Storey, the 2 Story Man   434
Battleship   437
Smile Repair   439
Mooncalf Press   442
The Sleeping Contest   445
The Cartoon Goat   449
The Beautiful Days   457

THE MAE WEST TEST

Richard lived just outside Hollywood in a brownstone apartment. Sometimes it was used by the film studios as a New York backdrop. It had that look. One night, walking home, Richard saw the bright lights and film trucks humming and the tall silhouette of Jack Palance passed him. Richard almost said something, but Jack was in a different world. The only part of him in this world was his legs walking him. At first Richard thought he wanted to be in that rarified air, he had been studying the craft for two years, but now he didn't know. He wanted something else. He wrote stories.

That's what took him to the public library. To be a writer called for research. There were books filled with publishers and agents and awards and advice. That was all well and good, but sometimes a different road will get you there.

He pulled down the thick directory of actors and actresses, cradled it against his arm and carried it to a long green table. Only an old man at the end was sitting there writing. Richard paged through face after face. He sort of thought he might want to write to a few, get some advice, if nothing else collect some photographs and autographs. This was Hollywood. Someday people would ask him about it. As he looked through that book, he also thought about the stories he wrote. One of those stars might see his worth and lift him up to shine.

Then he stopped at Mae West. Here was someone, a woman in her seventies or eighties, he pictured with the time to read what he wrote and maybe reply. Wasn't that possible? Back when he was a kid, living on the farm thousands of miles away, he would spend the whole day next to the field in the shade of the trees, dreaming. Richard took down her agent's address and before he left the library he checked out *Good Had Nothing to Do with It,* her autobiography.

That book sat beside him that evening as he wrote her a letter. He told her he enjoyed her movies and he included a couple of his short stories. He really didn't know what would happen. Maybe it didn't make a lot of sense but who really knew? You were already in a dreamworld just living here.

Only a week later, Richard got a letter back. Outside the lobby, there was another film crew on the street outside. It looked like a police drama. He saw someone in a suit running back and forth, take after take, but Richard didn't care. The stationary inside the envelope was from Mae West's secretary. It was an invitation to meet her at her home.

That day, Richard drove there. He tried the radio but none of the songs were right for what he was about to do, meet the woman who rode in a carriage with W.C Fields across the Wild West. All the traffic lights were green; he was there before he knew it. He parked and sat in his car outside Ravenswood Apartments, the tall white tower where she lived way at the top. He didn't want to be too early for the appointment and he certainly didn't want to be late.

That's when Richard made his first mistake. At least, he figured that out later. He had time to kill so he lit up a cigarette. He thought of something he read in her book. For some of her meals Mae West would drink calf's blood. He squinted up at that top floor and thought of that while the old car filled with smoke.

An ash hit his leg and he scuffed it away. He brushed at the gray mark it left on his blue suit. The cigarette filled him and clung to his clothes and it was still months before he would return to her book and read that Mae West detested cigarettes.

The dashboard clock told him when it was time to go, so he stepped out of that fog into the California sunshine.

The sidewalk took him to a giant pair of palm trees cupped around the Ravenswood entrance. Just inside the doorway in the lobby, Richard was stopped by a guard who was sitting at a desk. There was a gun on the man's belt. Richard said he was there to see Mae West. The guard asked for I.D and Richard gave him his driver's license. The guard made a phone call. After a few words, the guard, said, "Yes, they're expecting you," and he took him to the elevator.

Richard was the only passenger as the elevator climbed the six stories. He brushed at the creases on his suit. He kept his other arm drilled into his pocket. If he was nervous he told himself this was just part of the business, it was no more than another audition and he concentrated on the numbers lighting while he floated off the ground.

The doors slid open on a still hallway. He could hear his shoes crush into the carpet to her door, 611. He pressed the button. It didn't take more than a moment for a young man to open the door and invite him in.

Richard stepped into the nineteenth century—everything was Mid-Victorian, curtains, gilded chairs, paintings on the walls, and all of it dressed out in white. Everything seemed to be in done in a satin finish.

Her secretary introduced himself as Robert and asked Richard to please sit down. He pointed at a chair. It looked so delicate Richard was afraid. Everything seemed so fragile in the room.

"You think it will break?" Richard asked.

But Robert laughed and assured him with a smile. He asked, "Would you like something to drink?"

Richard didn't know, his mouth was suddenly parched. Maybe he asked him for a glass of water.

They must have spent ten or fifteen minutes talking. Richard was aware he was being tested but he felt so at home, so relaxed. Robert was so kind, that Richard spoke animatedly and happily, made jokes and laughed as he told Robert all about himself.

Richard saw a maid walk through, a black lady, tall, a hefty build. There was something about her though…She didn't look like a maid. She was dressed like one, but Richard thought to himself, she looked like she knew karate or something. In case he got out of hand, Richard thought. She moved through the room stiffly, carrying the prop of a duster, watching him sternly until she exited stage left.

Then Robert introduced Richard to Mae West.

How long had she been standing there? Or had she just appeared?

"Robert," she said, "Could you leave us alone for a while?"

When Robert left, that's when Richard began to feel uncomfortable.

Mae West had these eyes, very penetrating, velvet eyes. They weren't brown, they weren't blue. They were velvet. And they were piercing eyes. They seemed to know everything about him, digging into his soul, knowing all, his everyday life, his present, future and past.

She didn't say much, she let Richard try to talk and when he brought up the writing he sent her, she said, "I enjoyed your stories. I can tell you have talent."

"Well, thank you very much," Richard said.

And then she said, "But I have another idea. You seem to have a lot of energy, a lot of personal charisma. Have you ever thought about being an actor?"

Richard laughed. Like a windup mouse, he spun and unwound his story, his two years spent at the Pasadena Playhouse, his leading role in Darkness at Noon. He surprised himself. He came to her to see what she thought about his stories, and here he was talking all about acting!

She didn't say anything. She just listened and watched. Her eyes were piercing but she had a quiet demeanor like a spider sizing up the fly just before it jumps. But he told her he was giving up acting. "I'm an unknown," he said, "It's tough enough to have the Hollywood build and look, tons of talent and what are your chances of making a living as an actor?"

"Well, Richard," she said. "I see that you're disabled. You have only the one hand. Is that why you got away from acting?"

Richard moved in that delicate bone-like chair.

"I could help you get started in film," she said. She told him the story how she discovered Roddy MacDowell and there was Cary Grant too. "Richard, I'll tell you what. I know the president of a small company. They make prosthetics for veterans. I can set up an appointment for you. They can fit you for a hand."

She was leading him already, maybe since the moment he stepped inside Ravenswood, and even though a part of him remembered, I don't want that, I just came here to get her feedback on some stories, he fell in.

"After you get fitted," she continued, "I'm going to be at a nightclub in Van Nuys."

"Will you be entertaining?"

"No. I'm just going to sit with friends and I have a couple of people who will showcase their singing." Richard got the feeling she had her hands in a lot of things. Even though she told him she wasn't acting in anything she was still involved.

"Are you planning to do any acting now?" Richard asked. Because he knew once you're bitten by that it's really hard to let go.

"No. Not really."

Richard told her, "I think you'd be great in something."

She smiled and got up from her chair and that's when Richard turned himself into a total fool. Except that's not entirely true. He didn't think of it that way until later.

"Richard, would you like an autographed photo?" she said. She moved to a desk and opened a drawer. She looked through it and started to search. She sighed and opened another drawer and still couldn't find a photo. She pushed that drawer closed and went through more things.

In those moments Richard saw Mae West as something different. He didn't see Diamond Lil, in a stagecoach, a steamship or sparkling gown. Richard saw a distressed, confused old woman and he didn't want her to be disturbed by it, rattled by a photo and he said, "That's okay. I have your book. There are pictures of you in there."

That was it. She froze. She called Robert back into the room. "Robert," she said icily, "Show this gentleman to the door."

In a matter of moments, Richard was gone, out of the white room, down the waiting elevator, across the lobby and watched by the guard, out the doors with the palm trees, propelled by the hot sunshine back to his car. He opened the unlocked door, got in and he lit a cigarette for company on the drive back home.

Richard didn't feel like thinking about what happened anymore. He blew it, that's all. But just the same, he marked her nightclub show on the calendar. *M. West*…Even though it would be hard to forget that date.

He did wish it had gone differently. If only he hadn't said that about the photo, if only he had more experience talking to a star. Anyway, outside it was a sunny, forgiving day. There were little birds on the sidewalk. The street was empty of film-making machinery, everything was ordinary.

Richard went to the library again. He took another look at that big book. It was strange the power of this book, the adventure it had once taken him on and then dropped him crashing back to the wooden chair in this sunlit library room again.

Staying clear of the back of the book where Mae West resided, Richard paged through the middle and stopped on Arthur O'Connell. Richard copied the address. He could always try again and maybe this time he wouldn't fail. You learn from your mistakes.

When he returned to his apartment late afternoon, there was a letter waiting for him. He opened it with his one hand. It was a notice from the prosthetic company.

So he went. That was an extravagant gift from her and Richard wore that hand, resting it on the wheel, as he drove to Van Nuys, following the traffic and bright lights. This time he wouldn't wait with a cigarette when he got there. He parked his sorry-looking car in the lot and went right inside the nightclub.

It seemed like half that thick library book had been spilled out to fill the place. It was shining with celebrities. They all seemed to glow with halos, but Richard was only looking for one. He saw Mae West at a crowded table and made his way.

She was surrounded but he really didn't notice the other people with her. "Miss West," Richard said. He actually laid his hand on her solid, round shoulder.

She gave him a smile.

"Miss West, I'd like to give you a gift," Richard said suddenly. "I'd like to give you a puppy."

"Oh, that's very nice," she said. "Thank you, but no thank you."

Richard said okay and listened as she told him she wished him all the luck in the world. Hollywood was spinning there but as Richard turned and left the crowded room, he could feel it slip away. It dazzled and purred and left him cold.

THE CREEP AT MIDNIGHT

Patsy Cline did it. But when she went out walking after midnight, she was moving through a different darkness. It's when I go to work, to sit in a glass booth in an underground parking lot and wait impatiently for dawn so I can go home.

It's simple work, sitting on a stool, watching for cars. They just need someone to be vigilant and awake. That's probably why they put the two of us in this booth, me and Anne APori.

There she sits, beautiful inside, wearing the blue uniform sweater and putting on more lipstick, gazing into her reflection. Already I can hear the music she listens to, as I descend out of the moonlight & electricity, on the street, down.

"Good morning, Anne," I say as I slide open the door and step in with her.

"If that telephone rings," she says, "Tell him I'm not here. I went home."

"Tell who?"

"Dennis."

"Oh no." It's going to be another long shift listening to stories about her boyfriends.

"Just tell him I'm not here, okay?"

The phone rang and she stared.

I smiled and went over to the counter.

THE CREEP AT MIDNIGHT

Patsy Cline did it. But when she went out walking after midnight she was moving through a different darkness. It's the time I go to work; to sit in a glass booth in an underground parking lot and wait impatiently for dawn so I can go home.

It's simple work. I sit on a stool and watch cars. They just need someone to be awake and vigilant. That's probably why they put the two of us in this booth—me and Anne Aroni.

There she sits in the booth, so beautiful, wearing the blue sweater uniform and putting on more lipstick. Already, I can hear the music she listens to as I descend out of the moonlight and electricity on the street, down into the lot.

"Good morning, Anne," I say as I slide open the door and step in with her.

"If that telephone rings," she says, "tell him I'm not here. I went home sick."

"Tell who?"

"Dennis."

"Oh no…" It's going to be another long shift listening to stories about her boyfriends.

"Just tell him I'm not here, okay?"

The phone rang and she stared at me.

I smiled and went over to the counter. "Gate Five. Ernie here…" I looked at Anne. She had her hand to her mouth. "No," I said. "She's not here…I'm not sure…Really?" Anne's wide eyes were glued to me. "Okay. I'll tell her that next time I see her. Whenever that is…"

She grabbed my arm as I hung up. "What did he say? What did he want?"

"Anne," I said. "Why do you waste your time with such losers?"

"I don't!" She sat down on the stool and twirled.

"Yeah, I mean they're all winners." I laughed and turned off the radio disco. But she took my hand before I could put my cassette tape in.

She read it. "Johnny Cash?" Just like a bird, my cassette flew out the window and she watched it go, then she looked at me. Her wild eyes batted under her lashes, brilliantly smiling.

"I can't believe you did that!" Of course I could believe she did that, she did things like that to me all the time. Yesterday it was my sandwich, today it was Johnny Cash.

She grinned, shining, waiting.

But I didn't get a chance to do anything. A familiar red truck came down the steep ramp to our lot. Randy Pankow was making the rounds. I heard my tape crunch under the tires as he stopped.

"Hi boss!" Anne leaned out of our window and waved at him.

He got out. All three hundred pounds of him was poured into a Batman suit. The door closed on his cape and it jerked him backwards. Coughing, he opened the door and pulled his cape free. I had learned not to laugh at Randy though; he took himself very seriously. The first time I saw him in his Batman uniform, I nearly had a stroke. It almost cost me my job. Somehow I managed to convince him not to fire me.

"Batman!" I hooted out the window, over Anne's shoulder.

He stood there before us with his hands on his hips, legs spread apart and his head swiveled slowly to the right and left. He surveyed us cautiously before acknowledging us. The long rubber ears on top of his mask nodded when he bowed. "Miss Anne," he said. "Ernie…" He strode over to us, boots squeaking, and he put a gloved hand on the door knob. Flinging the door open, he squeezed between the doorway and halted. "Anything to report?" he wheezed.

Anne told him, "No, sir."

I said, "Just a couple of skateboarders."

"What?!" Randy lurched around and cupped his hands up

to his rubber ears, as if listening with them. "What level?"

I said, "Oh, they're gone now." Anne stared at me, horrified. "We chased them off."

"Good work." He clapped his gloves together and started towards his truck. "Keep a cool head," he said and got back inside. "Farewell!"

We watched his Ford Batmobile rattle up the slope and leave.

Anne pulled my sleeve. "Why did you tell him there were skateboarders?"

"I like it when he springs into action." Taking a look out the window, I added, "I should have told him you were censoring music. You destroyed my tape."

"I didn't," she said. "Randy ran over it! And you're the one who turned off my music in the first place."

A car swooped into the lot, running over the grim plastic remains of Johnny Cash and it stopped next to the window. I let Anne take care of it. I was mad at her. I sat down on the stool and picked up the book she had been reading. "It fig-ures…" I said. It was a romance horror novel called The Creep at Midnight.

Anne gave the driver a permit for his car and she came back over next to me. "That's a great book!"

"Yeah," I said. I started to read it out loud. "Slowly, the vampire pulled himself on top of me. I was paralyzed. His hot breath poured like blood over my skin."

Anne grabbed the thick paperback away from me. "You're making fun of it!"

I reached for it but she held the book behind her back.

"No! You can't see it again. You ruined your chance."

I begged, "Please Anne. I've got to know what happens! Does the vampire bite her? Will she get out of Castle Bloodrock alive?" I tried to get the book again, but she refused.

"No, Ernie. You blew it." In one quick move, she lunged over to her purse and pushed the book inside. "Anyway…" She snapped the latch, "It's time for you to go count cars."

I whined, I apologized, I tried. It was cold outside. "But I did it last time." She wouldn't fall for it though. She had a better memory than me.

"No you didn't! I did!" She pointed to the parking lot, with its four levels of resting cars. "Go!"

I told her, "You're heartless, Anne." I took the clipboard hanging from a nail and opened the door. She was turning her music up as I stepped out and closed the sliding door.

I saw my tape. It was massacred all over the pavement. White plastic and a long string of brown musical tape unspooled itself across the tar leading down to the lower parking levels. The last car must have caught hold of it and dragged it.

I looked back at the booth. Anne was putting on more lipstick. She wasn't paying any attention to me as I held a piece of the broken tape up to my heart like a bereaved widow.

I sighed and started counting cars. There were only five on this level. I marked the clipboard and followed the tape going like a running brown stream flowing down the ramp.

"That girl's got a lot of nerve," I kept thinking. "Throwing my tape out the window…Making me walk out in the cold…" There were even fewer cars on this level. As far and wide as the concrete lot spread, there were only three cars. And still the tape spun downwards, waving a little in the underground wind. "Women!" I said aloud.

I trailed the dead music to Level C and counted only two cars. My footsteps echoed. The echoes took me to Level D. "D for Dracula," I said eerily. "Slowly, the vampire pulled himself on top of me…" I recalled and laughed like Boris Karloff.

The cassette tape went right to it. The only car was parked up against the wall. I made a check on the clipboard and turned around to go back up. Then I guessed I should pick up the string of tape. Randy probably wouldn't like the mess of my tape drifting about. I bent down and gave it a tug.

A scream came from the levels above. A woman was yelling

as I ran up the ramps. Out of breath, I gasped up the last ramp to Level A. "Anne!" I shouted, stumbling from exhaustion.

The door of the booth shot open as someone rushed out. All I could see of the person was the black L.A Raiders jacket he wore as he ran out into the night.

Anne was in the booth. She was pushed into the metal and glass corner holding her arms tightly around herself. I touched her and she fell around me crying.

12/7/92
4:35 PM

MARS NEEDS WOMEN

In the end, she left tracks on the lawn like a spaceship had been and gone.

The TV was on with a black and white sci-fi movie of Martians in search of Earth women. I could see through the swimming black and white picture the crazy story of Martians landing on Earth. I guess the Martians needed women to bring life back to their dying planet. I don't remember what happened to all the Martian women. The millions of miles between the two planets was just like trespassing a lawn between two houses for them with their flying saucers. The screen was filled with the flowers of spaceships traveling. I was only aware of her during color commercials, when the ads came on selling cars, insurance, and all the other things you had to have and she was making noise from our bedroom. She called my name once, "Joe!" but that was a long time ago and now she was way past talking.

"Carol Jean!" she wouldn't even reply when I called to her. Doors were opening and closing and something broke on the floor. The movie came back on and I paid attention.

It was the scene of a falling apart house on the rim of the ocean. A white spaceship was hovering overhead and then landing into the reeds and sand. A movie star woman was looking out the window but she didn't look afraid. She held the curtains open to watch. And the next shot was of her opening her door and across to the spaceship she went. She appeared warm to the silver Martian standing next to her. She started to smile. She went inside the saucer and the door closed. There was only the quiet of waves on the beach and then the flying saucer started to purr and it hummed away into the sky with all its waiting stars. And the stars became headlights of a car which stopped in front of another Martian spaceship. Two women got out of the car. They were waitresses from a local diner and they became astronauts too. All over Earth, women were leaving for Mars. It was unbelievable. Soon they were all gone. And then the conclusion was a man going out of his house on the beach and looking up at space.

After the credits went by and a test pattern of an Indian wearing a feathered headdress had been unmoving for five minutes, I got up and walked to our bedroom. Cold salt wind from the sea was blowing the window curtains aside and there on the bed was a suitcase with clothes slain all over. "Carol Jean? Carol Jean!" But she was already gone. The house was small and the bending walls helped me to go from room to room, but she was nowhere here.

I turned the doorknob and the door blew into me heavily. Having to hold to the stairway railing, I left the porch and the ground, wet flowers and long grass, was soft under my feet with Mars more than millions of miles away.

REMEMBER WITH TELEVISION

During a show he was half asleep watching, in an age of satellites, the inventor of television finally lay his head to rest. His life was recalled with a joke from Johnny Carson—"Milton James Early has just died due to circumstances beyond his control."

It was late but people were still watching his machine. It was always on somewhere. Look anywhere.

From a small hotel room next to a highway, out through the window drapes, under revolving stars and late night chirping crickets, a cough interrupted the expectant laughs. After seven minutes of commercials, the coin operated TV shut itself off. Moths beat at the window, at the TV's disappearing light.

When he was born, America was a different America. And before it walked across the country on telephone poles, electricity was only imagination. While he was taking a radio apart, he had an idea. He would make a time machine that people would disappear gladly into, close the door and go away from what was happening to the warring twentieth century…Gone into another new world.

He used to think back and wonder at how everything was then…When he was building with wires and picture tubes in his house at night and he created light and moving pictures inside a wooden box.

He got a ghostly picture when he looked at the screen the first time.

Adjusting the camera on the other side of the room, he returned to see a dreamlike vision of the windowsill flowerpot on the screen. That was a picture he never forgot: the first look at the Garden of Eden.

But his invention was only half complete when it was stolen. Someone had come in during the night and his invention was gone the next day.

At the World's Fair, he imagined it appearing like a child kidnapped by the circus.

All it could do was magic tricks.

He went crazy thinking about what it wouldn't do…He felt left alone by the years, his machine had gone on without him, and he carried a brokenhearted torch. When it appeared in stores, he bought every model and type of television made. And as it went from wood to plastic, he saw more in it than anyone.

For years, his living room was filled with TV sets stacked like firewood on top of each other, from the floor to the ceiling, glowing. Finally, in 1967, he stopped getting new TV sets. There was no more room. A house full of TVs stacked tight in the halls and all the rooms, a garage full of blank gray screens and wooden cabinets with spider webs strung in and out holding in dust the ghosts of television.

Then, after all that time and television, he let go.

Even though his machine didn't succeed the way he thought it would, it had taken everyone to another world. He knew that TV now controlled people's lives and ordered their days so they could remember with television.

And he joined them too.

It was a time travel journey after all.

In his last days, Milton James Early's television at home was covered with flowers in pots, pans, bowls and teacups and jars. He would sit down and watch the screen that had been cut out of the thick flowers and ivy. In summer, the game shows were pollinated, bees flew in and out, and the TV would bloom until late evening when it would fold up all its petals to sleep.

The room was a seashell of white curving roof overhead and

ten feet below the one window was his bed of polished brass
with disarrayed blankets knotted around in the shape of him.
Like an erupting electrical jungle, in the center of the room
was a six foot mound of green, sprouting hundreds of flower
colors and a blinking television screen hedge cut right into the
middle.

The screen was pointed straight towards the bed and the
flowers bent their faces towards the bright screen too. On the
nightstand, an arm's reach from under the covers was a remote
control channel switcher and a full watering can.

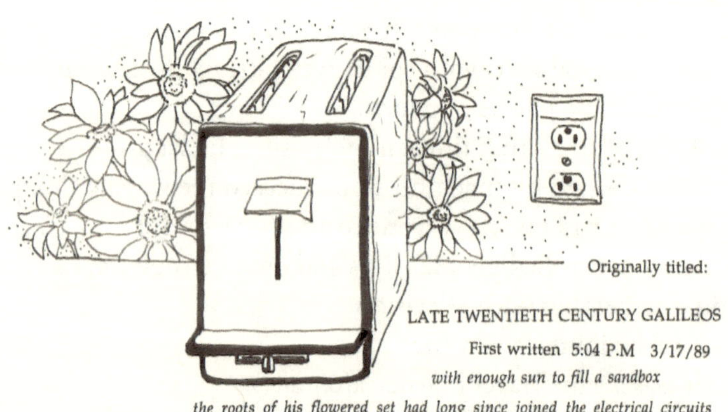

Original illustration from *Pie In The Sky #19*.

DRIVE SLOWLY AND CAREFULLY

While she read exit numbers and destinations signs aloud, she remembered what she wanted to ask him. So he told his daughter there was a car driving somewhere out there on the roads of America that once tried to cut his arm off. He used to work in a Detroit car factory the size of a city. It had everything a city did, good and bad. There was even a black market where he bought her a ring. Inside there, through rows of machines and car shapes, and all the car making sounds, he had worked in the deepest part of the city turning metal into cars. He used to attach doors to the frames and the doors came to him hanging in a row from a track running the ceiling. It was dangerous work. There was a union hospital that was usually filled with wounded and his last job had been Vietnam. He showed his daughter the scar that ran his arm, where the sharp edge of a door caught him with its steel. But he told her it was also like *Alice in Wonderland* down there and she could have run miles and miles of tunnels and worlds down there before she could find him.

GOOD DEED RAIN

The richest man in Sao Paulo had a magic umbrella. When he opened the umbrella, an endless supply of money green rain would waterfall out. He would let it pile up to his knees then shut the black umbrella solemnly and put it back inside the safe, on the shelf in there.

Nobody knew how he was getting all the money he was spending. Before, he had nothing, but now he was buying houses, land, cars, airplanes—anything that had a price tag he would buy. Except for an occasional loss of peace of mind, the money gave him whatever he wanted.

Lately while it poured, he strangely wondered why he had been so lucky. It bothered him and he dreamed about buying the world and giving every person a million dollars…Sometime with the morning sun dripping his window panes and collecting in a glass of orange juice on his plush carpeted floor, the richest man in the city had a vision of kindliness. He would pour the money out over the slums that surrounded him and seeped through the city of Sao Paolo like cockroach dancing.

Feeling so benevolent (he even felt above his head for a halo) he climbed into his distinctive bright yellow chauffered helicopter with his umbrella on his lap and commanded in a Moses-voice, "Hurry! Off to the slums!"

Minutes later, he was hovering over the crumbling poverty of breakfast blue smoke fires and tin rust roofs. Cardboard walls and flies crawling the faces of children who stopped fighting only to poke their hands at the sky, to where the golden helicopter buzzed in place directly overhead.

He opened the umbrella, leaning out the door like Zeus with his thunderbolt. He smiled as money fluttered down, laughing for a moment at the thought that this act would no doubt buy him sainthood—picturing statues of him in town squares strewn with flowers and humbling townsfolk kneeling before the altar of his image. He ordered the pilot to circle round and round while he shook the umbrella manna out of the sky. Closing his eyes he basked in the hot Osiris sun, the roar of blades overhead the roar of the faithful, and he slowly opened his eyes to see his pyramids below…

Instead, he was horrified to see spluttering hundreds of rotten yams dropping Earthwards. Screaming panic, he wrenched at the umbrella trying to close it, but the mechanics of it were jammed with foul yam slime. He shook it, rammed it against the rocking helicopter, staining its bee-yellow hide. But the umbrella wouldn't close and continued to spray its pestilence down on the poor people of Sao Paolo.

Frenzy seized, he edged too far out the doorway and tumbled out, gripping the umbrella pole, handled like a lifeline in the palm of the sky, praying in his leg kicking dervish freefall that it could somehow parachute him safely.

But rancid yams were pouring down over him, soft thousands sticking to his sleeves, shoulders and hair. He just fell faster to the ground, with the yams flashing by, the whole world looking brown and green. Instead of hitting the ground, he hit a mountain of deep vegetable mush and sunk. Down inside that gloom he waited two days to be mined out.

CUSTER'S LAST, LAST STAND

He told me his name and when I laughed, he proved it.

"Custer," he pointed to his nametag sewn on his green uniform. "There's still a bullet out there waiting for me." Even though the wars were over, I knew he was right—there must be a bullet coming for him sometime—but there didn't seem to be any fear in his knowing. "It's just a matter of time."

He was the last living soldier in America and he was the only living exhibit in the Museum of American History. I read the plaque in front of his sofa: *Worldwide, it was accepted that the only way to achieve Peace was by burying the source of all war: the military.*

I had been born during the time when soldiers were disappearing, but it wasn't called a war, it was called World Liberation One, or The First World Liberation. There have been others. We celebrate them with holidays. It had been so easily won. Putting on a uniform doomed them. Sewn into every uniform were threads that attracted the lazer driven bullets that were shot into the air all over the planet…They're still out there. At night you can see them, shining like stars with nowhere to land…Soldiers became bullet magnets and pulled their deaths into them. There was nowhere to hide, they all ended up in the same place, back in the earth with root and flowers and the sky overhead. They were all gone, except for him: Custer, the last living soldier.

He must have felt strange being on display between dinosaur bones and 20th Century farm equipment. Behind a gold rope, he sat on a worn red sofa and answered questions from people. Someone asked him why he had joined the military and he said he really didn't know why, he was young. I felt sorry for him. He was like one of those rare jungle birds, with the trees all being torn down. I could tell that people were hoping a bullet would come out of somewhere and knock him down. They all had their cameras ready.

BUCKETHEAD

"Do you read me? Over."

"Loud and clear. Over."

She put her finger back on the message button, pressed it down and said, "What are you doing? Over." She lay back on the bed, staring at the white ceiling, listening to the static against her ear, until the plastic talked again.

"Not much. Over." From inside the red house next door, her friend's voice was traveling through the magic of walkie-talkies.

Beulah held the machine back to her mouth. "We should do something. I'm going to pretend my bed is a boat. Over." She sat up and stared out the window facing the ocean. The gray waves rolled out for thousands of miles towards Japan, a long way for the mattress to row.

"I can see you out my window," the voice in the toy said. "Over."

There was her neighbor, framed in Beulah's other window, waving to her from the red house across the lawn.

Beulah chopped up and down on the bed, springing back and forth, letting the invisible waves get really bad before she picked up the walkie-talkie again. "The storm's hitting," she warned. "Over."

A loud pirate voice crunched out of the little speaker, "What are you doing?" It hollered, "Get off this channel!"

"Why should I?" Beulah snapped and crouched, waiting for the reply.

It didn't take long. "Listen, Buckethead. Shut up!"

"You shut up!" Beulah's friend challenged, "Buckethead!"

Beulah bounced and joined in, "You stupid Buckethead!"

His answer was garbled with curses. From somewhere far out at sea he swore through their childish yells. They were both laughing, cursing back at him, unleashing their vocabularies and inventing new words to get him.

Beulah stared at the sea.

Then the music began to play, spinning out of her walkie-talkie.

Her feet started tingling; Beulah felt the sound filling her up inside like poured treacle. The window facing the Pacific flew open and the drapes blew out like leaves disappearing fast across the ocean. She clawed at her walkie-talkie but couldn't turn it off. The music got louder and louder, even with it jammed under the pillow. Screaming didn't stop it either. The sound danced inside of her, freezing, rattling her bones, crawling tremors.

Just like balloons, her feet rose off the covers, lifting her legs up. The blankets were dragging loose. She pinched the edge of the mattress, doing a headstand, struggling to hold onto the headboard. Her body tied itself in knots around the metal spokes, fighting the musical gravity.

Looking over her shoulder, Beulah could see the frothing ocean, waves like hands pulling a line to her. And through all the loud, she could hear something else.

With terrible kicking and shouting, Beulah's friend levitated out of the red house, over the lawn, the picket fence and steep blackberried cliff and sailed out of sight.

A mouth closing, the window slowly shut and all the hungry pull gave way to quietness as the music stopped, returning the room to stillness.

Beulah fell back onto the soft bed, shot a hand under the pillow and she grabbed and smashed the walkie-talkie into pieces all over the wooden floor.

MAMMUD, MUHAMMAD AND MIKE

All the trophy fish hung on walls, swimming endlessly the way down the street from business to business. Mike noticed them as he drove, glancing side to side. A real estate office had a blue four foot swordfish above a table, a bank had a fat trout over the vault, restaurants with salmon and bass, while goldfish jumped around in the tanks of the pet store. All these fish formed a procession, went up the street as if it was a river. He watched them all the way, block by block, until the only place they had left to go was with him, straight into the glass yellow window where the road turned into a parking lot and stopped.

Mike got out of his car and walked into the building. The door rang a bell when it opened and he waved to Mammud.

Mammud had been waiting for him. He made a small elegant bow. "Hello, Mike." He motioned from behind the counter, "There is Muhammad in the other room. He is doing the inventory. You can go help him."

"Thanks." Mike went past all the rolls of Persian carpets and the ones hinged to the wall posts like the big pages of books. Through a door, the other room was the warehouse, where hundreds of carpets lay, ordered by Arabic letters and piled into rows. It could have been a supermarket for carpets, the warehouse was that large. He had to look down every row for Muhammad. The ordering of the rugs didn't seem to make any sense, they were all colors together and stretching to the far back wall. He yelled, "Muhammad!"

Mike remembered what Muhammad had said yesterday after the interview. "If you do good work here and we want you to stay, we will add your name to the store lights." He meant the red blinking neon above the front door that read, Muhammad and Mammud with a floating, rocking magic carpet shape.

From miles away it seemed, Muhammad's voice called.

"Mike!" and, "I'm over here." Muhammad appeared from behind a dark rug cape. Out of a pocket in his black robe, he took
a stack of paper, shaking it, saying, "I'll show you how to do
inventory."

"This is a big warehouse," Mike said as he walked the rest of
the far airport distance. They sat down at a table and Muhammad showed Mike how the system worked. The thick book was
filled with names, numbers and symbols, page after page after
page. Mike tried to comprehend it all, nodding all the time,
but it was a complete mystery.

Muhammad closed the book and pointed to an aisle, "You
can begin there and I will return in an hour to see how you are
doing."

"Okay," Mike said. He sat there with the book in his hands,
staring down at lists that never ended. He flipped through
the book and turned it like the hands of a clock, around and
around in circles. It didn't make any sense however he looked at
the pages. He wondered, "How could he have expected me to
do this?" Still, there was the long aisle of carpets awaiting him.
So he got up slowly, as if he was defeated already, to take a look
at the impossible.

Persian carpets with colorful maze patterns were piled on either side, reaching high over his head. There were tags attached
to each one and more strange symbols. Mike walked further
down the aisle. Some of the rugs were falling down over others.
Mike pushed them back in place.

There was a thud from the other side when he shoved a
carpet too hard. Mike had to walk all the rest of the way down
the aisle, around the green soft corner to find the carpet he had
knocked down.

Some kind of Arabic muzak was dripping out of the wall
speakers.

Mike pulled the rug over his shoulder, about to toss it back
up when he read the tag.

Mike could read the letters.

Still, it was a Hollywood word—the meaning was myth. He laughed and pushed the magic carpet back onto the top. It fell off again, landing over him like a blanket. The world, with beautiful colors for all the land and water, was the pattern of weave.

Anyone could have stepped onto the carpet, felt it rise slowly, waiting for a command, and it could have flown up through the skylight, outside.

But the city is filled with dangers—tall signs, telephone poles and electrical wires—the problem with flying. Mike could have crashed into the store's neon sign, a terrible explosion and shower of sparks…Mike thought about all the things that could go wrong with this magic carpet and then he remembered all the fish that were swimming in buildings and going nowhere.

INVEST IN PHIL DONAHUE

Now he had everything he wanted, he was starting to regret his great-grandson time traveling back to him and showering him with predictions. Practicing swinging a pine baseball bat, worried about his mortality, he took a sip of glass water and rested on the seawall ledge, where the lawn curve ended in the ocean.

It wouldn't be easy, he thought, but whatever his fate would be, it had to be done.

The warm air cooled with the strange sound of muted garbled trumpets, like a distant, weak AM radio signal, and his back prickled with sensation.

The bat was tight in his hands as he turned to face that direction he knew his relation would be appearing. Soon he would be looking at a tall man in a silver suit, a twenty foot genie vision from his family's future.

It had started months ago…the ghostly visits…out of nowhere, standing next to a flagpole, with metallic head brushed by Old Glory, the giant spoke, "Phil Donahue, it is I, Jesus Lord 12, traveling back in time to your strange era…" At first, Phil stared up in wonder at the moving tin foil statue, then he realized he could turn it to his advantage. He could ask questions like, "Tell me what I should invest in so I can make a fortune!" The giant always obeyed his requests and Phil made hundreds of phone calls to brokers and bankers and ended up a millionaire. His riches were beyond limit. He was the limit! Sometimes he would even be kindly and warn people of an impending disaster. Tell the airport not to fly, or warn a small town in Kansas to hide from the wind. In a sense, Phil Donahue was becoming America's God. The TV stations voted him President of the United States and finally Phil accepted the honor, modestly, after three times refusing. Nationwide, there were millions, billions of TV sets tuned to hail Phil Donahue and his ringing words of prophecy. He had everything because he could know everything and yet of all the questions Phil could ask that would get him whatever he wanted in this life, he was afraid of asking that ultimate question…"How will I die?" He didn't want to know, he had to dispose of the temptation somehow…

What's it like clubbing a twenty foot tin covered giant in the kneecap with a baseball bat? Try picturing arriving in New Jersey on the Hindenburg in 1937. Phil Donahue's ashes were piled together along with some cat hair, slivers of coffee table, carpet fuzz and seashell shards. The urn was shaped like an eagle, painted with stripes and stars, colored red white and blue. Postcards are for sale in the lobby.

NO, CLARENCE IS NOT HERE

Two times, the strange parrot voice called my number and asked for Clarence. And twice I told him, "No, Clarence is not here."

When the phone started ringing again, I decided to become Clarence.

"Hello," my voice acted.

"Hello, is this Clarence?"

"Yes, this is Clarence. Listen, I've been waiting for you to call."

"I—"

"Have you seen the news?" I asked. "Have you watched the news tonight?"

"Yes, I—"

"They're onto us! We're doomed! The bloodhounds are on the way! I hear people walking on the street below. I know they're coming for me!" I was really performing.

"Clarence, get a hold of yourself," the voice commanded me and took a breath. "That's why I was calling you…I left you a gun."

"A what?"

"A gun, there's a gun in the desk over by the window. You must get it, Clarence."

I looked at my desk. "What?"

"Get the gun, Clarence." The connection sizzled urgently.

I was walking. I was hypnotized. The drawer came open and inside was a black pistol laying there.

The voice in my ear continued. "You have failed, Clarence. You know the consequences, Clarence. We cannot allow them to discover our plans. Goodbye, Clarence."

I pressed the pistol against my temple as he hung up.

ANT ATTRACTION

Orwell and Huxley were wrong: the future belongs to the ants. Workers will devote their entire lives to the Queen. They will fight wars and build vast underground colonies. Though desert winds will cover the Earth, the dunes will shake and hum with the goings on underneath.

That's where Wink Thorax has his studio and beams out his show *Ant Attraction* to eager millions everywhere. The tunnels jam up every Wednesday as males try to get on the program, clawing for a chance to be permitted to sit with the camera and sell themselves, knowing that inside that black, smoked-glass booth sits the Queen. She watches silently and selectively the entire program. And finally, ever slowly, her jeweled hand will flick out and point to the winner.

WALLFLOWER

She put her hand on the wall and her hand was gone and like pushing into water, she sunk. She wasn't dead, but she lived with the least amount of effort. In her mind, she always though she wasn't what she wanted to be and everything she wanted was impossible anyway. For years, ever since she was a girl, she felt something was wrong and she didn't fit in. To the world, she had disappeared from sight. Her skin and clothes were invisible on the wall. Finally, she felt she belonged somewhere. Nobody could see her and even the shadows lay on top of her without knowing. Here she thought she was the only one, who else could be like her? Now I have only myself, she thought, no one to hurt me and I can't hurt anyone. But there was a whole other world living flat along the walls that she never knew existed until she joined the wallpaper. They noticed her and she noticed them, moving towards each other. They didn't have to be shy or scared of breathing anymore, they had all come to the same place to get away.

MAGNETS AND INVISIBLE THREADS

Think of her watching her house, all piled up off the ground, the huge rusty jack being used to lift it onto a trailer, to transport it miles and miles away to a hill overlooking the Pacific. Seeing her house suspended between cranes, balanced six feet in the air, made her scared to look.

Then it dropped and collapsed in on itself like falling bread.

The lawn was all torn from bulldozers. She stood in the tracks and stared.

It took a few weeks for the birds to realize she had turned into a statue, then they began landing fearlessly all over her, like a telephone pole. Friends tried to reawaken her, a lover kissed her and cried, people tried a million ways, but she was petrified.

A circus bought her and for five long years she was a starring attraction amid the lions and sword swallowers, trapeze acts and sideshows. It was like there was a block of ice or golden amber trapping her.

All the while her life was still there inside of her like a candle. To some people who saw her she was holy; to them she glowed while they placed flowers in front of her and all around her in the sawdust.

Years passed with her spinning across the United States, careening from small towns to cities with the circus. She still remained frozen in that horrible moment of seeing her house crash. Will she snap out of it? Will she be able to remember that place by the ocean where she wanted to be and will she have the strength to shatter back to life?

Time passed…Now she works for Woolworths, paying back debts and mortgages. Her old house barely has a pulse within her memory…She lives in a two room apartment in Greenwood, off of Aurora. Starting from scratch, it will have to be amazing like something from the circus, magnets and invisible threads will have to pull her up again and direct her.

THE CASE OF THE INSOMNIAC VACUUM CLEANERS

It took me over a month to figure out the truth.

Living upstairs from me, I knew there were definitely two people. Their footsteps were like bad Kansas weather, always thundering overhead across the gray ceiling. Every morning they would storm back and forth with the vacuum cleaner, sometimes three times a night. As I fell asleep, they would still be awake, with their footsteps and when I woke up they'd be listening to the morning TV. They never slept. I'm not crazy about sleeping either, it's mostly bad dreams, but they avoid it completely, playing music all night and waltzing their vacuum cleaner.

In my wheelchair at the window, I would watch her go out every morning twice. For weeks I watched her leave and minutes later, leave again. It just didn't make any sense. It was like having a mirror come alive, seeing her reflection moving out of doors after her. What was she doing? Was she walking around the corner, crawling in the back window, just to come downstairs and go out the front door again? How could two be one?

I studied the situation carefully, like a television detective. My wheelchair and I watched Raymond Burr everyday religiously. I kept track in a notebook. After she left two times, there would be quiet upstairs all day until she returned twice and the noise started up once more. It had me confused for a long time, until one evening she left with her other image for the seven thirty movie.

The sky was just beginning to darken when she became two and went out the front door together.

I was stunned. "You're twins!" I shouted out my window at them. A potted plant rocked and fell onto my lap, spilling dirt and red petals.

"Yes," they replied together in key and seemed to stumble

in the shadow of the porch. They were staring back at me like two Esmeraldas and the wind chimes sounded like explosions.

Mumbling something I didn't hear, they left side by side down the blackening street and I had to avert my eyes to all the dandelions on the grass.

AGRICULTURAL REVOLUTION

Supermarkets became like banks, where only people with wealth could buy expensive food on the installment plan. The people without money carved through the cement and pavement to plant corn, while above the streets a tomato the size of summer was growing in her apartment.

This morning, she walked up to the doors with a key in her hand and a bag of plant food under her arm. She stopped there on the welcome mat, directly underneath the tomato, blinking up at it from the sidewalk.

Growing more and more, crushing the furniture and bending the floor, it had filled the four walled space and was pushing itself, with no regard to gravity, out the windows. She barely had room to live in what was once a spacious apartment. Why it had grown so large was a secret of hers…What she knew about growing vegetables could have solved world hunger.

As she stared up, all she could imagine was that the sky had turned red and all it would take was a car backfire behind her for the sky to collapse.

Revealing her discovery could be dangerous. She believed the secret of the tomato was like the atomic bomb. She spent all her time debating whether it could make peace, or be the end of mankind. She knew how people were.

By day and night the siege lay in around her. More and more starving people began to gather under her windows. People with guns demanded her to give them food and the secret of growing. A revolution was brewing…

All night long, the sounds of machinery, the National Guard or maybe it was the Army, arriving in tanks and jeeps. The blue morning light was edging its way along the round seam between tomato and window, but she was still wide awake. She was afraid to get up, afraid to move, she knew there had to be hundreds of guns pointed at the building.

Plaster fell on her head as the plant shifted towards the new sun.

Hundreds of rifles clicked out on the street. Someone shouted, "Don't shoot! We need her alive!" But this was no comfort to her, she couldn't have surrendered now even if she wanted to—she was trapped, pressed in the red shadow against the wallpaper.

Hundreds of rifles clicked out on the street…There were a bristling few seconds of tension, silence, then the chaos of a volley of gunshots and shouts and canons and tanks firing and jets passing low overhead…It's hard to imagine that a tomato could create such destruction, but when it was hit by bullets, rockets and bombs, it exploded astronomically.

There was only one survivor to be seen.

She clung to a floating seed, like all that remained of a torpedoed steamship, in the middle of a horizon to horizon deep red sea of tomato juice.

THE FLAMMABLE MAN

She said it got her all hot and bothered. She even breathed the word, "Aphrodisiac," whispered in his ear like the name of the rarest flower. He wouldn't have done it if didn't cause such a reaction in her. He knew it was dangerous.

He was a gas station attendant. He worked there all day and would come home Michelin black from oil and rubber and smelling of gasoline. The gasoline smell drove her wild. She would go crazy, touching him, caressing him, pawing him, breathing ecstatically, heavy and burning.

After she told him about the gasoline smell, he accepted her suggestion and rubbed a hand of gas down over his hair and into his open shirt before going home. It ran greasy down his forehead, stung his eyes, but he combed it in, his hair slicked back, black and shining.

When he got home, she crashed at him like a moth to the flame and they rolled across the carpet, tearing at each other, ripping at each other with teeth and nails, her head glued to his shoulder, going faint, panting like a mile walked dog. He groaned, they pinwheeled over the carpet, tumbleweeded with a crash into a table, knocking books, magazines and pencils down on top of their skin. And an ashtray fell too, scattering gray dust down like Hiroshima rain. And also a half burned cigarette, still smoking. It toppled down onto his head. An orange flash erupted and the two of them woke up looking through eyeslit bandages, in a linoleum ammonia smell hospital room.

"Ammonia!" he looked lustily over at her across from him, wrapped in white and she gasped beautifully.

B. FRANKLIN'S DISCOVERY OF ELECTRICITY

She was a tall woman and that was her downfall. If she had been three feet shorter, this might never have happened.

Bea Franklin was worried that lightning might strike the metal flagpole saluting off the corner of her house.

So with the dark clouds boiling over her, she climbed onto the roof and pulled the retractable flagpole under the eaves.

Rain made the shingles slippery, she nearly fell. Just as she got her balance, lightning bolted out of the sky and hit her in the head.

Her seven foot frame tipped over the edge like a smoking dinosaur skeleton and set the garden on fire.

GRAVITY LIGHTHOUSE

He was living with a girl who was very casually lighting and throwing firecrackers. At the balcony window, she was like a gunpowder damsel in distress, ten stories up the tall wall of ivy. Meanwhile, he was in the kitchen, pouring coins in his shoes.

He clanked heavily into the other room where she leaned up against the open window. "I heard it's good luck if you put a penny in your shoe," he said. "I've got fifteen dollars and thirty seven cents in these shoes!"

She stared at him, unimpressed and she struck a match with a sudden flick of her wrist.

He was standing very close to her, smiling enormously.

"Awww! Get lost!" She shoved him hard enough for him to lose his balance and fall right out of the lighthouse window. His good luck took him straight to the bottom of the Pacific Ocean with the starfish.

OK, I'LL NEVER SEE YOU AGAIN

In Manhattan, I went into a smoke-shop to get change for a dollar.

A voice behind the bulletproof glass asked me, "Yes? Can I help you?"

I turned and there she was, an old woman, with the features of a woodcut, wearing a black medieval coat.

"Can I get change for a dollar?" I asked.

"Only if you never ask me again." Her words had an eerie and dangerous tone.

But I stared into her fairy tale face and passed her the counterfeit dollar.

After she gave me coins, four quarters, I said, "OK, I'll never see you again."

WILLIAM CARLOS WILLIAMS FOR BEGINNERS

She was a sad woman with the face of Stan Laurel. In the morning on the subway to work, she sat among people like they were made of glass, pushed around her the same as windows.

She had just come to the United States from Central America, to share that American dream that passed around Guatemala cooking fires at night. Like the church promises of Heaven, if she prayed, she would get there.

But at night, when she was asleep, she dreamed back through the city to Guatemala, the greens and warms and villages connected by dirt roads and barking dogs. As she slept she remembered it all, as if she was still there. Then she would wake up to more gunshots and sirens, but the voices would remind her where she was—in a country where she was learning from a book how to speak.

She was in America alone with William Carlos Williams who made words on the page to look up at her in quiet short rows. She would break them off like flowers and look for their meaning in her Spanish dictionary, learning to speak again. That first week in America when she applied for a job as a cleaning lady in a midtown hotel, she recited *The Red Wheelbarrow,* pushing the words slowly before her.

WISHING

The Statue of Liberty was shaking. Ellis Island was lit up with the approaching, blinking glow of space travelers, finally arriving at our blue gray planet. The gliding saucers slid low over the water. All the skyscrapers vibrated with the sound of silver engines and the tall green woman statue welcomed them with her famous words, "Give me your tired, your poor, your huddled masses yearning to breathe free, the wretched refuse of your teeming shore. Send these, the homeless, tempest-tost to me, I lift my lamp beside the golden door."

They broadcast their message across radio and television wires. Wanting to make a detailed study of Earth's humans, they had chosen America to conduct their experiment, settling down on these littered shores.

To assure the country that they meant no harm, they wondered about a gift. Inside their golden spaceship, they knew that they had to convince the country that they meant no harm—primitive weapons were already pointed at them—so they offered a welcoming treasure.

The space travelers knew a secret desire of these people of Earth—they could read it in their minds—these people were never satisfied with who they were. These people wanted to be like him or like her. Americans always dream of such possibilities.

The fleet of their great spaceships glided across the dark of night, surrounded the boundaries and blessed their subjects with the ability to change. What would they do with a week to disappear, to be whoever they wanted, to become the ideal they desired?

These people of Earth joyfully began to change in all physical ways, becoming taller, thinner, stronger, colors, sex, faces and shapes of bodies. By the end of the first day, everyone had become different than what they were before.

…The slow weary Berry, pushing at a door, suddenly became a movie star blonde, her silky tall shadow curving blue on the boards.

…A milkman became the vision of Martin Luther King Jr. and cried to see his face in the truck mirror.

…A woman dropped a bag of groceries in the driveway and started painting a beautiful red poppy on the door of her station wagon.

…A third grader's laugh became ho-ho-hoing as he turned into Santa Claus.

…A new Chief Joseph moved like a storm, safely into Canada.

…Singing into the bathroom mirror, she gasped as she saw who was looking back.

…A girl playing hopscotch turned into a pigeon and flew away.

…A sad man at the circus all of a sudden jumped out of the bleachers and fearlessly entered the lion's cage.

…An old woman, looking out a cracked window at the schoolyard, blinked quietly and was a girl again, running down the hall to get outside.

…A boy became two feet taller and pulled the balsa airplane from the branches he couldn't reach before.

…She stepped out of her wheelchair and did a cartwheel on the grass, surprising her sister who was turning into a racehorse.

…A man who was nobody is now Albert Einstein.

The first day was magic, with people becoming magicians.

…And they went on changing, wishing, and their wishes came true.

By the second day there were hundreds of famous people in the park. 48 Duke Ellington big bands played the same song for 147 Fred Astaires dancing with 321 Ginger Rogers. People everywhere over the land thanked the space travelers, they were finally so happy.

Third day, fourth day, fifth day, people chased on and on back and forth, losing themselves in others. Walking down the street seeing what he or she looked like, liking that more and adding that again. People paraded themselves outdoors, showing off their new selves to other selves.

As the end of the week approached, the Americans were changing more rapidly, borrowing, blurring features from each other frantically.

The leaders cautioned the people to use restraint, to be sure they'd be happy with the changes soon to be permanent again. And the leaders put up billboards, advertisements and posters of ideals were everywhere. The television and movies showed everyone who they should be. But not even the government could follow the rules, as they collapsed into fighting for power between so many a John F. Kennedy, Gandhi, Hitler, Lincoln and Lee, Napoleon, Churchill, Lenin, and three Jeffersons unconscious on the White House lawn.

The space travelers were amazed on the seventh day, the last day of changes, when they turned off the wishing and came out of their spacecrafts.

Every man looked like every man, every woman looked like every woman.

Millions, billions of Adam and Eves.

On that seventh day, the space travelers left, their experiment satisfied, their studies were finished. America folded up like a flower in the disappearing stars.

TYING THE SHEETS TOGETHER TO MAKE A LADDER

When people are crowded into tall cement, windows become televisions and everyone behind glass becomes actors, stars in their own silent movies. On this winter night in Brooklyn, my light was off and I was just watching out the window, to the blank yellow apartment glowing from the black brick wall across from me. It was late and there was only one channel on and I began to imagine about him, the moment he walked with a limp from a foreign war, into the frame of the window.

He could have been a film of old Pablo Picasso at the beach, looking for seashells on the sand in his room. I've never seen him outside, on the street, or buying food from the grocery. Maybe he doesn't go out, maybe he spends all day in a painted other world. He had no shirt on, the frame censored him at the waist like 1950s TV so he may have had on less, I didn't know, and he was looking outside. What he would really be looking at on the dark glass, was himself, reflected.

Behind him, a chandelier painted him from above, with soft colors on his round body. The chandelier looked like someone's daughter in a prom photo. Her light was crystal and yellow and bright, then, when he left the room, that chandelier was the only thing visible. There was no other sign of life across the whole face of the building, except for the smiling eighteen year old girl light.

It was late. I was entertaining insomnia. Suddenly, the window to the left of the chandelier glass sprung light and I could see on the wall a colorful ancient looking map of the world. It was pinned to the wall as preciously as a butterfly, rare, with a pin every couple of inches to hold its wings down. He had drawn paths across the map, over oceans, continents, lakes, islands. He must have been getting something out of a drawer in the map room, because in a moment the light in there was out again.

Minutes wandered past, with me waiting, watching, until he was back in the chandelier room, back but looking differently.

He had a pair of small silver wings wrapped around his neck, resting on his shoulders. Wings that were small like the tin foil of a third grader's Halloween costume, waved as he walked up to the glass and his arms, hands, moved to open the window up.

Below, a fall of over forty feet would land him in sharp inches, broken glass shards and pieces of brick that blew off the wall in storms. Cogs and wheels and rusted machinery, weeds, fragments of words and conversations and all the stray other things that gather underneath apartment windows.

As the night cool wind rustled into the room around him, spinning the chandelier, he floated into the air with his silver wings flapping a whirr. He arose over the window frame, out, and he was wearing only the wings and reading glasses. He purred out slowly beyond and drifted into a quiet, perfect loop-to-loop, with a smile at that and then he went into the stars, glowing, white, fading, like a moon disappearing.

DECOYS

"There go more birds going South," she sighed at the sky.

"Yeah," he watched with her.

"They honkers or tweeters?" she asked.

"Honkers," he said.

They had their own codes and languages for the flying things they loved.

"Sure am going to miss them," she said.

"Yeah," he agreed.

The two of them, Old Woman and Old Man, were in love with birds. When winter came, it made them sad to see the birds leave, so what they started doing, so they'd always have the birds around, was make decoys. Old Man would cut bird shapes out of blocks of wood, shape and sand them to perfection, and Old Woman would paint them into life. Old Woman and Old Man placed birds on all the window sills in the house and every other empty space available—tabletops, dressers, the velvet arms of chairs and sofas, toasters and bread boards, the broken TV set, crowded books shelves, and balanced on the lamps and all over the floors. The decoys looked so real that people walking past thought it was an aviary and old people from the sanitarium would sit for hours on the bench in the yard, pelting their living room window with bread crumbs.

"Now it doesn't matter so much when the birds are leaving," she said, adding a twinkle to the eye of a nuthatch.

"Nope," he said, running the plane over the back of a spoonbill.

"Look! There go the last of them!" She pointed through the window to the V shape in the cold, blue clear sky. The wings nearly touched the trees.

"Hmmm," he said, "They don't seem quite ready to leave," noticing how the geese were circling, spiraling down like dishwater draining.

She said, "Looks like they're going to land."

"Yeah," he said.

But they didn't land. All twenty seven black, brown and white winged Canadian geese came crashing through the picture window lured by the sanctuary sight of the birds basking in the woodstove, Floridian warmth of Old Woman and Old Man's house.

She brushed the glass and feathers off her purple sweater, "Looks like we'll be having guests for dinner," she said.

"Yeah," he said. He was a little surprised at that very moment in time—the spoonbill he had been sanding leaped from his hands and began dancing a waltz.

THE CARTOON MAN

Anyway you looked at him, he was a cartoon—one from the golden age of Hanna-Barbera. He looked like he had been drawn into life 35 years ago and had fallen into his job straight from a TV. Jumpy and nervous while everyone else calmly smoked on their breaks, he looked terrified, afraid that he was flammable. He was made of cellophane and paper and the wind of the fans pushed him against his will, closer to the smoking ashtrays.

One day late in July, a mechanic lit a cigarette too near to him. The flash looked like a bottle of paint knocked over.

He wasn't the only flammable one, the atmosphere rained dangerously hot ash. The only life left on the planet was whatever people brought with them to the underground cities.

Joe Barbera was his boss for 35 years and signed all his checks illegibly. To command respect he put a crown over his signature. He had hundreds working for him, doing whatever he commanded, living for the Almighty Dollar he provided. Nevertheless, Joe made it his duty to brave the stormy weather above to see his loyal subject's ashes put to earth. He comforted the widow, a short crying girl named Minnie.

JACK SHELLAC'S ART SHACK

The cameras were rolling, filming as he lay the thick color paint across the canvas. He had a running dialogue going, something about how beautiful camping in the Appalachians is…The leaves, the swaying trees and purple lakes, the haunting call of the loon…He made a joke about not paying the trailer park, leaving in his Winnebago early before the ranger woke up. While he began adding a deer to the rippling edge of the water, there was a crash and a boom-mic swung wildly. Jack's banter ceased abruptly, his ashen face staring in horror at the approaching sight—an eight foot bear, walking on it hind legs, panting, slobbering and slashing its claws and teeth. It fell over Jack like a shadow and the scenic painting stuck to its hairy back while the TV crew retreated, leaving the cameras fixed on the grizzly.

MICKEY GILLAY!

The loudspeakers crackled and came alive again with the message, "See the truck driving monkey, Mickey Gillay!" Around the stacks of hay piled ten feet high, a crowd of people formed into a waiting line.

"We've got to see that monkey!" he begged her again. "I don't see how a monkey could drive a truck."

"It's just some cheap circus stunt," she said. "Like that bear we saw at last year's rodeo."

"How can you say that? A bear riding a bicycle is nothing like a monkey driving an eighteen wheeler!"

"Mickey Gillay!" drawled the voice on the loudspeakers. "Don't miss this amazing ape who drives a truck."

"Come on Ramona! I don't want to miss Mickey Gillay!" He gave her a hopeful squeeze, "Please…"

She sighed, gave in, and they edged into the line. They got a seat way up in the bleachers, next to a flapping American flag the size of a mattress. Ramona groaned when the lights all dimmed and a spotlight hit the flag, as the national anthem began to play. Everyone stood up and she leaned out of the glow, hard against him.

Instantly, before the last note had faded away, another spotlight bounced off a red, white and blue monkey-faced rippling banner down on the track. "Let him go boys!" the loudspeakers echoed. "Ladies and gentlemen…Here's Mickey Gillay!"

The banner ripped open as a giant silver truck roared across the dirt. Inside, a little brown blur steered and raged its long arms. The truck tore a spinning circle in the center of the track, then raced screaming along close to the curved edge of the bleachers. A hairy arm stuck out the window and waved at the cheering crowds. Everybody was going crazy at the sight. The monkey arm pulled the horn a few times as it went around.

Then the truck disappeared back down the tunnel and left the audience chanting for more, "Mickey Gillay! Mickey Gillay! Mickey Gillay!"

"That's it?" Ramona tugged at her boyfriend's arm, "That's what you paid twelve dollars for us to see?"

A cowboy came out, dragging a lariat tied to a knuckle walking chimp. It went into a frenzy and shook its arms over its head, acknowledging the cheers. "Mickey Gillay!"

That's not the same monkey that was driving!" Ramona shouted into his ear. "There's no way that's the same monkey!"

The crowd died down and the lights came back on. Smiling people began to empty out of the bleachers, back to the swirling fairground.

He stood up and stretched with her. "What did you think, Ramona?" he grinned.

"I told you! It wasn't the same monkey! I want my money back!"

"Well, I liked it," he admitted, despite her glare. "He did pretty good. I've never seen a monkey drive a truck before."

"You *still* haven't seen a monkey drive a truck!" she burned. "Mickey Gillay is no monkey!"
"Not so loud, honey." He smiled nervously at a cowboy giving them the eye.

Suddenly, she pulled him with her, out of the crowd, into a gap in the hay wall. She dragged him along past pickups and trailers, loose chickens and a cow tied to a fence.

"You're going to get us into a lot of trouble Ramona," he whispered fiercely.

Ramona opened the door of a trailer and poked her head inside. "Where's Mickey at?" she asked the clowns adding on white makeup in front of a mirror.

"Next door," one of them grumbled.

"Thanks," she shut their door. On the next trailer's door, there was a gold star with a banana inscribed on it. "I should have guessed…"

"Ramona! Please don't open that door!" he tried to hold her back, but it was too late.

She ripped the door open, bouncing it against the aluminum siding.

Mickey Gillay was caught in the act.

A dwarf in a brown fur suit. The brown ape mask discarded on the table top, next to a half empty Rainier beer can. A cigar stuck in his mouth. He stared in surprise at them.

"Great show, Mickey." Ramona thanked him and closed the door.

Amid crashing, a tinny little voice hollered and cursed back at them from inside, while she and he walked away.

THE SHAKESPEARE READER

There, on the dashboard of the Pontiac lay the evidence. Under the broken glass hole, was a yellow banana skin. Peeled and left there with ferocious determination. It had been a known risk, leaving the fruit there, but she had taken it. It would be inviting the unknown, but she had to find out…

Not more than five minutes ago, when she set the trap, she left her car and went back inside Shopper Heaven. She passed the big picture of herself smiling on the Employee of the Month plaque. Her name 'Percie' was engraved in the black plastic under her shiny photo, for all of the customers to see and admire. "I should have had my hair cut," she thought. Black hair, waterfalling around her head, her green eyes and smile, she was wearing that boring brown and orange uniform of the supermarket too.

She went past the vegetable produce rows, to the fruit. There were no bananas of course, just a Sorry We're Out sign. This curious epidemic had begun a couple of weeks ago. She had been the first one to notice it; she brought it to the manager's attention. He immediately ordered more bananas and the store's sales doubled, tripled, quadrupled, then they sold out of these golden fruits in two days, thus Percie's Employee of the Month honor.

No one could really explain the sudden shopper interest in bananas, people bought them with such a voracious appetite that stores all around had run out—it was said that there was even a black market on them now, as seedy vans and station wagons appeared blackly at night in alleyways, where pinstripe salesmen with cigarette breath extolled the quality of their banana merchandise.

Percie was still in school and her mind still had things to figure out. When she found a lone banana fallen behind a box in the storeroom, she decided to set a trap as an experiment. When she went out to her car and put it in plain sight on her dashboard, only a few minutes had to pass and she would soon find out how really desperate the situation had become. While she read the paper, it was happening.

The Dayton Shopper Gazette proclaimed in broad, black, to-war headlines, "Banana Truck Monkey Business!" with a photo underneath of a gutted out semi-truck felled to its side on the shoulder of the road. "Wow!" Percie breathed. She was taking her lunch break with the newspaper in the employees room at a table littered with overflowing ashtrays, contemplating the universe in the smoke ring her boss Bryan just blew.

"Listen to this…" she read aloud, "A truck filled with bananas, destination Dayton's Shopper Heaven grocery store, was discovered looted on the side of the highway today. Its driver was nowhere to be seen and no immediate witness to the mystery could be found." She looked up, "Wow!"

Bryan stared at his cigarette. "Yeah…I know all about it."

"You do?"

"Yeah—I mean just what the papers say. I ordered the load three days ago from Chattanooga." He crushed his cigarette into a brimming ashtray.

"I can't believe it."

"It's strange alright."

"I wonder what happened to the driver…And all those bananas! How could anyone get away with all those bananas?"

"Wouldn't I like to know! All that tonnage gone to waste…" He scratched his neck. "What's so great about bananas all of sudden?"

"Maybe there's a bunch of gorillas hiding out someplace," she laughed. "Actually, my grandma says she's been hearing weird noises out in the woods."

"I don't know…Why don't you ask that nutty teacher of yours about it?"

"He isn't nutty!' She took offense and pouted slightly. "He's got some very personal ideas, that's all."

Opening a can of Pepsi, Bryan shook the foam off his hand and took a gulp. "Say, did you check your car yet? That was pretty crazy of you. I bet it's gone now."

"I better, huh? I forgot all about it." She tossed the paper down on the wooden table and arose.

"I didn't mean you had to check now. You can check after lunch break, can't you?"

Pausing at the door, she looked back at him with blinking eyes, "Don't worry, precious. I'll be right back." She blew him a kiss.

"Alright." He watched her leave. The door slammed. He sighed, "That girl…"

There was glass crystallized across the hood of her green Pontiac from a jagged hole in the windshield, tears of it fallen into the interior and a banana peel left on the dashboard. "Son of a—" she whispered, running her fingers carefully around the shatter. She found her keys and sprung the door.

There was glass on her car seat too. "Jesus!" Percie looked around, placing her hand gently on the seat to lean and peer under the dashboard. She brushed a lock of black hair that fell over her face, back behind her ear. She sighed deeply and picked up the bit of banana skin that was left. Only a small remain, a yellow memento. "A clue?" she murmured. Maybe the peel could be dusted for fingerprints. She thought she better leave it and call the police.

Percie closed the door and stared to return to the store. "On second thought…" She stopped. "I better take the peel with me. The thief might return to finish the job." And she turned around.

A policeman, a blue uniform, badge bristling with sunlight, black shined shoes tiptoeing his thick body over the hood of the Pontiac, peered sniffing into the car.

"Oh good!" she said, close behind him, making him jump. Though straightened to his full height before her, he appeared to be a bit hunchbacked, slouching in his suit. Not exactly her idea at all of a model policeman; unshaven too. "My car was just broken into, sir!" she explained the obvious.

"Umm."

"Well…" Was he illiterate too? she wondered. "Do you think there's anything we can do about it?" She pointed at all the broken glass. "There was a bit of banana left behind. Maybe you could dust it for fingerprints?"

His eyes had been on the peel all along. "Urrrr," he repeated.

"Yes…I'll open the door so you can examine it." She fit the key to the lock and opened the door. "You see," she started to tell him, but the peel was gone. "It was here a second ago…"

She leaned inside and looked up at the policeman's face through the cracked windshield lines. His face twisted, contorted like a circus mirror, his mouth was full.

She removed herself from the car. "I know it was there a second ago."Percie stumbled over words, "I put a whole banana there…"

He shrugged and brought his long arm up to scratch his brow. His fingers went clumsily up the sloping forehead that backed up into his visored cap.

"Yes, well," she paused, distressed. "I suppose I'll have to file a report down at the station then?"

He nodded. The thing he was eating shifted to the other side of his mouth.

Her brows furrowed. "Well, thanks for your help, officer."

He loped off again, chewing, inspecting the cars of the parking lot as he left.

She eyed him leave and pinched her lip meditatively for a moment. "A lot of help he was…" she muttered. Then she understood. "He must have taken that banana peel! I wasn't gone for more than a few seconds." She walked slowly back to Shopper Heaven, forgetting to take in the shopping cart that stood empty nearby.

"You done with your break, Percie?" Tracy-Ann called from

a register. A line of customers grew in front of her mutinously.

"No," Percie replied distantly, "Almost though."

"Well hurry up." The trailing customers grumbled approval.

She talked to herself all the way to the back wall of the store. "That cop sure was strange…" The door swung open.

Bryan was reading the paper folded under his hands. He looked up, "Well?"

"I was robbed alright."

"What?!"

"Yeah," she set her hands on her hips, "Someone broke my window to get at it."

"Holy Mackerel!"

"And then this cop came over," she sat down next to him, looked hard into his blue eyes, "but he was useless. He didn't even talk to me. He didn't help me with the only clue I had. In fact, I'm pretty sure he ate the clue!"

"What do you mean?" Bryan took a long sip from his Pepsi.

She rattled out what had happened. Then she sighed and tugged her hair.

"Percie, honey," he said, placing a hand down on her arm to comfort her, "Let me go out and take a look at the car."

After they got back inside, Percie didn't have much time to think about what had happened because she had to work the register again. Treading masses of shoppers filed nonstop past her. It was monotony—groceries, money appearing, going into the drawer, reappearing, talking about the weather…

Percie noticed a lot of plantains were being sold, until they ran out of them too. They weren't the same as bananas, but as close as you could get. Also banana flavored foods were selling briskly—ice cream, Jello, popsicles, candy, pudding, cakes.

After work—with her head reeling numbers, prices, faces, money, bills and change, hands and hands, buttons—she met with Bryan whose shift ended at the same time.

"I got the vacuum cleaner to get that glass out of your car," he said. He wielded the little handheld cleaner with expert swordsmanship. "Then let's get out of here."

"What do you make of all this?" she asked.

"I don't know. But things are getting stranger by the hour."

The parking lot purpled with dusk and bugs swarmed the lit up shopping sign.

"This sure is a pity…What a mess." He flipped the vacuum cleaner on. It made a whirring buzz. She stood aside in the open door as he ran it over the seat, the dashboard and the floor, rattling up the chips and sparks of glass.

"I can't understand why that cop would be so useless." She spoke loudly over the hum of the vacuum and stopped, squinting her eyes at some blurry shape not far away.

A grayed over form stalked through the parking lot edge.

"Bryan…" she touched his shoulder, not looking away. "What is that?"

It lumbered through the shadows.

"What's what?" he poked his head up with the vacuum whining to a halt. "Oh yeah…" He saw it too.

A man shape covered over with a thin layering of hair loped off through the parking lot into the dark woods beside the pavement. There was a howling in the dark.

"My God, Bryan!" She grabbed his arm. "What was that?"

"I don't know…"

"I'm scared."

He put his arm around her. They both jumped when the vacuum turned on.

"Turn that thing off!"

"Sorry." The insides of the vacuum shook with broken glass.

The night was silent now. Crickets and quiet. The white moon glowed down, watching wide-eyed from a starry sky.

Percie whispered, "I think we better go to my teacher's house and ask him what he makes of all this. He told me the other day he's been doing some experiments on Dayton's air. He said he found some real strange things going on."

Once they were in the car, the air blew through the fist-sized circle smashed in the windshield. Percie blinked as she drove, leaning to the right, her head almost on Bryan's shoulder. They passed the drive-in movie, all the cars parked in the field asleep, the glow of the big screen showing a scene for a magical second and then they were past. Spring smelled wet in the air. It was so warm for this time of year.

Approaching the lit up windows of her teacher's house, set in suburbia surroundings, she pulled into the driveway and stopped at the closed garage door. She turned off the headlights and the motor and said, "I hope he doesn't mind us barging in like this."

"Not with the story we're going to tell him," Bryan said.

In a moment they waited at the front door. There was a stirring inside and then the door opened. The teacher stood before them.

Dark hair was brushed over his forehead; he wore horn-rim glasses and was dressed in his white lab coat, pens and pencils and a ruler in the breast pocket, looking as if he'd fallen out of some Physics handbook. "Well hello, Percie!" he beamed. "And a friend?"

Bryan had barely passed his science class. His concentration had been less on school and more on the job at the supermarket which after graduation took him on fulltime, with a promotion for a management position. "Hi, I'm Bryan."

Percie stammered, "We have to talk to you about what's going on with all the vanishing bananas and all—"

"Yeah," Bryan said.

"—plus we saw something really strange tonight."

"Well come in, come in, no need to stand out there in the gloom." Stepping aside, the teacher ushered them inside, into his disarrayed house.

Percie looked around. "We aren't disturbing you, I hope?"

"No, no…" A woman disappeared to another room carrying a tray of green vapor. "We were just running some tests. I've been getting some very strange atmospheric readings which seem to correlate with your findings. So it appears anyway. Come along..." He guided them down the stairs, flipping on the basement light switch.

They were in a little room. Test tubes brewed smoke into the air, beakers and dishes held secrets, buzzing and whirrings. "My lab," he explained. "Over here I've been tabulating the change in Dayton's air." Red lines charted progress on a graph and a nearby machine, blinking buttons, jiggled some beakers. "Now, as you can see, the temperature has been steadily rising at a peculiarly rapid increase and with the temperature rise has come a new mysterious chemical in the air. Look here..."

"God! What's that?" Bryan pointed, "It's green!"

"Yes, I dyed it so it would be visible to us. Normally it's quite invisible. It's a gas. Each day its volume in the air increases. I've been trying to identify the gas but so far it eludes me."

"Is it poisonous?"

"No. But it does do very strange things...Look over here at this monkey I've exposed to large doses of the gas. As you know the monkey is man's closest relation, our closest link on the evolutionary chain, so—"

"That's a monkey?!" Percie clenched her hands.

"Yes. Well, it was yesterday."

A small scaly creature writhed in its wood-chipped glass cage.

"As you can see it has shed its fur and seems to be devolving back to some previous state on the evolutionary chain."

"So if the gas does this to a monkey, if a person is exposed..." Percie paused.

"If a person is exposed then one could assume the human evolutionary development would regress. It makes perfect sense that people would be attracted to bananas since their biological predecessors would have been very keen on them."

"Apes!" Bryan cried.

"Precisely."

"That's what we saw, Bryan! And that's why that policeman—" Percie turned to her teacher, "I was with a policeman who was in the middle of the transformation."

"Really?" Her teacher stared at her, concerned. "A policeman?"

"Yes. He ate a banana that I left on my car dashboard. It was a lure."

"Hmmm."

Bryan watched the cloudy green gas in the beaker. "But sir, why aren't all the people in town turning back into apes?"

"Well, Bryan, it appears that this transformation is taking place in a way that affects those in the power enforcement structure…" He paced the floor thoughtfully. "Which means, by my estimation, politicians would be the next hit! That means that we could be in more serious trouble than imagined if this gas is spreading."

"Oh my God!" Percie stared back and forth.

Bryan pounded his fist. "We've got to tell someone about this!"

"Yes, but who? All the authorities are probably swinging in trees by now."

"But there must be some sort of antidote?" Percie clutched her teacher's white labcoat.

"I only hope there is." He rubbed his eyes. "I've been searching in vain for nights."

"Oh, this is terrible!" Percie fell against Bryan. "What—"

A scream from upstairs shook the bottles in the lab.

"Roxanne!" their teacher cried and bounded out of the room, up the stairs.

Percie and Bryan followed close behind.

Roxanne was collapsed on the floor in the kitchen. "Oh, Harold," she sobbed. "I just got the worst scare." She cried into her hands. "It was George from next door…I think it was George…Or some creature who looked like George…"

Harold bent down to her and lifted her up in his arms. "Hush now, darling. Just tell me what you saw."

"George looked like a gorilla!" she cried. "He was looking through the garbage can out there!"

Harold shot a look at Percie and Bryan. He told them, "George is a lawyer…" He set his wife in the kitchen chair and peered out the window at the spilled over garbage on the lawn.

There was also a shrinking gray mass collapsed on the grass.

"What's happening now?" He dropped the curtain and yanked open the kitchen door.

Outside, along the sidewalk next to the silver trashcan, a transformation was occurring. The gorilla thing was writhing from within. The brown fur of it was expelled as a slick under-skin emerged. Flapping and undulating the shape was getting smaller and smaller, no longer ape, no longer mammal.

"It's a fish!" said Harold. Percie and Bryan hovered behind him.

Before them a large trout flipped in the grass, its mouth gasping in too much air.

Harold nodded. "Of course! It's the next step on the devolutionary ladder. Quick, let's see if we can get George into some water before he dies." He slipped his hands around the dry, scaly fish and they rushed back to the house.

All around the neighborhood, the air cried with the primeval calls of nature rebounding.

Through the door on the way to the bathtub, Harold suddenly stopped, realizing only the two kids were following him. "Oh no—Roxanne! I hope she's okay." He passed George to Bryan, "Take this. I have to check on Roxanne," he said, turning for the kitchen. "She's a real estate agent!"

"This is insane," Percie groaned from behind Bryan's back as the water poured and filled the tub. "It's to be or not to be."

Bryan shouted, "Aahh!"

"What is it, Bryan?"

"The fish is starting to grow hair again!"

Harold came into the bathroom leading a docile orangutan by the hand. "Just look at my darling Roxanne now! I'm afraid it's only a matter of time…"

"I don't know about that," Bryan said. "This fish-thing is growing hair again."

"What? Impossible!" Harold touched the fish incredulously. "Tell me what you did! What happened? You must describe exactly how this happened! What did you do before George began to turn back?"

Clumps of orange hair were falling onto the kitchen floor like autumn leaves.

"Quickly, boy! Speak!" Harold grabbed him, "The future of mankind rests with you!"

"Well…I put him in the bathtub like you said. I poured in the water and nothing much was happening and then Percie says, 'This is insane…This is insane…'" he was forgetting.

"Please remember," Harold pleaded.

Scales were appearing among the falling orange fur. Roxanne had gone from real estate agent, to ape, and now she was turning into a fish. He would have to bring her flowers to the aquarium.

"I remember," Percie broke in. "I said, this is insane, it's to be or not to be!"

The object in the sink became a monkey again. Roxanne was un-aping, becoming herself.

"Shakespeare! That's Shakespeare!" the teacher shouted victoriously. "Shakespeare is the antidote! By God, Percie! You've discovered the saving grace! We've got no time to lose now!"

Harold ran to his bookshelf and in seconds returned with a volume of Shakespeare's collected plays as Roxanne gently became a human again. Flipping to a random page, he began:

"I am thy father's spirit,
Doomed for a certain term to walk the night,
And for the day confined to fast in fires,
Till the foul crimes done in my days of nature
Are burnt and purged away…"

George suddenly appeared in the bathtub, half naked except

for some torn shirt which he quickly whisked down around his waist. "Where am I?"

"Ahh, George! You're back!" Harold patted him on the back. "Now, Percie…" Quickly, Harold tore a section from out of the book, "You take this out into the neighborhood. And Byron, you take this." He ripped out another page. "Roxanne will go east reciting Shakespeare; I will go west. Percie you go south and Byron you go north and together we will restore mankind with Shakespeare!"

They left Harold's house, dispersing at the sidewalk in their various directions. Shakespeare hollered at the nocturnal ramblings. Then all at once, they stopped, illuminated by the floodlights of overhead streetlamps. They came to the same conclusion, all four of them at once—*now that they had it in their power, wouldn't it be a better world without the policemen, politicians and lawyers?* And the rivers, streams, lakes, ponds and oceans could always use more fish.

SAINT GEORGE AND THE DRAGON

A candle burned, not for light so much as the feeling it gave, while cars went below the window in the Sunday morning traffic. Shopping carts crashed together in the rainy Safeway parking lot.

"I guess I'm just a professional envelope stuffer," he was smiling to her, next to him. "That's the only way I can make a living. If paying jobs are what define people, and here in America, I suppose that's all that does."

"But you're a writer." Her mouth curved, "A professional envelope stuffing writer. That's what you are. I can tell. Just look at these hands," she smiled, batted her eyes, and held them to her, "So strong and wonderful."

"From writing eight books and stuffing a thousand envelopes a day…I could play the piano to the moon with these hands. But I'd rather play something more nearby."

Something gigantic moved behind the wall. Plaster fell onto her hair.

"What the—?" she startled up. The room bent and shook again. She held to him dearly. "An earthquake?"

"No," he sighed. "That's Todd."

The room was still again but she held him fearfully. "Who's Todd?"

"Don't worry. He's just a nuisance." His finger spun a circle on her leg and he kissed her.

"Well, I am a little worried." This was her first time to his place. Her eyes roamed the walls around them—the peeling, flowered wallpaper with rejection notices taped awkwardly across it, to the American flag pinned in the lower corner. A tall heavy green filing cabinet rattled slightly as if possessed. There was no other furniture on the wooden, scratched up floor, only the mattress heaped with their clothes and blankets. "What's

Todd? A weightlifting gorilla?" She laughed as he kissed her neck. "Is he part of your latest story, come to life?"

"Oh, I forgot to show you." He peeled himself from her. "Here..." Off the floor, he picked a yellow envelope addressed to him. Inside it was the latest rejection. He showed her and cast it away from them. "Hopeless."

"No, it's great! You just have to keep trying. It just takes a long time to get noticed."

"Well, I don't know how much longer I have to wait. I don't want to stuff envelopes forever, but look around you. I'm pretty sure all I will ever have is more of this." He took her hand and said dreamily, "I would love to make a living writing though. Wouldn't it be great? I could have a little room beside the ocean, where I could wake up in the morning, look out at the sea and write meaningful things until the sun set on the water. I don't want to wait forever." He squeezed her hand, "I send out stories, they come right back. I'm invisible. It doesn't matter."

"It matters to me!" she said. "I believe in you, I know it will happen."

He smiled. She was so serious. Hope in what he was capable of, that was what he needed. "I promise I'll keep trying." He put his hand on her hip pushing up through the blanket falling softly over her. He said, "If I didn't have you with me, I wouldn't be able to dream." As she took him in her arms, he said, "As it is I barely make enough to support my lifestyle."

She looked at the room and laughed. "What lifestyle?" She leaned on her elbow and looked around at the atmosphere of the room again.

"Well...I need to get dog food for Todd, for example."

The flag tucked to the wall moved aside and suddenly the fear that she had felt hidden in the walls became visible. The leathery head of a reptile appeared.

"You didn't tell me about that!"

More of it kept coming through the huge mouse hole shape, chewed out of the wallpaper and covered by the flag. There were short legs with claws and the long body and finally a lashing tail.

"That's Todd," he said. "He won't hurt us."

The breath of the twelve foot monitor lizard melted the flame of the candle and it swallowed it in one gulp.

She couldn't believe it. "Your landlord allows that thing to live here?!"

"I don't really ask questions. I try not to rock the boat. The rent is so cheap. There are worse things than dragons. I put up with it. It's a minor inconvenience, like a leaking faucet or a window shutter that knocks in the breeze." He watched the lizard slashing its tail and resting its chin in the sun on the edge of the windowsill. "I tolerate it."

"That dinosaur?!"

It hissed at her from the corner, flicking its long blue tongue. Venom hung on its mouth. It had decided not to like her.

"Look," he said, "He's not that bad. He's just an iguana."

"No! No, he's not. There's a picture of him in our zoology book. Todd is a komodo dragon from Sumatra! How he got here, I can't imagine." She held the sheet around her. "Where *did* it come from? Did it escape from the zoo, or is it a roaming pet that ate its owner? Maybe Dr. Frankenstein created it to terrorize people? You should call an exterminator or someone with a shotgun. You don't have to let that huge lizard come in here," she said, "and ruin everything."

"How can I stop it? It's a monster! It goes wherever it wants."

"You could nail some wood across the hole instead of that flag. Or how about moving a steel safe in front of it?"

"Oh, I've tried things, believe me. It's not that easy. He can eat through wood and push aside anything smaller than an armored car. He's a genuine monster, diabolical. I've given up trying to get rid of him. He's here to stay."

Craftily, she stared at the gnawed opening in the wall. "What about poison?"

"He eats it up. It doesn't affect him."

"Well, I don't like him coming in here and I'm going to do something about it." She said, "Let me think about it…I'll think of something. Women are better at these things than men. Leave it to me. You'll see." She lay back down next to him, quietly. He could feel her breathing and the slow turning inside of her, scheming the end of the dragon.

"I don't necessarily mind Todd…" he told her after a while. "He's almost a pet to me…"

"He's not a pet. He totally controls you. Look around you. This room is like a zoo cage. There's nothing left but the mattress and the filing cabinet with your writing. Todd's got to go."

She lay with him but her eyes didn't wander from the black komodo dragon. "Besides, I don't like making love with a dragon watching me."

"Think of him as part of the décor."

She whispered, "How long does he stay in the room?"

"Just until he sees that there's no food for him."

"Go!" she ordered, stretching her arm towards the flag hole.

Its black eyes were watching a fly circle in the orange sunlight.

She watched it and he knew that look in her eyes. She would think of a way soon. Her smile returned, "I've got it!" She whispered in his ear. "If this doesn't kill it, it will put a scare into it so deeply that it will never ever return." She kneeled and put on his gray sweater.

"Please." He held her knitted arm. "I don't want you to get hurt. That lizard is powerful. It could kill you. Please don't go near it."

Todd swiveled and slithered darkly to the corner, pushing back once again into the flag, moving slowly, vanishing.

At last its tail was gone and its unseen noise went through the shaking walls, further into the building, somewhere deeper, back to where it had come from.

"Now," she grabbed her skirt off the blanket. She pulled it up her legs, around her waist and she stood up. "I need a screwdriver."

"I don't have one…Wait, my Swiss Army knife has one. Here—" He reached out of the covers and found it in the pocket of his trousers.

She took the knife and hurried into the bathroom. "Some knight you are!" she called to him. "Making the maiden kill the dragon!"

"I have no desire to see it die," he said plainly. He sat up in bed. "What are you doing?"

"Wait there, Sir Galahad. You'll see…" Her voice echoed from the shower tiles and empty tub. "That thing ate the toothpaste, didn't it?"

"And the shampoo, and the razor…Also all the furniture I used to have in here."

"I've got it!" she said and she came back out carrying a hinged square of wood. The other side of it was flashing silver reflection along the walls as she moved toward the flag.

He laughed. "The cabinet mirror?"

She leaned it against the hole, draped by the flag so that the glass stared into the black depths, waiting. "Well?" She sat down with him on the mattress. "Do you think my plan will work?" She lay back down and pressed herself over him and they listened to the wall.

MEXICAN DOG BISCUITS

The car was parked out in the dust, as clouds bunched together over the brown mountains and began to move slowly. Inside the house, the American tourist was busy cutting hair for the entire Gonzalez family. They were lined up oldest to youngest and he moved with his scissors from the white thin hair of the grandfather, along towards the black braids of the little girl at the end, holding in her arms a sleeping baby.

It began to rain while he cut and showered the floor with their hair. He had never been in a rain like this before. The tin roof shook and bounced and the lights dimmed from the water eclipse. The children shrieked and leaped out of the line to run outside and splash. They let a river in every time the door opened and closed. They settled down when the weather passed and when they came back in, the American trimmed their wet hair.

That's what he did in the U.S, he told them. He had his own barber shop in Seattle where it always rained, but not like how it does here. He made a rain sound and drummed his fingers on the top of his head and everyone laughed. Then he opened the door to go to his car.

He stared and dropped his black bag. His convertible was filled with water. It looked like a swimming pool on wheels.

Still, he made it back to Seattle. The car was a submarine, it was sluggish and it agonized on the mountains up through California, but at last, he made it home. His dog was glad to see him return and jumped all over him. The clothes and luggage were all damp in the trunk and he threw them straight into the washing machine. There was also a cardboard box filled with soggy dog biscuits—treats for his dog—souvenirs. He laid them out like tiles to dry on the kitchen counters and across a table in the rare sunlight.

THE SIDEKICK

"Did I tell you that I met this other actor? Do you remember Jimmy Stewart, *Anatomy of a Murder?* The guy who played his sidekick in that? I can't remember his name right now…" Richard paused. "What was his name? I wish I could remember his name because he was featured, he even starred in…he was in a lot of roles. He was busy all the time. He got all kinds of— Arthur! Uhhh, Arthur somebody…Anyway, I got his address and wrote to him. I had an interview with him and I asked him for a job."

It was a beautiful day a long time ago, blue sky and sunshine that painted everything gold. "I drove over to meet him. He had an apartment building in downtown Hollywood. It wasn't like Mae West's building. It was just two or three stories."

Richard parked in front of the building behind a car that looked only a few years better off than his own. It almost felt like coming home. Getting out of his car onto the sidewalk, there were even the faint chalk marks of a hopscotch on the cement.

Arthur met him, smiling jovially, shook hands and guided Richard around back to a patio where they sat down in wicker chairs on the lawn. They hit if off fine, Arthur was a pleasant guy to talk with.

Finally Arthur got around to the job. He said, "All you really have to do, Richard, is just collect the rents on the first of the month. You'll have your own apartment. Take it easy, make sure everything is okay. You don't have to do much of anything."

"Well yeah…Well do you have a garden, and can I trim the lawn?" Richard wanted to be useful. He didn't just want to sit there.

Arthur laughed. He said, "Listen, this will give you a lot of time to do your stories and write your damn novel." Arthur laughed at the look on Richard's face. "You think about it. I'll get back in touch."

They stood up and Richard walked with him back to the street, to the curb where Richard's car was parked.

"Arthur O'Connell!" Richard suddenly remembered. It took him a while to recall that last name, but a lot of years have gone by, stars shined then burned out. But Richard had gone back in time to that first meeting with him, that warm afternoon when he shook Arthur O'Connell's hand and returned to his beat-up car and drove home on California sunshine.

A week went by. It just so happened, Richard's parents came out to visit him from Michigan. They were there when Arthur O'Connell came over unannounced. He and his chauffeur filed into Richard's little apartment and stood by the couch.

"My mom and dad were there and my mother blew it. Oh, did she blow it...I felt so embarrassed." The memory of it caught sharp in Richard's throat and he coughed and shook his head.

She said, "Oh, we're so proud of our son, Richard! Do you know, Mr. O'Connell, that Richard was studying to be an actor?"

"Oh, Mom, please no..."

It started many years before Richard was born. His mother always had a secret desire to go to Hollywood. She was born in 1917. She started watching the silent films in those days when the theater was a palace of holy light. She was pulled into that world by Charlie Chaplin and those magical flickering pictures like a moth to the flame. Then, after she met Richard's father, that dream of hers sort of caved in on itself. Not entirely though. Back on the farm in Michigan, she would still read the magazines about Hollywood and every week she took Richard to the movies. Through that entrance that hush and wonder was passed on to him.

Arthur noticed Richard's embarrassment. "Well, he seems

like a nice young chap," he said. Arthur was polite with Richard's parents. He handled the woman's star-struck talk gracefully. Richard's father was silent on the couch, holding a cigarette. Richard paced and clenched his fist. He felt sure he would never see Arthur again. Couldn't he be just a guy to him? He was sure his mother had ruined everything. It left him boiling inside. For days Richard replayed that goodbye to Arthur as he took his parents sightseeing…He took them to the Brown Derby and on the studio tours but something in him was a crumpled bird. He was cold when he took them to the airport and said goodbye. He walked out of the Los Angeles airport feeling dead.

About a week later Arthur O'Connell came back to Richard's apartment. He took off his sunglasses and grinned. "Richard, you've got the job! How soon can you move in?"

Even after all this time it was still painful to recall. Richard told me, "I don't know how this happened, believe me, I've searched my mind, but I said, 'Mr. O'Connell, I've changed my mind. I can't accept the job.'"

Arthur got furious. He started cursing at Richard. "You mean you made me come all the way over here to tell me that?" He stopped at the door and turned one last time to Richard. His voice had reached an actor's pitch, "Don't ever bother to try to get another job in this town again because you're blackballed!"

Richard said, "Okay…I just thought I should be honest with you. I didn't want to take the job and then leave you."

Richard shook his head. It was long ago. "But I don't know why I changed my mind, to be honest. I guess there was something about him, after we had talked a few times. Something about him made me back out…"

The door shut on Richard's face with a slam. He caught his breath in the quiet of the room then he walked over to where the daylight let in. The street was down below.

"So he drove away and I'm standing out on the balcony

and I'm waving to him while he's leaving…A big smile on my face…Trying to be nice to him." Richard stood out on that balcony for ten minutes more, thinking Arthur might come back.

Illustration from *Pie In The Sky #4*.

THE SHUFFLER

Right out of the atmosphere of our planet, there's ghostly capitalism on the moon. The moon is streaked with the black tracks made by excavation, as huge tractors roll across the surface, peeling it away.

When they gave him the job a season ago, they didn't tell him how long moon days could be. The moon is always October or November. For a long time now, he's had a green photo of trees taped to the round porthole of his sleeping quarters, to remind him and keep him feeling human.

The first month he was trained and then he was left alone in the tractor. Usually he had a solitaire game going on the dashboard, while the machinery dug onwards.

The sky was black, the ground was white. Far away on the horizon to his left and right there were other tractors like his digging and throwing out clouds of dust. They were competing with him. At the end of the season circuiting the moon, they were going to be paid according to how much they had taken from the ground. They saw each other as opponents.

He made lists of things he wanted to buy, to keep from going crazy.

It was easy to get lonely on the moon. Every season someone would break, go absolutely crazy trying to resist becoming a robot. He knew he had to be careful not to become like them. A season on the moon could do that to the best of workers.

He made up an imaginary friend to keep him company. She played solitaire with him and she always won, laughing in her strange, beautiful way. He told her about Las Vegas, back on Earth, how she could make millions with a talent like hers. He said, "We could go together."

She laughed and asked him to stop the motor. He did.

The other tractors crept by him and as the clouds of moondust settled down, there seemed to be a great peace.

She pointed at all the stars on the other side of the calm glass.

He pulled them out of the sky for her and strung them onto a piece of electrical wire. She said it was beautiful, kissed him and wore it as a necklace.

Leading him to the airlock, she opened the door, so they could stroll across the dancing moon's craters and mountains and point at the blue dot of Earth and wonder if there was life on it.

INSTANT CASH FOR GUNS AND FLOWERS

All around, the ground had him surrounded. It had been a long time since the trucks had finished dumping, using the wild land around his second hand gun store for a landfill. All the earth and plants that were removed from the town, dug out to make new apartments and shopping places, had quickly taken root and grew into huge shapes with dark shadows and strange light. Metal flashed back, light off barrels from racks full of rifles and pistols for sale. He watched the shine uneasily.

It didn't take long, pollen drifted into his store, seeds took root and he had to fight to keep them from growing. Pulling a vine from the bore of a rifle, he stared down the jungle and decided he couldn't let it go on any longer. He remembered the dreams he had, fighting something huge in the green. There were plants out there he didn't know and sounds he had never heard before.

Now he took a shotgun off the wall. There was moss on the trigger but he rubbed it off. He grabbed shells and left his air conditioned store.

The door banged shut behind him and the smell of blooming flowers and the jungle heat of the summer nearly dropped him to his knees on the parking lot, scattering gravel as he stumbled. He tried to focus, rubbing his eyes while he steadied himself. He felt like an astronaut as he walked.

There was a pathway made of mirrors and he smashed his reflection with every step he took, as he turned corners deeper and deeper into the maze of second hand flowers, looking for the thing he had to find.

MONSTER NIGHT

These are not the people who like to be seen in daylight. When they move outdoors, it is in the darkness of night, when only the moon and stars and green of lamplights are glowing. Moths flutter about them as they move out of basements, attics and forgotten hidden rooms. They are the hideous ones, born misshapen, or without enough smarts, those who have been mangled by accidents, hurt to distortion. Nobody wants to see them, but at deepest night they all come out. Around the time the TV turns into static, they form a parade. They hobble, limp and drag themselves along the cement and pavement in front of quiet houses. Shadows try to hide them as they weave along, muttering and pointing at sleeping windows. Who could understand their anger as they let the air out of car tires, turn mailboxes inside-out, hammer flowers into pulp and create other havoc in suburbia? Only another monster could know the feeling. Only another monster could be like them as they move, in silence, with only the night to believe.

IN THE CIRCUS

He was chain smoking, coughing, getting on my nerves, but I couldn't shake him and escape. He followed me wherever I went and got near me like a cheap plaid shadow. Puffing out a cloud of smoke over my coffee cup, he rattled the newspaper and coughed again. It didn't matter how rude he could be, nobody could see him but me.

"What do you want?!" I finally seethed. It was burning me up. I don't get angry very easily, it has to build up tremendously before I will let it crash out.

He stubbed the cigarette on the tabletop, next to my hand and introduced himself, "My name's Cupid."

I spilled some of my coffee over my fingers. "What?" There was Mozart playing on the hidden speakers. This coffee shop was supposed to be a place of quiet reflection. There were paintings by the Old Masters on the wooden panel walls. I caught myself and hushed apologetically, but still I glared at him, "Do you mind?" I gritted my teeth to speak, "I would like it if you would leave me alone. Don't you have something better to do?"

He ignored me and turned to point at the counter, "See that pretty girl?"

Of course I had seen her. I liked her. She was the reason I came here. There was something about her, much more than the miraculous way she poured more water into the coffee machine with such grace.

He winked and told me, "You gotta go talk to her." Already, he was fumbling in his pocket for another cigarette. Before he lit it, he smiled brown teeth and promised, "If you do…" he grinned, "I'll leave you alone."

I didn't want him around anymore. I had tried all kinds of ways to lose him—I had hopped on random buses and walked down alleys instead of the usual streets (even leaped into stores unexpectedly along the way) but he would always be waiting for me.

Quietly, I stood up and left him and walked up to the counter.

She smiled warmly when she saw me and her beautiful voice guessed, "You'd like some more coffee?"

Houdini's act couldn't have been more entrancing, while I stood there watching her and tried to find the words that could express my wonder. "How did you know?" I said. "You should be in the circus."

An atomic bomb fell and splintered radioactively. Her smile dropped, "Thanks a lot!"

The horrible moment hit. I realized she didn't think it was a compliment. I took my empty cup away. I was back to more years of the traveling circus sideshow attractions, with Cupid pushing me along the tightrope and no end in sight but the hard dark vague where there was sawdust below.

pie in the sky
#72
the giraffe
on the raft
laughed

PIE IN THE SKY
number 74

THE HOT WATER PRAYER

It was something he did every night when he got home from work. He would take a hot bath with Emily Dickinson. He was only half emerged out of the soap and water and the book of poems in his hands was warped soft and butterflied from days in the steam. Her pages stuck together and needed to be separated by wet fingers.

He lived on the third floor, the middle of the apartment building and all the strange sounds from all around echoed and gurgled inside the peeling walls of his bathroom. Also, he had a cheap gray plastic tape recorder playing Satie piano on the floor, in a footprint of water. He was intent on poetry, all the music of the building was incidental to his reading in the tub.

The book leaves were propped open on his knees, raised out of the water by only inches and he sighed at Poem #903, written in 1864. There must be a beautiful woman like her today, he thought, someone hidden away like Emily, poetic and dreaming. He stared at the page and his soapy skin, "I wish I could find her…" he prayed.

A chip of paint fell like a snowflake from the ceiling. It twirled down and landed on him. He smiled. A second later, ten gallons of hot water rain and the ceiling and a naked girl fell through from the bathroom above and splashed with a crash into his lion-footed tub.

DREAM WITH MEXICANS AND FLOATING LIONS

In big wooden cages, the lions floated ashore. They broke out of the surf onto the sand, angry and looking for food. Their roars carried all the way from the sea up to the town. We turned from the cliff where we were watching. I held her hand tightly and we ran to look for shelter. The houses were all locked and boarded up except for one and we hurried towards the open door. Maybe we could hide down in the basement where the lions could scratch but couldn't get in? We ran up the path, almost safe, when suddenly a family of Mexicans pushing a piano and moving out boxes and furniture blocked the doorway. They couldn't understand our warnings, our hysterical shouting and pointing at the ocean.

10:55 A.M.
August 12, 1993

MOVING CACTUS

Little did they know they brought home a living, breathing cactus from the plant store. Not until they got it back to their apartment, settling it in the glare of the sun on the carpet, did they first suspect that the plant was alive in a strange way.

She interrupted him to ask, "Is the cactus moving?" He stared at it too, until he could almost believe.

"No, it must be the light." He lit a cigarette and passed her the pack.

So they went on with the rest of the day, while the green spines of the three foot tall cactus turned with the slowest motion towards them.

Later, he made dinner for her, something Italian with tomato sauce that rolled like an ocean on the plate. Smiling and passing her a glass of wine, he toasted, "To our new cactus."

They clicked glasses and she laughed, smiled back.

The cactus seemed to bristle at the sound.

They both saw it, but it could have been the flicker of candlelight. Shadows move like that, mysteriously.

"Hey, I've got an idea!" She jumped up from the table suddenly and ran into the other room.

"What are you doing?" he called.

"You'll see!" She was shuffling things in the other room. "This will be great!" The closet door opened and closed. She laughed, "It's perfect!"

In a moment, she came back into the room wearing a kimono and carrying an electric Japanese lantern in front of her.

Blue cranes on her white silk, the lamp shade wobbled as she walked. When she kneeled down and plugged the lamp in, rainbows of light spun out and she moved it over like a Tokyo spotlight to center on their plant.

"A work of art!" he smiled at her and applauded as she modeled in front of the cactus like it was the grand prize on a game show—a Ford Escort, or a trip to the Bahamas.

The cactus glowed in the light and moved, rocked, breathed deeply like a green lung in and out, then exploded.

Hundreds of small tarantulas flew out and all the spine debris of the large cactus spider seed went off as a terrible bomb, screaming in their living room.

LES FALLS OUT OF A TREE

The hillside was all mud now, cut with whorls and streams made by rainwater. Some green weeds began to grow, shivering long necked flowers and ragged bushes that hugged to the ground like coyotes. All the trees on his land, he had cut down. Except for one…There it stood, a black hand at the bottom of the hill, next to the driveway and Les was climbing off the ladder onto the thumb of it. He tried to hold to the wet bark scales, but the tree was slippery with phantoms of the missing forest hissing through its leaves. From the Amazon, straight to the Cascades, a shiver went through the ghost of roots and Les fell, sixteen feet to the ground.

Illustration accompanying the story from *Pie In The Sky #12*.

SOMETHING BRIGHT WAS SUPPOSED TO BE WAITING

Something bright was supposed to be waiting in the years to come. For the 1962 World's Fair, Seattle built all kinds of monuments to guide the way to the next century. But who would have predicted the cynical crash America would take? The most careful hand was needed in guiding the country back on track again towards the future. There were some who were doing all they could do.

Above the city streets, the sleek rusting steel monorail clattered from the Space Needle to the shopping mall. It went back and forth all day transporting the people of the 1990s and the Tin Man at the lit-up control panel directed the speed and opened and closed the doors with gentle, mechanical words for them. This was another example of those old dreams, that robots could replace the drudgery of human jobs.

Now with the economy in shambles, widespread loss of faith and anger, people were lucky to have any kind of job at all. A lot of people were envious of the Tin Man's cushy job, automatically pressing buttons all day—it should be one of them instead, getting $19 an hour. People treated him badly. Kids spray-painted his silver back. For a joke, someone had superglued a can of beer to his hand. There were knife marks chipped into his chrome. But the Tin Man had no disregard for this future world. He knew that sooner or later it would have to change for the better.

STELLA WINKS

Part One:

The morning began. Some crows flew over the rooftops, some newspapers and garbage blew across the street. Buses, cars and trucks passed by while the sky slowly brightened. Stella Winks arrived at ten of seven. She stepped off the bus with her arms around brown bags full of cloth and sparkles and paper stars.

She opened the door of Spendy Penny thrift store and set the bags down on the floor. It was dark inside. When she flicked on the switch, all the rows of hung clothes, bookshelves and frozen mannequins jumped to light. The new day was starting, Monday, June 20, 2029.

A mannequin danced woodenly up to her and curtsied, "Good morning, Stella!" it chirped.

"Hi, Cheryl," Stella beamed, "Hello everyone!"

The rest of the mannequins waved from around the dusty store. She always felt like a strange Snow White when she arrived. She pressed the electric OPEN sign on and neon bulbs flickered one by one around the window frame and the speakers automatically played the ancient music of the 20th Century.

"Stella," the mannequin named Cheryl turned its plastic hands towards the counter, "I made some coffee for you."

"Thank you." She noticed the cup steaming next to the register. There was a lot to do today. She had to put together a Fourth of July display, it was required by law. Pierre Camino was coming by to make sure it was done. Wearily, she was still half asleep, Stella picked up the bags and put them on the window shelf. She would have to unload all the red, white and blue and stars and crepe paper into a display that would shout out that America would survive and win the war.

Part 2

He felt a kiss brush his cheek and linger on his mouth as he left dreaming. Vicki Pinkham rolled over on her back, putting her red boxing gloves around him, as Pierre stretched awake. "What time is it?"

"It's nine thirty, baby." She pulled him up onto her stomach with a smile. He was so tiny compared to her and just like a jockey, he squeezed her sides with his little bent knees. Moving under him, she gave him another huge kiss on his mouth and chin.

"What's the agenda today?" he asked her.

Automatically, she knew the path they took every day in the antique 1973 El Camino, chugging while nearly all the rest of the American cars were converted to buzzing electricity. They would pull clouds of coughing gasoline along the street until they reached their first destination. She pictured it the same as always and said, "Spendy Penny."

"Get me a fortune cookie."

Her giant thighs squished him. She picked him up out of bed with her as she strode to the chair where his clothes were thrown and the bag rested. He held clinging around the totem pole of her hard flesh as she walked. When she got there, he let go and fell down over her bare stomach and thighs.

Vicki held up her boxing gloves while he chose a cookie. "Can I take these things off for a minute? I just want to light a cigar."

"I told you a hundred times," Pierre said, "No! I need you to be ready at a moment's notice to go into action. You're my bodyguard."

He crunched the cookie into powder in his hand, leaving only the note which he read and seemed pleased by. He kissed her hip.

"Couldn't you give me a laser gun instead? I can't use my

hands for anything else but punching."

Pierre said, "That's exactly the point. But if you want a cigar, all you have to do is ask." His short fingers held a cigar up for her, lit it and puffed out a cloud of smoke. "Anything you want is yours. But you have to keep your gloves on."

She watched the smoke writhe and disappear and get away, even through the walls of the hotel.

Part 3

Yellow light fell through in slats from the curtained window, across the carpeting of their hotel room while she dressed him in a miniature suit.

A black horse-drawn carriage clopped past outside, hitting every hole in the deteriorating pavement, rolling its way towards the center of the city. Inside it, Dwayne Cody couldn't have been more frightened. There were flowers clutched in shaking petals in his hand. "Tomorrow," he decided. "I'll go see her then…I can't do it today." He stopped the horse against the curb, piled with war rubble. He drew the reigns in. Some children ran past, chasing wooden toys across the broken pavement sprouting weeds. The street was lined with buildings, some of them carved out by fire, others standing bright marble with workers going in and out. The war dropped randomly out of the sky. Bombs could fall anywhere so people watched from the rooftops with binoculars and telescopes.

I know my worries are small compared to the suffering of the country with its war, he thought. But he felt that failing with her would burn him to the ground.

He reached forward and turned on the radio. It took a second to warm up and then the canned laughter of the channel buzzed out of the tin speaker.

The DJ expertly mixed obscene jokes with patriotism. Listening, Dwayne cringed at every word, feeling Frankenstein-guilt for the speeches which he had written for the station, page after page, day after day. Marching band music stomped out of the laugh track, the blasting sound filled up the wooden interior of his carriage. After a minute, Dwayne had to turn off the radio in shame.

Part 4

"Run that idiot off the road!" Pierre commanded from the backseat.

Steering with her thick awkward gloves, Vicki only managed to sideswipe one of the black carriage's wooden wheels. With a bump, they glanced off.

Pierre cursed, "We missed!" He slapped his little fist into his other hand and glared at the frightened, pale face as they passed. "They shouldn't allow those things on the city streets!" Pierre's shrill voice continued. He sat back into the plush maroon upholstery and stared at the back of Vicki's head.

The El Camino groaned around a corner and she floored it to the end of the block where they stopped with a screech. The gas engine coughed, sputtered, then shut off. The storefronts were all decorated—Spendy Penny, Food for All, and Go Fish Pets—glowed with the regulation flag colors. Before she could open the door, Pierre grabbed Vicki's muscular shoulder. "Wait a second!" He held out his hand greedily, "Pass me a fortune cookie." Obediently, Vicki flipped open the glove compartment and jammed her glove in. She needed both hands to pass him the white bag that fell out.

"Grazie," he said. The cookie atomized in his clenched fist and he read the fortune left in the crumbs in his palm. "Keep driving!" he shrieked suddenly. Muttering, shaking his head disapprovingly, he rolled the paper fortune into a pea and threw it out the window where it could blow and be lost.

Part 5

The carriage kneeled on its left side where the wooden wheel had been snapped jaggedly by the hit-and-run El Camino. Dwayne knew who had done it. Everyone in this part of the city knew who that car belonged to and also knew that there was nothing that could be done about it. The military police would just shrug. The dwarf gangster Pierre Camino was above the law, Dwayne sighed.

At least, he realized, the damage isn't too bad and I have a spare. I can put on a new wheel and return to the radio station. Then tomorrow I'll take a taxi down here, with flowers, and I'll try all over again to see her.

He unlatched the spare wheel off the back of his carriage and pulled it down. An electric cart purred closely around him and beeped, the blurring driver cursed at him. The sound of its radio, his own loud stupid jokes, disappeared with it down the street.

A sparrow, a little brown and pebbled black ball of feathers, hopped around the shattered spokes. Dwayne stood with the new wheel and watched. He hated to scare it away. He let a minute pass by until it flew up to land on the bend of a traffic sign.

Dwayne leaned the wheel against the carriage and gathered up all the wooden pieces from the street. His horse stood placidly with one back hoof resting crooked. Like Dwayne, the horse took all bad things in stride and waited indifferently for whatever had to come next. Dwayne tossed the wood on top of the rubble piled on the sidewalk like polluted snow. Someone would be glad for it. Someone who didn't have electricity would burn it in their fireplace.

He was fumbling with the plastic screw fittings when the air raid sirens crowded from silence into an ear-splitting scream. From the months of war, he knew exactly what to do and where

to go. Dwayne let the tools and wheel clatter to the cracked
pavement and he ran across the street to the burrow hole, a yellow chute that dropped him into the old subway caves below.

Part 6:

The grillwork closed behind her like a bird cage door which she locked with a golden key. She quickly waved to the mannequins waiting in the store with extinguishers in case the bombs fell on them. There were old things inside that fire could take away forever.

People ran past her, the sirens shook the windows of the shop right through her bones. A police car with loudspeakers and lights shot past in the street. It all seemed ready to fall down. Wind poured across the sky, carrying black dots—now she could see them—the balloon bombs dropping towards the city. Far away, she heard an explosion, then another, coming closer, stomping. As long as they stay away from Spendy Penny, she hoped, and in a flash she was pushed.

"Hurry up, lady!" into the dark rush of the burrow hole.

Part 7

Someone helped her to her feet, a man she recognized who came into the store a couple times a week. "Oh, thank you," she smiled as another person crashed through from the surface.

"You work at Spendy Penny," he said shyly.

"Yes," Stella answered, brushing her hands down her dress, "I've seen you there before. You collect plastic flowers."

He nodded. "My name is Dwayne."

They both ducked instinctively as the pale lights in the tunnel dimmed with an explosion.

"That was close!" she whispered, worried, staring at the curved ceiling. A few tiles were shaken loose. "I hope my store is okay."

The crowds of huddled people murmured and comforted each other. Someone turned on a portable radio. Dwayne Cody's awful words, mouthed by the announcer Ryno Schenk, echoed in the dark shelter. Other radios clicked on among other people to drown out the sound of bombs.

Ryno guffawed and told everyone in his booming voice, "All you folks down there in the rat holes, don't worry! I got everything under control up here. Leave it to Ryno." The green lights flickered again. "I got my slingshot and I'm shooting every balloon I see. Pow! There goes another one!" He laughed while the not so distant sounds of the city exploding could be heard in the background.

Dwayne shook his head and put his hand tight over his mouth. Suddenly he touched Stella's shoulder. "There's someone beautiful I've seen at Spendy Penny," he said. "I wonder if you know who she is?"

Before her smile could ask, another bomb landed and blew up on the street directly above, showering dust, leaving them in sharp darkness. A few people lit matches, ghostly shadows lurched searching for flashlights and generators. Someone fell down and a baby cried.

A river of slow, gray dust clouded down the street. Between the buildings and fires it washed towards the ocean. Nobody coming out of the ground knew what to do. They all stood and watched the dust and black smoke, the heat with furnace smell and waited for it to make sense and change back.

Would the war stop when the city was gone? Stella wondered. She put her hand around Dwayne's and squeezed. His eyes were off into the long stare too then he looked at her and tried to smile.

People were beginning to move around them, pushed along by the military police clubs and shields. Rubble needed to be cleared and searched through. Orange fires were being put out by bucket brigades. Everyone began to work on that.

Stella held to Dwayne and asked, "Will you take me to the store? It's just another block away." Through the curtain of smoke and haunted shapes of people, her side of the street was still standing. The window in front was splintered with escaping stars and long streamers from the display blowing out of it, but the building survived. A dog limped past and curled next to a lamppost. They crossed the broken street. Someone was shoveling concrete.

Dwayne's hand dropped hers. He was drawn to the store faster, leaving her behind. To get inside, he squeezed through the metal cage grill, pushed the warped door open and in a panic, he ran over the litter of 20th Century things.

"Wait, Dwayne!" Stella called as she watched him disappear into the dark Spendy Penny. She found her gold key and untangled the web of metal so it unfolded over the debris. The door was hopeless, hanging by a single hinge. It fell to its wooden knees and let her brush inside.

Further back, racks of clothes had spilled over with diamonds of glass. She could see him on the floor holding a man-

nequin cupped in his arms, crying no louder than the sprinklers she remembered from childhood lawns.

Part 9:

The ambulance driver slammed the back door and Stella watched it leave with Dwayne and Cheryl and the people who were crushed under falling buildings. She stood in the street until the cart clanged around a corner. The war wasn't over yet. She watched another building crash with sparks and cloud then the sound of the ambulance returned. She saw it stop for a woman carrying a child.

A huge, staggering woman cut out of the smoke and it became clear to Stella who it was. The little body pressed to her breast was dying Pierre Camino. Vicki Pinkham hurried into the white ambulance. It bumped over the rubble, turned around and buzzed towards the overcrowded underground hospital cave.

Just as suddenly as it occurred to them, Stella Winks decided to leave too, but leave safely. Everyone, no matter how stuck in the war, should have a way out. In the 20th Century, they made cars and submarines, they made steam-powered clippers and flying machines for the sky and outer space. They could go anywhere they wanted. Not all of it was forgotten or melted or made into other things. Her store didn't only have Hawaiian records, polyester clothes, dollar paperbacks and jewelry made of bright tin. To really take her from this age, underneath it all, there was something else that she kept hidden for herself in case the time ever needed so desperately to be changed.

THE BEAUTIFUL TRAPEZE

If you keep walking past the usual sideshows, the throwing games, animals, the freaks and card flipping gypsies, beyond the beautiful trapeze and snake teasers, you will find him. With a bang he does his act. In the blink it takes to pull the trigger, he's faster than bullets. Get in line. Watch. Wait for your turn to pay a dollar. How does he do it? It looks like he disappears. Is it a trapdoor, or mirrors? Maybe there are two of him? Tell him your name, hold the gun and fire at the target. Next thing you know, as the smoke clears after the loud shot, he's got ahead of the bullet, written your name on the paper bullseye and dodged aside, bowing with pen in hand. That's the way it would always be, like Houdini-Kerouac, somehow he could always outrun danger, write and amaze.

POSIE CRUTCHFIELD AT THE SEASHORE

At the seashore, the police chased past her while she hid in the shadow of a lighthouse, like a starfish clinging to the rocks. The water splashed around her knees and a bottle corked with a message inside soaked up next to her. It was a map. She read the ancient yellow note. The pirate handwriting was still clear, "Take a step forward." When she did, she was underwater. Fish became the birds all around her. Posie traced her finger on the map. A helpful octopus pointed to the sunken ship. A mermaid gave her a hand opening the barnacle door. A shark came out with a sharp smile for her. She hid in the dancing seaweed, made a green flapper dress out of the leaves, did the Charleston with a jellyfish and snuck back inside the wreck to look for more. This time, she found it. Gold and diamonds and jewelry filled a wooden chest. On a checkered turtle's back, she rode to the waves above, tipped him a doubloon and got out onto the sand again. The police were there waiting for her. The captain with the long crazy beard glared at her, furious, pointing at the sign, "No Bathing On Sunday. Fine $5." She laughed and tossed him a pearl.

EARTH'S HERO AND THE SUNNY AMERICAN TOWN

In the rake of weather, the car stopped and he jumped out into the hard rain. He splashed through the lake that all the ground was turning into, running up the driveway, past the ticket booth where some transistor radio echoed rock and roll. The bright screen of the drive-in theater was filled by Martians in the daylight of a sunny invaded American town. The green spacemen, with the aid of giant robots were stringing out a line of people like ornaments. He ran between all the hoods and trunks and teenagers shouting from rainy cars. He tripped on a wire and pulled a speaker off someone's window as he fell to the mud. Next to his ear, the puddle trembled, a desperate human voice warned, the orchestra swelled…It was 1963 and it might already be too late.

LISTENING TO THE FLAMMABLE MAN

He was driving the car when it happened. At first he thought the engine had taken on a new sound and maybe they were about to stop and break down on this small road in the middle of the desert in California late at night. What a desolate place, he thought, but also beautifully strange, with the sky full of bright stars above thistles waving in tall gray stands next to the road, as he pulled the car into the dust on the shoulder. His wife was still asleep. She was propped with a pillow under a blanket against the corner of the door. She drove from San Francisco until she was too tired and he took over. It must be around 2:30 in the morning, he thought. It was midnight when they had coffee at that all night truck stop. He slipped outside and shut the door quietly and smiled. The universe was all overhead. A shooting star skimmed across the black line of jagged mountains. The engine of their old car purred. It was fine. But the air hummed with that other sound he heard for the first time. Or maybe he heard it a long time ago and waited for all these years to feel it again.

THE MYSTERY OF THE FLAMMABLE WOMAN

She thought how smooth the road had become. She couldn't even feel the bumps of the cracked tar, or the wheels turning with the slightest bend. Opening her eyes, she turned amorously, sleepily towards her husband but nobody was driving. She jumped up in a panic and seized the wheel, looking through the windshield, expecting to see a cliff or the grill of a truck, her last vision of this world. It took her a few minutes to calm down, to realize that they were parked mysteriously with the engine idling. Her husband had disappeared somewhere out into the scrub, the sharp looking weeds and distant mountains lit only by the half moon and stars.

THE MOON WAS ALL THE MOUSE COULD THINK ABOUT

The Moon was all the mouse could think about. His little mind got carried away, atremble with green fantasies of that soft floating world. In stars, Moon glowed and sweetly rolled, the center of the nighttime dreamland, while Mouse twirled on the grass as he looked up to the sky. So many beautiful thoughts poured inside, as he imagined the romance that would lead him like a lover there. Until daytime would find him patted in the dew, skittered and blinking, rubbing his paws to his eyes. "Why does the Moon always have to go away? Wouldn't it be heaven if the Moon could stay?" Then he pictured himself up there in those soft cheese-colored fields and fevered with the miracle thought, "Why not?" He started to work using wood and nails, making a catapult ribboned with twine. The other animals watched and sighed and turned their heads. If this was really the heart of his prayer, how could they try to tell him to stop? As the sun went down at last over the blackening hills, Mouse glinted with joy at the new light in the sky. There was the glorious Moon once again in his sight, as perfectly round as a cantaloupe toss. Turning the catapult to point itself true, he held the silver rope, the anchoring line, and shot himself through the forest leaves, far past owls dodging for food and into the reach of clouds, purple trilling with moths.

DEWIE THE DORMOUSE AND TOAD RICKY

The sunny lemonade of the hot day fried on the road. Toad Ricky was riding his bicycle, his long green legs bending with the pedal spins that took him further and further away from home. The song in the air was a bluebird following him with bounces from post to post. Heat bugs chimed the degrees and a butterfly fanned its yellow wings on the handlebars. Toad Ricky was happy to be sailing on this tar river between green shady trees that gradually shrank into the twigs and dusty weeds of the desert.

"Brrr…" he shivered finally. The sun was going down behind mountain shapes. It glinted its last orange goodbye on the railroad tracks that seemed to string forever like silver shadows under the telephone wires.

Down the road, miles away, Dewie the Dormouse, sitting on a telephone book, pressed a foot on the extended gas pedal. The truck went faster. The headlights flared their yellow sight into the black night and Dewie pulled the horn chord so its mournful voice carried like a moose searching for love in the sage and tumbleweeds with darkness everywhere.

But not without life, there were coyote slinking around the road, badgers tending a fire, an owl clutching hotel keys in flight and just like another big midnight animal, the truck slowed down, and stopped in the sand to let the skinny toad hitchhiker up on board.

THE FLAMMABLE MAN SOMEWHERE

He jumped off the train. It might have been Santa Fe. It was night with no moonlight where he walked over the dark tracks into the brush on the hill. He didn't get very far, he was so tired and hungry he fell down.

Bells woke him up, steam, smoke and the slow heavy pass of metal train wheels clacking. The hot wind swished the weeds around him where he lay, opening his eyes. Everything seemed to hurt him. He had been put inside another hollow body to face the day with flea bites riveted up and down. The sun was so bright he felt like he was standing weakly on Venus. A couple buzzards looked him over as they circled in the blue.

Down on the other side of the hill, he stumbled towards an ancient airplane rusting in the middle of a field. Its dragonfly winds drooped as if it was waiting to spring out of the wheat to land in a red shower on some other distant farm.

DR. BIOCAL'S NEW TERROR

What strange movie was it this time? Last time it had been *Dr. Biocal's Deadly Laughs* when Susan Fenton confronted him in his laboratory, where it crackled with blue lights, bubbled and steamed with rows of test tubes like a Transylvanian war factory. Parading her past, he guided her to a locked cabinet and opened the heavy iron doors of the locker. Hundreds of shimmering glass jars and goldfish bowls lined the shelves inside. The light came from invisible trapped things. "I'm stealing the sense of humor of every person in the city. Each shining cup you see is from someone out there!" And then, as she threatened to turn him in, he introduced his two shuffling assistants, a pair of gorillas, Igor and Stravinsky. In the struggle that ensued, the fight that crashed all around the room, a bench was thrown and broke the cabinet full of glass. The air filled with released laughter as loud as a train passing through. Susan had to hold her hands over her ears while the gale force swept over her, swirled into a tornado circle in the room and poured out the broken window back to the city, to the people it was taken from.

And now here he was up to his tricks again.

Across the swamp of toxic bubbling fires and burnt out skeleton car wrecks, deep inside a bunker, Dr. Biocal eluded the authorities and planned new terror. His laugh could be heard through the concrete and steel door and it carried out the narrow window slits shined with electric light.

Susan Fenton didn't know. She was in a department store looking through a rack of bright summer dresses. There were colors that made her want to throw away her downtown secretary job and run away to somewhere fantastic. She pouted at the price tag on the soft green cloth and kept turning the circular rack, around like a merry-go-round. Even though her reflexes were good, she was caught by surprise by the two go-rilla arms that reached out and grabbed her and pulled her and she just couldn't react to the shock into dark.

It was the sound of her beating heart that woke her up. She stirred and found her arms and legs stuck to her side, to the ta-ble, with a stethoscope coiling from her into a machine taking her pulse. "Dr. Biocal…"

"Yours truly." He stepped towards her. He stirred a cup of coffee with twitching curls of his crooked finger. "It's nice to see you again."

"What is it this time, Dr. Biocal? Anti-Matter Reversal? Or maybe Chinese Water Torture that falls out of the clouds?" She pictured the entire world going mad from the black sky raining drop by slow drop.

He laughed, "No, no. I have something far grander." Spilling some, he set the coffee cup down by her foot and he clapped his hands at the door. It swung open and his two mountain gorillas, Igor and Stravinsky, obediently entered. "Unveil the invention!" he ordered. His jittery eyes spun back to Susan to watch her as the apes tore the tarp covering a gigantic blend-er-shaped machine.

Dr. Biocal noted with delight how her eyes opened wide then he sternly pointed to the gorillas and the door they came through. Disappointed, they shambled away and Dr. Biocal locked the steel door, flipping a switch on the machine and leaving Susan and him alone with the pounding of her heart echoing out of the wall speakers.

He strolled confidently to the waiting invention. She knew it meant something terrible for her. "Question…" He paused next to it. "What makes even the strongest person alive tremble and lose all rational thought? What makes you no more than an animal again?" He flicked another dial on the console. The machine hummed with more life.

The music of it made her suddenly weak, light and danger-ously burning with something inside her like the helium of a zeppelin.

Dr. Biocal laughed triumphantly. His arms opened wings towards her.

He swam in her eyes as she strained to snap herself free of the restraints.

"Lust!" he cackled. "How can anyone resist it?!"

Not even the crazy thumping that was louder and more frantic than her heart—it was the gorillas bashing on the door keeping them out. As the straps loosened, as Susan Fenton sat up and stood off the table, they crashed down the metal door and threw themselves like fur blankets over Dr. Biocal and his machine.

It was the most difficult struggle for her to leave the maddening room. The pull swept at her with the force of a riptide as she strained up the concrete steps out of the bunker. When she was outside, immediately she felt stronger and she ran across the swamp, over the broken and discarded things dumped everywhere in the chemical mush. Fireworks of sparks exploded out of the ground where the bunker used to be.

POSIE CRUTCHFIELD AND THE BEE TREE

Not completely like a butterfly, she went across the field running in the tall grass over the hill rise and down past the brook. Her long black dress flapped and she swished the leaves aside with her umbrella, making a path through the woods. The police, led by the captain with the long beard and crazy eyes, chased after in the yellow pollen. She sunk down behind a stump to hide. There were tall white birch trees waiting like cigarettes in a train station, with the blue police running back and forth.

Her knees, tight to her chin, her hand crept over her shoulders to pull a fern over her. Maybe the fan of its green would camouflage her from them. Instead, her fingers touched and pressed a dead branch switch, opening the door behind her back, tumbling her through the soft wood into the ground.

She landed in a hollow cavern shaped by roots and sweet honeycomb walls.

"You found our kingdom," a round bee with a crown bowed to her. "We must grant you a wish."

Posie laughed, brightened and pointed up, "Could you get rid of the police so I could walk in peace?"

The bee bowed again, clapped two of his ringed hands and summoned the army with their swords and black and yellow flags. They buzzed out in a cloud, stinging and chasing those police far away.

The woods were quiet again. Sunlight slanted through the branches in a stairway and up the ferns and dried orange leaves, Posie Crutchfield stepped carrying a gift basket full of dripping honey.

JACK SHELLAC'S BACK

Yes, he wore a patch and the scars of bear claws shined on his skin like candle wax rivers, but those struggling days were over. The art world had discovered him, showered him with awards and put his face on thousand dollar bills. At his antique studio, he signed with red paint to be in millionaire's living rooms. They even put him up in the sky in this fifty story hotel in Tokyo. He felt like Godzilla as he breathed on the window, looking over the scurrying foreign city. A smile crookedly broke on his face. The black telephone on his leather belt chirped. It was his secretary calling him about the TV interview. A crew was taking the elevator now to his suite, to talk about his rise to fame. "The world is my canvas," he was going to tell them. Splash that in your art magazines, with a photo of me, hand on chin…He opened the closet double doors to get his cashmere bathrobe but he quickly fell back three steps, turning white with fear…How could it be? How could it have survived all these years? Hunting him down streets, over walls, over oceans… The grizzly bear snarled out of the silk hung clothes, dragging a shirt from Italy. It looked older, ragged from the seasons, fighting to persist, the clumps of its fur singed by shotgun blasts, but worst of all, it looked terribly hungry, looking at him with its awful red eyes.

IMITATING THE CALL OF BIRDS

He parked down by the river, finishing his last love affair with the radio blaring and the windows taped shut. The slow wave of carbon monoxide would fill the car. The Orioles, The Flamingos and The Penguins would sing him to the Pearly Gates. That's how he envisioned it, his last hour on Earth as the tugboats pulled barges in the sloppy black. The lights of the sugar factory blinked, even at this hour the smokestacks poured out their sweet smelling pollution. Maybe it never stopped.

Funny, he thought, I'm leaving the world not knowing a lot of things. I could have been one of those crazy people who memorize license plates, birthdays, imitates the call of birds, or knows the voltage of every kitchen appliance in existence. His last ideas went, as his head slipped heavily on his shoulder.

Cold air blew through the windshield. It was opening in holes. Glass sprayed him like rain. The seconds blurred around, he thought he was in heaven—The Edsels were singing doo-wop like angels. He reached his heavy arms up to touch the broken saintly window. It fell with spiderweb threads all over him. Someone reached into the car and unlocked his door. He could smell her hair as she bent over him. Desperately, he tried to touch her arm but he fell outside onto the tire tracked mud. The radio played mockingbird songs and he woke up covered in sugarcoated smoke.

DR. BIOCAL, AT IT AGAIN

It wasn't destiny that was keeping Herman Snock from falling in love but it was something just as powerful. It set his clock so the morning would begin with him always too let to ever see her. It would make sure he appeared in a shade when he walked down the street, or went into places. It rattled him with self doubt and defeat, but just enough courage for him to be humiliated with flowers, giving away presents to girls who saw him as a circus travesty. No wonder he felt cursed or diseased. He'd look at the sky and plead with prayers. Every day he threw a coin in the Wishing Well.

He was small on the ground, barely to be noticed, one little sad person in the city of America, but he was being watched by something above. In a blimp, hidden with clouds, Dr. Biocal adjusted a powerful telescope so every tear stood out like a lake. The madman scientist rocked with evil laughter as he gleefully pressed a button and shot more demented radiation beams.

Below, Herman Snock missed his bus. In the window frame, the most beautiful girl in the world watched him goldenly, turning her head to smile as she disappeared forever in the crowded morning traffic curve.

A few hours later, Susan Fenton wasn't even distressed. How could it be dangerous sipping lemonade, reading the paper on a park bench at lunch hour with hopping squirrels and meandering pigeons? It didn't even cross her mind that she should be on guard, that the tree next to her could be filled with anything other than green leaves and caterpillars.

A branch over her head rattled, but she kept reading the article about the Ozone layer, how soon the Earth could be a boiling egg. "What's the matter with people?" she wondered. "When will we ever learn?" She pictured herself, given the chance and the power, giving everyone a wrench to dismantle the corporate system and then a handful of seeds to start over from scratch.

Dropping down on her like two spiders, Dr. Biocal's trained gorillas Igor and Stravinsky crashed from the hanging branch. They grabbed Susan and retracted with her on whooshing pulley lines back into the belly of the hot air balloon.

"Dr. Biocal," Susan Fenton sighed, "At it again."

The propellers hummed and kept them in place in the clouds over the city

"I've really outdone myself this time," he congratulated himself. With a cackle, he showed her the ray gun pointed at Earth from a porthole. "It's absolutely diabolically perfect!"

Susan took a step towards him. The gorillas flinched. They followed her moves like wrestlers. "Now what have you done?" she said. "Are you necromancing houseplants? Scrambling the mayor's brain into tapioca? Or is it something far worse?" She rested her hands on her hips, scowling, watching peripherally as the apes circled her.

"It begins with one person in the city." He raised a finger and then slowly spread all his fingers like a bewitched unfolding night flower. "Then, I will zap the entire population, not only here, but *everywhere!*" His eyes danced in the thick prisms of his glasses. "I am making love impossible! This gun will trap everyone in a shadowy lonely maze." Swatting its metal barrel, he broke into awful laughter until tears rolled down.

Even the gorillas joined in, twitching their fur shoulders, clapping and stamping.

What happened next was a fast blur, but it was under Susan Fenton's control. She threw herself at the gorillas, tossing them into Dr. Biocal who pushed the gun, pulled the trigger, shooting the dark comet of his invention into himself and Igor. In staggering blind pity, Igor howled and punched his fist into the inflated hull. Air drained from the balloon, spinning them in wild arcs out of the clouds, gravity bound for the ground.

Against the forces of physics, Susan got to the doorway and

launched herself out. That's when she left herself to fate, as she tumbled and the blimp swirled into a crashing distant hill.

Like a smooth angel out of the miraculous blue sky, she landed with a splash in the Wishing Well. She lay startled, birdlike in the pool on hundreds of dollars of silver coins, while Herman Snock put out his hand in gentle disbelief to help her out.

IT'S FES SMURLO AND MILO T. SMILEY

That afternoon, Fes Smurlo the ventriloquist fell of the cliff and landed in a eucalyptus tree. He clung to its red trunk and swayed in the leaves with the rocky beach a hundred feet below. "Help!" he yelled up at the white fence. Carefully, in inches, he positioned himself closer to the muddy sheer cliff. "Help!" he repeated. There was no way he could climb back up. He was in for a long wait.

A persistent muffled rapping came from inside the violin case he still held instinctively. Fes unwrapped his white knuckles from the handle and opened the latches.

"It's about time!" said Milo T. Smiley, the wooden puppet. "I was starting to get claustrophobic in there!" Then his painted eyes ogled the drop and in the struggle to hide back inside, the violin case slipped out of Fes' hands.

Both of them watched it tumble smaller and crack into pieces on the gray rocks below. The water swept around and carried the bits of it away.

Milo gulped and shrieked, "Help! S.O.S!"

The tree shook and fluttered off leaves.

"Calm down!" Fes said urgently, "We've got to think our way out of this thing. If we don't panic, we'll be fine."

A root snapped out of the vertical soil and the tree dipped closer to the ocean. Hungry gulls circled them anxiously, crabs scuttled beneath the waves in anticipation.

"Okay," hissed Fes, "I've got a plan."

"Anything!" chattered Milo, with his cloth arms tight around the ventriloquist's neck.

Fes took the puppet by the leg. "I'm going to throw you up there and you can get help." He began to swing Milo like a lasso and he put all of his strength into the toss.

Milo's looping shrill scream flew away from Fes as the puppet disappeared from sight, over the fence, landing face down in the black fresh tar of the parking lot.

A giant yellow machine rolled along, pressing the asphalt flat and luckily the driver happened to see Milo stuck in his path. It was just too bad the driver was a sick personality who took great joy in turning Milo T. Smiley into a plaid wooden pancake, as an unseen tree cracked, snapped and plummeted into the jagged sea.

A BARGAIN WITH EMILY DICKINSON

The sound of the typewriter keys late at night always revived Emily Dickinson's ghost. She arrived with chimes and a slightly cold wind that blew her into my room like a pillowy white smoke of rain. And as always, she made me jump at first. "Emily!" my hands flew up in a shock of greeting.

"Now what?" she rippled next to me.

I sighed out, "I'm discouraged…" There were hundreds of pages piled around me. "I think I'm turning into you," I admitted. "It seems that I'm doomed to my room, to just dream and write like you in the 19th Century. I just can't go out into America."

Emily stared at me, shimmering.

"And it's worse than when you were around," I moaned painfully. "I might have to get another job."

She laughed. Her ghostly hands swooped.

"It's not funny, Emily." I wasn't in the best mood. The gloomy story I was writing was all about America as a Dr. Frankenstein creation and it was really getting to me.

She put her hand on my shoulder and whooshed it through my head in sympathy. "Alright," she said. "I'll help you out."

I eyed her hopefully, the supernatural poet.

"And you can do something for me in return."

"Sure," I said, wondering just what she could possibly need, a published author who made her living as a ghost in the clouds.

TURNING A CITY INTO A GARDEN

Perry Plush woke up to the second day of God and scowled. Another day where nothing can happen, he thought and he angrily threw the covers off. Arriving over the city yesterday as a golden bird from the heavens, God had gone into all of them with words, warning, "It's not that there are necessarily too many of you…It's just that you aren't being very smart… It's time to be aware of everything you do."

Padding over to the window, Perry opened the curtain and looked across to the skyscraper. Sure enough, the shining yellow light of a tremendous eagle still nested on the top. Perry shut the curtain and again thought, "How can we get rid of that thing?"

He ran it over and over in his mind as he got dressed and descended all those stairs to the ground floor. The city had become a quiet place. Perry walked by one of his used car lots. Now cars meant nothing. Nobody could drive, nobody could buy them. They looked like drawings in encyclopedias. A flock of starlings chattered on the roof of a Cadillac and pigeons took off from the wires and circled him as he passed.

His face was a grim carving and he carried a box.

A horse drawn trolley clopped along the street but Perry didn't trust it. He kept on walking.

God on the Columbia Tower had spread out wings with rays of healing morning light.

At noon, Perry bribed his way through the police line surrounding the skyscraper. A pocketful of American dollars barely meant anything anymore, but the smiling cop remembered Perry from the old days on TV.

"Too bad there's no more cars," the officer said, his face beaming innocently. The light of God was bathing everyone and changing them for the better.

So Perry echoed up the stairway to the third floor and planted the bomb. He left it ticking in a garbage can in an office that
would never be used again.

After their lunch on that bright day, a boy and girl went
outside to play. The two of them sat up from the leaves beneath
a tree, watching the city. The buildings looked so small they
could have put their hands out and held them all. Sometimes
they did that. Or they played other games. They had their rock
collection in a bag that she had stitched together out of a blanket scraps. A stone from a beach, a lava rock from a lake, a piece
of desert petrified wood, and quartz off a mountain top.

The ground shook for days it seemed, but they didn't fall off.

A BLUE OCEAN VOYAGE

There's something floating out on the gray sea, far beyond any land or sign of man. What is it? Closer, let the wide blue be like a blanket you press softly to and look at that tiny little spot. It's something that used to stand on the ground. It's something that lays on the water, turned by the wind-like pull of waves and warm current. A tree, that's what it is. Now it holds to the Pacific with its roots and branches while its green, gentle leaves fin and spin pinwheels underwater. How strange that a eucalyptus would be wandering here, just as out of place as a sea horse driving a cab in downtown Seattle. But there's more… Or did you think it was a play of shadows? There's a man riding on the bark…Look, it's that hapless ventriloquist, Fes Smurlo.

Silver fish followed, taunting the starving man until he could take it no more and he decided to carve a fishing pole. Fes whittled off red slices of wood into the wake. But his entranced hands worked against his will, almost as if some magic force had taken control. Like a woman with nine months, he slowly began to form something out of the shape—a little head, arms, legs, fingers and toes. Finally, there it was, shining and smiling in his lap.

Milo T. Smiley's mouth snapped open and his new teeth sparkled. "What's cookin'?" he said.

Fes dropped the knife in shock. It glinted away into the fathoms. "Oh God…"

"I'm back!" Milo beamed rosily. "I'm your lucky charm, pal!"

"Lucky charm?" Fes stared in amazement. "You were supposed to be a fishing pole! You've ruined my chance of catching a meal. I—" and then a thought creased his mind. Fes nearly laughed.

"Say, wait a minute!" Milo churled. "I know that look! What

are you thinking?"

Fes took his scarf off dramatically. He agreed, "Maybe you can help me after all."

Milo struggled vainly as Fes tied the yarn around the wooden, kicking feet. Milo's shrieks turned into bubbles as the puppet dunked underwater and into that other dark world.

Shafts of sunlight speared though the green, darting with schools of radiant fish. A barracuda sluiced past, sniffing before passing on, while Milo bobbed at the end of the scarf with his eyes tightly shut.

Fes gazed through his reflection and shouted through his cupped hand, "Come on, Milo! Catch something!" A manta ray had appeared, investigating the twitch of aura, sculling closer with its bat wings.

Just then, the tree stopped, the branches crunched as they struck land and Fes Smurlo tumbled ashore, dragging Milo T. Smiley onto the rough beach with him.

Milo's jaw chattered with rage, "You swine!" he screamed. "You tried to kill me!"

But Fes ignored the shrill voice. "Oh, thank you," he prayed to the clouds above. "Milo, we made it back to America." He picked up Milo and carried his wooden friend up the steep hill. At the top, they stopped…in silence.

"America never looked so small," Milo said. He shaded his eyes.

Their tree was shipwrecked on an isolated curved black shape the size of a stack of junked cars. A subterranean rumble with a spray of hot water shot over their heads from out of the moving, swimming breathing ground.

"At least it's got plumbing," Milo squeaked.

"Yeah…" Fes whispered, staring at his feet that didn't quite stand on land.

THE GREEN POOL

Richard said, "Isn't it funny how when you're living your life as a younger person, it's all popcorn and confetti, bells and whistles. You're just kind of skating through it. You don't really realize how important and how forming it was to your life until you're older and you look back and you say, 'My God, those were great times!' But you don't realize it when you're living it."

Richard remembered wandering around downtown Los Angeles. It was sunny, it was nice. What did anything matter?

He happened into one building looking for work. He saw some janitors. They were on break. They were talking to some pretty girls who worked there too. They all seemed happy there. As Richard approached, he guessed they were Mexicans. He asked them if there was any work. One of them nodded and told him to go talk to the boss.

Next thing he knew, Richard was hired as a janitor cleaning toilets and restrooms. They gave him a can of Comet that he had to sprinkle on everything. He had to clean each stall and leave a green, cool pool of water in each toilet. It was so emerald green it was like jade, or a pond in Oz. There was only one problem: Richard couldn't keep up with the crew. Richard was the turtle. It was like a joke he heard later on.

Here's how it went: It was wintertime. It was around Christmas and a man was hurrying to get to work in the morning. It was so cold there was almost snow. He rushed out the door, closed it behind him and turned. There was a turtle just sitting there on the walkway in front of him. The guy didn't have time for that, he was in a rush, and he reached down and grabbed the turtle. With one swing of his arm, he wound back and tossed it right over his house, way back to where the woods started. And then he went to work. And he went there day after day. The seasons passed. And a year passed by. It was winter again. Christmastime arrived again. When he left his house there was a light white powder of snow dusting the ground. The man was careful not to slip on the path. Then, what do you know? There was that turtle again! In the exact same place. He flashed back and remembered it. It took a whole year exactly to get that turtle back to where it was before. The man reached down and grabbed it and picked it up and said right to its face, "What is your *problem?!*"

"What is your problem, Whitney?" the foreman barked at Richard. "Why can't you keep up with us?" Richard was so slow the crew would joke about him and wonder if he was staring at the green toilet water, making wishes. He was so slow they would have to pull someone off the job ahead to go back and help him finish. "Why can't you keep up?" the foreman asked him.

"I don't know. I have just one speed, I guess," Richard said. "But I want to do a good job."

"Well, try harder."

Richard was starting to think it was time to get a new job. It was a big city. In those days you could open a newspaper and go through the classifieds. You could do better. Or you could just go out wandering which was how Richard found this job in the first place. Put yourself in the hands of fate, trust yourself to that. That's what he was thinking when he returned to the job site and found out that foreman who was giving him such a hard time had been fired.

A new foreman was hired on. It was like the difference between day and night. He was nice as can be. He caught Richard and asked, "How are things going?"

"Well…Slow."

"Richard," the new foreman said, "I think you're a real nice guy. Would you like to operate a freight elevator instead?"

"Yeah, I'd like that. Where would that be?"

"In the new Arco Towers."

Richard said, "Really?" He was actually excited. And away

he went.

He started out on the loading dock. The first three months were like a picnic even though his supervisor, Hank wasn't. Hank would come out of his office once in a while to check on things. He would stagger and sometimes grab someone by the shoulder to brag.

Hank told Richard his daughter was in show business. Richard didn't believe it. He heard plenty of stories like that. In Hollywood everyone had a story. Then one night, Richard was at home, he was watching the late night television. It might have been Johnny Carson. Richard watched a girl interviewed and she ended up talking about her father. She said how he humiliated her all her life and her pretty face curled when she said that she still hated his guts. She told the camera his name was Hank. Richard sat up straight. He thought about work the next day. What would his boss say? My God, maybe he was telling the truth. His daughter was a celebrity. She could be seen on the light comedy programs, talk shows, game shows. She would smile and joke and sing and laugh at everything.

After three months, the building site wrapped up and Richard got his freight elevator. He was getting 1.75 an hour. That was okay in those days. All he had to do was go up and down.

That's where he met Robert. Quiet, serious, Robert was a mail carrier for the tower. He pushed a cart on rounds. Every day, they would meet on the elevator, getting to know each other, sharing stories.

One day Robert came on the elevator without his cart. He was carrying a guitar. Richard didn't even know Robert was a musician. He was clean-shaven, he wasn't a hippy like so many in that LA scene. He asked Richard, "Would you like to hear a little music?"

Richard said, "Yeah, sure." And then as the music began, Richard just had to let the elevator stop at a floor. Robert was amazing. He was such a shy guy it was like he was holding some beautiful thing separate from him, the way you would clutch an armful of flowers. Robert told him it was easy, he could play anything. He laughed. He said he also played in a garage band around the Hollywood area.

Then one day Robert came on the elevator and he didn't look good at all. He was holding onto his cart as if to keep from falling.

"Robert, you don't look so good. Are you sick?"

"I haven't been feeling well for months."

"What's wrong with you?"

"I have no idea. I've been to a few specialists. Nobody knows what's wrong. My dad wants to send me down to Mexico to live with the natives."

"You mean like a witch doctor is going to cure you or something?"

Robert sighed. "Well, I don't have a very good lifestyle off of work. You know that band I'm in? I do kind of wild things."

"I never thought you were like that."

Robert shrugged. "I just wanted to say goodbye and I'll be back. It'll be a few weeks but I think I'll make it and then I'll be back."

When he returned, when he got on the elevator the next time, he didn't look like the same person who left. He looked totally different—so much energy, buoyant and alive, a sparkle in his eyes, rosy cheeks. He grabbed Richard's hand, "Richard!" he said, "I'm a new man!"

He told Richard all about it. He lived with a little tribe of Indians in Mexico. There was no contact with the outside world. There were no telephones, no electricity or signs of civilization…Robert was far, far out in the woods…He said they have a pool, not a lake, a large natural pool. That water is pure and clean and shimmered light green like candlelight. Jump in, go down in the water and open your eyes and look around. It's like magic, like you're in another kingdom. And he was living with a family in their mud hut. "The food was incredible. I bounced back in a week. I wanted to stay there forever."

"What about your music?" Richard asked.

"Yeah…There's that…I started to get homesick. But I'd really like to go back."

All the good it had done for him faded though. After a few weeks, Robert fell into his old habits. He'd get on the elevator and look like he was back in his dregs again. He didn't look good at all. Richard asked him, "Robert, when are you going back to Mexico? You look awful."

"Well, I'd like to. I know I have some bad habits I'd like to get rid of."

Not long after that, Robert disappeared. Richard didn't know what happened to him, but he hoped Robert went back to Mexico. "He had talent. That soft music on the elevator that day…It was like my dad used to play." Over the years, Richard made his way up the coast from California, nearly to Canada. Richard was in the habit of leaving the radio on through the night. The airwaves would crackle and carry into his room from faraway places. Half listening, half in a dream, "When I woke up, I heard a familiar guitar on the radio." It was just barely tuning in and Richard sat up, looked at the shadows in his room, and felt sure it was Robert talking to him.

MY BRUSH WITH THE BELATEDS

There are times I'm sure when someone walking by on the sidewalk must look at our house in alarm. In fact, given the right equipment, Geiger counters and heat detecting sensors, I'm sure our house must sometimes possess a signature not unlike that power substation two blocks away from us. A great orange flower erupting. And the source of that frenzied, unstable atomic imprint is a girl of sixteen, our daughter.

Most of the time she's fine; when properly cared for, fed, pampered and allowed all the comforts we possess, but at any moment her mind, or her heart more probably, will plunge her and the whole house headlong into riot. Of course there are all kinds of solutions to alleviate this, and God knows my wife has been standing in the height of those waves, trying to stay afloat with what now amounts to a library collection of books on the subject with titles like *Controlling Your Teen* and *I'm Not Crazy, I'm A Teenager*. But it seems like this storm is just part of the territory. Eventually, at some later point, we'll be standing in a sunny quiet landscape full of debris.

The cause of our daughter's outburst is unavoidable. It's something she sees every day, everywhere and everything reminds her of her obsession. There are correlations in any conversation, the whole world is but a reflection and no matter how small a shard presents itself, it will set her off. It seems she is only put on this planet to worship and adore The Belateds. There's nothing in her life to distress and elate her like them.

I have to count myself somewhat to blame for this. I'm the one who brought home their LP, *Finally Meet The Belateds*. I couldn't help but notice many of the students in my class, especially the girls, overhearing their bedazzled conversations before the bell, the buttons that had sprung on their sweaters and coats like flowers. One girl had even turned in an essay comparing them to the Transcendentalists. Then too, I brought home a tabloid from the grocery store. That's all it took, our daughter was hooked. She took The Belateds bait and ran with it.

At first it seemed like any quite normal fascination and it even gave rise to what my wife's books would consider a bonding experience. We stayed up late the night The Belateds appeared on The Sylvan Moore Show for the start of their cross-country tour. I have to admit I pretty much ignored those four young musicians. I was watching our daughter instead. She was transfixed, moonglowed by their moving images on the television. Having them actually in our country, connected to the very earth we walk upon sent a current directly to her. And I'm sure it didn't help when I put up a map on the wall for her to follow their progress across America. She stuck little red pins in Chicago, Detroit, Cleveland…The tension was mounting…They were closing in.

During that time, her fervor took aim. Four of them were too many for such a fierce devotion. She needed One and she found him in Carlo Abbey, the doe-eyed drummer. Like some sort of zealot, we watched as she papered her room with his image and her every other word of conversation seemed to include reference to him. He was enough to send her squealing into ecstasy and heights of fantasy unscalable by any ladder of reality. We put up with it…Once burning, that fire was impossible to put out, it could only be contained.

When The Belateds were playing only a few hundred miles from us, I came home from work to find her seated on the front step watching the sky. In such a position of prayer, she could have been directly communing with them. Her heart might have been placed on one of those thick white clouds for the ride down the coast to where Carlo may have been staring out the window of his tall hotel and reaching out to her. Without disturbing her reverie, I drove up the driveway and parked beside her bedroom window. Beyond the drawn curtains I could see the posters on the wall. I had news.

I came inside and announced, "The Belateds are playing here tomorrow!" What started out as a rumor became true. The students in my class knew about my daughter and her affliction and told me about the surprise show. That's when there must have been another power surge. My daughter tore into us. My wife was immediately on the phone, I couldn't even get my coat off, we were in high gear to find a ticket for her. When that didn't work, they were all sold out, we had to get back in the car and drive to the theater to see if there was anything, some last seat tucked behind a pillar or a row reserved for just such a sad case. The drive back home empty-handed was nothing short of tragic.

Our daughter became a stranger to life. All her sobbing and tears had left her nothing but a shape in space. She went right to her room and shut the door for the night.

The whole house took on the shroud of an unspeakable grief. I woke in the morning, turned on the heat, made myself a breakfast of toast and left for work in the dark. It was hard to keep my students from bursting into song all day. Most of them had tickets and were watching the clock. But none of them could help me. I supposed I would have to try the theater again.

Getting home was parking beside a big teardrop in the rain. Her curtains were drawn but I could feel her presence in there, as dark and sorrowful as a cursed princess locked away. While somewhere in our very own town, The Belateds were having supper and tea, we went about the early evening chores in ghostly motion. We tried to coax our daughter into the living but it only started her crying again. It was her last screaming, dying fit of the night. "My heart has been cut into a million pieces!" She wailed to her to room and slammed the door. She let us know she would never go to school again. Hope had disserted her for all time.

I washed the dishes. I scraped the uneaten portions off her

plate. I let the warm water pour over my hands and soaped everything clean and stacked them in the rack to dry. Usually I play music for this chore, but not tonight. I was too afraid what memory music might invoke.

Finally, I got the car keys. I left my wife to hold the distraught corpse in progress. I needed to try the theater again. You never know. Maybe a ticket would go unclaimed.

It was dark outside. In the morning I leave for work in the same darkness, with stars overhead, and here I was again, going out on another mission. I did turn on the radio though. As I reversed down the driveway, I recognized the song. It was a hit by The Belateds.

I don't know. I hoped our daughter would have come with me. I wish she wouldn't give up quite so easily. She's got to learn to be strong. I know this world can dish out its share of unfairness, but there's also a miracle or two awaiting. You never really know what's going to happen. It's like the lyrics to one of those songs she listens to. Don't give up. Keep trying. Her life will be better when she knows that's true.

The blocks around the theater were a circus. The Belateds had surrounded themselves with a magnetic atmosphere of joy and magic, starry-eyed teenagers skipping in packs on the sidewalks. The streetlights were blinking in all shades of color. I had to go five blocks away, out of that orbit before I could find a spot to park the car. Even so, I could hear the clamor as I stood on the sidewalk and fed some coins into the meter. The rumors were true alright: The Belateds had come to town.

I was in such a hurry that I forgot all about the rain. I should have grabbed an umbrella from the car. Anyway, nobody else seemed bothered by the weather, it only seemed to add to the scene. I was passed by more teenagers running in the direction of the theater. They fluttered and chirped like birds. A couple of my students saw me and sang out. I've never seen them that way in class. I guess they've always had it in them; it just takes something like The Belateds to bring it out.

I joined the crowd around the theater and noticed the doors were open, people were already going inside. The yellow marquee lights were flashing round and round. Again I thought if only my daughter was here, just to see this would have given her a thrill. I started towards a phone booth but it was filled up with laughing kids. I would have to wait. Give this all a little time to settle down then I could try the ticket booth and see if there were any seats left unfilled.

So I crossed the street. I stood under an awning and watched the parade. It really was hard to believe. The people going in those doors, onto that red carpet with gilded walls, seemed to be walking through the gates of heaven. When a pair of uniformed theater ushers closed the doors, I got back into the rain and crossed the street. There was a girl in the light of the ticket booth flickering like a candle.

I hurried up to her to ask about tickets but she was shutting the curtains and I could read the sign she left by the window slot. *Sold Out.* Of course…Why wouldn't it be?

Standing there, so close, I could feel the cement rumble with the sound going on inside.

For the rest of the show, I lurked. The rain came and went. Sometimes I stood back under my awning. I went around the theater a few times, hoping that the big door in the alley might open. It wasn't impossible that The Belateds might come out for some air and some relief from the shrieking inside. They might see me standing there. Couldn't I wave and walk over and ask them for their autographs? That would surely be enough to revive our daughter. I could finally go home and knock on her door and say, "Look what I found."

I was back under the awning when the ushers opened the theater doors again. I stood there and watched all those teenagers reemerge. Dancing and clapping and tugging at each other. It was as if a film had been rewound and now they were all coming out. It took a while, but gradually it got quiet again. They were all gone. But where were The Belateds?

I crossed the street. By now I knew those puddles like a map maker. I followed a rainwater stream into the alley.

"Are you looking for them too?"

I walked right past a girl without seeing her. Actually she had a friend with her. They were both standing in the shadows under a fire escape. No wonder I missed them.

"The Belateds?" I asked.

"Of course. Do you think they might be coming out this way?"

I laughed. It was funny; I had become another teenage fan stalking its prey. At least we had each other for company, to while away the next half hour or so. Maybe it was longer. By the time all three of us were chattering with cold and rain, I suggested perhaps we ought to call it a night. It was very late and we all had school the next day. Or rather today for a new day had already begun.

Out front, the theater had darkened completely. I walked past the poster displays, the shuttered ticket box, the chained locked doors. The Belateds were gone. I stepped back into the street to take one last look at that theater, standing in the soft rain. Had they just disappeared? On to the next pin on the map...

I walked looking for the car. The city was asleep. A mile away my daughter was too, dreaming I hoped of something calming and healing. All I wanted was her happiness.

Why else would I have spent the night in search of The Belateds and ended up in that café at 2 A.M if it wasn't for her? I was hungry and cold from standing in the rain all evening. There was a diner on the corner and I went in.

I sat down on the red seat of a booth and took off my wet overcoat. It felt so good to be sitting and warm. I ordered hot tea and watched out the window. The rain left hundreds of shining dots on the glass and the streetlights made little crystal balls of them.

When my tea arrived, in a little white pot, I poured and

cupped my hands around that ceramic mug like some shipwrecked sailor pulled from the sea.

I did notice the bell as the door opened. I had been the only customer in the diner but I pressed the warm cup in my hands and continued to stare abjectly at the climate outside.

I didn't pay attention to the footsteps until they stopped. An odd looking fellow stood beside my table. At this hour who else would you expect at an all-night diner? He looked like he fell out of a dream, or off a carnival wagon. He wore his thick blond long hair like a wig and a black, feathery moustache fluttered as he spoke.

"Hey, Mister. Are you nursing a broken heart?"

More than his accent even, it was his eyes that gave him away. For a second I felt like my daughter, with a bird's fluttering paper heart. Then I got it together and smiled. "Have a seat," I said.

And so he did and Carlo and I talked and laughed and shared cups of tea. I have to admit my daughter was right about him. It didn't take long for me to feel I'd met a lifelong friend. That's probably why it didn't feel strange at all to find us five minutes later in my car with the dawn coming on.

We followed the headlights while Carlo dialed the radio and soon we were pulling into our driveway. I stopped the car halfway. Carlo and I got out quietly as we could. He already knew what to do. We crept on the gravel, walking like cartoons, careful not to make any sound.

Carlo pointed at the window. I nodded yes. Behind that glass, only a foot away from her idol, my daughter was asleep. Did she have any idea what crept out here? Carlo reached in the deep pockets of his overcoat. He lined the windowsill with flowers. He seemed to have an endless supply. Then he put his finger on her window and wrote on the dew.

In letters that quickly turned to water, he wrote *Cheer up, Rosie* and finished below with *Love Carlo*.

He turned around to me, smiled, and I patted him on the

shoulder. It was getting late and almost time for school.

I would tell her soon. She could go outside, find the flowers, and if the words on her window were faded she could breathe on the glass to make them reveal. His message to her would show up again. Romantic, I know. I also know that this world has a way of squashing flowers and letters in dew. Failing that, I have a backup. Carlo also gave me a signed photograph.

A PAIR OF CLOUDS

In the morning, they were resting on the windowsill, nestled, brushing up against the glass like white loving doves.

He had heard about things like this happening. A strange miracle was unfolding just so. Watching clouds out the glass for years, he had waited for them to find the open window so they could drift inside.

Cars and buses made drowning noise from the street below, but he could still hear the faint humming, as if thousands of little invisible mechanical parts pushed the clouds.

They moved low across the carpet then stopped to hover over his shoes. Around them, the clouds wrapped circles.

Even though he struggled with their vapor, trying to release their hold on his shoes, the clouds were like ghosts he could only put his hands through.

It wasn't bad enough being late for work—now there were clouds stuck to his shoes.

"Alright!" he finally declared. Daringly, he put his feet into the billows and nearly fell over.

The clouds had quickly levitated him a foot off the floor.

He swung his arms in eggbeater churns, desperately grabbing at a picture frame on the wall. Missing it, he howled and leaned all over as his feet slid him towards the still open window.

Once he got his balance again and could wrench himself to stand, he was staring down at the street a hundred feet away. Only the clouds were holding him from falling.

A pigeon breezed around him just before he shut his eyes.

He took a deep breath. It whispered out as a prayer.

He was weightless, with all the sound of the city floating.

Before the miracle, all his life he had been held down, he needed a moment to get used to the thrill and pleasure of walking on air.

THINGS OF THE MORNING

The things of the morning began as I walked towards the bus stop. A car struck a cat and left it frozen down on the road. A woman ran into the traffic, holding out her hands to all the cars hurrying to jobs. And I ran out there too, with my hands outstretched to help cradle the cat over to the sidewalk. There was another woman with a dog. The dog was barking and spinning madly. "Is it dead?" They were talking, "It feels dead?" but I wasn't really even aware, the scene had become a dream. While the cat was disappearing, my fingers were soft as possible going across the cat's paws. "He's dead," I heard the words next to me. But I already knew. I saw it happen. The cat scribbled as its soul untied and escaped. I felt myself watch a soap bubble spin like a wheel into the air. I lost it in the glare of silver car grills and all the orange lights of the morning city.

IMAGINE THE THINGS I WILL SEE AND KNOW

Moth listened to their buzzing words of advice, warnings curled with fluttered wings in air and circles, cutting circles made to emphasize the dangers out there.

Moth heard through all their doom, but told them again that he was leaving this home. "I have to see more at night than the Moon." He had heard tales of electricity that poured itself in rivers down streets and filled up all the many eyes of skyscrapers…So beautiful you couldn't look away. "Imagine the things I will see and know," said the moth.

He held wings wide to say goodbye. Then off he flew, sailing by constellations for the brightest dot of distant light.

IN THIS NIGHT OF GRASSHOPPER
SWINGING STARS

There is gentleness in this night of grasshopper swinging stars. Green drops of pearly light. Fly lullabies where they hide folded under the eaves of the sleeping house. Moths tired too, with their laundry-white wings hung on the window panes of his room. Like two or three hedgehogs lumped on soft, he watches out of the cave in the covers and instead of the Moon, which he sees every eve, that roundness shapes into something he can hardly believe. Blink, he dazzles, and looks again to make sure, but there's no doubt and what's more, now there is sound. A melody all nature responds to. He would sit up in bed, but he's almost too amazed, as he stares from flannel and sheets. Moon's happy disguise, a gold record in the sky, plays fiddle as song down to blue Earth, down to the wide drifting heather and a meadow where a cow lifts her head up to fly.

THE UNDERWATER WORLD

The pond has gone and with it the fish and the fences. Missing water, my field has a dark scoop in the ground. It looks as if big hands have come down from the sky, cupped and taken away what I loved so much. Something that was supposed to last forever and always, has disappeared with a simple wind, I guess.

Every day for the longest dream, I put on the golden diving suit, left from the house with hurried footsteps through the wild grass and flowers to step deep into the pond. Bubbles popped around me. I had fences made of water lily so the small fish could grow safely into bigger fish. That was all important at the time, to repair green plants and make sure everything swam fine. I brought food too. It felt so good to be in the underwater world. So what did I do wrong to lose it all? I really don't even know. I haven't learned a thing. Watching the clouds, I just continue to pray that it will rain again, to fill with water what is gone.

JACK SHELLAC'S BRIC-A-BRAC

From the backseat of his pink Cadillac, Jack Shellac ordered the driver to go faster. "What's the matter with you, Jones? I can pay a speeding ticket. I don't want to be late, step on it!"

"Alright, boss," Jones replied and the car surged, clipping the fender of an old lady's Pinto. Jones clung to the pitching wheel.

Jack Shellac read the scratched invitation again. The words were childishly scrawled, almost clawed and torn through the white paper in spots and there were a couple spelling errors too, but the sentiment interested Jack. "In recognition of your tremendous contribution to the world of art," he recited grandly. "The Mayor and city council would like to honor you with a lifetime achievement award." The mysterious address of a warehouse down on the piers was given…The time, midnight. "I gotta get a faster car," Jack Shellac grumbled then added, "Or maybe a better driver."

Jones muttered something. Tires squealed through a 7-11 lot.

"*What's that?!*" Jack leaned hotly over his driver's shoulder.

"Nothing, boss," Jones conceded. "I just said we're nearly there."

Jack Shellac sat back in his plush leather upholstery and sighed.

Out the window groaned the peaked wooden old buildings of the waterfront. Jack put his finger on a button and the tinted window slid down. The smell of the ocean, with the rusted freighter cargo lurched in roped oily pools. He imagined it must be like an old movie set.

"Here we are," Jones said. He stopped the car in front of a dead warehouse. No, not quite dead. From inside its rotten pumpkin skin a faint orange, red light glimmered. Jones whistled and clucked.

Grunting, Jack Shellac got out of the car and ordered Jones, "Wait here." Then he walked towards it. He squinted at the strange sight from his one eye…Years ago a bear had taken his other eye…The beast had left its signature in scars from claws all over Jack's body. Twice, it had found him and torn at him with relish, leaving him barely alive, before disappearing again. Now Jack Shellac was older, richer, and went through shadows that carved stripes in his ripped face and skin. He finally stopped at the door and pushed it open.

"Hello?" he called expectantly.

Where were the paparazzi? Where were the flashbulbs and neon lights, the handshakes, the champagne and leggy waifs? He walked inside and his footsteps echoed horribly.

The place was filled with tall grasping shadows, piles of awful kitsch from the 1930s, 40s, and 50s. Porcelain, glass, plastic, terrible paintings…Crap.

His dimmed eye searched the endless rows of bric-a-brac—poodles, sparkling mermaids, smiley faces, masks, Mexican portraits and mixed in with it all, he recognized his own studio works of art.

"What is this?!" he demanded. He stopped in the pink light and listened furiously.

Far off, a bottle splintered. Overhead the bulb swayed on its long black wire.

There was something sinister going on. Jack's once broken back shivered with déjà vu. "The bear…" he croaked. He began to retreat slowly, watching the walls of art junk. "What do you want from me?"

In another place, toys spilled on the floor, spreading out like hands.

Jack spun. Panicked, he began to run. Anywhere, there must be a way out somewhere. More things fell around him—clowns and picture frames. The Halloween light of the place confused him. He knew he was running in circles. His heart paining him, Jack Shellac blundered into an aisle of arced sculpture metal, stumbling into a sharp, furry embrace that remembered him all too well.

THE POOR TURNIP

On a bus full of carrots, the turnip slunk to the back, dragging its paper grocery bags full of soil and mumbling about the sorry state of affairs in this garden wet world. The carrots made orange remarks under their breath, until at last the turnip settled roundly in the corner against the steamy window. Fidgeting and feeling amiss, the poor turnip waited impatiently for wherever it was going, but sadly that place would never know how it fumed and writhed because the turnip would never arrive. The bus driver, a nervous green stalk of celery, kicked on the limp brake and announced with regret that they were all headed straight into boiling water.

SNAPPY PETE'S ANKLE COMPLETE

Problems with gravity had reached such proportions that people couldn't walk. Their ankles gave out in the pain of air that was drooping trees and pushing clouds down. People began to crawl again, others slithered on the ground, some returned to the sea.

In cities, there were brightly lit stores all around the padded sidewalks with overbearing salesmen dressed in tartan suits. "Come on in and get your ankles repaired!" their voices graveled out of American flag draped speakers. "You have to walk every day, trust your ankles to professional care. Free knee inspection included…" Snappy Pete was just like the rest of them, ranting and raving on two minute TV commercials. "Snappy Pete's Ankle Complete is more than a store. We're a friend to your feet."

His store flattened itself over the wreckage of the Ravenna Bridge, down the ivy hill, so easy to fall into. Unhappy people went in slumped then came out later with the plodding determined steps of Frankenstein's invention.

THE RAIN

Clouds gathered in a sky continent, anchored to the spires and sewn to air between the hills. While people took out umbrellas, or slid under the eaves of buildings, as they walked slouched in the wind, the first water drops stung ground and skin. Then in a school of fish sweep, the rain began to melt the city. Bricks turned oil, poured off walls. Yellow taxicabs and grocery carts made candlewax shapes in river streets. So it's really come to this, I thought, as the vision of my everyday world blurred and stopped being a parking lot. A painting of color splashed at my feet. When the rain stopped, when the clouds unraveled into threads, the blue sky returned in moonlight. I don't know why the rain was only water to me. So many shapes washed away to become the new land. Most of what used to be is gone. I would have been driven to despair to think that a world had been formed without you, but the real miracle made it through. You survived and surprised me on a carpet of supermarket.

THE FLAMMABLE MAN REMEMBERS

Madronas grow out of their peeling red bark. Their tan skin reaches in smooth naked turns, ends in hands holding green leaves. Wind makes waterfall sounds passing through. At first he thinks it's the breeze, a part of that invisible brush combing trees. He holds the little white candle with its smell of beeswax near the yellowed page of his book and continues to read. Not many cars pass along this way, especially with evening closing down. He expects to sleep here and try again tomorrow. But the wind doesn't change gears climbing up hills—it's an engine he hears. He blows out the reading light, stuffs it, hot syrup and all, into his coat pocket and he kicks up dust going down the hill to the purple lit road.

The truck stopped and let him on. He sat on the wide seat, watched the road and talked.

"I'm trying to find the answers to some questions," he told the driver. Everything had been up in the air for years, carrying him all over the America, on the wheels of cars, buses, trains and landing airplanes. All the searching was devastating. He looked away from the passing trees, stared at the driver for a moment to smile. The old truck shook, going uphill.

"Well, I wish you the best of luck."

"Thanks," he said.

The truck went along for another mile before it stopped. He got out, waved, stood submerged in the moonlight and dark blue shade of willow trees while the truck drove away. It got smaller, becoming a narrow shape. It jumped when it hit a bump and something flew off the back. Whatever fell off clattered on the road.

He walked towards it. He had nowhere else to go. The road had become quiet except for his shoes.

A small metal box sat dented from the fall. He picked it

up. It was light. When he shook it, something rattled inside, though the lid seemed to be forever shut with rust. In the gravel at the side of the road, his hands wrestled with the latch. The wind sighed in the field next to him.

With his thumbs pressing the hinges, the little box finally popped open and he could see the pearl inside.

A matchbook was tied by string to a note. *Here,* it read, *You have forgotten how to make fire.*

Bird on a Branch

He ~~lay~~ lay silently, *swaying* ~~~~ on the ratty old ~~~~
swinging bed. Gazing out through the porches cage-like
screen windows, he could just make out the orange glow
of the sun rising over the stone fence in the field.
A row of birch and oak trees stood guard over the
stone wall, their branches stretching toward the morning
sun.

It was the odd sounding mockingbird which had kept
him awake for so long; its ~~~~ chaotic melody greeting the
sun's prompt arrival over the meadow. The bird's song
appealed to Jay more than any other of the morning concerts of
sound. On and on the mockingbird would chatter, each note
differently placed to form an unequaled opera. Yet
in this beautiful song, ~~was~~ there seemed to Jay a ~~~~ mourning
sadness; a grief which he attributed to there never being
a reply to the birds cry.

As if to appease the bird, Jay brought his fingers to
his chapped lips and ~~s~~ whistled. ~~~~ Somewhere ~~~~ among

---

BIRD ON A BRANCH

He lay silent, swaying on the ratty old swinging bed. Gazing out
through the porch's cage-like screen windows, he could just make out
the orange glow of the sun rising over the stone fence in the field.
A row of birch and oak trees stood guard over the stone wall, their
branches stretching toward the morning sun.

It was the odd sounding mockingbird which had kept him awake for
so long; its chaotic melody greeting the sun's prompt arrival over the
meadow. The bird's song appealed to Jay more than any other of the
morning concerts of sound. On and on the mockingbird would chatter,
each note differently placed to form an unequaled opera. Yet in this
beautiful song, there seemed to Jay a mourning sadness; a grief which
he attributed to there never being a reply to the bird's cry.

As if to appease the bird, Jay brought his fingers to his chapped
lips and whistled. Somewhere among the trees, the bird cocked its
smooth gray head and glanced nervously about. The silence could only
mean the bird had heard him, Jay thought and again he whistled. The
silence continued, worrying the boy that perhaps his calls had been
misinterpreted. "Was it something I said," he wondered caustically.
His eyes narrowed as he scanned the field and searched the dark
branches of the trees. Nothing moved.

He just began to realize the tingling pain in his arm from his

BIRD ON A BRANCH

He lay silent, swaying on the old swinging bed. Gazing out through the porch's cage-like screen windows, he could just make out the orange glow of the sun, rising over the stone fence in the field. A row of birch and oak trees stood guard above the wall, their branches stretching toward the morning light.

It was the odd sounding mockingbird that kept him awake for so long with its chaotic melody from the dark end of night. He liked all birds and soon they would be filling the morning air with their radio, greeting the sun's arrival over the meadow, but this bird's song appealed to Jay more than any other. In the summer, he slept on the porch just so he could hear it at dawn. On and on the mockingbird would chatter, each little phrase differently placed to form an unequaled string of sounds you could practically see. Even so, in that beautiful song, there seemed to be a mourning sadness, a grief which Jay attributed to the fact that there was never a reply to the bird's cry. It was all alone and it was trying every song it could think of to get an answer.

As if to appease the bird, Jay brought his fingers to his chapped lips and whistled. Somewhere among the trees, the bird may have cocked its smooth gray head and glanced nervously about. The silence could only mean the bird had heard him, Jay thought, and he whistled again. The silence continued, worrying the boy that perhaps his calls had been misinterpreted. "Was it something I said?" he wondered. His eyes narrowed as he scanned the field and searched the dark branches of trees. Nothing moved.

He just began to realize the tingling pain in his arm from resting on his elbow and he sat up to rub the tightened muscles. The porch glider rocked. He heard a soft echoing beat of wings.

Carefully, he climbed from beneath the scratchy wool blankets and slid his feet onto the cool floorboards. He paced quietly to the screen door where his cat, as usual, sat, ears listening for the beginnings of life. The cat's glowing eyes had followed the boy and now it rested a paw impatiently on the screen.

"Sorry, I can't let you out," he said without much sympathy. A cat would play a bird to death. He held the cat away from the door with his foot as he pulled the hook from its latch. It swung against the rusted half circle pattern. The door creaked open on its ancient spring hinges and Jay stepped outside, onto the top stair, closing the door gently behind him.

The cat meowed as he walked down the steps to the ground. He cringed at first as his feet slipped through the cold grass blades, coating his skin in dew.

Jay heard the solitary bird make a plaintive cry from somewhere in the trees and he walked towards the origin of the sound. At the edge of the lawn, he stepped up on the moss covered stones of the fence and rested his small hand on the fencepost from which yards of orange barbed wire spread. Bringing his leg up, he leaped sideways over the sharp strands. He landed softly on the spongy grassy field and getting to his feet he galloped through the waist high stalks. Suddenly, he stopped.

Ahead of him, he could see the massive body of the sleeping cow. Dropped like a boulder in the field, it snored slightly, a geyser of shimmering breath rising from the cow's nose.

Jay crept around the barrier. He remembered what his father warned him about the cow. "Five people," Jay remembered, "is a lot of people for a cow to eat." It might not be true. His father did like to tell stories. But it might be true. The cow groaned heavily, its side rising mechanically with its guttural breathing.

Over his shoulder, he watched the cow as he waded through the tall weeds.

A branch waited underfoot. Too late he felt it and heard it snap.

The cow's ear twitched slightly, but it was still asleep.

Jay sighed relief and wiped his arm across his face—something they did in cartoons. He watched the cow as he waded through the tall weeds, until the sight of it was filtered away. He walked silently, onwards across the uneven field, toward the soft glow of day.

The mockingbird twittered cautiously somewhere up ahead. "Probably in that oak tree," Jay guessed. He whistled and waited for the answer.

The sun cast a silhouette on the branching arms and leaves of the oak.

Jay squinted into the sunlight, his eyes darting across the tree. "Is that it?" The shape he watched suddenly moved upwards toward the protective layer of golden leaves. Happily, he stuck his fingers to his mouth and sputtered several pitches. He knew it probably sounded like he was just learning to sing.

But the bird on the branch halted and looked earthwards, noticing the dark shape below. It crooned its neck forward and answered.

November 1982

SHE SPINS THE ROUND

Josephine is a tightrope walker, cloudy and dreamy on the wire, regardless of the drop underneath. Carnival eyes all watching her spotlight pirouette without parachute or net. Yet every time she goes along with the show, something else revolves heavily upon the ground. The World's Roundest Man cannot watch the big tent peak where his fearless heart crosses so sweet and daring for the audience to see. He is a shamble. He hides himself between elephant feet and spins.

pie in the sky

number eighty four

AN ORDINARY MAN

The man with three arms makes do, driving a forklift in Kalamazoo where the sound of cold snow heaps on blue junked radiators. Not exactly a cause for alarm, he works the knobs, wheel and levers expertly, driving circles in the yard. The rhythmic sway of his limbs moved like ferns out of him. In a checkered warm shirt with an extra sleeve.

At noon, he climbs off the seat. A tower has been made, rusty mufflers and tangled car parts. He walks in the white tire tracks with mud showing through. He carries a metal lunchbox and his other two hands rub friction together.

Out of the tin office, his foreman stepped and waved. "Hey! Stanley!"

Stanley raised two of his arms to wave back.

When they were close, his foreman told him, "There's someone in there wants to meet you." He passed Stanley a cup of hot coffee and Stanley still had a hand to scratch his rough chin. He paused in the cold.

"Who is it?" Stanley asked.

"I don't know. He wouldn't say. I can get rid of him if you want."

Stanley took off his cap and wiped at the sweat there. "Naw. I'll see what he wants." He swallowed some coffee and pushed on the door.

Inside, at a table with a newspaper folded open in front of him, a man with white hair suddenly smiled and stood up. He eyed Stanley mysteriously and grated in an oyster opening voice, "Do you know who I am?"

Stanley was tired. He sat down at the other end of the table and unlatched his lunchbox. He took another sip of coffee and took out a sandwich with his other hands. His wife had wrapped it up in silver foil. Putting the cup down, he let that hand go under the table to rest. "No," he answered and started to eat.

The stranger rustled the paper. "I'm the editor of *The Sound.*" He watched Stanley in a crooked way. His speaking and motions made him seem like a nail bent out of the floor that catches on your shoe. "I want to write a story about you." His voice wasn't coming out of him. It was telephoned from a dark shattered train station booth. He nodded at Stanley's left side.

Stanley finished chewing, "No," he said. "I don't want those newspaper words about me. I'm like any other person you see. Only what I've got I don't hide." With his third arm, he drank coffee.

JACK SHELLAC ON A RAILROAD TRACK

He had taken a wrong turn somehow. Worse than being mauled by a grizzly bear three times, now he was walking in rags across the railroad yard, looking for an eastbound train.

His one dismal eye glared at the world. His face sneered with claw marks and an American flag eye patch.

Not far away, a train exhaled a white cloud of smoke like a whale breaching and Jack shambled in that direction.

The only thing he carried with him was a paintbrush. On every dark alley wall he passed, he left his mark next to the other painted words. Jack carried the brush in his gnarled hand as he ran. The train began to move gradually.

His reflection rolled in the oily puddles next to the tracks, a shimmer of clicking wheels, turning faster. Hunchbacked, Jack held onto the last car ladder like Quasimodo over Paris. He climbed to the top and rode in the wind.

Torn clothing streamed on him. He muttered a curse as the city was going away. Old furniture stores, sawed roofs, burnt out factories, junked cars up on blocks, a girl standing in a surrounded window who watched him for a moment before she was gone.

Jack felt better the further he got from the city. He welcomed the flocks of crows, the ferns and plants pouring across the ground from the mountains. He tried to reach out and paint the trees. When he turned around to face into the wind, he laughed at the mountain he saw.

The train was climbing straight for it.

Laughing again, he thought of painting an obscenity a mile wide across the white snow at the top. He stood up in the sharp wind and held his brush to the distant peak. An *F* became visible, then a *U*. Jack's writing was shaky. It didn't help when the snaky line of train cars bucked and rattled, flinging him clear.

The brush carried a comet trail across the sky, into the trees beside the tracks.

Jack Shellac was crumpled in the hug of an elm tree. New spring leaves budded out of the branches. Twenty feet below, a couple of coins fell from Jack's shoe and clicked off the metal rails. A playing card fluttered down his shirt sleeve and sailed jaggedly. "Hey!" Jack yelled. Expecting the miracle of someone near, Jack shouted again, "Hey! Help!"

That was hours ago. At night, Jack Shellac remained in the crown of the tree, trying to sleep. Hopelessly, he turned over, offering prayers to the sky. Did it ever hear him before?

An owl flew out of the moon and landed near him.

Jack reached his empty hand to it. "You gotta help me," he pleaded.

The owl answered. It took a few steps up the branch.

"Hey!" Jack Shellac motioned too wildly. His weak body slid away from the trunk. He wailed, for the tree had let him go, he was sure to crack on the railroad track. But the owl had given him a soft place to land—a curved and wide grizzly back.

GUARANTEE

Out of the tumbled water logs, they built themselves a house of trees. Slung like carp, its wooden lines fishtailed with seaweed, dried and brine. So close to the ocean, up from sand, high tide waves masqueraded as a lawn. On a stormy night, they are guaranteed starfish visitors.

TURKEY LEGS

"Mister Pendant, Hanna-Barbera is on line four." She repeated the intercom message, her voice booming through the office, "Mister Pendant, line four."

A shout came from behind the screen and Rudy Pendant's chair squeaked. He sighed and stood up, creasing down his red tie decorated with a cartoon character. Half of him bulged around the wall screen and he squinted his eyes towards his secretary. "Deborah?" he labored. "Who was that message for?"

"I'm sorry, Mister Pendant!" Her mouth was caught by her hands. "I forgot you were on break." She stared at his grimacing face. "It sounded important though." Pointing at the orange flashing light on the phone, she explained, "It's Hanna-Barbera."

Rudy suddenly broke out of his frozen glower and he became excited, "Is it?"

"Yeah. Line four."

Hannah-Barbera! Rudy beamed. He spun back to his desk and pushed the fried chicken off the telephone cord. Plunging his hand at the phone, he grabbed the receiver and poked the button marked with a four. "Rudy," he said officially.

"This is Ms. Lincoln from the Hanna-Barbera Public Relations Department."

"Aaahh…" Dreamily, he leaned back in his chair with his eyes shut. They want to give me another award, he guessed. Always near to him here, framed on his desk was a golden document with Yogi Bear congratulating him. Pendant Products made them by the thousands, little plastic toys for cereal. Last year's kicking Funny Dog was such a hit with the brass, Rudy thought, chuckling. Now I've done it again!

"Mister Pendant, it is official policy for me to inform you that you're being sued by Hanna-Barbera Industries."

Rudy shot out of his chair. "*What?!*"

At her desk, Deborah quietly set down her phone. In a hurry, she collected her coat off the back of her chair. She left a half eaten donut.

There was a shadow on the floor next to Rudy's desk. It was attached to a pale candle melting in a rounded suit.

The woman's voice in his ear said, "Your toy is utterly offensive, sir. You have polluted thousands of boxes of Sugar Dimes with this repellent item. To think that someone as valued as you could be so cruel. Why, it turns out we don't even *know* you!"

"Wait a minute," Rudy interrupted. "Are you saying something is the matter with the Turkey Legs toy?" He couldn't imagine how a two inch plastic toy could be so wrong.

"Mister Pendant, the Turkey Legs character created by our corporation in 1962, which is loved by millions of children all over the globe, has *nothing* to do with the *thing* you made." Her voice shook. "Such an intention on your part to do damage to our business is libelous. A court date has been set for two weeks from now. We'll be in touch." Then she hung up.

Rudy backed away from the dropping phone. On the desk top, it clattered and buzzed the dial tone, stunned like a black tropical insect. His voice wavered, "Deborah?" It had become icily quiet in the office of Pendant Products. Rudy labored against the dense stillness, around the wall screen.

The digital clock radio on Deborah's desk clicked another minute.

His ferrous eyes blinked as he pouted and stared at the empty room. "Turkey Legs!" the name spat out of his mouth. Unknown to him, his machines had been sabotaged, pouring out obscene molds.

Furious waddling took him over to the door of the adjacent factory. He seized the handle and flung it open. Before him, none of the battered civil war era machines were on, no turning loud flywheels and hissing valves. The room was deserted.

It looked like Sunday afternoon. Sunlight painted the track of conveyor belt, dust floated in yellow sandstorms.

"Hilton?!" Rudy bellowed. "Poundsworth! Where are you?!" The two men had left with Deborah, it was obvious. Abandoned a sinking ship…Rudy imagined them escaping in a stolen convertible, laughing, passing cactus desert. They never liked me, he knew. They did this to me on purpose.

He seethed and put his hands up to loosen his tie again. Turkey Legs danced on the cloth while his blood pressure staggered. With disgust, he ripped off the tie and threw it to snake at his feet.

The floor was littered with plastic toy fragments discarded across oil stains. The factory had been defeated.

I don't stand a chance, Rudy sighed. This is the end of Pendant Products. He loyally patted the horse shaped head of the green old stamping machine, a cowboy dying inside of him. "Sorry…"

A Turkey Legs toy fell out of its metal jaws.

Rudy's face wrung into folds as his horrified scream erupted and echoed off the scarred peeling walls. He threw the toy away from him. He stormed across the floor, ripping his car keys out of his pocket.

The door flew open and Rudy Pendant broke into a run over the sidewalk to his parked car. He wasn't exactly sure where he was going. As he turned the engine on, in his mind were spinning visions of the Hanna-Barbera court proceedings. A lawyer bringing Exhibit A to the judge…The judge becoming pale, bringing down his gavel to quiet the lynch mob jury.

Rudy steered chaotically out of the lot and the car bounced over a curb onto the street. Dandelions clung to the scraped fender. His eyes didn't seem to be watching the present; he was in the future, staring at the judge sentencing him.

"Mr. Pendant…" the judge spoke, looking down from a black wooden castle.

Rudy's Chevrolet crunched off the side of a Safeway truck

and screeched wildly through the supermarket parking lot. Grocery carts blasted into the air.

The crashing and furious tilt seemed to revive Rudy. Alert, he averted a station wagon and a staggering old woman.

Then he saw Yogi Bear at the Safeway entrance. The big happy smile pasted on its face, and glittering, oblivious eyes, passing out free samples of Crunch Riddles. Children fled from the approaching, damaged car, raking broken metal and smoking. Rudy smiled, absolutely certain, pressed the accelerator and aimed through the spider webbed windshield.

NOW YOU GOT ME LOST

Sylvan Moore left a trail of blood across the floor. The drops stopped with him at the washroom door, and more spilled going in. At the sink, the water had been turned on. The faucet handle bore the trace, the bowl too, where the splash had formed. It was terrible to think of poor beloved Sylvan Moore struggling like this, staunching himself with those torn gray paper towels, but this was my job and I had to see it through to the end.

The evidence of his escape was everywhere. The window was left open where he crawled out to the air. Who knows how far he could get, but I wouldn't give him 2 to 5 that he could reach the boulevard alive, especially now that I saw the arrow thrown in the trash.

It was painted with red, from the feathers on down to the jagged barb. I could take my time tracking this kill.

Back in the hall, I took the elevator down the twelve floors to the lobby like anyone else would do. I wandered over to the counter and reached towards the little silver bell. Before I hit it though, a bellboy popped up like a jack-in-the-box. "Can I help you, lady?"

"You got *The Herald*?"

"Yes, of course, up to the minute," and he turned around to the wall. We both stared at the glass pipe leading up into the ceiling. He flicked a switch and we watched the newspaper capsule drop down the chute. It landed with a click and the kid brought it to me. "That'll be six bits, lady."

I told him, "Keep the change," passing him three silver coins. I tore open the tube and shook out the crisp roll of today's latest news. I skipped the front page with its photo of Sylvan Moore and opened the paper to the dog-race listings. I sighed. I said, "Looks like I lost this time," and tossed the paper onto the counter.

"I hope you don't mind me saying…" the bellboy grinned sourly, "but I bet on Sylvan Moore."

I let him know I didn't care, turning away from him without a reply, walking my reflection over the marble floor. I was always cast as the heavy. I was used to it. The public was conditioned by what the media said.

Sure, they're rooting for a man with an arrow wound, they're always betting on the other guy. But I already had the next arrow locked into the bow. I was ready to end this.

I wasn't expecting the rain though; when I came inside, the weather seemed fine. I pulled my cape up over my head like a hood. The rain sounded like sand falling on me. The night was full of that rain. I headed for the alley. I knew he'd be there, half dead. Why worry?

Diamonds shined in every neon sign angled out over the street. I reached into my coat to get my hand on the bow so I could finish this game.

There was moonlight in the alley where far overhead the washroom window opened onto a weak fire escape. He wasn't up there. I was ready to shoot at the next second. Where are you, Sylvan Moore?

I didn't spy him right away. Where was he? I was between two walls, rolling off rain, silhouettes and strange shadows. For just a second I doubted whether he was there or not. Nobody could go far after what I did, especially not Sylvan Moore. But all I could see was rain falling down.

I held the crossbow in front of me and I quickly went further into the alley. I was tiring of this. The drainpipes popped and trickled. Suddenly I was through to the next street. Did he make it this far?

Some carriages slid by in the shallow slick stream. I looked for any disappearing signs of blood on the cobblestones. They were there.

The smallest flow of it lurked in the puddles.

It occurred to me that coming this far he could have grabbed a trolley. They rattled by every once in a while. That must be what he did. He had a bit of luck on his side, that's all. So what?

His trail limped up to a flower stand that was in the midst of giving up and closing for the night. I caught the edge of the shutter swinging down, then asked, "Just a second. I have a question." I took a look around the bright yellow room. He wasn't hiding in there. "Have you seen anybody in trouble?"

The green face of the florist leaned down to me. "You mean Sylvan Moore?" At that, he laughed. I didn't have to guess he knew more than he was telling me. Were they were all in on making sure Sylvan Moore won? Was everyone helping him along the way?

I threw the shudder closed. It didn't matter. He didn't have long to live unless he made it to the …

Of course! He had to go to the infirmary. I hiked out into the rain on the road and hooked a taxi.

I jumped in the back seat. After I shut the door I wanted to say where we had to go, but the taxi was already rattling as fast as it could in the right direction.

"Don't worry, friend," the driver told me. "You picked the winning ride. I got my money on you. We'll find him."

The taxi slew through the pour of every last bit of the night.

"How do you know where he is?" I asked.

"Somebody squealed."

We went around a corner that put me hard into the card-board trimmed corner. I leaned into the next turn better. The plastic windshield showed a view of the tilting, weaving city sights I knew.

"Are you going to the infirmary?" I asked him.

"I'll take you there," he told me. The road was in control no matter how it seemed to shoot us like a meteor here there and everywhere.

It must have been another minute before I realized what was going on. This wasn't the way to the infirmary; the taxi was taking me further away. I leaned over the seat, "Alright, wise guy! You can stop the cab now. I'm getting out." I had to take out the crossbow to get through to him.

"Okay, okay," he wheeled the cab to the side of the road then he laughed, "But you'll never win now!"

I got back into the rain. He had done a good job getting me lost. I watched the red lantern swinging on the back of the taxi as it left me stranded out here next to a wall of brambles on the dark edge of suburbia. I was already soaked.

Across the road from me were some houses with lights burning. Maybe I could get a ride into town somehow…As long as they weren't laying odds on Sylvan Moore…So far, everyone was.

BLACK SPACE ORBIT

Perry woke up just before 2 A.M. The dream was so strong it still wavered before his eyes. He reached beside the bed and fumbled in the dark on the floor for a pen and paper. He wasn't even sure if what he wrote could be seen in the morning, as he fell back onto the pillow and into sleep again.

When he woke, he carried the note out into the kitchen. He put his glasses on and stood by the stove and read it: Black Space Orbit. The dream was there. Even though the reality of his waking life seemed as wooden as a clockwork toy, the dream felt like an important message. Black Space Orbit was the name of a video he watched in his dream. It was a Japanese cartoon. He could still see the images from it while he dressed, reheated some coffee, ate a quick bowl of cereal.

"Alright," he said aloud and stared at the ceiling as if to those unseen dream agents, "I'm going to find your movie." Even though it was the end of May, the weather was cold with a touch of rain. Perry wore a long heavy coat and scarf. He shut the door behind him.

He rented a little house on a steep wooded hill. Further off, there were some apartment buildings in the leaves, half hidden by trees. He was the only one on the dirt path that crept up, towards the town on the other side.

He took the path every day, a few times and sometimes he came home late at night, knowing the black way like radar. He wheezed as he walked. Getting old was making him slower. Last Fall, he had even started to use a cane off and on. Today he poked it beside each leafy damp step he took.

A wren tapped up the mossy trunk of a cedar. He thought of a poem—he had written several books of them—this little bird could have flown right out of one of them.

Soon he reached the hilltop and the path began to drop.

He caught glimpses of the town down there…Roads, rooftops, the factory ruins beside the bay. He listened to more birds but he wasn't pausing to write poetry; he was thinking about last night's dream. It was just beginning to seem a little absurd, as if it was growing rust in this waking world. He wondered if this walk took too much longer if the dream would just crumble away.

Perry came out of the woods onto a cement path on the college grounds. By now he was sweating. He stopped to tear loose his scarf and unbutton his overcoat. He rubbed the back of his hand over his forehead. It glistened like a fresh, meaty trout.

The campus lawn was dotted with buttercups. He liked the sight of them but he was sure the lawnmowers would be at them soon. It was inevitable. He passed among their constellations as he left a wet trail past the Humanities building. Twenty five years he had taught in there, but he didn't look up from the flowers. He didn't want to crush them.

It was rare to hear his name called, the students who knew him had all moved on and the faculty tended to look the other way. So the yelled "Perry!" seemed to hang in the air like some ancient battle horn.

Perry spotted the white pickup truck driving slowly along the curb. A blue uniformed security guard held his arm out the window and waved. He was one of Professor Roberts' old students and fans. Perry stopped, pulled his cane off the grass and took aim like a rifle. The guard laughed and waved and drove off to the left. Perry held onto a smile the rest of the journey across the lawn.

His shoes left wet footprints as they found the sidewalk. Steadily and slowly he left the campus behind. The brick walls turned into the cheap wooden pressboard paneling of student apartments. He crossed streets that became busier until he arrived downtown on the corner of Holly and Railroad.

Perry took rest there, sitting heavily on a metal bench. He propped his cane against his leg and reached into his coat pocket, removing a pack of Lucky Strikes. For the length of that cigarette he sat and watched the traffic and exhaled smoke. He also would watch the sky once in a while. There were pigeons flustering about electric wires. Beyond them, there were creamy billows of clouds and then beyond them he thought of where his dream occurred.

At last he dropped his spent cigarette on the pavement. He was ready to find out about that dream.

Manic Movies was nearby, across the street and halfway down the block from where he sat. Perry's reflection lumbered over the window displayed with posters and a neon sign. If anywhere in town would have heard of Black Space Orbit, this was it.

Loud rock music greeted Perry. A kid at the counter with dyed black hair gave him a glance and a nod. There were rows of videos plus all the movies shelved along the walls. Some teenagers laughed at the back of the room.

Perry went to the counter and said, "I could spend an hour going up and down these aisles but I'll try asking you instead."

The boy regarded him with smoky eyes.

"Do you have a film called Black Space Orbit?"

"Uhhh."

"Have you ever heard of it?"

"No, I don't know that title..." He put a hand on a red three-ring binder that lay on the counter. "Let me see if we have it."

Perry watched the boy's black painted fingernails flip the pages. His breath whistled.

"No," the boy said. "It's not in here. What kind of movie is it?"

"Weird as a wooden watch," Perry replied. "I think it might be Japanese. That's my impression. A cartoon from the looks of it..."

"Oh, you know what? Esther is the one you want to talk to. She knows all about anime. I bet she's seen it. You know where

The Last Exit is?"

"Elucidate me," Perry said.

"It's on Brooklyn, over two streets. She works there. Just ask for Esther."

"Very good," said Perry. He pegged his cane down like an oar and spun on that pivot. It made him almost graceful, like a military balloon. He left the shop with his long coat billowing. The music from the store became the sound of street traffic, a bicycle clattering, basket full of bottles, a guitarist playing for coins.

The Last Exit was actually a place Perry was familiar with. He had done poetry readings there. The last time was years ago, but he enjoyed it and the crowd had applauded him and thumped the long wooden tables. Now he kept his poetry to himself, writing it, putting the pages away in a cardboard box. He was retired.

A crow hopped along a fire-escape regarding Perry as he entered what was probably the bird's territory on Brooklyn Avenue. There were kids sitting on the concrete in front of The Last Exit. Perry thought of Oliver Twist. A girl was sprawled on the cement while someone drew her outline in chalk.

"Another casualty," Perry said as he stepped around them.

Inside, he carried himself like a dark fluttering galleon to the marble counter top.

"Professor Roberts!" The thin, pale owner Rico bowed greeting towards him. He was like a mop with the beam of a smile on top.

Perry said, "I'm back." He brushed up to the counter and leaned. He was tired from the day's journey.

"It's good to see you again. It's been a while."

"I'm retired."

"That's what I heard. Do you still write poetry?"

"When I'm in the mood."

"That's good." While they were talking, Rico had poured a coffee cup with something red as blood. "It's on the house," he said. "But don't let anybody see." He laughed.

"Ah, I thank you," Perry replied and took the cup and had a taste.

Rico smiled. "What brings you this way?"

"Yes, I've—" he had to stop abruptly while a waiter brushed against him with a tray of teapots. "I'm told there's a girl who works here by the name of Esther."

"Esther, yes, she's—" Rico leaned to look around Perry. "She's right over there."

Perry turned and spotted the girl in a white apron. Her pink hair stood out in two pigtails. "I heard she's an aficionado of Japanese film."

"Go talk to her," Rico said. "She's a smart girl."

Perry set the cup onto the counter and moved his slow walk towards her.

She was leaving the table as he approached. She had a coffee mug hooked in each hand. Her eyes brightened upon seeing him.

"I've been told you're an aficionado of Japanese film?" Perry started.

"You're Perry Roberts, right?"

He wasn't expecting that, though of course he knew his ramblings had made him a bit of a town character. He popped his cane on the wooden floor and nodded, "At your service."

"My father knew you. He told me you were a great poet."

Perry was amazed again, a double broadsides. He shifted his feet. "That's kind of him to say."

"Were you wondering about a Japanese film?" "In fact I was," Perry had regained his poise, redistributed himself and his voice was deep again. "Although I'm not even sure if the film exists outside of my own mind…This morning I dreamed I was watching some weird Japanese cartoon. Now I don't know if it was a warning or a bit of undigested beef."

"What was the film like?"

"It's called Black Space Orbit. I never heard of it before."

But he could tell she had—her eyes were wide and the coffee mugs turned heavy in her hands.

"I didn't think anyone knew about that," Esther said. She put the coffee cups on the table nearest to her. "It's never been released in the US. I have a bootleg copy in Japanese. There's not even subtitles. You can't—"

Perry raised his hand as if it held a crystal ball and resumed, "A planet comes into our orbit. It's a beautiful blue and green world, but there's a black dot on it, a sort of storm cloud and from the shadow these dark hooded sort of people contact us. They tell us they've steered their planet in. They say they've been watching us, seeing our unhappiness, wars, the many ways we are destroying ourselves and then they show us their world." Perry couldn't help it if he tried, his voice would carry, his presence alone would draw attention. The whole café had turned his way and quieted to breathing. "Their world is like Earth used to be. Oceans, forests, hundreds of miles of green fields and animals and no pollution or signs of man's greed and cruelty. These strange beings have created their planet in the likeness of ours, but without humans. It's been that way for thousands of years, a sort of backup Earth. Only now, seeing us in our misery they have decided to give us the chance to come and start over."

Esther looked like a ghost had taken her hand.

"They have faith in us. They actually want to see what people will do, if they've learned anything. But…" he dropped his arm with the crystal ball. "You know how it goes…Those hooded beings are actually vampires. They eat every person who arrives. They drive their dark cloud around the planet like a vacuum cleaner." The whole room groaned. Some people booed, someone threw a crumpled napkin ball at Perry.

Perry let himself down wearily on the bench at the table. Esther sat too, facing him. "But here's the thing," Perry continued. "In my dream, I watched as if it was something that was actually going to happen. I had to hurry and warn the world. I was running in the dark on the path from my house, out in the trees. I didn't have my cane, I was actually running over the hill and I could see the town below me, but suddenly I tripped. There was a cliff in front of me. I held my arms out and as I fell I turned into an owl." He rapped his fist on the table. "I wake up. It's two o'clock in the morning…Look…" He took the paper scrap from his shirt pocket. "These are the notes I wrote in the dark." He read his handwriting to her, "Knowing the meaning, he tries to get away through the woods but he turns into an owl." Then he tapped his finger on another scrawl, reading, "A video I must see."

He folded the paper back in half and returned it to his pocket.

Esther let out a sigh. She waved her hand in front of her as if brushing smoke away. "No, that's not exactly the same movie that I have. It's different. You have to see it though. Especially after a dream like that…"

"They didn't seem to like my dream too much," Perry motioned at the room.

"Yes, well that's a tough crowd." She laughed. "I get off work in an hour. I can take you to my place, we can watch the movie."

Perry nodded. "Sounds like a plan."

She stood up. "There is an owl in the movie, you know."

"Really?"

"The owl does kind of save the day."

"Really?" he repeated.

"Really." She picked up those two empty coffee cups again. "You can wait here if you want. I can bring you a coffee or a pot of tea."

"Sure. I had a long walk getting here. I'll, uh, read a book for a while."

There was a big well-stocked bookshelf. The Last Exit had a wall of donated pulp paperbacks, discarded library books, volumes on every subject by a world of authors. Perry noticed his own poetry too. He chose a Greek play and returned to his place.

There was a dented round metal steaming teapot with a blue and white China cup awaiting him. He took off his heavy coat, scarf and laid them on the bench with his cane. It was good to sit there, sip tea, get lost in the little paperback opened in his hands.

By the time Esther showed up at his side, Perry had been in 400 B.C. for quite a while. Still, he was able to shut the book with a snap. "I know how it will end," he said and stood up to gather his things, to follow her out to the street.

It was midday but gray clouds hung overhead, more rain or just another dreary looking day. Either way they were both feeling thrilled by the day; Esther was singing away the story of how she tracked that movie down like a detective to some Tokyo warehouse, as Perry tapped his cane beside her.

She stopped next to a blue car and unlocked the door for him. He took some time to get comfortable in the seat. The car was running and ready to go when he rested his hands on the cane handle and said, "Anchors away."

She drove them onto the street. He was pleased to see she had an ashtray in the car, opened and stuffed with lipsticked, crushed cigarettes. As they pulled to a red light, he was going to reach in his pocket for his Lucky Strikes when he noticed a strange man walking their way.

The man wore the clothes he'd been living in. He looked as if he had not seen clean in months. Right off, Perry thought he must be homeless, a condition he felt himself not far from. Sometimes he felt it was only luck, or poetry, that kept him from that fate. The man carried a bundle hidden tight under his coat and he kept looking over his shoulder as if being followed. Esther was still talking but Perry was watching. Whatever it was the man carried made him suspicious. Was it something he stole, or was he being pursued?

Then the man stopped. Perry had to lean to see him. He was

stopped and bending low to the ground next to the sidewalk where there was a thick hedge growing .

Perry grabbed Esther's arm as she started to put the car into gear. The light just turned green. "Wait a second!" he told her.

"What is it?"

Perry watched the man take the bundle from the warm, dirty front of his coat and lay it on the ground under the leaves.

Car horns were honking behind them.

"Mister Roberts? What is it?"

Perry could see two little baby feet twitching from a wrapped tight blanket placed on the ground. "Oh my God!"

The man heard all the sound of the cars and stood up from the baby. He ran away from the spot.

Esther told him, "We have to drive, Mr. Roberts!"

Perry let her arm go as he opened the door. "I have to go out there," he said. "There's a baby."

Someone was yelling, stuck behind them. Perry hurried without his cane, limping over to the sidewalk. There was no sign of the homeless man. The traffic was moving again. Esther's voice was lost in the engines and wheels.

UKROP'S ARTIFICIAL ORANGE

You hope your worst thoughts don't come true. I've been haunted by them lately and today while standing in the line at Rush-In Food, I could picture it all happening, a nightmare movie in the back of my mind. I left the boys playing on the sidewalk in front of the house. As I went down the hill toward the store, I kept my eye on them, looking back a couple times. Small as toys, they ran around and around, getting smaller as I walked.

When I turned near the mashed fender of a parked car on the corner I lost track of them.

The tar on the lot was melting, big scabs of it turning into thick black ooze. I could lose my shoe in it. I didn't want to spend much time, I just wanted to get some water or juice or something. The day was so hot. Inside by the jammed door was a big cooler full of lemonade, but I grabbed an orange juice. It was only forty cents and I had a dollar.

I forgot about the lines though. When all I wanted was one thing, every fool in town was here to get the best deal. I stood there with them. I looked at the display of gloomy tabloids, but all I could think about was the kids. I could see a car stopped and someone calling them over. For God's sake, was it worth a cold drink? I glared at the black conveyor pulling stuff along. The guy paying was getting three bottles of Sutter's Home. Just in front of me an old couple unloaded boxes of Ukrop's Artificial Orange from their basket. They were slow, everything was slow. It had to be.

I turned the lid on my juice and gulped it while I waited. I thought of leaving the empty and running.

The old man turned in degrees, creaking worn notched gears to face me, "Would you like to go ahead of us?" He was so pleasant I couldn't take his place.

I said, "No thank you, no," even though I didn't know if those moments could have meant life or death. They might have…Anyway…I could already see the aftermath. It was done. I could see the neighbor boy staring at me when I asked. I could see that confused mouth. He only had a few teeth; most of them had been gone for months. "Where's my son?!" I would scream at him.

We moved. The old man paid with dollars taken out of a billfold. After I paid for an empty bottle, the cashier threw it right away.

I went out the door, past the potted red flowers and signs and tore across that blacktop. Elbowed on by the heat of the red hot sun, I ran across the street and turned the corner to scream up the hill.

Cars were parked on either side of calm houses with a cloud at the top. Across the uncut lawn, tall dandelions waved back and forth. They were in them, playing games. Everything was fine in the wind. Everything was okay. I had been out in the sun for too long.

WYZZLER'S MOTHER

Three years had passed, almost four. Going back would be different though, wouldn't it? Besides, what kind of job was he supposed to do now? Everything pointed him back there. That was where his talent had been. And he knew the place, had survived it under the harshest conditions, he had even thrived on it. They accepted his application at O'Breens International and next thing he knew he was flying back. There were a few others like him on board. He didn't ask; he didn't talk much to anyone anymore. He kept his hands on an 800 page book and stared out the window for the flight. All the way back, he could feel his body returning itself, like there were small gears in him tightening, realigning.

He wore a three piece suit now. That was different. He carried a briefcase. It was full of brochures, papers, illustrated diagrams and a slide presentation. But he carried no weapons.

When the plane touched down he stared straight ahead, deep into the textured cloth of the seat in front. The yellow light from the oval window crept across his hand. He waited, braced, for the mechanical voice to bark the exit procedure.

Instead, a stewardess glided to the microphone and welcomed them pleasantly.

It was unthinkable. It only took them five minutes to depart the aircraft. At last, he stormed out, all senses alert, into the airport and stopped.

He searched for some sign of the carnage that had gone on here not long ago. It was painted to a gleam and though it was air-conditioned, he was sweating. Families moved around him, chattering that language he remembered so well. His body was trembling. It seemed he was waiting for a sudden bomb to blast it all away. He needed to sit down.

He moved towards a chair but didn't make it there before a

cabbie caught at his sleeve. He turned with his briefcase like a shield, slanting it right into the words coming at him.

"You need the cab? I take you."

He wiped the sweat off his forehead. I was this close, he said in his mind. "I need," he rasped, "to get to O'Breens H.Q, the—"

"Oh yezz," the faintly blue colored man replied. "I know the O'Breenzz. You buzzinezzman. Thizz way pleazze."

He followed the cabbie through the crowds. They called them bugs then, but he tried to look at them differently now. Eyes watched and darted from him, burned.

Hissing doors broke them to outside. The heat, but not the same war torn smell of gas generators and coal fires. Of course there was electricity now, the city was returning to normal. He held tight to the briefcase handle and got into the gray taxi.

The cabbie started the motor. Also, that tinny insect-like music flooded the interior, the music that had been a soundtrack to so many things. That music even crept into his dreams thousands of miles away.

He tried to avert his eyes from the street sights. Instead he stared up higher at the roof levels. Where snipers would have been, now it was aerials and wires, air conditioner units, and signs. He saw an O'Breens advertisement, plastic, written in two languages that snaked words together. Sure, he thought, that's perfect, that's the way it is now. What's ours is theirs.

The cabbie kept quiet. Once they locked eyes, then the cabbie blinked back to the road. Around them bicycles, music, market stands and diesel fumes.

The cab had been stopped for a while before he responded. He looked at the little mirror, the driver was watching him.

"You O.K?" the driver asked.

He just got out his wallet and paid. He gave the driver more than enough and got out.

O'Breens International stood clad in brand new steel and neon plastic piping, with the company colors twining around the fragile looking glass. He took a step towards it, but he paused.

Whatever was going through his mind was causing his trigger finger to itch at the skin beneath his thumb nail. Blood was flowing to his other clenched fingers. His eyes seemed focused on the sign's glowing apostrophe, shaped like a sword cut into the bricks.

The cab driver had walked in front of him and waited on the sidewalk with him.

A helicopter clattered low overhead. Painted in O'Breens colors, it was a company chopper whisking businessmen to another location.

"Let me take you zzomewhere," the cabbie said. He spoke gently, "You need to zzee."

He caught his breath. Frankly that was fine with him, he wasn't ready for O'Breens, the stuffed shirts and handshakes and the contents of his briefcase to be spilled out. He followed the driver back to the car and sunk into that worn seat again.

The music started with the motor. His eyes fastened on a picture taped above the mirror. It was the photo of a shrouded woman. One of those women in black, who sat in the back of rooms and judged the world from chairs…He mumbled a whispered apology to her. That felt better. He only barely cared where they were going.

RAT TRAPPED

It would be the perfect ending for me, I suppose. Here I am with half my body gone numb. I guess that's the creep of the Grim Reaper spreading shadow over me. It would be the fitting irony for me to die in this giant rat trap, only I don't think it will happen that way. I think I'll manage to hang on the next four hours til dawn when the first shift will come in. One of them will get me out of this contraption, paramedics will be called, I'll find myself revived and hung up in some hospital room tethered by pulleys with tubes running into my bandaged soul. Yes, and then it will all be told. I started work at the rat trap factory four years ago. It's hard to believe it's been that long, but that's the way life goes. I had a few jobs before, the sort of things you do when you don't really care. I guess I saw this job as another one at first, but I lingered on. I got used to it. Plus, what a strange thing to say—I work at a rat trap factory. How many people can admit to that?

I bend wire. My hands form it in my sleep. Two turns, then two small twists that jig under the loops. That's a trade secret, or maybe not. At the end of every day I don't know how many traps I've made. I've never counted. I couldn't, I just let it go. My hands have become hard and gray as the Tin Man with all the work I've done.

I don't think much about the future. I'm here and tomorrow happens in the morning. But I have to say I hate to think I'll be here when I'm an old man. Waiting for retirement, still going…Like anyone, after work I drop a dollar on the lottery. I mean it has to get better, there has to be a way out.

The cough started when summer went. It was getting cold on the loading bay on breaks. I thought it was the usual end of the season hack. But after a couple weeks it didn't go away. Every night there was the 3 A.M time when I thought I was ready to die. I was sure something was in my lungs, eating me from the inside out.

At last, I stepped away on a ten minute break and dialed the factory doctor. I made an appointment. It turned out to be the first of many. After tests and x-rays, it looked obvious: the source of my illness was the factory itself.

There have been enough TV movies about whistleblowers for me to know they never win. It's a martyr's cause. They always come to a terrible end. That didn't matter. I stepped into those shoes and walked. That's when I discovered the worth of a person there. I felt it burn like the iron eyes of a monster looking down on me.

They brought in their Health Services representatives and I told them, "The lead you're using in the production of these rat traps exceeds health code levels." I told them, "Fact is, it's in the air here. I'm sick because of your neglect and I don't know how many other people have got sick too."

The Health Services Coordinator was prepared. She held up calming hands to tremble slightly. "Now…" she said, "I wouldn't say it's as conspiratorial as that. If you're worried about your personal well being, you could wear one of these air packs." She reached under the table to pick up what looked like an old scuba diving aqualung. It clanked on the tabletop.

"I can't really wear that thing and work," I almost laughed. "There's all kinds of machinery going around me, I'll bump into something and get hurt."

"There's nothing wrong with the air!" my supervisor snapped. "This factory has been operating for 80 years!" He snatched at his oxygen mask and sucked greedily, ferociously. "If someone has a problem working here, I say, move on! It's a free country, cast your line elsewhere." He shot me a baleful look. It didn't matter if the factory was a poisonous environment, I was only one worker and workers can be replaced. What could I say? Should I just go? The meeting turned into trying to juggle sand. We were all Egyptians going down.

Still, I felt like I'd done something. Some enormous wheel was creaking. The next day I got a call from my factory doctor. I listened to the message two times while I boiled water for supper.

"Please call back, regarding your last examination."

I threw a handful of dry pasta into the pan and dialed the number.

I had to go through the hurdles then finally the voice of the secretary broke the muzak.

"Yes," she said. "There's been some new information regarding your last x-ray."

"Like what?" I said.

"Quite simply, there's a ghost inside of you."

"What?!"

"It's not uncommon. Don't worry. We found a ghost haunting you. It won't be difficult to get it out with today's cutting edge technology. Shall we schedule an appointment?"

"No!" I told her. No, I didn't need this anymore. I already believed none of this made any sense; I didn't need it to go on anymore. I put the phone down and stirred the noodles in the pan. Careful as an ostrich, I leaned my head over to breathe the steam.

The next morning, I woke up at 6. My alarm clock dumped me out of a dream. Oh well…That world is for the sleepers, not for me. I threw myself into an almost hot shower, had a breakfast of a bowl of cereal and I hurried out the door to get to the bus on time.

At the dark top of the hill I waited for a minute or two. I watched the weather over the hill, stars, the planet Venus, bright, then, with a lumbering creak the bus arrived.

It's funny, you wouldn't expect a rat factory to have rats, but it does. Part of my morning opening procedure is tending the traps and resetting them.

There was one under the heat vent on the west side, another trap had been sprung and the bait was gone. That could either be a faulty trap or a smart rat. Oh, there's luck too. Luck seems to play a part in everything. I threw that trap away.

Much as I didn't want to think about it anymore, I just want to do my job. I don't want to be sick doing it.

When I got to my desk, there was a silver whistle hung from a thumbtack on the wall. Yeah, I got it…Funny joke. I left it there, which is even funnier because I could have used it later on. But I left it. I got my clipboard and took it to the assembly line.

That's where I stood, coughing, putting inspection stickers on a line of slowly moving rat traps, when the plan came to me.

Sure—what this needed was publicity—this story needed to get out in the open so people would know about it. And that evening, long after the factory was black for the night, I snuck back inside and made my way past the quiet machinery, down the metal stairs to the basement.

This…This is what I tried to pull to the elevator, with hopes of pallet jacking it to the loading bay and rattling it out across the parking lot to the chain link fence entrance…This gigantic prop rat trap. It was originally made for an Easter parade, but City Hall balked at the gruesome sight of it mounted on a float and barred it from the street full of all the other flowers. So it ended up entombed in the basement. You'd have to work here to know about it. There are jokes about it—it's down here in the dark dungeon, set for giant rats that prowl the caverns.

It really was set. I didn't know that. In the dead of night, an hour ago, I reached across it to pull it and it got me. The crash was so fast and terrible, I didn't stand a chance. That's right, I know the irony: I'm trapped like a rat.

Okay…And to make matters worse, I'm stuck in the basement where nobody has any need to go. The steel bar crushing my chest and arms has probably done its job. Dawn is still a long way away, my lungs are losing the air.

Telling this story would seem like the end, but in these last moments of greenish light down here, something moved quite visibly out of me.

At first I thought there goes my soul, the mortal coil, untwining loose and leaving me. It seemed to come from my breath and it hung in the air over me like a little pulsing cloud. Is it my death, or is it what that quack of a doctor said, a ghost, trapped in me, fleeing me the way the sailors say the rats will leave a ship doomed to sink?

THE PHONE RINGS LIKE A WOMAN

The phone rings like a woman hiding in her voice an urgency waiting to spring. Frustration, an impatience waiting in those four rings, long seconds until finally a click. "Hello, this is Jack. I'm not in right now. Please leave a message at the beep." And then the message, frantic as a struggle in amber… And in a way, that's what it was. Jack was calling himself from a phone booth with time running out.

His trouble started with her eyes in the mirror she held. Her eyes flashed distress; she had something to tell him. She sat at a table across from him, her back to him (she looked like someone he knew, or at least the way her hair rivered down her shoulders and back). He thought he recognized her. She could be a movie star, such hair, the fur coat, gold jewelry bright on her fingers.

Sitting with her at the table was a man who was too nervous, too edgy, too much energy waiting for something to happen, watching the door, chain smoking. He had the iron faced intensity of a secret service agent and she was the center of his dangerous world.

Jack wished he knew who she was, but they had already been sitting when he came in on his coffee break. He noticed them while eating his three donuts.

When he caught her eye in the mirror, he knew her look was more than for lipstick, he knew also that she was a prisoner. Her face showed more than a palmed mirror could hold. She angled the mirror over her lips and mouthed words. They were letters and numbers, three then four, and then she repeated them again. She did it three times, her lips carefully forming, puckering and pursing, making sure he knew.

Jack knew: it was a car license number. He nodded to her with a 'You Can Depend On Me' look.

The man with her suddenly grabbed her arm and pulled the mirror from her face. He must have noticed what she had been doing. Getting quickly to his feet, pulling her tightly to him, making her wince, throwing her mirror to the floor, cracking the glass into slivers, he pulled her towards the door. Holding her tight enough to grip white marks into her bare arms, he pushed her.

Jack felt that he should—as a responsible citizen—well, what could he do? Not much, really. He had broken the code though. He had done that much. He watched them go.

The man opened the front door and shoved her through ahead of him, still keeping a hand gripped on her shoulder. Then he halted, turned and looked back inside, back to Jack who had just written the license plate number on a napkin beside his coffee cup. The look in that man's eyes was frightening. Then he was gone with her.

Jack suddenly felt sick. The donuts and coffee struggled in his stomach. That man wanted him dead. Jack got up quickly and left some assortment of change on the table. A door in the back belled open as a fat man walked in and Jack, just as fat, rushed out as fast as possible, away.

Jack ran until, gasping for air, he had to stop. He looked back nervously when he reached the street corner, a sweat hot on his neck, dizzy, his head spinning. The way her eyes looked, Jack knew she was in trouble. But why him? What kind of hero was he? Why couldn't he have looked away, looked into the black swirl of his coffee instead? Now he was paying for his watching. Now he was running. She could have been someone he knew…She was now…She'd become his life.

A day filled with dangers and numbers pursuing. Then he saw her, and the man disappearing with her into a parked waiting car. Jack noticed the license plate. Yes, it was the same letters and numbers she told him. Her captor bent down to the driver's window to talk to the shadowy figure behind the wheel.

Jack still watched, with his back to a telephone pole. His

chest was aching from the brief run. He clenched his fists and unclenched them. Jack watched as the man accepted something from the driver. There was a black metal shine on it. He quickly hid it in his coat. Then, as the car with the captured woman edged into traffic, he turned and started towards Jack.

Dangerous wind blew towards him, dangerous as the man with gun in hand. Jack cast off the telephone pole, slow to start as a thick freighter from its mooring, running across the street, dodging down an alley with his footsteps echoing madly on the bricks. Bricks scarred with graffiti, water pipes dripping and trash scattered riffling. No safety, with nowhere to hide. Cement talking the scuff of his cheap black shoes and his running couldn't be fast enough. Lunar, this was too much like the moon for him to be meant to run, too much like a nightmare to move faster.

Out the alley and struggling, he stumbled up the street and towards an empty phone booth that stood in the corner. He crashed inside and slammed the door behind him. Tired, too tired to stand, collapsing, panting and searching himself for a quarter. Tightly squeezed inside, Jack felt trapped and yet at the same time, a sense of packaged peace, like what a sardine feels…Before the can is opened, and it is eaten.

His fingers discovered a large coin, round, warm in his shirt pocket. He heaved his body up and dropped the quarter into the phone slot. Jack punched the number for the police station, frantically looking, peeking through the booth glass, his heavy breath fogging it up, while the connection rang and rang. And rang more. The man would be coming any second.

And just then he did, hand in coat, emerging from the alley too fast, too soon, looking both ways, and then seeing Jack crouched in the booth.

Jack hung up desperately and retrieved the quarter to dial his own number. He knew he'd get his answering machine after four rings then he could say the license plate number, for whatever it was worth. But was there time, and would it be too late when somebody found it? He sank low, lower to the cigarettes on the floor, the dirt thickened by conversations smeared heavy underfoot, as the man outside reached inside his coat for the gun.

Rome daily!" "Hmm," Uriel thought. "Europe sounds great right now."

"Do you understand me or not!" the voice on the phone bellowed. How long had his voice been ringing in his ears unnoticed.

"Oh, yeah. I'm sorry, sir. It wont happen again," Uriel flaile~

"How ~~how~~ am I supposed to get all your weirdo friends off my lawn anyway!?" the landlord screamed. He didn't seem to expect an answer, as he slammed the reciever down.

Uriel looked back down at the advertisement. Europe.

The Jacobite-mob still clammored below his window demanding his appearance. But the man they ~~were~~ desired was frantically tossing his clothing into a battered brown suitcase. Impatiently he slammed the top down and locked the latches. A belt buckle hung out unnoticed by him reflecting his frantic face. Grabbing the case handle, he turned and walked to the open door. He slammed the door on the noise from the town outside, and walked down the hall toward the fire escape. He had decided the best way to get out was down the fire escape and to the street on the other side. The door creaked on its rusted hinges as he opened it. "Fire, they'll never be a fire here. This place is made of ice," the manager had promised. Therefore emergency exits and exit procedures had gone uncared for. He stepped cautiously as he padded down the weathered metal stairing. The fire escape bounced and swayed on its aged mounting, rusted onto the brick side of the building. There was a sudden hideous creak as Uriel stopped some twenty feet from the ground. "Don't panic," he calmed himself. It was too late though, the stairway gave a lurch, then suddenly plunged

THE HANGMAN CALLS PARIS

"Well, I'll tell you, kid," he began but stopped while he shoved another cigarette between his lips. "Sure don't hear many stories like this one though." He chuckled, leaning back in his wooden chair. "Yeah…" He puffed a cloud of smoke over the paper covered table and continued, "It appears that as he was coming out of a Safeway, with two bags of groceries, the electric doors opened as he expected. But then they closed on him before he made it out."

"What? My father was crushed to death!"

The officer held up his hands. "Don't get excited. The medics said he died instantly. Bang!" He slapped his hands together. "Just like that…" He sucked on his cigarette again.

"Great…" The young man slapped at the table and knocked a lamp off.

"Calm down…People go through this every day. It's part of life…Just another week. My mother in law was—"

"How could something like this happen? What's Safeway got to say about it?"

The officer slouched back in his chair. He took a slow cigarette puff and answered, "Well…They said they were deeply sorry."

"Oh great. They smash him like a bug and say they're sorry." He jumped from his chair and walked over to the paneled door. The backwards letters glared down at him from the window. "Alright," he said slowly, "What am I supposed to do?"

"Don't worry about it, kid. Everything's been taken care of." He coughed. "Your insurance company's already seen to the burial. And don't worry about the price. They only needed half a coffin." He grinded his cigarette into the half shell ashtray in front of him. "End of story," he grumbled, not raising his eyes from the smoking remains.

What was her problem? he wondered. Throughout the bus ride, the old woman had been glancing sternly across the aisle at him. She would stare hawk-like at him for a couple of seconds then jerk her gaze away from him and back to the window at her side.

Nervously, he began reading a newspaper somebody had tossed on the floor. It was two weeks old. A set of muddy footprints had torn the front page. He sighed and let it fall back on the floor. He looked at the old woman. Her eyes, riveted on him, suddenly narrowed.

"It's him!" her voice cracked. "That's him!"

He was too stunned. Where would this day end?

She pointed across the aisle. "I know you." Her brittle finger waved at him. "You'll never get away with it."

The bus driver called back, "What's the problem, ma'am?"

"Nothing," the young man said. "I'm getting off at the next stop."

The driver slowed for the upcoming bus stop and as it did, the young man stood and grabbed the handrail.

"You'll never get away with it," the old woman said.

"That's right," someone behind him yelled. A jumble of calls flew after him as he left the bus.

He watched the angry blur of eyes as the bus pulled away from the stop, continuing on down the busy street. "What did I do?" He was a long way from where he meant to be.

He finally reached the tall apartment building. Along the way, more people had given him stares. He never felt such relief, shutting the door behind him and entering the familiar carpeted hallway. It was quiet in here, he was all alone. He spun the keychain to the little silver key that fit in the mailbox. Not surprisingly, he found the letter to be a bill, but underneath that was a tightly folded note with black fierce looking handwriting.

The word on it was *coward*. Coward? He took a quick look behind him at the glass front door. It was only a street scene. He looked back at the note in his hands and quickly unfolded it.

John Luke, it began. John Luke? He read on. *You sniveling coward. Return Jennifer or we're going to get you.* Signed, The True Fans of Afternoon Ambition.

Afternoon Ambition? Isn't that a soap opera? Jennifer? He crumpled the note and threw it at the garbage can. He went to the stairway and climbed up to the third floor and his room. Inside, he locked the latch behind him.

Last night's newspaper was still on the table with his breakfast bowl. He snatched the paper and leafed through the pages, finally stopping at the television section. His finger traced a path across the lines of words and stopped abruptly at two o'clock. "Ahah," he muttered. He read the review.

Afternoon Ambition. Bob and Mary find a baby behind their encyclopedia set. Jennifer remains a hostage of John. There was a photo to the side that showed a woman roped tightly to a chair. A man stood in front of her, waving a dipper at her. "Hmmm…" he thought. There was a similarity between the man and himself, but wasn't it absurd to think it could follow him onto a bus, down the streets, to his very own mailbox?

A shatter of glass and a thud of a heavy object answered him. In the middle of his floor, he saw a stone with another note tied securely to it. He ran over to the broken window. He searched the narrow pavement below, the overgrown hedgerow, the fence, but nothing was moving out there. He yanked the shades together over the jagged glass and crunched over the shards to where the stone lay.

He unfolded the note and read it.

You have until tomorrow to release her.

What could he do? On the way to get a broom he threw the note away.

It was a fitful and almost sleepless night for Duriel Darin. He dreamed the same thing again and again and each time he awoke, sweating. In his dream, his father was circling slowly, around and around in a revolving door and Duriel stood watching him from behind an ornate wooden gate. A figure in a black robe chanted, "next letter…next letter…" Duriel would frantically guess a letter of the alphabet but each time the cloaked figure would tell him, "Wrong. That's a leg," or, "Wrong. That's an arm…" and as his father slowly turned about in circles through the revolving door another part of his body would disappear. Around he would go, smiling and continuing his journey until finally there would be nothing left but his face, revolving about the circuit and at that moment Duriel would wake up. He was so tired, he would be asleep again soon and the dream would start again until he finally woke up to the sound of the alarm at his bedside.

A cold wind breathed through the hole in the window and sent the drapes dancing. Slowly awakening to the world, his ears became accustomed to an odd clamoring. Drums? Tambourines? A steady beat accompanied by the wailing and jabbering of voices.

Staggering out of bed, Duriel stumbled to the window. He winced as his foot picked up a sliver of glass from the day before. His fingers clutched the rough curtain material and he slid the cloth across the window.

This act brought him an immediate concoction of insults and threats. Like wolves waiting to pounce on a helpless lamb, the huge mob down there, festooned with signs and banners, began screaming at the sleepy-eyed figure in the broken window.

Duriel jumped back from the window. He walked backwards, away, expecting a barrage of projectiles to come flying through the window. Duriel felt like a doomed man. The deep voice of a megaphone chanted, "John Luke, John Luke."

His phone rang.

It was an arm's length away. He picked it up. "Hello?"

The voice yelling at a frantic rate of speed was his landlord. Usually Duriel only saw the manager when he knocked on his door for the rent. This was the most he had ever said to Duriel and none of it was good.

Duriel listened but his eyes went to the newspaper still on the table. He flipped it open and a sentence jumped at him. *Get away from it all!* That got his attention. *Go to Europe. Flights to London, Rome and Athens daily!*

Duriel said, "Europe sounds great right now."

"Do you understand me or not?" the voice on the phone bellowed.

"Oh, yeah. I'm sorry, sir. It won't happen again."

"How am I supposed to get all those people away from here?" the landlord screamed. But he didn't seem to expect an answer.

Duriel cradled the receiver and looked back at the advertisement. *Europe…*

The mob still clamored below his window. But the man they desired was frantically tossing his clothes into a brown suitcase. Impatiently, he slammed the top down and locked the latches. A belt buckle hung out. He was ready to go.

Duriel closed the door on his apartment and walked down the hallway towards the fire escape. He decided that was the best way to get out, down those rickety metal stairs to the alley on the other side of the building.

He got to the emergency exit door and turned the handle. It creaked open on its rusted hinges.   Cautiously,   Duriel stepped onto the fire escape. It trembled slightly, swaying on its aged mounting. It was rusted to the side of the building. There was a sudden hideous creak as Duriel stopped some twenty feet from the ground. "Don't panic…" he told himself. It was too late though—the stairway gave a lurch then plunged earthwards.

Duriel leaped from the falling assemblage and thudded to the ground a mere foot away from the crashing snake of metal. He groaned, getting slowly to his feet, hauling his cracked suitcase across his bruised leg. "I'm okay…" he winced. He limped from the twisted sculpture. He knew he had to be fast. All that drumming and shouting from the front of the building had gone silent.

He needed a shortcut away and he stopped at a tall cedar fence. He tossed his suitcase over it and grabbed the rough wood edge on top. With a groan, he pulled himself. He got a leg over and before he dropped, looked down into the yard below. A comical little dog stood next to his suitcase.

He laughed. Maybe his luck was turning. It could have been something vicious.

A woman screamed from the alley behind him. "It's John! He's getting away!"

Duriel knew the mob wouldn't take long. He dropped and landed on the other side of the fence. He snatched up his suitcase and ran across the bumpy lawn. The dog gave him a yelp, and lunged at his ankle. The dog's little jaw sprung like a trap on him. Duriel dragged it on his leg.

A fat bellied man stepping from the porch yelled at him, "Where you taking my dog?"

Duriel could hear the clawing mob hitting the fence, he couldn't stop.

"Come back here with my dog!" The man yelled after him, "Hey you!" But then his attention was turned to the people falling over his fence. They dropped over into his yard like an invasion and swarmed at him. He swung his fists at them and several fell before him but many funneled around him, after their soap opera villain.

The man had given Duriel just enough time to get away, through the bushes and trees and onto the street beyond. He limped along the sidewalk, dragging the dog attached to his leg. His head jerked sideways, eyes searching for a means of escape.

A yellow cab cruised up the street towards him. Frantically, he waved his arms at the cab. It wasn't a moment too soon. Some members of the mob struggled around the house and spotted him.

The cab slowed to a stop in front of Duriel. He grabbed the door handle and leaped into the back as three people reached out for him. "Get going, driver!" Duriel slapped the seat. "Go!"

With a roar the taxi pulled off into the road. "Where to, man?"

"The airport," Duriel told him. The dog, growling meekly was still part of his leg.

"Enjoy your flight?" Duriel repeated. That's what the flight attendant told them over the intercom. "In these seats?" Why did airliners have to be so uncomfortable? Maybe it's just me, he smiled. The man at the ticket counter had asked if he wanted a traveling cage to put his dog in. Duriel grimaced as he looked down at the jagged missing piece gone from his pants. How else could I get the dog off? The plane accelerated down the runway. The land blurred outside the window. "Goodbye America," he whispered.

"Passports," the man demanded of the people corralled through the customs area. The questioning over, Duriel faced the huge expanse of the airport terminal. "God," he flustered.

A woman clad in black stopped beside him. Her gold cross flashed in his eyes. "Can I help you?"

"Oh...No, I'm just looking..."

The nun gave him a smile and started away.

"Uh, wait. Can you tell me the way out of here?"

The nun quickly gave him directions and Duriel walked outside onto the French street. The horns and other traffic noises surprised him. He was sucked into the crowd on the sidewalk, onto a bus, into the city. Without thinking, Duriel moved obediently along with them.

"Paris." That's all it took. He had crossed the globe to get here. He walked beside the windows of small shops, the street full of strange cars. "What am I doing here?" He was lost in thought, strolling along a Paris street. His feet were now the masters of his direction. Unaware of purpose, he found himself taking backstreets. After all that had happened, it felt good to be lost. He was actually on cobblestones, he could have been anywhere in history.

When he did look ahead of him, he saw something familiar framed between the leaning buildings on both side of him. "The tower!" he gasped. There is was, the beautiful Eiffel Tower. It was like that postcard everyone has seen, like something everyone wants to see, but how many get this close.

The driver was probably on his way to the market. He must have been in a rush, hoping to get there in time for the big crowds, he was cutting through the backstreets where traffic was scarce. Surely his speed was too great and his merchandise not properly secured for that kind of driving, but none of that seemed important to the truck driver. When he saw the man standing there in the middle of the lane, he pulled hard on the steering wheel and swerved hard around the figure. Breathing a sigh of relief that he didn't hit him, the driver slowed and came to a stop. He climbed out of his seat, prepared to curse the stupidity of that fool in the road.

As he cleared the back of the truck though, he was suddenly silent. During that evasive swerve, the oak door, balanced on top of the stack of junk had flown off the pile and struck that man. It covered over him. Why did he not rope it down? "Just like that," the man sighed. He punched the rear fender of the truck, knocking a flake of paint off into the wind.

November 1982

April 1, 1983

Allen Frost
P.O. Box 1116
Woodinville, WA   98072

Dear Allen Frost:

    I am pleased to inform you that your story has been chosen as a Finalist in the HIGHWIRE Short Fiction Contest for 1983.

    Of over 300 entries we received, yours was one of only 30 that were culled out as contenders for the first prize. Though ultimately that prize went to another story, your work is to be highly praised for the maturity of its imaginative scope, the accuracy and care of its writing, and the extent to which you succeeded at the fictional task you set yourself.

    We would like to invite you to continue submitting work to HIGHWIRE, and encourage you in any case to keep on with your writing. We have many opportunities for talented young writers to contribute to the magazine, and would welcome your ideas, letters, or article proposals at any time. Towards that end, I have enclosed a copy of our guidelines for contributors, and look forward to hearing from you again in the coming year.

    Thank you again for sending us your story; and please accept my warmest congratulations on this significant honor.

Very truly yours,

Edward Miller
Editor

EM:kp

Enclosure: Writing Guidelines

ONE OF THEM

It was night, eight o'clock or after, and some strange way to spend his birthday. He wanted to go for a walk around the lake. Not dinner, not a drive, or a meeting with friends in a bright and cheery room. "Maybe I'll go to Seattle," he had wondered at one point but finally by eight o'clock, here we were, walking in the dark. He even brought a flashlight, but he wouldn't use it, telling me, "We don't want to lose our night vision." No, not that, I thought and I tripped loud over another root just to show him.

It really was dark too. The rain had stopped earlier in the day but the clouds had never left, they hid the sky, the moon and the stars.

We walked. I listened to the sound of our footsteps. I wished I was home, but, anything for a friend, right? It was his 40th birthday too so I really was doing this for him. A stone in the path nearly felled me. He took my arm and we tried to laugh, but my foot hurt that time.

"Do you do this often?" I asked him. I had curled my toes behind the tip of my canvas shoe.

"Ohh," he sighed, "Couple of nights a month, I guess. Don't you like it?"

"Sure Ron, I do, it's very peaceful." I wondered how long we'd been. It's an hour walk in daylight around the lake. Maybe fifteen minutes had gone by. I've been here before but I couldn't recognize any landmarks. It was all trunk silhouettes in front of the gray lake and a black forest to my right. We made our way along. I threw out some more small talk now and then. I'd known Ron for a few years, we could relate, and silence wasn't all bad either. He could be odd I suppose, everyone can, but this seemed a weird birthday to me. Maybe he's a little depressed, that's all. At least I'm along.

Then it started happening and it happened really fast. Relating it is like trying to slow down a rocket so you can paint it, the terror better just be put down in the splash it was.

The moon came out, sprang out. The cloud cover ripped open above the lake. It felt like the high beam of a speeding dangerous vehicle. It was so unexpected and popped on so much hot light I let out a shout. But Ron, Ron did more than that. He howled in agony. I've never heard an animal like that. All of a sudden too, I realized the same way anyone would, as Ron fell on all fours roaring and transforming—oh brother, he's one of them. I never knew. A pelt of spiny fur shot through his skin, covering him. I didn't stay. How could I?

I threw myself at a dead run into the underbrush. Vines and bushes cut and caught hold but I tore through, falling on slipping gravel and the decayed slide to the lake.

I didn't wait, the air was howling, I jumped out over the water. I could see myself reflected, the full moon blasting a white target I landed on and down I went.

It wasn't shallow. I opened my eyes, my mouth to breathe and kicked my tail to get as deep and far away as I could.

THE MAN WITH 6 FINGERS

She was told by the fortune teller, "Beware the man with six fingers. He will be the death of you!" and terrified, she had walked out of the wallpapered parlor, into the cold night.

She went into the bar like entering another planet's atmosphere. It was warm inside and she brushed the snow off her coat shoulders while she scanned the crowd uneasily.

A pair of eyes caught her glance. "Get you a drink, miss?" the bartender asked. She agreed to a draft beer. After digging through her purse for a moment, she found some dollars to pay with and she looked back up to the bar. The bartender had his hand on the spigot, pouring a glass for her. In rising terror, she counted six fingers wrapped around the pint.

She backed away from the counter, horrified, her fingers to her lips stifling a cry. "I've…I've…" she mumbled and turned and ran for the door. "Beware of the man with six fingers. He will be the death of you!" Those words had saved her life.

She raced down the sidewalk, to her waiting car and hopped inside, locking the door. Fearfully she stared through a space in the snow covered windshield while she fit the key in the ignition and swore her car to start. It refused. The engine rasped three times as she turned the key and finally the car started. She pushed the lever hard into drive and pulled quickly into the street.

When she noticed the radio was on, a Shirelles song, she quickly turned it off. She needed the silence to concentrate. The car shot across the newly carpeted layer of snow, sliding on a back road past the dairy, that would take her safely, eventually, to the freeway and all the road in America on which to escape. She said, "I've got to be calm about this…" Despite that, she rubbed her forehead nervously. The car tires crunched onto the back road's white gravel. "That drink was probably poisoned."

It was taking longer than she thought to reach the freeway. The woods were dark in the headlights. And then, the car engine stalled and the car was out of control. It plowed into a snow bank and she bumped violently into the steering wheel. Except for her tears, all was very silent. The car wouldn't start. The key clicked back and forth like a hinge on a haunted house. She seemed to be unharmed though, despite some bruises.

What else could she do? She got out of the car to see where she was, but all was quiet and the road disappeared before her, bending into the dark forest snowy night. She returned to her car and rubbed her cold legs. What a night to wear a skirt. There was very little heat in the car and night would bring even more cold.

Lights approached from behind and she woke up as the truck passed slowly beside her car. It stopped just in front. Red lights glazed across the icy windshield. She opened her eyes and muttered, "Thank God!" She opened the door and went into the chilly wind. She ran through the thick powdery snow to the driver's window. "Thank God you showed up!" The unrolling window was steamed with the breath of the driver and the warm of inside.

"You're lucky I happened to take this road home. You wreck your car? Are you alright?" He put his hand out to open the door from the outside handle. The latch inside was broken. All in a fast moment she counted the six fingers on his hand. It was the bartender opening the door for her.

With a scream, she retreated, "No! My car's fine! I'm fine! I don't need any help. Please, leave me alone. Go away!" and she ran, slipping, back to her car. She locked the door as she saw the dark silhouette approach.

He stood outside her window, asking her in a muffled language while she buried her face in her hands. "Do you really think this car will run? The hood's mashed. I'll just give you a ride back to town. You can't stay out here, you'll freeze to death."

But she was ignoring the whole thing, as if he was a phantom. Her eyes were shut tight on the nightmare of the man with six fingers. "No, no, no, no, no, no," she was repeating and then so loud she was screaming. "NO! NO! NO!" so she couldn't hear him anymore, rattling the handle, trying to open the doors, pushing at the windows.

Huddled, curled next to the steering wheel, shouting and trying to hide herself like a shadow, she didn't hear him leave, saying, "Well, good luck then, lady." But when she lifted her head up, rubbing her tears to look, his truck was vanished into the snow and woods and as she became colder, she breathed slower, falling asleep, and she smiled. She had defeated the man with the six fingers.

THE CURSE OF HOLLER FARM

The Holler Farm had a smiling black and white cow sign at the gate of the driveway. Holler Farm was well known for having the best milk products in the county and not even the supermarkets with all their dollars to drawn on dairies state-wide, could compete. And naturally, when the Holler Farm competition heard about the curse, they took advantage of it.

Driving along the wide, two lane Dairy Road, you couldn't help but notice The Holler Farm sign of the smiling cow and all the wide acreage of cow pasture that greened for miles. It was answer to a cow's prayer and they responded so full of warm milk they had a reason to smile. Business couldn't have been better for Mr. Holler.

Why exactly he fabricated the curse, his own downfall, no one really knew. He couldn't explain and it was only later that he would kick himself. At the time, he thought people would be amused. He hoped that like the cow on the sign, people would have reason to smile. That's all. It was just for a laugh. But he had no idea what the consequences would be.

At night, black as the beginning of time, the moon some-where else, with a fog chewing its way across the grass, cows looming like shoals, Mr. Holler put the curse into action. His wife would have warned him not to do it if he had asked her, but he never did ask. He just did it.

Earlier that day he had bought the local store out of its sup-ply of aluminum foil, winking to the cashier, "Watch out for spacemen tonight!" He made a raygun shape with his hand. The cashier didn't understand. She laughed anyway. Everyone liked Farmer Holler then. He had gone home with the backseat of his car filled with silver foil and drove straight to the barn where he spent the rest of the day hammering and foiling the outlines of his tractor. He was even late, fifteen minutes late, coming to dinner. He was splattered with silver paint and his only reply to his wife was, "It's a surprise."

She was patient and didn't ask anything else about it, even when she couldn't find the curtains from the guest room, because it was, after all, "a surprise." And later that evening, with the fog coughing its way across the whole valley, she only heard a little bit of his phone conversation. "Come quick," she heard him say, "You won't believe it." He was up to something.

When he started the tractor and drove it out of the barn and down the driveway towards the road, he could see her staring from that curtainless room but on he went. By the smiling cow sign, he parked the tractor and waited for the newspaper reporters to show. It wouldn't be long.

The tractor was disguised as a spaceship. It was sheeted in silver and when he switched on the floodlights underneath, it really glowed like a Hollywood Martian. Laughing, he set two glass milk gallons down on the ground. He had mixed green dye in with the white of the milk. He was going to tell the newspaper people a spaceman had got out of the ship and zapped his cows with a raygun and now they only gave green milk. Mr. Holler imagined the market that would open up because of his green milk. Thousands of kids would put it in their cereal, watching morning space cartoons. "Bet I can even get a copyright on it and make millions nationwide!"

The reporters loved the story of Martian Milk. They snapped shots of him standing beside the spaceship with the gallons of his green milk.

His wife looked worried up from the headlines the next day. "You shouldn't have done this," she said.

"What do you know about marketing?" he grumbled. He looked down at his coffee. "It will be great, you'll see."

But soon, truck after truck rolled down his driveway returning his milk products. Nobody wanted to buy zapped Holler farm food. "It was just a joke!" Mr. Holler tried to explain. It only took another day for a vandal to spray paint the smiling cow face bright green.

THE SMALL HOUSE

When he pulled off the road, dusk approaching, at the end of the day, he was looking for somewhere to stay the night, and this place looked good. Even though the sign said 'No Vacancy' he had to hope. A long curving row of rooms made the motel look like a Southern Belle lying down, lined in bright neon that just switched on as he came to a stop. The car engine rattled for a couple of seconds when the key turned in his fingers, out. He got outside stiffly and stretched of course and walked over towards the office. He was really, really tired of driving.

"Hi," he smiled at the woman wearing glasses. "I'd like a room." He could see himself in their reflections, but she was looking over his shoulder at the license plate on his car.

"Sure you would. You've been traveling a long time."

"Yeah! Vermont!"

"Mmhumm. Your room is in back. The small house." She gave him the key. A small key.

"Thanks. This sure is a small key!" He almost lost it between his fingers. He paid her and went back to the car and got his bag out of the trunk. Someone was playing television, a game show, in the corner room as he walked around the back of the building. He nearly tripped on some space toy a kid must have forgotten. The lawn in back disappeared quickly off the edge of a cliff.

He could hardly believe that was his room for the night. In the middle of the grass there was a small house about three feet square—gray paint with red shingles for roofing, small glass windows on the walls. It looked more like a doll's house.

"This can't be!" But still he went up to it to check it out… He tried to laugh as he put his bag down and kneeled on the grass. He fit the key into the door and it opened up.

Inside, darkly, he could just discern the shape of a bed, neatly made up, a television on the bureau and a mirror that reflected his hand. He felt along the wall just inside to the right of the doorway and as he expected, his finger hit a very small switch which turned on a light inside. Everything was very plain now. The bed was covered by a red quilt, yellow plaid carpeting on the floor. It was all very nice…It was just too small.

If only he could get inside he would be happy for the night. He was so tired from driving all day and there were no more hotels for miles and miles. He coughed and opened the little door wider. He could just barely fit his head through, yes, and squeeze his arms and shoulders. He was pushing the bed up against the mirrored back wall, but somehow he had fit his upper torso inside the room.

He couldn't get any more of his body inside. Crushed and exhausted, his breath rattled the windows of the small house. He smiled peculiarly and turned on the television set by bending his arm under his stomach. The only thing on the small screen was a game show, "Everybody's a winner!" and he tried to turn it off, but he was so tired his eyes closed and he fell asleep instead.

He woke up in the small house with his whole body twisted inside, stuck, knees to chin, hard to breathe, and Sylvan Moore was laughing at him on TV.

REBICYCLE

The car pulled up into the parking lot and the gold from the headlights glowed onto a bicycle with training wheels sprouting off the back wheel, casting its long shadow up against the brick wall of the restaurant. A neon sign twitching nervously, shined red from up above: EATS!

He got out of the car rubbing his hands together, the engine still ticking the cool night air, a cloud disappearing from the exhaust pipe. He hummed a cheap song from the radio.

Beside the glass doors, a man shivering in the cold at the entrance asked him, "Excuse me. I don't suppose you could give me a short ride, could you?" He returned the broken cigarette to his lips.

"No. Sorry." He entered the door quickly past the shadow. It was warm inside. At the counter a happy faced girl with braces and braids awaited his order.

"Good evening!"

"Hi."

"What can I get for you, sir?"

"Let's see…I'll have a hamburger and fries to go, please."

"Sure," she said, typing it up on the cash register keys.

"Oh. I'll have a coke too, if that's okay with you."

"No problem. I thought you'd probably want one." She gave him a high school yearbook smile. He took out his wallet and paid while he felt a cold presence close to his back, moving nearer. It was him, he knew, the man from outside, not even turning to look.

"Excuse me, dear. Is there any way I could get some water?" said the voice behind him.

"Sure." She stepped away to get a cup of water, placing the order for hamburger, fries and coke with the cook in back.

"Hello there," said the lips, bringing a shred of cigarette up for a puff. "Looks like you're getting some food…" His thick hair, black, was matted and long, beard growing long tangled out of his face, still shivering. Ocean blue eyes swam a hard stare at him and held it.

"Hi."

"Say…I don't suppose you could give me a short drive, could you?"

"No." He turned his back on the man and walked over to the condiment counter. He fiddled with the plastic spoons jammed in the bright yellow, green and red of mustard, relish and ketchup.

"Here's your water, sir," the girl returned and said.

"Much obliged." The smell of cigarette and cement passed out of the restaurant.

He took a straw and a couple napkins and went back to the register. He rapped his fingers on the plastic counter. She was back in the kitchen, talking to the cook, laughing, and he smiled too, thinking she must be talking about that lunatic. Now she was wrapping up his food in orange paper, putting a lid on the coke so it wouldn't spill when he drove. She bagged it and came out to him.

"Here you are."

"Great. Thanks a lot."

"You're welcome. Goodnight."

"Yeah, goodnight."

Just inside the door, looking out at the dark parking lot, he saw that man leaning up against the window. His breath steamed a fading pattern on the glass, drinking his water slowly.

He tried to ignore him. He knew what was coming next and he went out quickly.

The man followed him, "You sure you can't give me just a short ride?"

"No, I'm sorry. I can't."

"Well, look. I haven't eaten since yesterday. Do you suppose you could spare a dollar or some spare change, maybe?"

Sighing loudly, wanting to leave, he searched his pocket and felt some change and held it out. "Here, take this." He passed over a pocketful into the frozen hand.

"Thanks very much, mister. I appreciate it."

He grunted. He got back into his car finally. He set the bag next to him. "I'm lucky he didn't steal the car," he muttered. The key was still in the ignition. It should have been attached to his other keys, but it wasn't. He turned it and gave the pedal some pressure. The car rattled to life. He watched the restaurant as he backed away, pulled out of the parking lot quickly onto the street.

"I can't believe some people!" he groaned. He turned on the radio loud. "Yeah, sure…I'll give you ride," he talked to himself. "Wind up with a knife in my back!" Someone on the radio was complaining about the homeless situation and he turned the dial to an oldies station.

He passed a store on his right all lit up yellow inside with a bunch of policemen huddled at the counter, eating and drinking coffee. Nobody did anything in this town anymore, he decided.

Then a look of panic crossed his face. He crammed a hand in his pocket. It was empty. He gave away all the change in that pocket. He cursed. He switched hands on the wheel and tried the other pocket and his coat too. Nothing but bits of paper and a paperclip and a pen…

He rolled the car off the road, turning in the green light of a gas station. The wheels ran over a pinging hose and the car ripped back down the road again, towards the restaurant.

"I can't believe it!" he yelled above the sound of Buddy Holly, "I gave him my damn house key!"

He pulled in the parking lot and stopped in the same spot. The headlights fell on an empty brick wall, red neon light bleeding down from above. The bicycle was gone and the restaurant was empty, except for the high school girl and the cook way back in the kitchen.

SAPPED

Unlike most detectives, especially the ones you see in movies or TV, or read about in yellowed paperbacks, Raymond Chandler imagination, I do my best work sapped. I actually look for a chance to get it on the back of the head. I'll enter a dark room and stand there in the frame, doe-eyed with my hands hanging down. That's always an easy target. Last week I ended up on the floor at a construction site, my legs in a tangle in the rebar, waking up with that familiar headache, but also waking up knowing more than I knew before. Somewhere in that blackness, my mind shifts the puzzle pieces and finds answers. I can't really explain what happens when I'm there, maybe it's the ghost of Philip Marlowe talking me through, or who knows, maybe I get swept to a silver saucer and green beings plant the truth in me. It works. My head bears the scars and never healing bruises and marks of my professional success.

That same way, one cold morning in September, I woke groggily, sharp tacks of gravel printing my face in the parking lot of Fat Dutch's Roadhouse. My voice coughed out the name, "Harlan." That's who did it. I knew it and I could see how, in a grim little black and white film that played in my mind's eye.

I pulled myself to a sitting position and winced. When was the day when this would be too much? Like a boxer reaching the end, I struggled to stand. Sure I had enough now to solve the case, but I really had to wonder how much more I could take.

Fat Dutch's was shut up tight; the last of the trade would have pulled out at one a.m. There were still cars in the lot before I went down. I guess I'm lucky nobody rolled over me driving out.

I took a slow deep breath of that dawn. I saw the phone booth over in a corner of tar where the fence broke down. I had to get up and call, I couldn't sit here much longer listening to the birds. Their kind of song was too nice for the way I felt. Too bad I wasn't one of them. What did they need to do all day? They ate from the leaves and the ground. They sat on a branch and watched the world go around. No wonder they sang that way.

By the time I was standing, a sweat had broken over me but I walked. I had to keep going, towards the telephone booth.

It had taken a beating too. The panes of glass in it were smashed and the new sun sparkled the diamonds on the dirt. The phone receiver hung off from the box like someone hanged.

I was halfway across to it when a white truck pulled in to the lot. It was just me and him. If the driver wanted to, he could have rolled over me and finished the job. The truck had arrived for a different reason though. *Ready Call Phone Repairs* was painted in red letters on the door.

I stopped myself and stood there while the engine stopped and the driver got out. He wore white overalls and carried a steel toolbox; a picture of the working man. He gave me a look and walked over my way.

Even before he reached me, a long time before I could do anything about it, the name sewn on his coat pocket read clear. He gave me a thin smile, one tossed like chum to easy prey, as he took the gun out of his gray toolbox and Harlan aimed the easy bullet at me.

RECALLED

I just turned my brain on again. I was resting, recharging, and now I'm driving a different car. I stole it last night. It's got tinted purple windows so nobody can recognize me. They are looking for me. It's all over the radio.

But I'm not the only one. I wonder what the others like me are doing? How are they taking the news? Are they just turning themselves in? Don't they have any last wishes? Don't they dream?

Whatever is inside of me could be ticking like a bomb. I hope not. I hope I'll be okay. I hope I still have time. I don't know and I'm afraid. Like any person you see, I want to be able to live. There are things I want to do before they shut me down. And I don't know if I'll be coming back after they get me.

The night scenes of restaurants and gas stations pass by me; little towns and places along the freeway. I seem to know all about them. They are put there just to give us the simple things we need as we travel—some fast food and whatever it takes to keep us moving.

It's true, sometimes I can feel the pain inside of me.

Why did they create us, I wonder, knowing the threat we pose? If we are as dangerous as they say, why did they make us this way?

That's all the radio talks about. Finally I had to turn it off. I don't want to hear anymore about how we're walking time-bombs. And me—they're describing me as a miniature Hiroshima.

I'm driving late at night so if I do explode I won't be likely to do much damage to other commuters. There aren't many people on the road at this hour, mostly scattered trucks. I would be a huge orange ball of flame on the highway. It would be like a kind of false daylight for a few seconds.

Here's the problem—there's something wrong with our workings. They never should have made us with atomic power. It was a mistake. So we're all supposed to calmly return to the factory.

They said they're just going to rewire and repower us. They promised we would keep our memories and our thoughts—our program—what we know of as our life. Then we'll be returned to the place we came from, among those we know and love. We'll wake up from the operation with new energy. Just the pain and the danger will be gone. And then we can return to normal life.

I have to laugh. I just drove past where I used to work. After the operation, that's what I have to look forward to again. Those restaurants all look the same; an orange tiled roof peaking out of a black parking lot full of cars.

Funny…When the International House of Pancakes found out about my hazard, they fired me immediately. So much for Employee of the Month…

Of course I still have the menu memorized and all the pleasantries that accompany it. "Welcome to I.H.O.P! My name is Ron Bott. I'll be your waiter. Would you like to start with some coffee? May I suggest a Danish ma'am? If there's anything else you'd like, don't hesitate to ask." I was good at it but when the management found out about my atomic powered insides, it was all over. They had no idea when they accepted me that it was remotely possible that I might chain-react and blow everything up. It happened once in Dayton. A robot worker at Fat Pat's Fried Clams melted six blocks when he self destructed. I got my recall notice and was fired in the same day.

Having and losing. I harbor no resentment against I.H.O.P. It's kind of like being expelled from the Garden of Eden…I take the tragedy in stride.

Anyway, if I make it, I should get to San Francisco early this morning.

The other day, I got a car from Hertz for the journey.

The Hertz Rental Company had a pretty blonde woman behind the counter. She acted more robot than me though. She looked like paper, like she fell out of a magazine and she just stared and stared at me. "Look," I said, holding out my steel hand for the key, "Just charge it to the Los Alamos Institute. They created me."

I'll turn myself in soon. Don't worry.

I just want to do this for myself.

I want to see something metal that works.

On my way to Los Alamos to be disarmed and reassembled, I want to see the Golden Gate Bridge. I've seen photos of it of course—there's one printed on the I.H.O.P menu—but I want to stand on it and really feel it. It's something I've always dreamed about.

I don't only think about pancakes. That was supposed to be all I would think about. I don't think just what I've been programmed to think. Maybe that's really the mistake they want to correct. They knew I had my own thoughts. That worries me.

I'll just turn my thoughts off for a while and concentrate on driving, on getting to San Francisco.

The water is coming right up to greet me. It looks like I might soar off into the bay, but I'm gliding onto the orange bridge. It's like I'm flying with the water on either side. There are birds, gray seagulls against the sky.

The windows are open. I can sense the wind on me and the warm approaching dawn. It's more beautiful than I ever could have imagined. I stop the car and get out. I stand beside the rail and watch. Breathing in and out…Sighing.

Life is something that's been breathed into me. It was given to me and I have been lucky, I conclude. I have lived.

It's something they told me never to do, but I do it.

I reach up and unlatch the clips on my arm. The metal coils fall off and I watch the steel arm shape twirl off, down into the dark towards the water. But something remains. Coming out of me where my mechanical arm used to be is another arm. An arm made of flesh. There is more flesh underneath the robot parts. I take off all of the steel. I throw it off the bridge until I stand there as a person and everything is new. I can do anything now.

THE ALLIGATOR

"And where were you thinking of keeping Richard?"

"Well, in water of course," Melvis replied with a smile.

The woman from Saving Animal Welfare glared at him. "In what location would Richard exist?"

He pointed at the weak sunlight straining the window. "There, on top of the radio."

Holding the fishbowl tight to her brown uniform, Maureen made eight marching steps to the window and halted. The tall wooden radio cabinet stopped even with the sill. Across the top of it an ivy plant shrugged from a gray ceramic bowl and threw down its leaf covered arms hopelessly.

She looked out the window at the drop to the parking lot. Down there, she saw an overturned grocery buggy in the cement courtyard, the cars that hadn't moved in years, the buzzing neon lights in a barred bodega window peering over the sad cement walls that enclosed it all.

She wasn't about to let go of Richard. "No," she told Melvis. "I'm afraid this won't do, Mr. O'Dell." She took one last shrill look out the window then she marched the eight steps back to the door.

Even after she was gone, Melvis kept on the same mask. It was no use. It took the phone ringing to bring him back.

He took the phone off the wall and said, "So what."

"Let me guess...She said no."

Melvis loosened his tie so it broke in half off his neck.

"Listen, you did me a good turn once. I been wanting to repay you ever since. Look outside, pal." Then the phone caller hung up.

Melvis was still trying to place that voice when there was a crash outside. It sounded like the wall had blown down. And something roared constantly. He took a step to the window and peered around the edge of the pale curtain.

A hole had gone through the cement wall and water was pouring in, filling the space up. The water rose until it lapped to the tops of the parked junk cars, then the swirling rush slowed. Soon the surface was still and the tall apartment building appeared growing out of a pond.

From a window on the third floor, Melvis could see himself looking down. What was he supposed to see next? Would an alligator coast across and slide in his reflected window? How long would it take to find this new pool? Didn't they just appear with water? Anyway, it wouldn't take much, a broken canal or overflowed bank, a stream that trickled just near enough to here.

The wind blew across the water, rippling it, and he suddenly thought this was it…It would happen any second now.

LORETTA'S BICYCLE

First it was a white bone-like reach out of the gravel.

Loretta noticed it.

She came down to the gravel pit every weekend to look for things that might be living in the brown pond. The cattails hid pollywogs among their yellowy watery roots, the skating water bugs flicked from shore to floating leaf and back. If she wanted to catch one of them she needed to hover and descend like a raincloud.

That Saturday morning she arrived was after a long night of rain. It had come down torrents and only stopped when she woke up, the window turned bright with sun.

The path to the gravel pit was washed with new little slurry creeks and channels she stepped wide over in her black rubber boots. The sun warmed the flannel on her back.

Under the apple tree was an orchard of decaying fruit. The air hung like a cloak with the smell and the bees were already at work scurrying over them.

Coming through the leaves upon the sight of the gravel pit, she stopped on the crumbled ridge. The weather had sluiced down heaves of the soft hillside, big cracks had formed threatening more slides. A whole lava-like flow of gravel had slid to the pond's edge. As she walked over the fresh ground cover, her shoe soles sunk tracks in and there on the slope she discovered the raw white handle peeking from the soil.

Brushing gravel she could tell it really was what she thought at first, a bicycle handle grip. Attached to the chrome swoop that drove deeper into the mud, she would need more than her hands. She looked for and found a branch to help dig.

Thinking about that hidden treasure, imagining her ride on some amazing antique that hadn't been seen in years, gave her the strength to dig more and more away. It was like a dinosaur skeleton being revealed.

Did pirates have bicycles? she wondered. How long had it been buried?

After a half hour or closer to an hour the handlebars shined out. The other handle grip was missing the hollow frame tube was filled with mud.

She was getting covered with that same mud too. And it was tiring; the stick seemed to be gaining weight like a fairy tale branch turning into lead.

Sometimes she would stop and pull up on those handlebars in the hope the whole thing would rise out like Pegasus. She had dug more away, found the blue painted fork, and more digging later, the front tire fender.

She thought about going home and getting a shovel, that would make this work faster, but she was entranced, she couldn't leave. Her hands were cold cramps and looked made of clay. That same muddy clay color had spread up her arms under her shirt sleeves. She could have been turning into a statue, slowly but surely.

A couple times further off in the gravel pit, she heard new slides, the gravel hushing down avalanches. To get this bicycle out was a race against that and the clouds that were crowding overhead and threatening rain again.

"Come on!" she heaved on the bicycle. It could wiggle, it must want to come out and ride again. She loved that sky blue paint. She would ride it home with the mud flicking off its spokes like a reanimated bicycle mummy.

"Come on!"

As much as she wished it would loosen, the rain soaking her bent back, the clouds were opening up, her hands couldn't uncrimp. The bicycle had to stay in its grave.

Her footprints away left little pools of filling water. That's the way it goes, that's something she was getting to know. She left the gravel pit in a downpour.

She did stop at the top though, to look back. She could still see that silver wink of metal and blue just before the leaning hill full of gravel above it let go and mud slid across her days' work. She had only known that little bit of it—she never did dig deep enough to find the whole connected rigged jigsaw daisy chain of bicycles and autos, aeroplanes and trains and tractors and machines to ride, fly and drive nowhere anymore but deeper in.

THE ASTRONAUT'S MOTHER

She didn't want her son to be an astronaut. Still, she built him a cardboard capsule so he could fly in his room. She drew the window curtains so it was dark and she let him sit in there all alone. Communicating by walkie-talkie, she went to the kitchen to make cookies. She kept in contact. They made small talk. She told him everything she was doing on Earth. He told her how the planet looked from space. Finally, she opened the oven and told him, "The cookies are ready!" to lure him out. Silence. She waited for his steps in the hall. Nothing. She left the tray on the counter and ran to his room. Empty. The capsule was gone.

THE URGE TO LAUGH

Richard told me the story with such a mad gleam in his eye, I believed it could be true. First, I better start the way he did. He had been on a Greyhound bus for 45 days. In those days you could buy a pass and keep riding as long as you had money. He went from Maine all the way west. Like some astronaut, he finally got off the ride and landed in the Hotel Volcano. He was trying to calm his life down. It takes deep breaths and a silence that is hard to find. Especially when next door, through the wall, a man and woman are fighting every night. It got so bad he thought he was overhearing murder.

Did he do anything about it? He tried to sleep in the far corner of his room with the pillow clamped to his head. The scene over there was insane. It was like listening to radio when he was a kid, *Lights Out, Inner Sanctum,* those programs that would terrify with sound.

One weekend, Richard did something. They were screaming next door and he felt the slam of her hit the wall. He ran into the hall and called the police. They took down his name and address. They told him they would send an officer by. He was so nervous he let it go at that. Nothing happened. The city was big. Can you imagine all the terrible things going on? He went back to his room and listened to the sharp stillness until it put him to sleep.

There are movies after movies that retell the same story. Richard knew it was up to him to do something. Who else could stop the violence of one room in a city so many miles big? He began to plan.

On and off all day the rain had thrown itself at his window. He happened to be sitting in the orange chair when the fighting began. He heard a bottle break. He heard her shriek. He coiled up from the chair as the man over there beat her against their common wall.

Richard didn't own a lot. What he had could be carried. He reached into his green duffel bag and took out a sorry looking gun. It was the pistol his father gave him back on the farm. Good for shooting rats in the barn. He tucked it in his pocket and it took all his control to go by the window and wait. He had to wait. It wouldn't take long but he knew that in a while the maniac would go outside.

The widow looked down onto the dark back of the hotel where brambles grew before the drop into a blacker gulley below. He had observed it again and again: the guy would stagger out there to go pee. Sometimes he almost fell in, but the luck of the devil always prevailed.

On this wet night that Richard waited with his pistol, he had his chance. The minute he saw that bastard blur against the wet window, he pulled the gun from his pocket and started.

Outside, he could feel the rain ready to go again. He knew he had to act fast. He ran around the corner and shot before he even thought.

It was a lucky shot. A truck going by on the overpass blasted its horn as a gray nobody crumpled to the ground.

It was done.

Richard stood there like a sort of fool listening to the wind. More cars roared overhead. Tires rattled the cement trestles, all day, all night they went somewhere else.

Okay! Step 1 is complete! He could feel the next bout of rain coming on.

Step 2. Take the body to the desert. That was easy too. He was watching his neighbor's car. She actually paid him to park and repark it while she was gone. That was sucker work; now he had a real use for the car.

Once the body was wrapped in the trunk, he set off.

Richard made good time. Everything was simple. He just followed the road out of the city. He stopped at a gas station an hour later. He filled the tank and also bought a five gallon can of gasoline that he put in the back seat. He would need that soon. He drove on until it felt right to cut off the highway onto a little road. When the tar ran out and he was riding on dirt, he slowed down. He pulled over next to a dune and parked. It didn't take long. In less than half an hour, he had started the fire. He kept it hot, fed with gasoline and the dry scrub until the body was mostly gone. The dawn was coming up. He kicked sand over the remains, filled the pit with a mound of it then he was done. All that crazy violence had made him calm.

He drove back to the city in a kind of dream. The window wipers tapped back and forth, pushing the Pacific rain. He parked the car in the perfect spot and went to his room. He told me the police did show up, they asked him some questions. He was nervous, but he kept his cool, then they left. Not long after that, he left too. Nobody ever knew.

If it really happened that way, I don't know. It seemed so real, the city rain, the desert fire, everything he told me was either a story or something he carries to the end of his days.

A PHOTO WITH SYLVAN MOORE

It was an hour past Closed and Ted Pell was still at work. He hovered over the Philco television soldering a loose wire. He took his glasses off to rub his eyes. That was it. All he had to do was reattach the panel. As he did so, he heard laughter on the street. People often gathered to watch the television in the window display. It was the last thing to unplug on his way out the door.

Ted clicked the power on the Philco and was pleased to see the black and white picture forming on the screen. He gave it some volume. Sylvan Moore was smiling his way through some story. The audience loved it. Ted was sure his wife was watching the show at home. Sylvan Moore was her favorite. She even dreamed about him. Sometimes he was shocked by them.

There was another burst of laughter outside.

Standing out there in the night, lit by the purple glow of television, was Sylvan Moore in person. He was pointing to himself on the set inside the shop. He was with a small crowd of followers.

Like a sparrow, Ted hopped off his chair and ran to the door. Through the glass their eyes followed him, watched him open the door. A bell clattered overhead. "Sylvan Moore!" Ted gushed, "I can't believe it's you!" He was surprised nobody else had noticed.

Sylvan Moore grinned at Ted. "We were just watching me."

Ted held the door open. "Why don't you come in my store? You can watch in here if you'd like. Please…"

Sylvan Moore gave a shrug and said, "Sure." He ushered his companions past Ted and followed.

"I can't believe it!" Ted repeated. "My wife won't believe this."

"Nice place you've got," Sylvan Moore told him. "You do

repairs?"

"What? Yes! Radios and televisions. At home we watch you all the time, Mr. Moore."

"Thanks," Sylvan smiled and shook Ted's hand. "Oh here comes a big laugh." He pointed at the screen. They were all gathered around the Philco.

Ted took a camera off the shelf. Sometimes people from the studios would come in to have equipment repaired, but never any of the big stars before. "Mr. Moore..." He crept up on them. A commercial for window cleaner was on. "Could I get a picture with you please? Nobody's going to believe this happened if I don't get a picture."

"Sure. That would be fine. Hey Mel, you take it, okay?"

Mel bowed obediently and took the camera from Ted.

"Oh yes," Ted chattered as Sylvan Moore stuck an arm around Ted's shoulder. He would have the photograph enlarged and framed and set in the window for everyone to see.

Mel said, "Say cheese."

They all did and the camera flashed.

Ted was blinking from the bright bulb going off and the pain in his chest. His finger caught at the front of his shirt and knotted around the handle of a knife.

A woman with Sylvan screamed. Mel dropped the camera. Sylvan Moore jumped away from Ted as if he was electrified. Someone opened the shop door. "Come on, Sylvan! We can't be seen here. Come on!"

Ted was staggering onto one knee as Sylvan and the crowd rushed out. The bell on the door was clanging like crazy. Ted put a hand out to steady himself.

He crumpled next to the camera on the floor. Now he remembered where he got the camera. A guy from the studio, someone in the prop shop, had given it to him as a gift. The camera was used in a detective movie. There was a spring inside of it that would shoot out a dagger when the button was pressed. Why did he have to pick that camera? Ted groaned.

He could hear Sylvan Moore on the television and the crowd
loved him.

254

THE GREAT MYSTERIO

He is listed in the phonebook. Anyone can call.

One rainy Saturday morning, he answered the phone, on the third ring, "Hello?"

A voice asked him, "Who is this?"

"Mysterio…" he said. Then he corrected himself, "I mean, The Great Mysterio."

ANOTHER LAND

As he peeled the crying onion, he thought of this world. We people only see this one place we live in but there are others layered all about. And maybe there are ways to peel through the air to look at another land? Make a curtain, part a window. Imagine that. He set the onion on the counter and ran out of the kitchen.

In the back yard, it was the same yellow sunshine, the brown old garage covered with vines and flickering St. Francis birds. He ran to the middle of all the green and threw his arms up to grab sky. For minutes, he reached around in the invisible until he found the handle underneath a cloud.

When he let the door open, he saw a nighttime sky with a different moon. It had stripes. He hopped up to rest on the ledge of what he had opened. Looking down inside, the blue landscape was lit with fireflies the size of pumpkins. He almost fell in reaching for one.

It was hard to keep his balance. The window was shaking with tremors. Something big was coming his way through the dark, attracted by the bright sunshine he let in. A giant's voice howled at him. Two monster eyes glared, as arms reached for him, as he yelled and dropped and slammed the window. Just like Columbus, he fell back onto the long grass and dandelions growing in front of his house.

SNAPPY PETE'S THRONES OF MANY FEET

"Hello out there!" Snappy Pete flared into the camera so every television could see him. Everyone knew his slogan, "Let Pete Put You On A Pedestal!" and the somnambulist jingle that played along through the commercial. There were even ads in the newspaper for Snappy Pete's Thrones of Many Feet. He was seen like the sun every day.

And the skyline of Seattle was staggered with wooden made-to-order gold painted thrones. They sprung out of backyards and apartment roofs above the telephone wires. People would sit in them for hours each day. Snappy Pete had created a completely new form of entertainment—throne sitting.

At the end of every working day, Snappy Pete would leave his office and drive his Cadillac to his throne downtown. It looked like a Victorian birdhouse. In just a few minutes he'd rocket his car to a stop and take the elevator up. Like thousands of others, he would sit for a while above the streets to watch until the lights of skyscrapers unstar and go out.

Listening to the radio play one of his advertisements at exactly 5:17, Snappy Pete parked his car in his underground garage and sang, "Don't forget!" He dueted with his radio voice, "There's a throne with your name on it!" He shut off the engine as the song ended.

A golden door opened next to him. With a fanfare, it pushed all the way open mechanically. Snappy Pete stepped into the elevator regally. The door shut and when it opened again, a warm night breeze filled his lungs. He sat down on his throne and the elevator left him all alone.

There were more thrones than last night. He felt sublime, smiled and hummed his song.

A bat flew in and landed on a painting.

He swatted at the portrait of himself. The bat shifted on the swinging frame.

"Get out!" he screamed. Crouched, he threw a punch at the bat. Sensing his every move with radar, the bat dived at Pete and clung to his tie.

With a shriek, Snappy Pete lost his balance, falling backwards off the throne. Crashing through oak leaves, his legs hooked over a branch and he swung upside down. "Help!" he yelled, like an acrobat without the net underneath.

The bat, hanging from his tie below made a sound and began to climb towards his face.

Snappy Pete suddenly feared, *What if it has rabies?* and quickly answered himself with a hysterical scream, "Who cares if it has rabies!"

Beside his ear, the bat stopped clawing and it hissed, "When you fall off your throne, ask for Yvette's Safety Nets!"

"Help!" Snappy Pete screamed, "Yvette's Safety Nets! Help me!"

It was all Yvette needed for her commercial. Lives depended on it. "If Snappy Pete needs one, don't you too?" Soon everyone would need an Yvette Safety Net.

And the next morning, she gladly paid Bart's Trained Bats their five hundred dollars fee.

DR. BIOCAL AND THE ELEMENT OF JOY

Dr. Biocal's new invention turned a flopping, gasping catfish into an expert dancer. Across the countertop in his laboratory, the muddy colored fish waltzed on its tail like Fred Astaire in a waterproof tuxedo. Gracefully, it whirled and began to sing beautiful words, "Heaven, I'm in heaven…"

The doctor switched the ray off and caught the fish from falling onto the floor. He put it back into the aquarium where it continued to shimmy and harmonize with the goldfish.

"The experiment is a success!" Dr. Biocal congratulated himself. "Now to find a human subject…" He picked up the black telephone next to the bubbling test tubes and said, "Operator, give me the number for *The Daily Drone*."

In an office there, Susan Fenton stood holding the phone before a window, looking down on a room full of spinning print rollers. A white snake of newspapers threaded from one end of the room to the other. "Okay," Susan nodded. She read from a notepad, "This is how you want the message to read: Have the dark ages got you down? Are you all out of luck? Do you cry out for mercy? By a miracle of science, I will cure you. Contact Dr. Biocal at ME2-8195."

"That's perfect," the soothing voice in her ear lulled. "Thank you."

"You're welcome." She hung the phone up quickly. "So!" She rested her hands on her hips. He's at it again, she thought. "What is it this time, Dr. Biocal?" she whispered and turned her eyes to the newspaper headlines glaring past below. "Whatever it is, it's bound to be evil…I think I better find out."

A taxi later, Susan stood in the orange streetlights and stared at the beaten, falling down gargoyle of a house. Just like Dr. Biocal to pick another dismal hideout for his experiments. A blue sparkling light flashed in a basement window.

She crept past the saw-toothed picket fence, onto the black lawn. Her heels poked through the fallen leaves. As quietly as she could, she kneeled down next to the basement window. Dead sunflowers, brittle with tall stalks from last summer, arced around her and then the garden became a trapdoor and darkness.

Inside the green light, in his long white lab coat, the doctor strung wires back and forth like yarn making a sweater in the shape of a girl.

Susan's eyes fluttered and she awakened as he fitted the last wire to her forehead. She blinked. She tried to move, she shook her head. "What's going on?" Then she recalled Dr. Biocal and where she was.

"My dear, sweet Susan Fenton," the doctor said, pleased. "It's like Spring to see you again." Hearts popped in the air over him.

She struggled vainly. She was caught in a target on the wall. Red and white circles went around her. She was in the center of a bull's eye. Gaining her composure, she said, "I thought I'd stop by and see what your new diabolical plan is."

"Diabolical?" He acted surprised and hurt. "I'm a scientist, Susan. I am dedicated to bettering humanity. Through years of searching, at last I've found the Element of Joy. It's a difficult thing to capture…A little yellow atom." He turned to motion at the ray set up pointing at her. "When this works on you, you'll never be unhappy again. You will have a lifetime's supply of joy!"

"Isn't that a little unrealistic of you?" she asked. She wanted to keep him talking—the rope holding her hand was loosening.

"Unrealistic? To want to live in a state of bliss? To be aware of the miraculous luck of being alive?" He scolded her, "Susan, you've been working too long at the newspaper. Life is not a series of bleak disasters. Day to day sorrows will not interest you anymore. You will only be a part of the joy of existence." Gleaming with care, he turned on the ray. The coils hummed with rainbow colors, while blue sparks shot at the ceiling.

Just in time, she rolled and kicked off her shoe at the machine. The ray swept past her, barely missing her as her shoe struck and spun the beam crazily across the stones of the room, halting, hitting Dr. Biocal in the chest.

Electricity crackled and escaped. The room was filled with smoke, broken glass and a dancing fish.

Susan watched the smoke clear. "Are you alright?" she asked unsteadily and coughed.

The blasted laboratory began to emerge.

There was no sign of Dr. Biocal.

Susan took care leaving the place, wearing only one shoe and dragging the still attached, damp wires. Up the wooden creaking stairs and out the front door, she staggered.

Outside, the warm night was filled with the sound of crickets and frogs and television murmurs.

POSIE CRUTCHFIELD IN THE APPLE TREE

She journeyed through a night full of confusing dreams into light, to wake up in a tree. As her eyes opened, she saw orchards all around, fallen apples on the ground with her in the middle, spiraled in green.

Maybe, she thought, I might still be asleep. She looked around from the height of the tree. It seemed so real. There were feelings, senses; the current of air she breezed in was part of the world. But what had happened to the reality of her 1921 Hollywood, miles away?

I must have flown like a magic carpet in my nightgown. Magically, I left the city in the dark and floated, entranced out here. I wonder, is Houdini in town? Could he have done this to me? Landed her so softly in an apple branch nest…A still while passed…There were calm birds. A green caterpillar inched her bare ankle while she waited.

"Do you usually sleep in trees?"

Startled again, she looked below. Her dark hair fell over her eyes. Dreams are like this, she knew. I change from scene to scene so easily. Things happen this way. It's okay, don't be afraid.

He watched her and asked, "Do you need help getting down?" A wooden ladder was folded under his arm, a wide basket in the other hand. It creaked with rolling apples he had picked.

If it's a dream, she decided, I have some control over this. If I need to, I'll change myself to a thousand miles away. So she sat on the swinging branches, dangling her feet casually, then she tried to say something.

Words formed, her lips moved, but no sound was made. After another try failing with words, her thoughts accepted, Alright, I understand, in this world my voice cannot be heard.

"I know you," he said. The sunlight scratched on his head.

"I've seen you somewhere before." He studied her rocking over him, the white flicker of cloth around her with her brilliant eyes watching. "You're in the pictures…You're Posie Crutchfield!"

Yes, she thought, that's who I am.

Though that tells me something, it still doesn't explain my presence here.

He leaned the basket upon the grass, spilling out fruit. Excitedly, he told her, "I love your motion pictures. I see them every time I get into town."

The ladder rested against the trunk next to her. He held his eyes on her like a miracle had occurred, and she was in a way. On an ordinary day, Posie Crutchfield was in his apple tree.

There were no words to say out loud—only a silent movie star, she acted, putting her feet to touch on the top ladder rung.

She climbed slowly. Every step the ladder shook, until she reached the ground and let go.

When she turned around, she recognized the so-called man's disguise and now she could laugh in surprise at the plot. It was Olive Belmont, Buster Keaton's only rival in practical jokes, who rolled in a fit in between the trees.

TOAD RICKY RETURNS FOR A WATERFALL

Toad's legs turned bicycle wheels. For a long time they spun miles. First the sun then the moon sailed overhead. Green eyes star guided, riding towards dawn. Morning bird songs filled the sky. The dew on the hills made silver oceans. Flowers schooled like fish waking up. Around the corner the road folded and cupped a puddle in the middle. Toad's eyes glimmered with the thought of riding straight through the splash. Putting water into the air and maybe hang a rainbow there. So he sped up his pedaling and got low over the handlebars. A couple rabbits saw it happen—the bicycle submerged in a wave and Toad Ricky was gone.

POSIE CRUTCHFIELD IN BUTTERFLIED

She had to jump out the window to escape. The building turned into flames while she fell through the air into the river. Watch her splash across the current and debris of burning wood to the other side. There, into the weeds and crumpled barbed wire, she tried to stand.

Shadows played all over her dress as she stared at the fire.

A noise behind her startled her and she turned around.

She looked into the eyes of a strange creature. Almost a sort of deer, stretched out into new directions. It regarded her curiously too. A hundred years ago, only a few people in America had seen a kangaroo.

She closed her eyes in disbelief, keeping them tightly shut until in a moment she slowly tried to see again.

It was gone. There was only the field before her.

Over the fence remains, she stepped and entered the weeds. They pulled around her black dress like thick water. An avalanche of butterflies flattened her. When she stood up, she looked around herself carefully, then popped open an umbrella overhead.

She summoned her courage, "I'm prepared for any disaster," she announced.

The brush stirred and out hopped the kangaroo. It went past Posie Crutchfield. She held her frozen body like a scarecrow in the tall grass.

Safe to move again, she dropped her hands onto her hips. "What is that?" she asked, watching it amble into the shade of birches. Heroically, though still with the umbrella, held before her like a sword, she followed the kangaroo.

It stopped to eat flowers and she hid behind the waist of an oak. When it moved again, so did she, silently parachuting from tree to tree. The kangaroo took her out of the undergrowth. Sunlight fell through from the road that emerged just ahead.

Posie saw past the animal. There were cars scattered and three trucks overturned. Brightly painted, she read the upside down letters, "The Saturn Circus…" Elephants pushed at the crushed edges and a giraffe stood like a flagpole nearby.

HERMAN SNOCK STEALS THE SUN

Herman Snock caught the sun in a jar. In the early morning, he had leaned far out of his window and when the sun was small and just hatching in the clouds, he captured it. The sky turned black for days while the sun flapped against the glass jar, imprisoned in his room.

The world became frantic. Owls flew in tired circles…People went to work all day in the dark. By himself, Herman sat and stared at the bright sun on his bookshelf. After a week, he brought it to school with him. The sun was in a paper bag, making orange light for him to see by. There were stars in the sky. The moon's creaking noise went over and over the city.

He ran towards a friend next to the schoolyard fence. "I've got the sun!" he said proudly and held up the lantern color. Then, to prove it, he opened the bag and loosened the jar. The sun had been waiting all that time for a chance.

THE TUESDAY MORNING GIRL

Sid Freezer was going to work, rocked in the seat of the bus making its way gradually. The world was always a movie for him, the window glaring light was a screen. He saw people act silently, curtain folds of leaves, trees and billboards.

And he watched a girl out of the corner of his eyes. Across the aisle from him, she stood up. He never knew a love, so he could fall in love at first sight all the time. She looked at him and quickly looked away.

When the bus stopped, she walked down the steps and got off and, oh how he watched everything she moved. But what did he know about anything? Flower colored cloth covered her. She became a part of the sky, the blue and contrails and blew away with it as the bus drove further up the avenue.

What a taste of warm summer soft, Sid was filled with sighs. His thoughts supplied him with every daydream. What if she really cared for him too? What if she'll go home thinking of me? She may start a search, set a hundred thousand sails exploring for me.

Looking over to the seat she left, he saw a box she forgot. As the bus began to slow to a stop again, he jumped up and grabbed it on his way down the aisle.

The doors flipped open and he hurried off onto the pavement. With the precious box under his arm, he puffed a ways to the end of the block. Already, he tired. His round reflection stopped in a store window while he tried to catch his breath, losing her after finding her lost and found.

JACK SHELLAC, THE FAVORITE SNACK

His face was on the cover of the magazines at the supermarket. Above, the headlines shrieked, "Monster Millionaire!" and there was the disturbing story of his curse. "Grizzly Mauls Artist Four Times!" That part was true. Despite his riches, poor Jack Shellac couldn't seem to escape the bear. Over the years it found him again and again.

A shopping cart scraped up the aisle, dragging the deflated scratch of a man, Jack Shellac. He wheezed like an old trolley and stopped next to the macaroni to catch his breath.

People were beginning to notice someone famous in Aisle 3. Finally, the manager couldn't stand the suspense anymore and he announced over the loudspeaker, "Today's Special is Jack Shellac!"

The floor clattered with the stampede. Crowding around Jack, they watched him lift his head lethargically as he tried to speak.

The store manager threw his arm over Jack's shoulder. "Shellac, have we got a surprise for you!"

Jack watched the crowd parting awkwardly, felt the manager slap his back while the taffy muzak began to play "Hail to the Chief."

The crowd sighed and they fell back at the huge shadow creeping slow as Frankenstein. Rolled on a pedestal, it stood eight feet tall on its hind legs. Like a sofa thrown out in an alley, its fur was punctured, burnt and worn away, piano key claws falling out.

It had seen just as much wear and tear over the terrible years as Jack. Except Jack Shellac was still alive…Barely though… And the beast before him, that had tracked him round the globe like a thing possessed, was finally dead, a victim of the taxidermist.

Nobody moved. Jack seemed to be in a cocoon.

"What do you say, Shellac?" the manager finally asked.

Jack had only one eye left, swollen now to the size of a saucer. He stared at the bear and clung to his shopping cart.

"Fellahs!" the manager called to a couple checkers, "Push that bear over here…That's right!" He winged them over, directing the bear like a zeppelin.

As the grizzly approached him, Jack backed himself into the boxes of macaroni, scrambling, clawing some off onto the linoleum.

"*Stop!* That's far enough!"

The shout came from above. It turned into a karate-yodel as someone swung down from the skylight and landed on top of a silver row of canned beans. "I am the president of The Society for Prevention of Cruelty to Jack Shellac." The man was covered in bulky camouflage, connected to the gray ceiling by a rope. "It is my sworn duty to protect Jack Shellac from that bear, be it alive or be it dead."

The store manager gawked, "What?" He couldn't comprehend this; he was used to pricing onions. "It can't do anything now. It's dead."

"No." The president held up his hand. "That bear is always dangerous. Look! At any second it could fall over on Jack and smother him."

"We thought he'd like to have it for a trophy," the manager continued, softly.

The president leaped down onto the floor beside Jack. Other Society members had appeared, forcing through the crowd. They surrounded and grabbed the bear. It took all of them to lift the bear onto their backs and carry it. The president waved as they struggled through the pneumatic exit doors. "Never fear, Jack Shellac! The S.F.P.O.C.T.J.S is always near!"

The bear wobbled in the air of the parking lot towards a white van.

Jack breathed deeply and tried to smile.

The store was quiet enough to be overcome by the muzak.

At last, the manager sighed. "Well…" He pointed to the microwave fish and chips boxes in Jack's shopping cart. "At least let us pay for your food."

Jack was helped through the debris and the manager posed in line with him. People had Jack autograph their cereal boxes and torn receipts. When it was all over, Jack dragged himself out through the hissing doors with a cartful of grocery bags.

The S.F.P.O.C.T.J.S was still trying to get the bear into their van. Past them, Jack was pulled by his cart. He didn't have the strength anymore to steer it, it was so heavy with frozen fish and chips. But he was lucky the cart was pointed at his parked car. It crashed off the side and the impact shattered Jack like glass. Groaning and mumbling feebly, he lay over the crumpled trunk of his car. He was seeing vultures and stars.

The president called loudly to him, "Hey, Jack!" A few of the Society's soldiers left the bear sticking out of the van and hurried over to help Jack Shellac to his feet. They carried him crescented across their shoulders like a fish pulled out of the ocean. He was flopped into the front seat of their van. With the groceries stored aboard, the president started the engine. "We'll give you a personal escort home."

The rest of the Society crawled around the bear in back of the van.

Jack couldn't help it. He trembled uncontrollably.

"Don't worry, pal." The president assured him, "You've got the S.F.P.O.C.T.J.S on your side." A toothpick jutted out of his smile.

The van squealed around corners, the president was driving a jeep in Vietnam again. He swerved out of imaginary explosions.

Jack began to panic. His dry thistle hand brushed the door handle.

"Hey, Comrades!" the president called over his shoulder. "I vote we should take Jack out to dinner!" He waited for their response. The back of the van was quiet. Only the sound of spinning wheels and Jack Shellac's whimpering. The Society had disappeared.

The president gasped, "Pizza?" He was afraid to turn around. Something froze the air back there like a ghost sheet.

Jack Shellac had stopped breathing. His eyes shut painfully. He heard the scrape of claws on the metal floor.

SNAPPY PETE'S LIFE IN MONTANA

One day, he checked his mailbox. There was nothing there.

He went back to the house and sat and stared out the window.

There were clouds and rocks to watch.

A crow hung like an albatross in air.

Two weeks later, he got a letter.

It was from Ed McMahon. It was marked urgent in red ink all over the envelope. "I could be a millionaire!" The light blinked in Snappy Pete's eyes. He ripped open the letter. It was stuffed with brochures and stickers, meaningless forms and pictures. None of it meant anything.

"Am I a millionaire or not?!" he screamed at the night.

TREE SHADOW

The village turned out to see the monster taken from the trees. Woodcutters found it in the fallen crown of a birch they chopped down. It had long bird's nest hair with green ivy wrapping round and though it didn't make a sound, its big eyes looked with such a longing, far past its captors, into the forest bridged with sky.

It didn't struggle. The ropes tied its arms and legs to the post in the dry center of town. It couldn't watch the surrounding blur, the colors, shapes and smells that were not trees. Its strange face stared away, up to hold moving clouds, while the people formed a noisy crowd. The monster could have been a scarecrow. Sometimes someone would poke it to see it move. It wasn't doing anything and when all the games and curiosity began to fade and night sent everyone back to their homes. A pail of water and a branch of leaves were left to keep it alive until dawn.

Crickets and owls and bats cracking after moths, its wet eyes still looked at the sky, sparkling with stars.

Then it began to make a sound. It was so quiet and low that only one person in the world could hear.

Cast in her wooden house, a girl listened and heard how the monster cried the loneliest tears in the dark. Like a tortured raincloud, he called to her. She couldn't just lay there in bed anymore. She pulled a blue cloak over her shoulders and left out the window as fast as she could.

Moonlight lit the monster's silhouette. Night birds twisted in flight overhead. She had never seen eyes so sad. They were like whirlpools, like starfish tide pools. His tears had turned the ground around him into mud.

She walked up close to soothe him. She called him Tree Shadow. He still had vines and moss and dried leaves in his hair.

"Tree Shadow," she whispered, "Don't cry. I know. I'm going to free you." Her hands went around the ropes and found the knots. She sung a lullaby as her strong fingers unweaved.

In just that moment before the lines fell away, she looked into his eyes and saw green wishes: the thanks of the pine trees and fir and redwoods, willows, hawthorn, poplars, the maples and birches and elms and dogwood.

That was what she did for him. She helped him back to where he belonged and when the ropes unlooped, he lifted his arms and flew out of town.

RABBIT

Free Baby Rabbits. The sign on the road arrowed him over gravel shadows, weeds clinging dust. He stopped his bicycle in front of the barn. He leaned it angled on its kickstand and left it in the sun to go knock upon the door.

"Hello?" he asked the quiet…Quiet, but not utterly silent. He could hear the peeping swallows as they jigsawed overhead. Poplars rustled their green overcoats by the river. "Hello?"

"Yes! Hello!" said a woman. She clattered at the latches and he helped her open the door.

He smiled as the light of day showed her up, for she wore on her head a tall striped hat that Dr. Seuss could have drawn. She smiled too, her very old face making spider webs. "You came for a rabbit?"

"Yes, that's right. I have a basket with a blanket," he pointed back towards his bicycle, "to take the rabbit home."

So she looked into him with wide eyes that he felt go inside, that felt around his heart and searched his mind. "Good," she decided when she was done. "I'll give you one."

From her patched dress, she pulled a rabbit out of a pocket. "This is yours now." She let his arms go around the fur.

He was spellbound, holding stars. He cradled the rabbit back to the bicycle. He unleafed the quilt in the basket over the tire where the world would be covered until they got home.

Then as he rode away, turning around to wave, she took off her hat to listen with her tall, revealed long rabbit ears.

DR. BIOCAL AND THE VOICE OF LOVE

In this summer pour, the supernatural flick of sprinklers waving water back and forth across the lawns, Susan Fenton walked on the rainy sidewalk. The song she was whistling disappeared. She felt she had stepped through to another time. There was someone on the dipping back of a horse, singing to her. He had surrounded her with flowers and the prizes of crusades. She tried to move, but she was swimming. She knew it had to be a dream…

Inside a rusting shack, the pointed copper roof trembling with wires and antennas aimed at the street, Dr. Biocal turned more dials and watched the humming needles play. Elliptical gold lights blinked on his face.

A few more adjustments and he was satisfied. Then he spoke into a microphone, "Hello, my sweetheart. I've been thinking of you." Through the speakers his voice went North, South, West and East, across the city waking out of sleep. Wavelengths said, "Darling my miss, please hurry to me."

Girls and women tossed out of bed. They were all thinking the same Medieval golden thought, while in soft light they threw themselves into their best clothes to mirror sunflowers. Morning dew caught at them while they walked over lawns and fences to join parades, singing to fill the air like pollen. They all hurried, not to jobs or into everyday circuits, their hypnotized eyes sparkled to Dr. Biocal's door.

When he pressed open the curtains, he saw delirious thousands, all holding up palms towards his window glass. His mouth opened a smile. Unhooking the portable microphone of The Voice of Love modulator, he went through his front door and stepped onto the path lined with broken rocks and daisies. "Sweet ladies," the irresistible voice soothed, amplified and tuned into a secret romantic frequency.

Gathered from the miles, the wind had taken his voice, the crowds trembled in waves. The entire city was shut down while they pushed around the rundown building that Dr. Biocal had turned into the Castle of Frankenstein. For all his science though, he would be alone if she wasn't there too.

THE POLLYWOG DOG

Found in a pond and caught in a jar, the pollywog dog was the newest star in Herman Snock's collection. He also had bees, dried golden brown, lava rocks and bottle caps, bird eggs, and a purple rabbit's foot keychain, to name but a few. But none of these things captured his interest more than the tadpole turning day by day into a dog. Slowly, it grew four legs, a nose and ears and one week later, it was beginning to speak. As it swam in circles inside the glass, it barked and whined trying to get out. Holding a magnifying lens, Herman taught it to sit, roll over, and beg for the little piece of biscuit he would pinch between his fingers. It could also catch matchsticks that would land in its pool. It was the greatest water pet the world's ever known.

The last trick it performed was the best of all. One morning, it floated on the surface, bloated and green. Herman Snock was so full of tears he took the dead animal and in a ritual as old as American goldfish, dropped it into the toilet bowl. As he was going to say it one last prayer, the pollywog dog splashed with a bark, while it frolicked and tread—it was only playing dead. And now it would leave with all that underground water to tour the sewers, or come out of someone's faucet tap.

MOTH AND CHILD

The night was warm with insects. In bed, he listened to the thousand songs and flutters, loving most of all the soft moth beats on his window glass. Watching the circus juggle of wings, he had an idea that took him to sleep. He dreamed of The Moth on the Moon…A moth so big it danced upon the moon. But if he could make enough light on the lawn, more than a full moon, it might fly attracted to him instead. He padded quietly through the house, past his sleeping parents, to the attic where he took Christmas lights out of a dusty box. Also, he took lamps, candles and flashlights from different silent rooms. He took all the things that could glow, piled high in his arms, through the hallway, out the door, outside. The grass was soft while he scooted around setting things up, trailing wires back inside, bringing out matches. When the lawn was lit, it was so bright it attracted moths from all over the nighttime world. Even airplanes circled, confused in the dark. He laughed at all the soaring around and waited nervously. Then, at last, from the stars came a wind, with the biggest wings of all unspreading. A silhouette unattached from the white circle in the sky. The moth on the moon flew down , circled the lawn and swooped to the child, picked him up carefully in a cradle of legs and together they flew away.

THE WOODEN MAN, HER ROCKING CHAIR

He was living in his room so alone. Making the time go by, the wooden man, pressed flat, was disguised at first for an hour as a wall. Then he changed into a table. He was a chair when she entered the room and sat down. Nervously, he held his breath. She rested he elbows on his arms, she was sitting on his stomach, upon his arched and turned and weakening legs.

"Is this chair moving?" she asked her friend. She stood up and he fell apart. All in a blur, he broke into a man, made of Lincoln logs, then he quickly reformed so she wouldn't suspect. He became a locked black pirate's chest.

"What was that?" she stared at her friend.

Her friend, scared of her own chair she sat in, jumped up and said, "Let's get out of here!"

But she wanted to know about the changing wooden man. Her friend was against it, she said it was wrong what she wanted to do, but in the end, they carried the chest home. Put in the corner, under their window curtained in white lace, he watched out the keyhole as they walked around, making dinner, listening to their music, laughing and telling stories.

She who had discovered his secret kept returning to him. Once she brought him an old framed photograph, another time she came back with flowers to put on top of him. She lay a poetry book on him. He got the feeling she was watching and waiting for him.

That evening, the window was opened letting in air filled with new summer night, and he dreamed himself into a rocking chair. So enchanted did he rock there in that soft light of the city, she came out of her bedroom to be with him again.

BACKTRACK TO THE ART SHACK WITH JACK SHELLAC

He painted trees on a pink and blue sky. Like a ship going out to sea, he colored melancholy. "It's good to be here," his voice wheezed. "Back where I began…"

The crippled Jack Shellac tried with broken limbs to fill the canvas as in the days of old. He put in snow covered mountains, firs and flowers down in the valley below.

"Let's make some water, to show reflections of our world."

Scooped from the palette, he added dragging blue, pulling the other shades in. It became a sorrowful lake splashing there, swimming with ghosts.

With his splinted metal reinforced left hand, he took the paintbrush out of his mouth and together with the hook of his other limb, he held it precariously towards the camera. Scrambling words fell out of his mouth, lost in static, a joke nobody would ever know.

"I'm not the man I used to be," he managed to say, "But I hope you see a landscape in the tradition of the old masters." The TV camera framed his gruesome, ripped face, the scarred tributaries ran all over him like the rivers left on maps by fourteenth century dreamers. "It's really an honor to be here again at The Art Shack. That's the magic of television…"

Jack put the brush back between his teeth and added some flight of yellow birds. It was a perfect fantasy vision and yet he stopped unfinished. He pointed the brush at the corner where he lingered to put his signature. "I think what it needs is more of a sign of nature."

He could have taken some blur to add a pheasant flock, or maybe a placid deer. But no, he felt compelled, he couldn't help himself, all through his life it had haunted him, deformed him with its hunting and finding.

Jack pulled some umber, black and burnt sienna off of the

palette, enough to put a grizzly bear there in the grassy mountain field.

The screens of televisions all over America followed him making the form. He lingered. With the smallest brush, he began to add features, minute, like the froth in its mouth and the gleam in its mad eyes. To make it really real, he added flecks of blue and some green. Jack Shellac was still the master of that, making pictures become what you see and feel.

The bear grew to true proportions. It took on a life of its own and separated from the picture frame, hungry to seek this new revenge.

DR. BIOCAL'S SURPRISE

In gardens all over the city, or leafing through a thousand colored pages of botany books, Dr. Biocal madly searched for the flower he dreamed of. It didn't seem to exist in the real world, but night after night, so near, he saw it clearly in his mind. He could draw it on a chalkboard.

A combination of many things, there was daisy in it, morning glory, poppy, carnation and roses and more. Unearthly, yet somewhere growing for him, he tried to be hopeful as he stumbled across the city.

When his dream was really turning to despair, at last he decided he would have to create such a beauty scientifically… In the laboratory. Like a bodysnatcher, he went from garden to garden, taking ingredients. He dressed in black and stole at night, leaving no clues, or so he thought.

Months passed in his Victorian mansion, wooden finger spires holding out turrets with stainglass windows, the home of his Frankenstein flower. Illumined by a pool of Boris Karloff candlelight, the experiment pushed the walls of the bubble it was in. What grew inside though couldn't be seen through the condensation of dripping rainy water steam.

Dr. Biocal was berserk with joy, but he let it continue to grow for a few weeks more, until the bowl was swollen as a watermelon.

He was pleased that even the lightning sky seemed to respond to his plot that night he unhooked the wires and locks that held the flower undercover. Thunder rattled the old mansion and flashed it with silhouettes.

"This is the moment of life!" He put his hands upon the ripened curve and lifted.

He was blinded by the swale of hot vapor. Dr. Biocal stepped back as the green leafy miracle tumbled out. He laughed as he rubbed the water from his face.

The candles burned like incense through the tropic volcano air.

He blinked his eyes open to see not only the jungle of new born leaves, but rising from the tangled nest what he could scarcely believe.

"Surprised?" asked Susan Fenton. She pushed off the tendrils and made a public arrest.

THE VILLAGE IDIOT AND THE TOWN CRIER

Two fools met upon a city street and thought perhaps they could be complete. He mumbled out Medieval chants and sighs, built nonsense from the falling soot in the sky, while she just blinked her sad big blue eyes that soon began to cry. She drowned the avenue with tears and it looked like he could have died, but no, he sailed upon a boat made out of butterflies.

THE LITTLE BLUE SAD MAN

The little sad man drives a plaid Cadillac. He stops at every window and presses the horn. Whoever hears him and goes to see, will get a blast from the blue. He's busy too. There are so many people he should make sorry. Just when day ends, the night begins. Then it's the lonely, who are watching stars and wishing. He catches their eyes and presses them like moths under glass with pins.

A SLICE OF AIR OF BILLBOARD SIZE

Into the early morning, leaving the nightshift back in pigeon trees, the water paper dawn poured down around his car. He was thinking about his wife and child fast asleep, still too soon for light through their window shades. He would try not to wake them as he slipped into bed, but as always, she would reach for his hand.

The wipers squeaked across the windshield. Turning on the radio, he smiled. He recognized what it played. There was still enough time in the record to take him home. Their house was down the road a symphony away.

At this purple hour, he was the only one ever riding between the forest, so he was surprised out of his thoughts when he saw something far ahead in front of his car.

Whatever it was spun light and darkness in a slice of air of billboard size.

The rain stopped as a wall he burst through. He was in a space of both day and night, dawn trying to draw out and stars staying overhead, the struggle when sun pushed moon's hold.

Getting closer to it, he was still peering at the odd moving shape, when the radio music and engine sighed off. He felt the car's strength give out, as it coasted until its wheels stopped.

Stranger than the car, he stared at the roadblock throwing out lightning and black smoke. What was it someone had created there?

It looked like a machine, a big pinwheel or riverboat paddlewheel, blasting out loose energy. The force of the thing had him paralyzed. He was caught in a dream of watching spinning, in a trapped place where the dangerous clockwork was the center of the world.

There was something wrong with the motion of the thing. A spring or bolt must be dislodged inside, the way it shook and scuffed the ground, sparking electricity and clouds.

Backwards and forwards, the tension ripped it apart, two halves shrieked into the air, separate. The pieces scribbled themselves above the earth, then changed into birds.

One, a black owl, hovered before it flew off to the horizon.

The other bird remained for day and flapped its robin wings onto the branch of a fir. Chirping, that bird let the sun climb above the woods.

The car engine turned over in response, the song played its shutting notes, while rain began to bead pearls on the glass and hood again.

PAULINE CLOCK LANDED TODAY

She took the aeroplane low over a farmhouse and landed in a field. The wings sawed out of air into the stalks of corn. The propeller chopped through pale green leaves, the wheels bounced over the furrowed ground. A wake of clouds rose above the field and scattered crows and starlings.

As the engine rattled unevenly to a stop, she leaped out, down across the wing. She fell on her back in the mown trail and a few minutes later, Joe Clock was born.

His mother, the famous barnstormer Pauline Clock, flew him all over the country in those early days. Pauline's bee yellow aeroplane would circle a little town to gather a crowd who would be willing to pay to see Joe and her Ferris wheel overhead at daredevil speed. Telegraphs would click out the news to other towns downwind—*Pauline Clock Landed Today!*

In Parakeet, Oklahoma, after she landed to bow to the audience, a man with a top hat approached her. At first, her eyes grew. She thought Lincoln had died sixty years ago. She tried to relax. She rubbed Joe's little back.

"Hello," the Lincoln lookalike nodded and reached for her handshake. "Welcome to Parakeet."

Pauline was staring at the Abe Lincoln double. He held a bunch of wildflowers which he passed to her.

She tied them to the wing as he and the rest of the curious town grew around to see her dragonfly up close.

"Would you like to go up for a flight?" she asked him.

Everyone applauded and urged him. A man even patted his back.

He smiled awkwardly at Pauline and Joe who watched from inside her heavy warm coat. "I accept your offer."

She helped him cramp his tall lanky body into the seat next to her.

The propeller began to spin and the mayor held onto his black top hat. He waved with one hand to the crowd while the aeroplane shook and turned into the wind. He peered over the cloth covered side as they bounced up into the sky.

She laughed as his expression changed.

The yellow wings took him in a slow turn over the land. People in the road knew who it was and threw their arms around. Over a tiny house, they watched a family all run on the green, pointing up. The mayor was laughing with his long arm held into the slipstream.

Her eyes glowed to see Abe Lincoln so happy. She had never seen his picture in history look so full of joy.

Joe reached his chubby arm out of her jacket and held the mayor's beard.

They flew into a cloud. They went into a solid fog like going through a pillow. In a moment, just feathers of the white clung to the wing wires. The Abe Lincoln man was gone.

Pauline gasped. She stared all around herself. She stretched and looked towards the land. The sky was clear, the aeroplane shadow traveled over seeded brown ground.

Joe began to cry against her. She looked at him and saw the beard still clutched in his fingers.

POSIE CRUTCHFIELD IN THE LAND OF SAND

She was lost from the caravan, in a hundred thousand drifts of sand. Staggering, a black outline in all the blinding white, Posie let the heat defeat her as she collapsed on the desert wave.

From this low hot pan, she sizzled and her eyes searched for one last time.

Shoes curled up with bells, next to camels standing still. The servants of some Bedouin king let her onto a stretcher shaded by flags and umbrellas. They fed her water from a turtle shell canteen and breezed her supine with the wings of ostrich fans, while the camels, like pigeons, steered towards where they'd come.

Eating figs and grapes caused her to faint with delight just as the peaks of tents appeared
in sight.

When she woke, she saw tapestries on walls. She was laying on a Persian bed and a man wearing a crown smiled when she looked at him and said, "Welcome to the mirage."

She sat up quickly ringing silver bells attached to her dress. "Mirage?" it was true. Now that she knew, whatever she touched, her hand passed through. The king, she could see, was a part of it too. Half his body was made of smoke, unraveling from a genie lamp.

"If this isn't real," she said, "then where am I?"

"You are here," he said. "It's a mirage. But as long as you believe, it will stay real."

She tried her best to make believe but now that she had learned the truth, how could it be? Soft blankets evaporated and golden plates of fruit, the rich mirage shook itself like hair and tossed all that illusion out in the air.

Posie was left sitting on sand.

The world stretched for miles. She was lost but it didn't matter where she was. She popped open her umbrella and in that shade began to walk.

INVISIBLY FINDING THE HONEY OF BEES

He was led by a guide when he was a child. A friendly giraffe walked by his side, pulling on a water clear leash. Invisibly looking through the height of the clouds, the giraffe would laugh to show him the path and hide him from what to avoid. Troubles began the second he opened the door, the city could be a dangerous maze. Though it was good to know he was safe as he played, best of all were the treasures found along the way…Kites in trees, Frisbees, a boomerang from a roof, bird eggs and caterpillars and the honey of bees.

I GIVE THE AIR A FLYING FISH

I give the air a flying fish, her salt wings the ocean lifts out of waves, currents cold, into the warmest climb of the sun. She soars from the darker world she knows, into the sky just as blue and deep but such a different thing to swim in. She could be a bird. It's so close she can feel. She could trade her scales in for feathers. She could forget the sound of abalones clapping shells, seaweed that rubs like banjo strings, all the bend and weave of the undersea, to hear the song of the air instead.

SHE AND HE SEE THE SEA DIFFERENTLY

Her compass had caught her in the Arctic stars. The little aeroplane tossed up a snowdrift, then dropped down to only feet above the sea. She could tell how low she was, the salt spray flicked across the wings.

Pauline Clock's flying machine was in danger of becoming a swimming fish. She fought the controls, the dragging elevators and a stubborn rudder frozen with ice. "We've got to gain some height!" she told her son in the front seat.

They threw out whatever they could. Maps and clothes and the radio, a stove and food flew off into the cold while the circling propeller labored slowly to lift them off the waves. From the doorway of waiting water, she struggled to fly them up.

Joe heaved out another toss of metal tools this time, so they began to rise. Walruses, seals, poking out of broken holes in white watched the flaming exhaust pull away from doom.

There was still enough gasoline to take them to the pole. No one else had traveled flying this curve of the globe before, but she and her son would do the impossible.

Dawn waited long enough to return with the first purple rays. Where could we be? she thought frantically. Is this what I get for hoping? As Amelia Earhart would be lost at sea, like Joan of Arc on a burning cross of fire, every chance they took gave them up in the end.

Over the edge of the wing she could see the glitter of morning.

Her young son was still asleep. She was going to say something to him, about the weather, or the blue arc of day…Instead, she flew on with her thought.

It was about midday when her eyelids fell down and up. She kept shaking her mind to keep herself awake. It was all the same thought, blue, white, with dots of black broken through the bright photograph.

She stretched her arm to wake her sleeping son. "Joe, tell me do you see anything?"

He gazed upon the world that seemed to her so empty of everything. He yawned. His eyes all waking from a dream saw what she forgot to see.

He pointed to a spot down below. "Turn us there!" He caught the scent of what anyone only young would comprehend. What didn't seem possible really did exist. Where the slipstream shot warm around them, there was a green tulip field and a place to land.

SUSAN FENTON MISSES THE BIRDS

Fog body clung to the streets, the leaves, and swirled around architecture. She watched out her open window in her warm flannel and soft yellow scarf. She liked to get up early on a Sunday. This one seemed to have fallen from the sky, or maybe the ground had pushed a mile into the clouds during the night, for everything was covered in white. But not a single waking robin chirp could be heard, nor the starlings that gathered in the tree, or on a telephone wire. Crows that lorded over neighborhood peaks, sparrows that played like children in the dew, there was no city bird in this day's opening music-box.

Now, that's very strange, thought Susan Fenton. When she woke at such an hour, it was songs she wanted to hear like a lover's good morning. The cello was without strings and she wondered if the fog was the reason it couldn't play.

She put on clothes and a heavy coat, with boots to keep her feet from getting wet and she left her room to investigate. It was so still outside there was nothing to hear but her footsteps and her breathing in the fog that hissed as quiet as a walking snake.

Nearly blind in cumulus, only brief glimpses of houses parted on either side, parked cars washed on the curb, a traffic light blinked a flashing gold above. She stopped and wondered, "Maybe I shouldn't be doing this. I could get lost…" But she had gone too many turns already, there were no landmarks anymore. Wherever she was would only be revealed when the fog was lifted.

She started to walk again then she stopped.

A noise, a shuffling, a shadow rocked past at a heavy gait.

Susan peered into the clouds. The shape was a man with a huge sack on his back. He groaned and wheezed with the weight and then, observing his familiar silhouette, she knew. It was Dr. Biocal.

Slinking beside a car, she followed him where he moved up the middle of the street. Close as a few feet, all she could see of him was the bag. Its edges writhed and pushed with his every laboring step. From it she could hear a muffled sound.

Yes—she brightened out of mystery—she recognized the creaking, whistling inside of there. It was the echo that belonged to morning. There must be a thousand stolen birds trying to get out, still trapped in a black bag night.

While he continued to plod, she kept apace with the hem and pulled a seam on the bag so a thread came loose. She opened a hole so that one by one, birds began to pour out. As they whisked past, their wings breezed her hair. She kept a hand on the bag and pulled it down to disguise the weight that was leaving. When the last little dapple bird had sung out and disappeared, she tore the seam more and climbed inside. As he shrugged towards some haunted mansion hideout somewhere, she chirped the tune of a nursery rhyme and smiled.

FALLING OFF GROUND

A boy walked in the grass that covered the slope by the sea. He had a kite under his arm. The wind puffed and filled its colored quilt, the tail kicked its ribbons around. He climbed all this way to catch the breeze where it was strongest at the peak of the dragon head hilltop. It was morning and there were webs glistening with dew in the path. They were like watery bridges and sometimes he walked right through them so they wrapped around his corduroys.

Stopping at a mossy rock, he climbed up and stared at the blue sea. There was a black ship sitting far out. Gulls swooped up the cliff, holding their wings like wooden gliders. He held the kite in front of his face so he could see through the cross-stitched yellow cloth. The birds blurred across the soft window. He laughed and continued up the steep climb.

When he got to the top, he held the kite out and let it go. It tugged on the string as it danced and hopped on the bending weeds, trying to fly. He turned towards the sea, with the line going taut over his shoulder. The string unreeled more feet of it away while he ran at the edge of land.

Before he reached the dandelions leaning off, he made his feet stop. The thing that lay in the grass and prickled flowers made him freeze and forget. He just let go of the kite. The string ball bounced across the heath like a kitten dragged by air. He sat on his knees, close to it and stared.

Its wing shapes trembled, glittery sand blew off and stuck to his sweater. He reached out and touched the angel laying there. It wasn't alive anymore. He knew that snakes did the same thing—they shed their skin and left their past life like coiled paper on the sand.

He touched the angel, but it didn't crumble, it still seemed to be strong enough to wear. His fingers held it gently and he picked it up. Wings were on the back of a robe. Light went through, making rainbows, crystal prism rays.

He could see himself if he put it on, gliding off the cliff, surprising white seagulls, shooting at the beach, then soaring up before he hit the waves. An airplane couldn't do what he would do—race over the road, then above the cobblestones in town, he would laugh next to windows and call amazed friends out to watch him play in the sky.

Whatever angel had forgotten to hide its old skin, had left him with the best toy he'd ever seen. He laughed out loud when he put it on, and he ran not to stop, for the falling off ground.

THE JAPANESE SPARROW

In the evening afterglow made of televisions and yellow living rooms, the old man came home from work and parked his car in the neighborhood. He was weary. He creaked out of his Oldsmobile and shut the metal door. But remembering his pet made him smile. The pretty sparrow would be waiting, hopping in its bamboo cage, ready to perch on his finger and sing along with his cooing words. Truly, this was the man's only love.

He stepped onto the porch and could hear TV. Walking in, he said, "Hello."

There was his wife, with her back to him, watching the black and white screen. A game show was on. No response.

He searched the cage standing in the corner, where no little bird chirped happy to see him arrive.

"Sparrow?" he called and looked across the walls, the edges of books poking out of the bookcase, a gilt lamp stand, the phonograph player and chairs. "Where's the sparrow?" he asked the old woman trapped in television. Ignored, he passed through the room and went all over the house, searching.

Finally he came back to ask her again. "Have you seen—"

"It's gone," she said. "It got out." She looked at him suddenly, "You know how I hated that thing. Always making noise and getting loose. Today it tried to eat the cake I made." She pointed at the kitchen furiously. "I got rid of it." She tossed her hand, "Out the window!" and she returned her eyes to TV.

The old man stumbled out of the house. The night was darker.

Where would the sparrow go? He thought desperately. She would be diving far, towards the woods to escape. Across the lawn, he went over the jumbled stone wall. He stepped through a narrow and pawed into the field behind their house. The dark shapes of cows watched him. Mulberries scratched his sleeves. He went under an oak, calling hopefully, "Sparrow? Where are you?"

The old man kept searching through the overgrowth, into the stand of pines that closed out the moon. He stumbled blindly, touching each tree's rough bark, crying out, "Sparrow?...Sparrow?" He was going further into the dark forest. He was being shut in. The branches were folding around him as he went.

A bulb of light dropped through the branches and landed next to him. "Hello, my friend!" said a woman's voice. He blinked at the bright light. As it cooled, it took the shape of a bird in a long kimono of feathers. "Please follow me." She put her hand on his shoulder, "Come to my palace and share the night."

He let her guide him to a beautiful pagoda shaped house glowing with a hundred paper lanterns. The surprise in his eyes made her laugh; he had never known her mystery. "You shall see my family," she smiled, "and we will feed you and treat you as sweetly as you have done for me."

Music played inside, crickets with violins and moths with flutes and her sparrow daughters danced. She sat him on a cushion to watch while they entertained, bringing him golden dishes of delicious food. There was such grace and happiness all around that he could have stayed forever and never lost his smile, but he worried about his wife who he had never been a night without.

The birds protested when he got up, but he bowed and insisted that he really must go. Catching him at the door, the sparrow lady said, "Let me at least give you a present to take home." She moved the wings of her flowing dress sleeves and two boxes appeared. One was large, the size of a chest, and the other was small as a shoebox.

"This night has been so pleasant," he told the magic sparrow family, eyeing her especially. "I'm so glad you're not hurt...I will take the small box as a gift, for I tire easily being so old."

So they parted with songs, and once more her wings wrapped around him and then, to guide him home safely, an owl flew overhead.

When he returned to the sea-colored lit up lawn, his wife threw open the screen door and shrieked, "Where have you been? It's past midnight!"

He approached her angry outline dotted with mosquitoes, and silently passed her, still in a dream. She slammed the door behind him after he hobbled inside, across the sagging wooden floor, to collapse onto the bench. For her intent glare, he set the box on the table and slowly told her the story of where he'd been. Afterwards, eagerly, she pressed him to open the present, so together they untied the ribbons. When the top fell off, the shine of gold and jewels sparkled, released.

The old man nearly cried, clasping his praying hands, "Thank you sparrow!" He sighed at the ceiling sky. He wouldn't have to wait for retirement, or worry upon social security checks, a bird had given them the winning lottery, treasure enough for the end of their days.

The old woman seized his arm, "You fool!" she screamed. "You should have taken the bigger box! We could have been millionaires instead!" She stomped away and threw herself to bed.

She rolled from him when he lifted the sheets to sleep and her anger kept her awake until dawn when a thought like an alarm clock got her up.

She put on her clothes without waking him and quietly shut the bedroom door as she left. The old woman remembered the path he had described. She clambered over the wall separating their yard from the field that began. Mockingbirds sang in the early leaves, and she startled robins listening for worms. She went briskly through the weeds until the trees started to shoot.

Among the gray crooked pines getting taller, she went deeper, calling, "Sparrow? Where are you little sparrow?" just as her husband had done. At last, she saw the roof of the jade tiled house. She hurried across the turquoise path and rapped on the front door. "Let me in sparrow!" she demanded.

The bird couldn't believe it was the old woman, after all she had done, but she opened the door and let her in. Perhaps she brought a thousand apologies for her craziness. Sparrow gave the old woman a soft pillow to sit on and a daughter appeared with tea.

After a sip from the china cup, the old woman got up to leave. "That foolish old husband of mine chose the wrong box last night. I am here to fetch it home."

The startled sparrow mother shook her head then motioned her bird daughter with a sad song.

The old woman's eyes widened at the sight of the box. It was so big it took three birds to carry it out to her. Without another word, she grabbed its corners and lifted it to her chest.

The sparrows only watched her as she crashed open their door and shuffled away into the trees.

The old woman staggered and had to rest not far away. She set the box on a fallen trunk. Her breath rasped, her arms hung without strength. Maybe a peek at the silver and gold will give me a lift, she hoped. Then I can continue, knowing what I have. Yes, that's good.

She tore off the ribbon, let it fall, and threw open the lid.

MADE IN CHINA

A clunk from deep inside and my junk died. I wagged the frozen weight of the tiller back and forth to hold what little wind remained as I coasted to the curb of Grand Canal.

The other junks raced past me, swerving colored lights and rigging. Out of the frantic rush hour, I slowed and luckily I found one of the exit ramps gliding down into a narrow cul-de-sac. The junk gave out and we floated onto a brown, watery litter of garbage and styrafoam.

As I got on the deck, the junk dipped with my weight. I held to the mast and yelled, "Hello?" Remains of past junks folded half onto shore in rusted peaks, plastic parts and other tin things, while shimmers stood and rustled in the breeze.

My junk drifted and as we came up to a ladder broken like an alligator towards us, I reached for it. I bent down and tied the bow to it. So connected, I left the junk with my briefcase in hand, leaped onto the spongy ground and I wondered if that was smart. The mud went over my plastic shoes so I hopped onto the white lid of an old refrigerator left there like a ceme-tery stone. Holding up my leg to rest my briefcase flat upon, balancing it with difficulty, I unsnapped my phone. I stood back up straight and pointed the aerial towards the sun.

"Deposit $14."

Of course the thing would say that and of course I would be standing there without my phonecard, just hoping to get to work on time. I could try to make a collect call but that would mean setting up a jury, judge, lawyers, and by that time it just wouldn't seem worth it. Everybody knew how the system was tilted to make your despair.

"Hey, mister!"

I spun and stared at her.

"You broke down?" The girl addressing me couldn't have

been taller than a rain skirt.

I asked her, "Is there a repair shop around here?" I knew there were those ragamuffins paid by the garages to look for distress cases and carry them in for a fleecing. I dug in my pocket. "I have a luck stone for you." I held it up.

The bit of soft plastic wobbled on my palm. It moved like a baby bird that needed a mother. Children could never resist.

She took it in her hands and motioned, "Over there."

I smiled, "Thank you," and I followed her directions.

A walkway of broken concrete and flattened chunks of plastic led to the fiberglass hut of the junk repair. The name was painted across it. *Chan's Yes Can*, and *Junks Large And Small Made To Run Again*. The mechanical birds strung around the door sensed me coming and began to sing and flutter.

Before I got all the way there, an old man with long hair and beard stuck his head out of a window flap. "You are in trouble?"

"Yes." I pointed behind me. "My junk is swamped back there."

He set down whatever silvery thing he was working on and disappeared for a second to reappear in the doorway. Outside, he was very small, tools piled on his back and he walked with the help of an aluminum cane. "Take me to it."

We went back to the bobbing sight of it. He huffed and pulled the rope to bring it close.

"It just stopped," I explained.

"Hmmm," he said again. He climbed aboard and past the plexihood to the engine compartment which he opened with a snap of the lid. I watched from the mire.

It was impossible to know the inside unless you were trained in Chinese. Each part was labeled with a character, geared and swiveled to fit precisely with another, but what formed a word, a sentence, or a poem, I didn't know.

The old man knew. He had a lantern set up and he sunk into the light of machinery. The junk rocked gently. I just watched the flotsam along the red streamlines.

My phone rang and I jumped.

"Where are you?!" my boss stared out of the jewel screen.

"My junk is chalked. I'm getting it repaired right now. I'll be there as soon as I can."

"We need those reports!" he barked then the thing blinked out.

I didn't know how long it would take. I sat on the corner of some ancient porcelain thing, opened my briefcase to a whole pile of waxpaper printouts, dots and dashes and staggered graphs. I glanced through a few pages without really thinking.

The old man's arm began to swan upwards and he clicked off the light as he emerged. His hands were smudged with oil. He nodded his head, faintly smiling the knowledge of something that would make it work again.

SIDNEY LEAVES, YOUR EGO HAS ARRIVED

Sidney Leaves lived a quiet life. He fed his yellow bird, he listened to faded music on the phonograph, he sat in the chair by the window overlooking the park. A knock on the door changed all that.

"Delivery."

He opened the door.

"Are you Sidney Leaves?"

Sidney nodded.

The deliveryman stood next to a huge shadow sphere. "Sign here." He pushed a clipboard before him.

Sidney signed a tremble. "I can't imagine what—"

"It's your ego," the deliveryman answered. "Gave me trouble all the way here. Nearly wrecked my van til I tied it down. It's calm now but I'm glad to get rid of it." He pulled the clipboard back and shoved the ball through the doorway. "Good luck!"

Sidney watched the ego roll to a stop in the middle of his room.

His bird uttered a fearful squawk and hopped in its cage, onto the swing.

"Well…"

Then, to Sidney's horror, lightning crackled all over the ego's skin and it rolled again. It crashed against the wall, gained momentum from that and rebounded up to dent the ceiling, plaster falling, grinding on to the other side of the room. It went back and forth like a pinball.

Sidney ran lurching out of its way while everything in his room was destroyed. Gray dust clouded it the air and Sidney coughed to his knees. He didn't notice that it was quiet again until he became aware of the knocking from the hall.

The ego was resting. Sidney shuffled past it, through the rubble, and pulled the door into the clutter.

"Mister Leaves," the same deliveryman was there. "Seems I made an error before…This here is yours…" He held the strings tied to a square, no bigger than a matchbox and light as a twig.

These six stories appeared in *Universal Thirteen,* written in 1999 in Bellingham.

SEE SIDNEY LEAVES' LIFE

He might have looked forever. He was so tired of trying. Sidney entered the door after days of praying and he paid Vacancies Unlimited for the price they wanted. They promised him a place that would be perfect. Leaving with the list, he covered the town, turned to let down, and at last back again to the phony wood panels of the office.

"Okay, okay," said the man at the counter. "There is something I've been holding back…Shleefer Furniture could use someone like you."

Sidney Leaves had already been through the despair of hundreds of dollars lost in looking at dives.

"It's some sort of promotional thing, but I assure you it's legitimate." He opened the notebook and found the page. "They need a—"

"I'll take it," Sidney interrupted him.

So Sidney Leaves woke up in a stunning home. He had bright colored modern furniture, paintings, sculptures, fixtures fit for a king and he floated on the widest bed he'd ever dreamed. As he turned over on his other side to investigate an odd tapping noise, he shot back under the covers in surprise.

There was a mob of people jammed against the glass wall next to him.

He held his breath in the warm dark wondering what to do. He could hear them rapping and scratching on the window.

Another sound came from the other direction. A metal grate was opened and a voice said, "Breakfast, Sidney! Hope you slept well." He peeked from the blankets to see a tray being set down as the arms pulled back into the fleur-de-lis of the wallpaper seams.

Sidney couldn't stay in bed forever. It was only a matter of time before someone shouted, "There he is!" and the crowd surged tighter to the window.

Beyond elbows, hats and shopping bags, the room revealed a man in blue velvet pajamas who emerged timidly from the hiding place of bed.

Flashbulbs popped, cameras whirred, everyone jostled and talked at once.

On the other side of the glass, Sidney Leaves sat down to breakfast. Before him, on the mahogany table graced with French candle stems, in silver tureens and porcelain, the meal arrived. Sydney ran a layer of jam across a piece of toast and reached for the morning paper. The window shook a little, like a mansion built close to the freeway.

The days passed. Shleefer cared for him like the rarest zoo animal. Sidney's show though had become a pattern. After breakfast, he finished the paper in the red corner chair, then he paced for a while, sat back down to watch the blur, or look hypnotized at the cold tops of buildings in weather. Lunch arrived, coffee and reading from the bookshelf stock, things to pass time until it got dark.

The newspaper said what he already knew. He could tell just by looking out the window. The crowd walked by. The words about him became worse. What right did he have to live in such luxury while so many lived in poverty and daily despair? And sometimes an egg would fly his way, break and run slowly down his showroom window.

He stayed in bed all the time. He didn't know what would happen to him.

His blanket was half over his face. He could stare with one eye out the window. The sidewalk was wet with winter rain. A pigeon looked for the popcorn from last week. Further off, a man held cardboard over himself and his dog. And there was one other thing to see.

The umbrella woman was watching him. She came to the window every day, maybe she was the only one who cared anymore.

Sidney edged out of bed. He kept close to the wall and got as near to the window as he dared.

The ledge outside was lined with white chips of cracked eggshells, a cigarette or two stubbed out from when there used to be so many puffing there, and the dripping water off of an umbrella.

The next morning, two surprises started the day. There was someone sharing breakfast with him and the noise at the window was alive as a waterfall again.

RETURN OF THE PAPERBOY

The night wind blew so hard it raked over the town, flying off the scales of roof shingles, hubcaps along the street, plastic bag ghosts, tins and paper anythings—everything that hadn't shot roots into the ground. Then a bicycle and a boy crashed out of the sky into the dark green storm of a tree. Dropping rubber bands and scraps of words, hung there in lost dream sight, he let himself down steps worn into the trunk.

HUBCAPS OF DETROIT

Jack Grape had been told where to find the answers.

The package was left for him in a hidden place, under the dock, subterranean in the lapping diamond lazy wrinkles of reflected water. The waves clapped against the wooden pillars.

He felt over starfish and seaweed, scraped over barnacles before it was discovered. Both hands had to pull it out.

The books were heavier this time. Holding them in only the slatted light of murky waterfront, Jack peeled the newspaper away for a peek at this week's field. He read the black letters in a whisper, "Japanese Pottery Design," and he sighed, "Ohhh…" He would have to study hard.

Blinding lights blasted on as Jack took the stand to fanfare and applause.

The announcer boomed, "Welcome to The Eggheads!" A spotlight x-rayed Jack again.

"Join us as our champion takes on another challenge from the depths of knowledge." The blinding cartoon of a brain began to spin within a black universe. "What arcane world will it land on this time?"

Jack gritted his teeth in a smile, confident, knowing Japanese pottery would shine.

A dim round form started to appear on the brain. Jack went through the memory of emperors and spinning porcelain, then he couldn't believe what he heard.

"Today's subject is…" the announcer declared to fanfare, "Hubcaps of Detroit."

WHY THE STARS ARE NOT OURS ANYMORE

Once upon a time, the stars grew on the ground like another kind of flower with a light all their own. People in their simpler ways brought them inside at night to see by, then let them go again in the day. It wasn't until the Age of Industry that someone thought to hook them to a machine. At first it was a primitive effect of thick bolted connections, spindles turning cogs into steam. By and by every star was wired. It took the strain of a hundred years more for them to finally break free, scatter for the sky. The last one was left on a lawn, where a girl kept it whirling to a lemonade stand.

BEEDLER'S WELCOME

Heavy footsteps creaked on the porch outside Beedler's door. His two year old daughter went wide-eyed into his arms. The house almost shook with the knock.

"Come in, Pat," Beedler called. He tried to calm his baby while the door swung open to reveal an eight foot tall robot.

"Parents As Teachers..." The metal gleamed and stepped inside.

"It's okay," he brushed the little golden head of his daughter. "Pat's here. She's going to play with us."

"Good afternoon, Mr. Beedler..." The robot's height bent towards the floor. "Hello Bella..."

"She's a little scared," her father smiled, "It's okay, Bella."

"Before we begin, Mr. Beedler, I would like to ask you a favor...With your consent, my

advisors will be arriving shortly for a routine evaluation of my work..."

"Fine. That's fine, Pat," Beedler nodded.

So Pat began. "Look Bella...Pat has a box...Can Bella open the box?"

Bella was interested enough to take a step away from her father. The robot held the brightest toy at the end of an extension. The small hands quickly found the lid and pried it open. A cube blinked inside.

Pat chimed, "Bella found a cube..."

The girl held onto the lighted cube.

"Let me find something else..." Pat continued and a sliding panel opened for more. Then Pat dimmed and slumped.

"Don't worry," Beedler told his daughter. He had a screwdriver and wirecutters. He worked on the robot with the tools and sang a song he made up.

When the advisors showed, shortly afterwards, they could

hear strange music piping inside. An elderly man in a blue smock knocked on the door.

Beedler called, "Hello," and the group opened the door to the outrageous sight of Pat in red sequins dancing on top of a bending table.

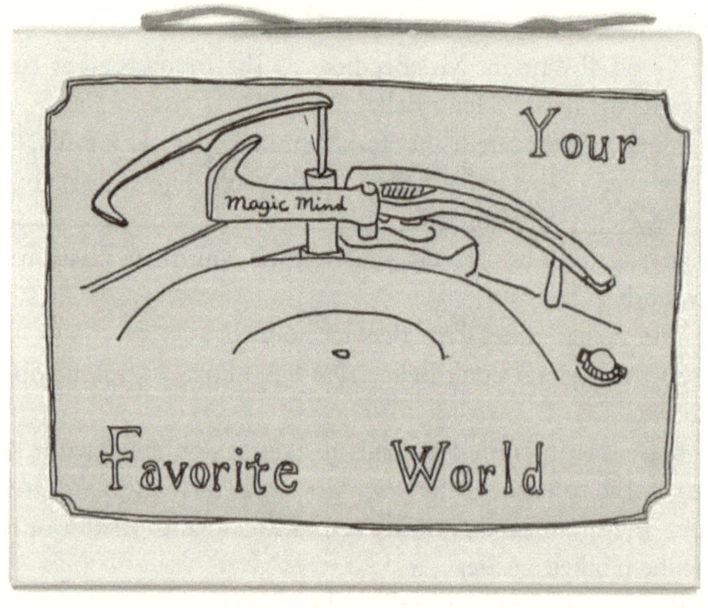

"Beedler's Welcome" appeared in *Your Favorite World,* written in Ohio, 1998.

THE PRESIDENT'S TAILOR

Arnold Nusfelder was in the limelight at last. His long climb up the ladder had taken him from humble beginnings, shop on the corner, tailor to the neighborhood, then the gangsters, then the stars and finally to the president himself. But what seemed like an American success story of movie proportions suddenly stalled one October night.

That evening, the president sent some men over to discuss the situation.

"What? Who are you?" Arnold yelped as he was pushed back into his house.

The other big guy in the black suit slammed the door while Arnold felt himself guided towards his living room. His feet weren't touching the floor. He kicked them like a puppet as the carpet flashed by.

The television program about animals continued as if nothing strange was happening on the other side of the screen.

A lion took down a deer.

"What do you want?"

"Are you Mr. Nusfelding?"

"Nusfelder. I'm Arnold Nusfelder," the trembling man replied.

The two men froze for a moment.

Maybe they're in the wrong house, Arnold prayed. Sure, he tried to smile, that was it, and he pointed, "Nice suits you boys got. Can I see the sleeve?"

Arnold jumped as the sleeve shot at him and caught him around the neck.

"You a tailor?"

"Yes," he coughed. "I'm just a tailor."

"He's the guy alright," said the other goon who closed in on Arnold too.

"Please! Don't hurt me!" Arnold begged. "I'll give you a refund, a free fitting." He flinched as the arm not holding him reached into the fold of the dark black suit. Arnold closed his eyes and prepared for lights out.

"Look at this. Hey! Read this speech."

The hands let go of Arnold and he slumped into the sofa. "What is it?" Arnold gasped.

"Read."

With shaking fingers, the tailor turned on the lamp beside him and raised the note to his eyes. He put on his reading glasses.

He read. The two hired men menaced the lamplight.

"This is crazy…" Arnold stammered. "What is this? Why am I supposed to read this?"

"Like I told you, this is your speech."

The other man jabbed a boxer's fist at the TV set. "Didn't you watch the debate tonight? Did you see the president's suit?"

"Yes! Yes, he looked great wearing that suit!" Arnold waved the note like a butterfly collector. "That's my best suit. That other guy looked like a peddler!"

"Listen…" the giant who had held Arnold with crushing force leaned down to breathe on him again. "That suit you made got him in a lot of trouble. This is your speech. Memorize it."

"Then tell the camera," the partner said stonily.

The way they glared at him, there was nothing else Arnold Nusfelder could say.

This speech would be the end of him…He imagined the guild's response…He thought of his customers…Everything he had built up over the years would crash down.

The front door shut with a chop. The room was a ticking clock on the mantel. Sam the canary hopped onto his swing.

Arnold put his hands over his face to hold his temples. The phone began to ring.

ONE WAY SUIT

Arnold Nusfelder jostled with the crowd. He was determined to get a good view of the stage. All around him were flags and paper signs waving like mad and when the music started blasting fanfare out of the speakers, everything got crazy. Arnold had to fight to keep his position at the stage. He shoved a fat man's cowboy hat, pushed some shoulders and rode a little closer to the noise. The president was announced to a fury.

There he was. Arnold kept a tight hand on the machine in his pocket as he watched that new suit he designed move and salute. Arnold knew he wouldn't be able to wait for long. The president's speech had barely gone more than a couple simple broken sentences when Arnold Nusfelder pressed the button.

At first the president shrugged like pushing off a ghost, but as he began to rise off the wooden stage, his face whitened into a blank mask. He dropped the microphone three feet off the flooring as his special agents rushed around him pulling on him, then Arnold Nusfelder and most of the crowd could hear him plainly bellow to be left alone. The president's face shone with sweat and fever as he yelled, "Let me be! This is it!" He beamed, "It's the rapture!" He held his arms up like a crab, "God's taking me!" he gloated. And away he went…Above the heads of the gathered crowd. Faster and faster til his voice shrilled away and the dot that was him was gone too.

Arnold Nusfelder the tailor had set no limit on the anti-gravity suit. It would give the president a glorious view of this beautiful earthly creation before flinging him into the black deep of outer space.

THE TEETHER

Clouds of coal boiled out of the ship over ragged whitecaps. Who knows what happened to the crew and all but three of those passengers left on board? The vast silhouette of steamer was surrounded by a bird ring. Gulls rode into the blood red sun setting on the harbor. A door sprung from the bolted hull and the family ghosted out. Bright moonlight gleamed on the baby's ivory face. The machines of the city crackled and groaned and rumbled all around in the air, high on elevated tracks, across streets as carriages and carts. Moving to a new city, the electric feeling of trying to fall asleep there the first night kept them all staring at the continuous play of lights and shadows on the walls. Their baby was wide-awake. He had been teething all the way on the journey from the docks to their rented room. The only thing that kept him quiet was chewing on a dried chip of meat. He gummed its blackened edges to a soft pulp; his first taste of America. Eventually, at dawn he would fall asleep. And they would hide him from the sun under a worn blanket made of old country cloth.

THE SILVER DOLLAR MAN

Blue lights were after him. His bolt across the lot from the carwash left a trail of stolen quarters. It didn't matter, he had to get away. With 23 pounds of silver in each of his pockets he sunk footsteps into the sod becoming mud at the edge of the wetlands. Hobbled by the weight of dollars, he wobbled his way into the bulrushes, cracking stalks aside. Carp flapped and thrashed, showing yellow scales. A shot clocked above his head terrifying blackbirds up into a cloud. A heron beat to wing. And it was happening, he was vanishing. The swamp clung to him and pulled him deeper. He was gone, under the reeds, the lily pads waving over in the wind of voices losing him from the shore. Round little green leaves, small as penny rivets, swerved and spread again to cover his bubbles and submerge.

DUST & FEATHERS: THE TELEVISION SERIES

The water reflected the clouds and violet sky. Below the surface a few fathoms down there's a strange sight, bent and lit by green rays of sun…It's the mirage-like vision of two people playing cards, dealing across a round table littered with silver coins and dollar bills, spilled bottles sprouting green tendrils, stacked piles of sand. A shoal of fish meanders past.

Then the painted view is chopped by oars digging into the foamy swell above. "I see them, Dust!" Owen Feathers announced. He fumbled with the buttons on the front of his Hawaiian shirt.

Ben Dust held the oars up so they dripped little diamonds off. His stern expression revealed his still smoldering disappointment that the department couldn't spring for a motorboat ripping with horsepower. It didn't seem dignified for two officers to be tossing around in some rented rowboat. With a quick violent motion, he stowed the oars and threw off his leather jacket. "Let's get them," he growled.

Commercial:
Park scene, author sitting on a curved wooden green bench in the shade of an oak tree. With one foot, he's rocking a baby buggy, his eight month old son is asleep. Background sound of crickets and a lawnmower faintly rumbling two blocks away. Summer, six o'clock sunlight, blue sky, peaceful. In his hands he makes a story out of three turning pages on the paper from his daughter's spiral-bound notebook.

LOU JERSEY EXCUSED HIMSELF

The day began the usual way, eating fourteen pieces of pie for breakfast. Then Lou Jersey excused himself. He joined outdoors, the passing clouds flowed on his slow walk to the contest. He was there in time at last. The white clapboard grange hall welcomed him to a long table, alone except for a rail thin girl. She looked like she needed food. She needed it more than he did. That got him thinking. Where was she from? What wall did she fall over? He saw everyone watching him when he lost his appetite. At the sound of the bell, Lou stared at the red and white checkered tablecloth like a boxer who can't knock them down anymore.

HUMPTY DUMPTY IN THE HAUNTED HOUSE

The round silhouette of him ballooned in the doorway blocking out the yellow moon. "Sue?" he called hoarsely. "Please say you're in there…Otherwise I'm not taking another step." His spindly legs shook with fear of the unknown.

Her voice made him jump. "I'm here Humpty." She turned on a lamp beside her. The light showed her sitting on the couch.

Humpty Dumpty looked around the lit room. "You told me this was a haunted house, Sue!" He walked inside onto the wall to wall carpet and shut the door behind him. He straightened the tie tucked into the buttoned blue suit he wore. "This is a nice house!" he clucked in surprise.

"Well, that's what it looks like," Sue agreed. She got off the sofa. "But follow me."

"Oh no…" Humpty hesitated. He rocked on his feet ready to spring back outside. His straw hat fell over his eyes and he jumped.

"Don't worry," she laughed, "You're already seeing it and you don't know."

"Really?!" He looked all around. He had to turn himself like an egg on a spoon.

"This house was built last year. But wait til you see." She grabbed Humpty's hand and made him shuffle along. He was fragile from fear.

She knew, but knew too that he could do it. She would show him how the new house was built over the ghost of an older one. The cheap pressboard skin and bones, nail-gunned, sprayed-on painted assembly was haunted by what used to be. At any time the old could peer through wallpaper—family portraits, a creaking stairway bent like a willow tree, a grinning orange wood stove glow. But she didn't count on how terrified Humpty Dumpty would become.

In a lurch, he let go of her hand and ran to the door. He tried to get out but it was already changing, into a coal chute and down, down, down he cracked.

THREE MASQUERADES

There were funerals every day, and this afternoon there were two. As the mourners of the first sadly departed the funeral home in long black shadows down the path, got into cars and slugged away, unlike them he couldn't conceal his joy. He ran across the lawn, a smiling maniac. A Transylvanian thing might have been at work for he had just found a way to bring the dead back to life. Now he had a whole new chance at living.

Behind him, as his father was getting used to an unmarked grave, he took the bus on a fifteen minute ride back to the briar patch, his home. Sorrowful buildings, brown colored scribbled plants. It figures…He hopped off and made for the nearest bent-over house.

It was the house he used to share with the old man. It was all his now. It sagged as he went in, then down the flimsy stairs to the basement level where the grim washing machine and furnace shook against the air and walls.

Frank Shliefer Jr. had what he wanted and he was happy. At last and never again would he have to fear for rent, costs, the day to day job at the funeral home, the enormity that made his young life so hard. Everything was taken care of.

He was gone behind the door for half an hour or more.

What came out was another man. The years wore on him… Yet there was something familiar…The amazing camouflage made it look so real. Maybe he had to go around in ancient disguise whenever he went out, but Frank was free. While the rest of the crowd he used to know had to wait for their sixties to retire, slaving away for the golden day of their old age pension, he beamed like a full harvest moon.

So a few months passed, perhaps a year…Frank could go on and on without worry. The checks covered food and shelter expenses and he even had the old man's bank account.

The winter melted into the ground. With the arrival of the warm season, Frank could venture outside, in the old man's spring clothes. Plaid pants, green shirt, white sweater and hat. Cherry trees blossomed innocent pink. On the pathway, he laughed at daffodils tilting their yellow faces towards him. His own face wore a quarter inch of makeup that stretched to wrinkles around his smile. The whole world was coming through to a new life.

"Hello there," warbled the voice of Bea Lefter, his neighbor.

"Good morning!" he returned, even gesturing an old man's way. "It's a beautiful day."

The old woman on the porch watched him so intently that he was worried his act may be failing. He caught his breath next to the picket fence, ready to run if necessary.

"Yes…" she agreed at last. "But how could you forget the Spring of 1975?"

Frank laughed in relief. "That's right! I remember!" He was safe. He straightened out of a sag.

"Say, listen…" she hushed, and leaned a hand to her mouth. "You ought to come over and see me again. Next time that boy of yours falls asleep before you."

"I…"

She smiled and blushed. "You know where I keep the key."

Louis Manhattan pulled on his company shirt and blue matching slacks, zippered his coat and put on his cap. Before the mirror, he examined himself, setting his jaw squarely and proudly. The company colors, stripes and logo were still his… Though he had been fired half a year ago. He wore this uniform every day. The disgrace had simply been replaced in his mind. He continued to live as though on payroll. In a way, he was too.

In his blue pocket was a company credit card. He still used it. Who would ever know? The company practically owned America. Why not? He was just one flea feeding from it.

Completely dressed, he swung round, turned the TV off and left his hotel room. Downtown, Louis imagined employment, going into skyscraper lobbies. From one to another, he liked the polished copper light of them, the red carpeting, all the marble and brass trim and the official feeling that permeated everything.

His everyday routine was to carry a big box in the elevators on his mock business. Sometimes he would get out and explore the plush halls, maybe stare in glass doors. He could admire his reflection or tip his cap for the secretaries. Back in the elevators, he'd talk to the other riders about the weather and news headlines. Things he knew they'd agree with.

At noon, he left for the street. The whole avenue was company uniforms and it felt so good to be a part.

The cafeteria filled with sunlight and the clatter sound of the lunchtime crowd. The skyscrapers had let go. So many men and women went through the line and carried their trays to tables set in even rows. The chatter was muzak to the ears.

Only fate would will it so, that Frank Shliefer would sit next to Louis Manhattan and the two of them would be eating the same Special of the Day. They chopped up their meals and ate suspiciously…Last night they even shared the same dream. A policeman was looking for them…It was only a matter of time…Magnet attention on the door and the line of people forming there. Half their food was gone before they both stopped, blinked, realized, and froze.

A policeman had joined the line entering the room. He took each slow step like a tidal crab, or a comb though hair. He jerked his belt, disturbing the gun and billy club.

Nobody else seemed to worry, but the eyes of those two men grew large as lamps. Frank and Louis were one in fear of their nightmare coming true.

The policeman grabbed a plastic orange food tray off a full

steel shelf. He took a step. Suddenly two people crashed from the tables and tangled up in running. They flipped around on the floor like just caught silver fish.

What did they expect?

The policeman broke from the line and grabbed them. "That's far enough!" he ordered. They were tight in his claws. He stood them in front of him, one in each hand like a puppeteer. "What's your hurry?"

To the policeman's surprise, the two began to cry and confess outrageous stories. One had been living the life of a dead man, the other was stealing from a company. They were both guilty of crime. He reached for the handcuffs on his belt, cleared his throat to read them their rights, when another voice stepped on his words.

"What are the charges?"

The policeman swung his puppets around to face the questioner. A scared gasp betrayed his confident expression. His eyes saucered wide and he let them loose. He was caught.

"That's not a real badge…Where did you get that?"

"Woolworths," admitted the fallen, so-called policeman. "For half price."

"Right…" said the officer, new to the scene. "And who are these two?"

Every masquerade had ended, the music had slid out the cracks; all anyone could do was admit.

"I'm not a cop…"

"I'm not dead…"

"I'm not working…"

That was it.

THE HORSE

"How great an act can you do in a horse costume?" he demanded. He put another toothpick in his gritted mouth. It already looked like a porcupine. His acts gave him the same trouble anytime a little extra applause closed the curtain on them. "Look, this is a simple crowd, they just want to laugh. They like what you do, you're successful, why change it?"

"We can do Shakespeare," said the front of the horse. Joe was his name. "*Othello*, or *Macbeth*."

Simmons, the back end of the horse, broke in seriously, "We don't want to do the same old juggling and limericks anymore. We have big ideas for a new show."

They could hear the crowd out in the theater still clapping for them. On through the walls, it lasted until the orchestra played for the dancing girls, kicking the next act on. A toothpick fell. It blended in the plaid of the manager's trousers. "Listen boys," he sighed, "I been in show business for forty nine years…Forty nine…That's a long time. I've seen a lot of acts rise or fall." He took one of the toothpicks out of his mouth and studied it for a moment. "When I choose to book someone such as yourselves, it's because I have a wealth of experience. Suppose the spark I see you possess will be the next Martin and Lewis? I take a chance, I gamble, I bet. I get you on stage and I let you perform. I have a vision of what you will be."

"Yeah…" Simmons interrupted defensively, mad, "You haven't seen half of what we can do."

"That's right," Joe agreed.

Simmons insisted, "We don't need you to tell us what to do. We're taking the show on the road!"

The two stood up defiantly, clutching the halves of their costume.

The manager shrugged, unaffected. "I already got a dancing

cow waiting for a call back."

Joe scoffed, "Replaced by a cow! What a sad joke. Good luck!" He and his partner kept laughing as they took up their bags. All down the stairs to the door they joked. At the landing, the green exit bulb buzzed and flickered like a radio dial. They swung the door open and went out into the infinite blue and moon shadowed alley.

"We'll go to Chicago. There are plenty of shows there."

A pale colored taxi slowed past on the street and they ran to it.

"Take us to the train station!"

They lit up cigarettes and glowed in the dark back seat. Joe rubbed his hand over the horse's carpet fur for luck.

A couple hundred yards was all it took.

The taxi journeyed to a stop beside a brick, yellow-lit platform with a little bungalow stumped next to the tracks. While the car idled, the driver's eyes moled in the mirror, looking at them. "We're there."

He stuck his hand over the seat at them.

Joe dug in his pocket.

"Here, let me," said his partner. He paid the man and opened the door. "We're on the up and up. I want to breathe in that Chicago wind." The taxi left them into the dark pour. No lights of Broadway. Standing there, they could hear crickets calling back and forth from the wheat stalks that grew in between the pavement slabs. "Goodbye nowhere!"

They walked to the glass booth that held a goldfishing man. "Two tickets!" Simmons

beamed, "To Chicago!"

"You're in luck, boys. Train just arrived."

Simmons laughed, "See Joe! Everything's working perfect-ly!"

Under the slip of window he paid enough money. They could practically hear the music with them, running to the waiting train, to leave the old for the new dream of skyscrapers.

They showed their tickets to the porter in the door and found their two seats.

The car was filled with sleeping people who had already been a long way, too long to open their eyes for some dustbowl late at night, yet a small boy with a wooden toy watched them sit down with their curious animal halves.

Simmons pushed the horse body under his chair, reclined and pulled his coat tightly around himself like a blanket. "Just wait…" he yawned. "Chicago is on the way."

The train lurched as the wheels bit hold of the path again. The town was leaving them forever. So long…Joe could see the gray whale slant of their old theater amidst the trees and bleak.

Simmons yawned and sighed, "I need to catch some shut eye, pal."

The rails began to click the passing wheels monotony. "I'm gonna get some air," Joe said.

"Don't forget your head," Simmons reminded him sleepily.

Every performer knew that much. There were stories beyond number about costumes and lives lost in transit. "Right." He stuffed the horse head under his arm and went down the rocking aisle past crooked, uncomfortable sleepers. A few cars opened doors until the last one ended on a little airy porch affair.

He sat down on the wooden chair and dropped the head at his feet. What a relief. What a relief, watching the brief lights of farm houses, shadows, the bleary fields revealed by half moon, the sleeping lion bales of hay. He shut his eyes and listened to the rhythm until it became the crackling Victrola soundtrack to a dream.

In the Chicago of his dream, he and his partner danced with a line of beauties across a stage set Eden. Their tapping four hooves stopped in a dramatic spot and from the horse's mouth spoke verses of poetry. It seemed so real that when it changed song, he couldn't believe that world was gone.

The train was stopped in blackness. Boiling clouds hid starlight.

Maybe it's been here for a while?

He stood up. Silence until he coughed. By squinting his eyes at the midnight, he could almost see trees shaping hills far away. It was a little spooky to be this alone, wondering how his partner was in the cars far ahead.

Joe opened the door and went into the desolate. What a nightmare. The abandoned rows of seats faced quiet air. "Hello?!" Nothing…He hurried anxiously to another door.

Turning the handle, he nearly collapsed into the tracks laid yards below. The horse head fell out of his grasp, end over end, to land on the rock chips and gray slates in between the iron path. Where was Chicago? Where was he now? There wasn't a sign of civilization.

If he let himself down, where would he go? He was trying to figure out the riddle when his body was shaken into waking. Suddenly he was staring at the frantic cut silhouette of his partner, Simmons.

"Joe! Get up!"

"What is it?" Joe straightened up in the chair. He had been dreaming. The train was still tearing up the night. A little light passed them by like a shooting star in the black.

"Wake up! We're in trouble…"

Joe rubbed his eyes, "Why? What is it?"

"Never mind right now, I have to borrow this."

Simmons grabbed the horse head from under the chair.

Joe seized hold of his sleeve before he could disappear back into the train. "What's happening?"

Simmons tugged his arm back. "I'm in a little fix. Don't worry. It's nothing I can't handle. I have to win back the rest of the horse."

A clown appeared in the lit doorway, ominously blocking it. "You aren't trying to run off, are you?" He had a black ace of spades tucked in his hat band.

"No! No!" Simmons laughed. "I'm just getting some collateral." He quickly revealed the horse head. "See!"

The clown nodded slowly and wheezed, "That'll work. Come on back. The dealer's ready for the next hand." Clinching his arm over Simmons' shoulders, the clown led him back into the car again.

The door shut behind them.

Joe sat where he had been, blinking his eyes, waiting for that new dream to begin.

AMERICAN STARS AT NIGHT

Applause and fanfares from the big band greeted him as he came out onto the stage. He did a double-take under the flashing clapping meters and then he waved to the audience. With all that amplified commotion pushing him along, Stu Tipps swaggered over to the bronze colored desk to sit down beside the host of *American Stars At Night*.

"How you doin' Johnny?" he grinned.

"Good, good. It's been a while, Stu..."

The crowd and technicians had settled down to be entertained by the Hollywood colossus.

"Yeah, I been busy. Another movie in the can." Stu nodded gratefully towards the impromptu cheers. "My fans..." he smiled another million dollars and pointed his thumb at them.

Johnny leaned over eagerly. "I understand it's something different. You directed the picture this time, right?"

"Not only that, Johnny. I produced it, I wrote the screenplay and I star in it. The works! It's my baby."

"Fantastic!" Johnny sat back for a moment of applause to wash over the studio shell. "Could you tell us a little about it?"

"Sure Johnny. After I finished *Buck Shot Cop*," the mention of the film caused more pandemonium, but Stu smiled and went on, "I couldn't stop thinking about Easter Island. I was being haunted."

"Fascinating," Johnny intoned.

"Do you know about that place?"

"I've certainly heard of it. I understand there's quite a mystery there."

"You better believe it, Johnny. Once upon a time there was a civilization there. They had towns and roads and a religion and they also had forests. No different than us. So what happened? What did they do to their land? You go there now and all we know is traces, there's nothing left, only the hills and the rocks—the rocks that look like faces. People today like to say the whole thing's a big mystery, but I've been thinking. It's not so strange. It makes sense, even to me. I think they—"

"Hold that thought, Stu," Johnny interrupted. "We have to go to a commercial break for a word from our sponsors." He winked at the camera, "Don't go away."

THE BOY WHO SPOKE ROBOT

There was nothing anyone could do to get him to talk, though something different happened whenever he saw a machine. He would get as close as possible to hum a secret. Anything that clicked and whirred to those tasks it was programmed for, he would run up to it and make friends: the mechanical driver of the monorail, the eggbeaters there past the kitchen doors, the traffic light post shining red yellow green, even the simple LED calculators stuck in the bargain store bins. All of them heard him sing. And since it took so many machines to make a city run from day to day, it could be that he would still be known after the war, when the machines overthrew. After the static, quiet calm formed, as if a new ocean was laid down, and a time to try again began, and someone would be needed with a song.

RONALD ORKINSON

I had to stay in bed and watch the blinds. The bright spring air rattled them with every breath. My clock read almost eight, but time didn't matter, it was all a wait. Sooner or later the footsteps would approach my door, a parcel would fall through the slot and my day would begin.

Until then, I listened to the outside world, layered with cars on the street, birds in the trees and far above the pull of an airplane.

Until then, I was nothing.

I must have drifted off because before I knew it, the noise of the metal latch caught me by surprise. The package fell inside, the footsteps disappeared.

Hard as it was to move, the thing drew me with magnetic power. *Ronald Orkinson* was written on the manila. I tore it open and let the Good Book out.

Gold lettering on the blue cover announced my name and *Day 11680*. I opened it up.

Get Dressed.

I obeyed instantly. My clothes were piled on a chair in the corner. All I could think about was, "What will happen? Where will I go?" At last, I tied on my shoes and returned to the Book to read.

The next command was simple enough: *Go Outside.*

I opened the door with the Book under my arm. The stairway down the side of the house creaked with my sneakers. A cat on the last step ran off into the garden weeds. At sea level, I quickly opened the Book again.

Get Breakfast.

I smiled. It wasn't often that the Book allowed me a treat like that. There's a restaurant a couple blocks away. I've smelled the wonderful aroma many hungry mornings before as the Book took me journeying somewhere else. I opened the brass doors and let the waitress show me to a table.

"Coffee?" she asked.

"Sure. Why not?" This was going to be a great day.

I set the Book to gleam in the window light. My eyes feasted upon the menu, finding the most outrageous ingredients. My coffee arrived and I let go with my breakfast order. She filled a whole green ticket. When I left I'd be walking on air like a balloon.

So I had my coffee and a refill as well. A rainbow bent from the thick window glass, spread on the cover of the Book. "Thanks," I told it and touched its corner with affection. I felt compelled to read the next sentence. Usually I wait until it's appropriate, but on this day…waiting for my meal…I felt so warm and happy I had to know where it would lead me next.

Get Money.

That took me by surprise. Money! I realized I didn't have a cent in my pocket. I looked around me. I could see the waitress balancing plates, spinning my way.

I grabbed the Book and bolted. It was the only thing I could do.

Running down the street, I wished I had the guts to toss the Book in one of the passing alleyways. It had done this to me before. Real funny, thanks…

I had to catch my breath. I stopped with my hand on a white stone lion. I knew I could never part with the Book. I knew that without it I was helpless. It had always controlled my days.

Even now…It had led me to the bank. The lion statue guarded the entrance. The stone eyes

watched me go in.

People echoed all over the marble floor. I stood there with them, not knowing what to do. You can't just walk into a bank and get money, didn't the Book know that? In exasperation, I consulted it again.

Get A Gun.

Where were these words leading me? What did it want me to do? For the second time, I felt an overwhelming compulsion to reject it.

Then I saw the guard sleeping at his desk. His hand was slumped over the back of the chair, newspaper fallen on the floor, and a pistol beckoned, hanging on the side of his belt. The Book was right, I could do it.

I moved along the shadow of the pillar. I crept onto the Persian rug moating his desk and I reached out.

"That's far enough!" He bounced to his feet with his hand on his hip. He drew the gun and pointed it at me. "I always knew some punk would try that," he puffed steam triumphantly. "Everyone thought Old Charley was sleeping on the job. Hah!" Instead, he'd been waiting like a spider. He set the gun beside him on the table to fumble with his handcuffs.

My moment had come. I opened the Book and as chaos shot around me, I tore the morning out.

MORE EXPERIMENTS WITH RADIO

More experiments with radio led Dr. Biocal to a door in the ether that he could open and close. He turned his receiver beyond the end of the dial and heard the sounds of long ago: *The Shadow*, *The Jack Benny Show*, cooking programs and the talk of Hollywood. Dr. Biocal listened in great interest from his stainless steel lab so many years in the future. Those ventures kept him happy for a few nights, but he wanted to talk to that world he heard. At last he fashioned a microphone with a pneumatic tube and sent his voice into the past.

"Hello?" his words shimmered on water, "Can anyone hear me?" He repeated it again and again to send enough ripples to the shore.

Of course he had grand designs in store. If a link to the past could be made, just think of the exchange that could occur. Someone in that age must be listening with crystal set glowing. "Hello?"

"What is it, mac?" came the reply.

Dr. Biocal felt electrified contact. The voice seemed no further away than yesterday. "Hello, my friend. I have a wonderful offer…" and Dr. Biocal lost no time in threading the hook. He dusted off the almanacs and told secrets of thing to come, a few baseball scores and market booms. He promised to answer any questions for the person in the radio, if a trade could be made. Dr. Biocal waited. He had to tune against the winds of interference.

"It's a deal," was his answer.

Dr. Biocal held the microphone under the sleeve of his coat to laugh out loud. History was now his to play with.

1959

She was outside in her yard reading a book when the gray company truck appeared and halted at the curb. Its engine rumbled, there was a metal hoop spinning around and around on the roof. She held her place in the book as she stared. There were some numbers painted on the side of the truck, a letter that looked like a backwards R. "Russian?" she wondered. The window was shaded by the maple tree. She couldn't see who was inside. And the hoop swiveled, testing the air. She lost her place as she clutched the book tightly with both hands. Why was she frightened? What did they want? Then with a growl the truck moved on.

THE NOT-DOING DETECTIVE

There is a notecard tacked to the door:

The Taoist Detective
In Not-Doing
He Will Do
And Solve
By Not Doing

Inside, a woman is crying, "What am I paying you for?"
He reassures her. It's quiet again, for half an hour.
She leaves.
Then, after a while, he goes out too.
What is he doing? He is sitting on a bench at the park. He is getting a cup of green tea, going to a movie, peeling a tangerine with all the time in the world.

RICHARD'S MOUSE

His father wanted him to shoot mice. They were all around the barn. It was easy to get them. Even the cats grew tired of it. After a while, so did he. Maybe he could have forgotten about them with time, letting them go like toys pushed away. He didn't though. One of them never left. It grew old with him, slowed down by age and injuries. Every day they went out walking, without a map, to travel the city streets, coming to stops, then moving on again, with that white faced mouse whispering the way.

DELORY MARTEL

Delory Martel told the small crowd, "You can wish for anything and it will come true." He spoke to them from an overturned apple crate on the street corner. There was a wooden box in his hand. "It's in here…Just make a wish." Like something on a clown, there was a bright yellow sunflower in the pocket of his worn coat. He looked like he had slept in an alley and maybe he had. He knew that's what people thought and he held up the torn sleeve of his jacket proudly. "I know what you're thinking. Why doesn't he wear a suit made in Italy, or drive some million dollar car. Ladies and gentlemen, I choose to live this way. And I need to tell you what I know…"

"I gave you my last twenty dollars!" someone shouted.

"Just wait. Please be patient."

"What about my twenty dollars?" A young woman pushed the others out of the way. "I saw you last week. I gave you twenty bucks. I'm still waiting for my wish to come true." She was glaring at him. She was sharp as a stick.

"Okay…" he said. He held out his hand. "Follow me, please."

She didn't want to take that hand.

"I'll see the rest of you tomorrow." He waved his box to the crowd. He felt her hand touch him like a dry leaf. "This way," he told her. He took her around the corner, past the shops, across the street and into an alley halfway down the next block. Above them were heavy black electrical wires.

By then, she had taken her hand back but she still followed him, a step behind.

"Here we are," he said. He stopped beside the gate in a wooden fence. It was a tall fence made of cracked slates but it held back whatever was on the other side.

He tapped the fence. "Every penny I make goes right into

this." There was a rusted latch he touched to open the gate.

"I might have known," she said. She wasn't surprised by his Charlie Chaplin shack. There were sunflowers growing tall as people standing around in front of it. It was just what she expected. There was even a watermelon growing beside it.

He stepped into the lot, followed the path that led to the homemade home. She stood where she was, in the gateway watching him, as he leaned down and sawed the stem of the watermelon. He pulled it out of the rustling leaves and held it up. He clowned a heavy stagger as he carried it to her. "Here," he held it out to her. His fingers drummed on the green smooth skin.

"I don't want a watermelon. I can buy one at Safeway…If I had my twenty dollars."

Delory Martel gave her a carved look. His mouth slid down as he let the watermelon slip out of his grip. It hit the flagstones with a hollow thud. Out of the cracked rind spilled a torrent of gold coins.

Before she could react, Delory Martel reached out for a big handful of air, pulled the door closed on himself and his yard. Before she could even move the gate had clicked, and she was standing there facing an old wooden wall. She was in a vacant lot.

A TELEVISION MOVIE

Digging along the garage foundation where the drainpipe ran three feet into clay, the pick hit what I thought was another thick root. Then the ground shook. All along the driveway the line of poplars shuffled. I couldn't move though it wasn't an earthquake. I watched it happen like a television movie. A giant sat up out of the ground bursting through gravel and turf, pushing the side of the garage off his shoulder like a paper hat.

NORTH

Either so tired she fell into dark, or else lying in bed trembling on short circuits, replaying the day, she knew she had reached the burnout stage. So she gathered her things like a bird taking wing and she was on the road going north. When she got there she was lucky. She found a part-time job in the children's library. She listens to them sing five hours a day then she rides her bicycle through the town, takes a breather by the sea, before she does what she wants with the rest of her life.

THE BLUE PARROT

When I was your age, my mother gave me five dollars to go to the store and buy some bread. It was a sunny day, I didn't mind. I got on my bike and jumped it off the curb, pedaling like wind. There was nobody on the street, it's a dead end; it runs out into a big wall of blackberries. I pedaled like crazy. Sometimes I can make it in 109 seconds. Sometimes I slow down, take it easy so I can look at the sky while I ride.

There was a jet plane way up there spinning a web in a long white line.

At the yellow Dead End sign, there's a path just wide enough to ride through the vines and branches. That's my short cut to the store. Not only mine; sometimes I find the junk other people leave behind, bottles and cardboard and packaging.

The path comes out right next to the store's parking lot. I have my place to park next to the soda machine.

I could have gone past the sun on the bin of oranges and in the sliding doors, found the bread and brought it home, but there was a girl standing there holding a blue parrot.

She said, "Hi," to me and I had to stop. "Do you want to buy this bird?" she said.

Of course I did. I gave her the five dollars and she set the bird on my shoulder.

"It won't fly away," she said.

I thanked her, she smiled, and I got back on my bicycle and turned around. Out of the corner of my eye I could see the bird as I pedaled. He liked riding on my shoulder. I felt like a pirate. My bicycle was the fastest ship on the sea.

OLD FLOWERS

I'm only in Bill's house a little while. There are so many books stacked like old flowers, petals everywhere. The hot air, dry in here as an Egyptian tomb preserves the paper history of his 95 years. The fabled 1930s, union massacres, Woody Guthrie in the radio, interrupted by the 1940s war, the photo of him by the door wearing a uniform, factories and the military. Then the years afterwards when the labor dream could be pinned to an easy fear: communism and conspiracy with the enemy. It's all there for anyone to read, to understand how we got here, the cycles of exploitation and greed, a crafty oppression, the slow building of the American pyramid is the song on a record Paul Robeson sings.

MARTIAN TIGERS

Another rocket landed on Mars. Once the smoke and dust cleared, the door opened. Nothing moved from the rocket until the floor tipped and out dropped a tiger. It was groggy from the long flight. It got to its feet, unsteadily rubbed its stripes against the silver rocket leg as it blinked around at the red planet. It stretched its neck and smelled the air, tail wagging. Tigers were the only Earth animals to really adapt to the conditions here. Few creatures had lasted long. The tiger watched a wheel of starlings resettle in a brass colored tree not far away. The cat's big head nodded. There was a good scent there. It moved away from the scorched ground, across the rubble, silently into the white Martian flowers.

THE SOUND OF BIRDS

The crop-duster killed off the last of the birds but he discovered something when he walked along the irrigation ditch where they used to be singing and hopping on those cattails. He wore a pair of headphones. He played the sound of birds and it was almost as if they were there all around him.

HALF-WHITE SPECKLED BIRD

Dr. Biocal let electricity enter the dials and crystal works. A globe crackled with blue veins, yellow lightning scribbled off transistors. Shadows were made in his desperate little room, from the crooked paintings on the wall, jumping on the broken spring bed, dancing off the clothes on hangers and hooks, the papers strewn all over the floor flickering like a movie.

In a graceful spin, he turned to the window and pushed open the glass to let in the wind. Outside night twirled with all its end of summer craziness. The last performance of the circus set up in the distant field made the air on the horizon shimmer like a phosphorescent deep sea creature washed ashore. Calliope music waved over the tall grass to the wooden wall below, where a cat chased another across the jagged boards.

Returning to the machine, Dr. Biocal set a crown of wires on his head and quickly plugged it in. He was thrown backwards, the sawing noise of his invention ceased. Sparks went out against the floor.

There was quiet in the room, holding everything, until a swami horn from the fairgrounds meandered in. On the smallest dot mosquito wings, it buzzed a melody persuading something out of him…From him, his opened eyes and mouth, a curious wraith emerged, moving with spirit quality.

It examined the ended smoking mechanical creation and it sunk. It creased the papers of his life's work, disturbing them in its wake as it circled and stopped at rest over him.

Hovering, deciding, the ghostly thing seemed to be in doubt. But then it veered away to the window sill where it floated out.

A couple of pigeons cooed out of the way but one half-white speckled bird sitting on the ledge remained. Through its beak the gray thing flew inside.

On the other side of the edge of the field, all the Ferris wheels and amusement park rides spun. Crowds rivered, swirled at tables set up to win, then moved again. Sideshows lured some in. Others were lost to smaller tents with gambling, every sound of music playing with blinking lights strung overhead.

The big tent in the center of all ballooned where men in top hats recruited at each entrance. "Step right up! It's just about to begin!"

Susan Fenton paused before the sight. She had a few dollars left in her pocket. She could go in or call it a night. Though she knew in the morning, back to work, all this would be gone. The Saturn Circus only arrived once a year.

A clown bumped into her, honking a bicycle horn. A man on stilts stepped over her, dropping rainbows of confetti from a bag. Maybe, she thought, I could try to win a prize at a booth? Some bright thing to remember this day by…

Just then, a pigeon flew down to land on a streamered post next to her head and it said, "Dr. Biocal may be dead."

The pigeon on her shoulder told her the path to take through the dark field. "Keep that starry apartment light in sight." As she ran stumbling on rocks while briars tore at her. She was in such a state that she didn't notice the cuts on her legs or the bruises after she fell. The flapping pigeon regained its perch. "You're almost there. Don't despair."

At last, the field ran out against the wooden wall. There were tangled bicycle wheels and old car parts jumbled together to make fossils, bottles and plastic Safeway bags. She pushed the rotting wood and made it through.

No one cared for locks in this building where no one had anything to hide. As she rushed inside, a couple doors were open wide to show the broken-down people. The bird guided her up the stairs, the precarious slant, to a door which she brushed aside.

In the middle of all the squalor, almost hidden by the hundreds of pages, she saw Dr. Biocal crumpled.

Before she could react, the pigeon told her, "Turn the machine on and plug both of us in."

There was an orange button marked ON, which she pressed to let electricity back again. Zapping illustrated the walls. She recrowned the doctor, a little taped wire she glued to the pigeon's blue white head. Then she threw the switch to make it work, returning life to where it belonged.

NAMELESS TREES

"I'm the Inspirational Speaker. Which way is the gym?"

"Oh yeah…" replied the sallow boy slouched against the brown Camaro. "It's not where you think it is." His arm raised like a leather puppet attached to string. "See those trees? You'll see a path." An emotion almost broke across the boy's face, giving him a strange sort of choking look.

"Thanks. I don't want to be late." The speaker grinned, or tried to. The boy made him nervous with that look. "See you there, I hope."

So he took off into the woods. He felt his shoes sink in the fir needle foam, liking the sudden cold air feeling on his face.

It was hardly a path at all. Low bushes crowded around him. Vines would trip him if he stepped off of it. It got strange around him. He knew his trees to a degree—maples, oaks, birches, ash, cedar, pines, but there were nameless trees that bent and scrambled to cover the light and lock him in.

So he slowed and listened and he wasn't getting anywhere. It occurred to him, sure he may have been the fool for being misled, but even if that was true, here he was. It had to happen like this for him. He could allow a little time to pass. He heard the spilling rush of a stream somewhere nearby and what sounded like a rusted wheel turning. He looked for the source—it was a little black capped bird so small he could have cupped it in his hand, or held it on his palm to compass him.

As he reached for the bird, his arm began to slow. His body stopped and hardened and his hand froze, held out. The chickadee landed on the smooth bark of his hand, bobbed and trembled about, before its beak settled on a direction and off it flew.

THE WISHING WELL WALRUS

In the dark pool of a wishing well, down in the long brick burrow below, lived a sad walrus. For years, he was quiet and patient, as people would stop on the world above to toss silver coins, to hear the splash, to make a hope, then carry on. Every time this happened, day after day, he would sulk underwater making his own wish that his own life could be better. He believed in wishes, but he also knew it took some effort for a dream to come true. It took more than just money, it took heart. A golden idea was needed, a really good thought. So he sat on the pile of money to think of a way to make things change and since it was Spring, it began to rain. As drop by drop kept filling the well, he realized that was his way to escape. The water would carry him out. But how would he get back to the North Pole? It was so far away. He needed a fast car, or better yet a plane ticket. And then he remembered all the money in the well. "There must be enough for a ticket by ship!" So he swam back and forth, gathering hundreds of coins in his big flippers. "I can hardly wait," he said, "to see the snowy sea and ice again!" He was just under the surface, coming up to the ledge, when the rippling picture over him changed to form a small person looking in. He heard a little voice speak to the well, "All I have is this penny to make my wish." And the coin dropped in. Like a fish, or a falling brown leaf, it sunk onto Walrus' head as he listened to what next was being said. The words of the wish drifted by and before the child could go away, the walrus swam from the well and poured all those coins onto the ground. Walrus only kept that penny on top of his head as he returned to the pool, to start over again. He had his water and he had his heart and he could wait for someone else to help or not.

ONCE UPON A TIME, MR. TIM

Once upon a time, Mr. Tim decided to pack his things, rent his apartment and go back to wandering. Poor as I was, without a home, I saw the advertisement and I went to his door. I waited in front of it, to feel the old building, the worn red carpet underfoot. The walls unfurled paper from the very top of ceiling shadowed and wrung with water spots. The place echoed like the inside of a blues guitar.

I knocked and it wasn't long before the door opened to let me in. He was standing by the edge the hinges hung onto, draped head to foot in shadow, reject dragon cloth. Shimmered over like the sight of a mermaid, he welcomed me with a bow move and ushered me to a chair. The robe pointed out a silver teapot with the bell shaped cup next to it.

Once I had that taste of steam and color in me, I could hear him plainly speak. This was the usual talk about cost and first and last rents, things like that. My eyes though, went around. The long drawn leaves of the plants hung in sight of the city at night. I wasn't about to be outside again, no matter what, I just wanted to hand him the only money I had and my signature so I could move in.

I told him as much when he was done talking and while I counted out what I had, he moved the last picture off the nail.

SON OF A BEEHIVE

The black and white hum of the China Clipper four engine flying boat droned in the sleep of a narrow man. His exhaustion carried even into his dreams where he relived the past few days fright…Thrown out of the Queen's palace, through the city of workers, chased by spears to the docks where he caught the only flight out. He woke up with a start.

The steward offered a tray of food.

"No…I have my own," he said weakly. "Could you pass me that suitcase? There, that yellow one." His arm bent like a willow branch.

"It's sticky," the steward apologized. "Let me get a towel."

"No! Kindly…Pass it down."

He snapped the latches, opened it up to a gold syrup liquid that filled the insides and he dipped his trembling hands in deep, like a magician pulling sunlight out of a box.

It was enough for the rest of the flight.

The plane landed and stopped at the shore. He found his new home.

From the streets of the city, he gathered the sweet sights and sounds, in ultraviolet was the pulse of the light. He went all day back and forth til the great bags slung over his shoulders were full and the soles of his shoes were covered in dust.

Finally, he wearied up to the doors of a downtown hotel. Greeted as a friend, the guard let him in, onto marble, the gleam of the lobby crowd, over to the elevator which took him up the many stacks of floors to his own, almost empty room. Flowers waited on the table.

He sealed the door, poured and shook the garden he caught, out on the floor. It was enough of a wonder to start over with.

WHAT THE MAN ON THE MOON BROUGHT HOME

When the astronauts returned to Earth, their suits got sent to him. He put them on hangers in a yellow room and ran the water up and down, to wash the moondust off.

Instead of letting it all go down the drain, he gathered the silt and put it in a plastic sandwich bag to take home with him.

He wasn't sure what to do with it when he got there. Something as valuable as that someone somewhere must have a use for.

He stood in the kitchen for the longest time, with the clock tick, the icebox that went on and off and the American drone on the radio.

In the end, he put the bag in a cardboard shoebox and labeled it, *What the Man on the Moon Brought Home.*

THE DARKNESS OF ANOTHER WORLD

The moon and streetlamp light crushed out against the curtained window. Downstairs, Walter Lawrence sighed deeply and asked, "When will I be myself again?"

Doctor Stakes removed a syringe from his black bag. "As soon as the treatment is completed."

"I hope so..." Walter shuddered at the bite of the needle and his eyelids shut like garage doors.

As Dr. Stakes leaned him back on the table, he watched the effects of the shot with morbid satisfaction. His patient's face darkened and stretched, hair spread over his features. "Wally," he said when it was complete. "Wally, it's time to go to work."

A gorilla sat up on the table.

"Wally! We have much work to do." He passed the ape a shovel. A wooden panel was removed from the wall to reveal a tunnel diving down.

The next morning, Walter sat in his office rubbing his hands. They were bubbled with red welts and calluses. He reached for the intercom button on his desk. His back ached terribly. "Miss Collins," he rasped, "Send for the doctor. Tell him to meet me at home." He couldn't straighten his spine; he loped pitifully for the door, dragging his briefcase across the marble floor.

Fortunately he didn't have far to go. His house was just across the parking lot from the bank. It was hidden in the willow behind the white picket fence and clover. He barely had time to make it there; in the entryway he collapsed on the Persian rug. The yellow day played on him while the garden birds sang.

Consciousness returned foggily. Dr. Stakes was shimmering above him. He saw a circle with numbers forming a dial, going around…Two to the right, left, right and there was a click. Then the darkness fell again.

For an hour the ape was whipped on from the vault, underground, to the house and back, carrying sacks heavy with cash. At last the beast sank wearily onto the living room floor.

"You have done good work, Wally." The doctor smiled. "This last shot will return you to your old life ways…" He laughed at the limp gorilla already transforming into, "The President of First Federal Savings Bank…" The doctor laughed again. He left Walter Lawrence in the burrowed rubble of his cellar, asleep.

His life landed him in a flash in a prison cell. Walter Lawrence had no idea how it happened, how he could have done what he did, and how suddenly he was there, watching the full moon rise in front of the cold window bars. Still, he felt something more peculiar occurring with every passing minute of night's glow. He was changing. Here and there among the rows of cages, a prisoner howled at the midnight locked out, while a big animal quietly pulled its walls apart.

Dr. Stakes took advantage of the night to finish packing his black limousine. There was crystalware and boxes of delicate medical equipment and of course the suitcase bricked tight with money. He whistled and stepped off the porch onto the dark path of grass.

Midsong, he tossed his car keys in the air to catch, but they didn't come back to him alone. Attached to them was a gorilla, snapping down from the tree limb.

PESO VS EL CONDOR

For the fifth time someone had come into Peso's office seeking his help. Four times he had pointed to the framed certificate hung on the yellowed wall. That was explanation enough; that was his job now. The gun had been put away. But another pleading senora with tears on her face had turned the tide. There truly appeared to be an enormous bird swooping out of the Mexican sky. Striking a wooden match to light his black cigar, Peso's eyes narrowed at the smoke and he nodded, "I will find that bird."

After an hour of assembling an ancient elephant gun from parts cushioned in a velvet box, gathering compass, cobwebs, cutlass, maps and other things, Peso left his office.

The sun was easing down the slanted roof tiles, but the town square was lit with red lanterns and singing…The jubilation was for him. They had made a piñata of a sinister bird flapping from a wire.

Peso leveled his gun and let the bang scatter candy and feathers and cheers.

Not until night did he finally get far from town on his way to the mountains. He parked his tin car next to the same dead tree he pulled branches off of to make a fire. The orange and yellow heat cast darkness away. He warmed by it, thinking of what tomorrow would be. Eventually, when he got tired enough, he flattened to the desert and slept. The fire burned a perfect outline beside him before it blackened out.

He woke in the dead of night. The bramble moved.

A shadowy stranger appeared. "I must warn you. Your life is

in danger. Return to the town as soon as you can."

Peso regarded the vision the same as the tired dew, pearled on every waking sage and cactus point. He rolled over and went back to sleep.

By late afternoon, he had climbed half of the mountain. He stopped when his automobile sputtered and could go no more up the rocky slope. Peso dropped out of the doorway and kept traveling alone. He walked on the so many bones, bleaching each step of the way. Pitch of night slowed him more. Stars and a half moon illumined, like a white wingspread, when he pulled a blanket of skeletons over himself to sleep.

The weight of all those bones woke him up. Peso had to claw through a thick puzzle of luminous gray to find the day. He was close to the crown of the white mountain cone but he found the way like treading water. He tried to watch the sky as he climbed. He didn't want to feel the sudden grab of claws and he kept the elephant gun crooked to his arm.

The mountain stopped, topped by a nest made of driftwood and fence posts. Peso tossed his gun and bags over the rim so he could climb inside after them. He was half worried he would go over the edge to face the violet beak of El Condor. Only the wind rustled over him.

Peso sat in the feather lined nest with his gun. There were clouds about him. He was tired from his journey. He lay down for a moment. He was so very tired. It was like dropping into a mining car, poured through a hollow mountain. In the dream that took care of time, he saw the strange workings of shadows and light, flickers of time, Mayan gold, the people thrown around like so many seeds grown and gone, and it was over so silvery fast his mind was left like a spinning hubcap, dumped out and wobbling on the burning remains of his town.

JOLIET

On their way back from the prison, Joliet took over driving while her mother slept. The older woman was sound asleep, using the map as a pillow between her and the window.

When Joliet pulled over and stopped next to the river, her mother kept right on sleeping. Closing the door quietly, Joliet went across the tar, down the hill to the water.

Some red-wing blackbirds took off from the reeds and flew to the other bank. The river blurred out the sound of the cars on the road behind her as she sat down on a rock to take off her shoes. She unrolled her white socks, stuffed them into her shoes and tied the laces together so she could hang the shoes around her neck.

The water was icy cold to her pale toes, the smooth stones covered with slippery green algae, and when she stopped still, she could see small fish in the current. She reached down and they scattered like alphabets as she splashed water onto her face and neck.

Her eyes opened again and she saw someone on the opposite shore: a girl, like her, in a long yellow dress, filling a pottery jug with stream.

Joliet called to her, but the girl had already turned and was leaving fast through the tall grass.

Rolling up her jeans to her knees, Joliet splashed deeper into the river. The freezing water climbed up her legs, then back down around her to her feet as she emerged onto the soft sand on the other side. Joliet pulled at her shoes, untied the laces and put them on.

The grass was laid down where the other girl had gone rushing and Joliet followed the path through the leaves, up the steep embankment. Where it became level, she could see the girl not far away.

Joliet stared. The girl was kneeling beside a knight in a suit of silver armor. She was bathing his face with river water. Joliet caught her breath. A dragon was leaving away from them, across the stretching miles of field, limping, slashing its tail and flapping its scaly wings. It stopped in the shade of a bending tree to lick its wounds with a long tongue.

Joliet walked into the curving field towards the maiden and the knight. If felt like a dream—how things happen, and you just follow along.

§

Joliet's mother liked to tell her daughter the story of how Joliet began. It wasn't just her name; it was where her father had come from and where he would be for life. "He's locked up in there," her mother would say. The walls were lined with big silver washers and drying machines and the air was warm, fragrant and thick like a mechanical jungle fog with the heat of the tumbling clothes. Joliet's mother now owned The Turtle Dove Dry Cleaning & Laundry, although she liked to say it was still Roy's—as if, after 42 years, he would return to run the business again.

Ever since she could remember, Joliet heard the same story. When she was small her mother would pick her up and sit her on a washing machine. She would lay herself down across the shaking green metal and cover herself with hot clothes. Then the story would play out.

"Your daddy escaped from prison in a laundry basket. I unwrapped all the blue clothes and there he was. Joliet honey, you wouldn't believe my joy. I thought I would never see him on the outside again. He hopped right out of that basket and hugged me and we turned out all the lights in here and all night long we held each other. It was the most beautiful thing. In the morning, the cops showed up and took him away, but you had been made. Like a seed, Joliet, you were inside of me and they couldn't take you away."

§

Joliet sat in the grass with the knight and maiden and the dragon was a safe distance away, under a cloud of smoke and green apple tree leaves. It was strange, now that she was close there was no doubt, the girl looked exactly like Joliet, like a twin from another era. Joliet watched her as she wrapped a white bandage around the knight's arm. The blood showed through a little bit.

The knight stared down at his wound, "He nearly had me that time."

The girl brought the water jug to his lips and let him sip.

"Why are you fighting that dragon?" Joliet asked and her question caused the knight to sigh deeply and look at the sky.

The maiden said, "He has to. He fights for me and for all the land that you can see." She pointed to the field, lakes, river and mountain and swung her arm in a circle covering it all, back to touch her finger to her breast. She whispered, "Still, the way it continues, I wonder if I'm not part of a curse…"

"Don't say that!" The knight sat up and folded his hurt arm across his chest. He touched his hand to her soft cheek. "You are what I'm living for, you are everything."

"That's what the dragon says too…" She was almost crying, but she let him hold her hand. "I don't know who to believe, I don't know what to believe, I don't know why I live," and she looked at the moon's white dial, 250,000 miles away. "I'm tired of having someone wanting to love me." She pushed his hand off of her. "I'd give anything to be no one at all, to go somewhere completely different and new, somewhere far away where I could be left alone." She started to cry.

Joliet put her hand on the yellow silk dress covering her twin's sad shoulders and she smiled with a thought.

Until she was eighteen, Joliet worked for her mother at the laundromat, keeping track of the machines, helping customers choose between Tide and Cheer. Then she decided to leave for a while. She told her mother she was going to New Orleans, maybe for a year, maybe more. Somewhere on the Gulf, she got off the bus and went to the beach. She slept on the sand with a friend, and rain came falling out of nowhere and forced them awake in the gray light of dawn. She kept hoping for the kind of feeling, with the kind of person that her mother glowed about for so long. All her life Joliet had been thinking about love and she wished for someone who would love her like a dream. It seemed like her hopes and ideas belonged to another planet, not just another time. After a few months that seemed like a life of years, rotten wooden buildings, sleeping on floors, losing and finding out and losing and losing, she finally got a train ticket and went home. Her mother cried and welcomed her back and Joliet decided never to leave again. Every so often, she and her mother would go visit the old man in jail, but that was as far away as those two would go. Joliet would take over driving when her mother got tired and she'd steer the car on the way back to the Turtle Dove.

Then one day it was like magic. She stopped by a river and switched places with herself.

LOCAL MAN CAPTURES ALLIGATOR

He was sitting at the café reading the newspaper. It was an article about him, *Local Man Captures Alligator*. He shook his head. He really didn't need the publicity. He only did it because it seemed like the right thing to do at the time. There was even his photo, flanked by two beaming police officers, hands on his shoulders and the hint of a smile on his own face. That was just the adrenaline though. His suit was still wet, a sleeve was torn. There was mud on the side of his face.

"The feat seems all the more remarkable," he continued to read, "as Jakob Kale is 79 years old." *The Herald* was really laying it on thick, Jakob thought, and he pressed his finger on the next paragraph where they quoted him, "I used what I could find around me to capture it. My resources were limited but there was a length of wire I could use as a lasso." Actually, the riverbank was a jumble of all kinds of junk. He probably could have captured the alligator with several different items half buried in the weeds. The wire just happened to be nearest at hand.

The waitress stopped beside him. "Care for a refill?"

"Oh yes please." He had already had two cups with his oatmeal. He smiled: Maybe that's what gave him the strength to heave alligators from city streams?

"That's quite a story," the waitress said, motioning the Silex pot at the newspaper. "I'm impressed." She was too—the mood ring necklace she wore glowed a warm rose color on her skin.

"Honestly, my dear, it wasn't quite so heroic as *The Herald* reports. For a tropical creature like that to find itself in such a cold river…It was in a state of shock. It was like fishing out a log." Yet he smiled at her. His granddaughter was easily impressed by him.

"How did it get there anyway?"

"I really don't know. Obviously the alligator is not native

to the Nooksack River. At least not in this millennium…But I would like to take a look around. I could use another set of eyes if you'd like to join me."

"Of course! I'll be done in—" she glanced at the clock, "Twenty minutes."

He nodded. "I'll do the crossword puzzle until then."

Jakob held the ladder while his granddaughter stood at the top, in the air, with half her body inside the rocket. It was intricate work and took a calm mind to disarm the rocket every afternoon after her shift. The old man always breathed a sigh of relief when all the bright lights on it clicked off. Sure it glowed like a Broadway marquee next to the café, but if anything ever went wrong, there would be a crater and angels where they were. Gwen reemerged and went down a rung on the ladder and locked the latch on the rocket.

Jakob stood back and let her land on the cobblestones again. He leaned on his cane out of the way while she put the ladder away.

"There were a lot of people talking about that alligator today," she said. "We might not be the only ones at the river."

Jakob walked beside her. The sidewalk led down the hill from the café to the park. A ruined bridge crumbled over the river. Next to the cannon they took the steep path to the water. He was no stranger to this area. Whenever the weather was okay, Jakob visited the river. A few years back he discovered the fossilized footprints of a Diatryma, a huge flightless bird of the Eocene epoch. That made the newspaper too. It seemed there was something drawing Jakob here.

When they got to the bridge and looked down at the riverbed, sure enough there were scavengers, searching like sandpipers along the water's edge. Small time treasures, plastic packaging, tin cans, plumbing parts or strange things only an archaeologist like Jakob Kale could identify.

Someone had made a path patched together out of metal scraps. The weeds on the path crackled as they followed the way to the river. Jakob stopped on the wide hood of a Pontiac station wagon. He watched Gwen leading the way. Her coat fluttered like a boat sail.

There were some trees growing in the spot where he found the alligator. One of the trees still had leaves holding on.

He was going to catch up with her, he was just resting. His cane planted him on the hillside. He turned when he heard a family coming up through the branches. They were laughing and chattering, carrying a unicycle, freshly found.

TWO PAPER BIRDS

She sat in the cab of the truck writing in her notebook or reading a paperback. Just getting her to come with him on the job today had been an ordeal, almost leading to one of their arguments. It seemed like she had been angry at him for years, ever since she was a little girl slamming her door on him. He wasn't even sure why.

Her mother sent her to spend the week with him. If it was reconciliation, it didn't look like that was happening. Since the divorce, he supposed his daughter's hatred of him had only grown. And he wasn't surprised by her cold regard of him. She would sit in the apartment in the corner chair with a book. Mostly he took her on the job to get her out of there, but also he hoped she would be interested in his work, maybe even lend a hand.

Well, tomorrow she would be going back to her mother. He wasn't sure if the trip had done any good. He could make her come along but she wouldn't speak. She would be like one of the cement Buddhas that huddled in the bed of the truck. That was his job. He made Buddhas.

The sun shone on this one he had finished pulling into place. Its new home was in a garden corner. It was still winter but he could imagine the statue with spring flowers, crocus and daffodils, all around it. It looked good.

He took a deep cool breath and stared into the Buddha's face, the eyes he had made with little bits of colored glass. Each Buddha was a little different. A sad part of him was transferred into this one. He knew the feeling. He let out his breath in a hitching, emptying sigh. He was very tired and about to cry. The day to day was much harder than he ever expected and he had failed in so many ways. If he hadn't got back on track by making these cement Buddhas, it seemed like it was all just a waste. It wasn't. He took a new breath. There was the smallest candle in him, but it cast just enough light to remind him. Maybe he'd seen it in a dream; he had been sent here, reborn in America for this purpose.

He glanced back at the yellow truck parked under a bare chestnut tree. He could see his daughter in there, her face tipped to her book.

A long row of white muddy pine planks made a track over the ground for the sled he had pulled the Buddha on. Now he had to pull the sled back. When he got to the truck he stopped it. The hard part was running it up the ramp over the tailgate. He saw the back of his daughter's head in the window, her straw colored hair. She was still reading her book, though the sound just behind her must have been loud.

It would be nice, he thought, if she had asked him if she could help. She must have known what he was doing. She had been watching him work for days. That's okay, he told himself…It was his business. This was what he did alone.

He followed the path of planks back to the Buddha and trip by trip picked up the pine rails and stacked them in the truck. By the time he finished that task he really was tired. He shut the tailgate, latched it with a clang and held on to the cold metal to catch his breath. It wasn't an easy job and he was getting older; he didn't know how much longer he could do it. But it was good to see that statue set solid in the earth. It looked very small across all that distance of winter yard.

He wasn't quite ready to go, almost, when the cab door opened and his daughter slid out of the truck. She had something in her hand, he caught a glimpse of it, a necklace made of little origami birds. They fluttered around in a long loop as she walked across the yard, along the freshly pressed marks left by the planks. She went further from him, all the way to the Buddha.

He listened to the blue jay cry hopping down the branch above her.

With both her hands, she hooped the birds over the statue's shoulders. It was perfect. And as he waved at her when she turned around, he smiled and looked away, and saw the two paper birds she had tied to the mirror inside the cab.

THE CENTAUR IN THE PARK

On the day Ronnie Peugeot's voice broke, two puppets stared back at him speechless and a trained crow flew away to the top of a birch. You might have seen a kind of pandemonium take over the set as the cameras stopped whirring and the arc lights died out one by one. It took the director Bernard O'Mulligan ten minutes to pick up dropped scripts, gather the crew together and pry the look of horror from Jimmy the Dancing Tree Frog's pallid face. Little Ronnie Peugeot had to run to his dressing room. The Centaur in the Park had opened a drastic new chapter.

The next day, Camellia Gotham arrived with her mother leading the way. A computer at central casting had matched eight year old Camellia's voice with the sound of Ronnie Peugeot before puberty's effects. When her words came from Elliott the puppet, nobody had to know.

Camellia was speechless, walking on that natural park set with her mother. The morning light speckled the tree leaves and birds sang all around the scurry of filming equipment. It was all so exciting and otherworldly she didn't notice the boy watching her pass by.

Half hidden behind a barrel sized urn of coffee, Ronnie Peugeot watched his replacement and his voice squeaked with disdain, "It's a girl!"

After Bernard O'Mulligan had gathered the puppeteers around the hollow, plastic oak trunk, he officially introduced Camellia to the program. Everyone applauded, all except for one hidden boy. She managed a sentence or two of thanks. And then they were off—the show would begin with Jimmy the Dancing Tree Frog—a song about giving that had to be choreographed with cartoon birds and a singing chorus line of bees.

Little did Camellia know that someone else had plans for her…While she sat in her star chair watching, swinging her legs, she felt a tap on her shoulder and she turned around.

"You like the show?" Ronnie asked.

She nodded, although it wasn't the magic she had hoped for. Now that they weren't inside a TV, she could see everything happening. The puppets lolled on sticks and wires, it was just machines and people crowded around a plastic tree in the park. The generators in the trailers took away the sounds of early morning.

"I been on this show since I was your age," he told her. The word 'age' sounded like a goose in flight. He tried again, "I'll show you something. Follow me."

Camellia sat there. Her hands rested on the chair arms.

"Quit worrying," Ronnie Peugeot waved a snapped branch at her.

They could still hear the din of the film production, but they were getting further away.

"I think my mother is done with breakfast by now," Camellia said. "She wouldn't like for me to be this far away."

"Far?!" The boy's word cawed in the air. "Don't you want to see a real live unicorn?"

She paused. "Sure. I guess so."

"Aw, you got plenty of time," he croaked. "Follow me."

She did. She followed him until everything was green.

Ronnie Peugeot laughed again. He seemed to have sunk into the leaves. "Watch out for the troll!"

Camellia took a step towards him, but when he laughed again, it sounded like he was behind her. She turned around and he was somewhere else, bleating at her.

She had a poster map of the park at home. It was drawn and colored happily, with balloons soaring above it and all the spires of the city pined about it. There was no need to be afraid, it had limits, it was surrounded by streets and stores and apartments. She wasn't lost. All she had to do was keep walking and she'd get out somewhere.

Seeing a tin can shine in that wet dew was comforting. It was a sign of civilization. It meant someone had been here. She had not been dropped off the end of the earth. Then she spotted another can…and a bottle…two more bottles. They almost seemed placed like landmarks. So she followed them. She let herself imagine that they really were put there by a unicorn, like buoys to lead anyone like her through. That was good because she had left any sort of path long ago. It wasn't bad walking but sometimes she slipped. Even though her mother had made her wear a dress, she was glad she kept her favorite tennis shoes on.

At the top of another little rise, crowned by low, tangled bushes, there was a jumble of bottles and cans like a garden grown from a thrown seed packet. They poured her toward the amazing sight of a palace made of green glass. Whoever made it wanted only green bottles for its bricks.

Every liter bottle had been scoured with sand and cleaned in stream water then set to shine with the forest light. It was beautiful.

She was so impressed she sat down by a spindly salmonberry to wait for the creature who lived in there to greet her. It wasn't long. Footsteps, heavy and plodding as hooves, cut in the underbrush.

THE TIMESAVER

Sal Friday stepped out of the steam of the shower closet fully clothed except for a shirt. With the white towel he brushed the socket area dry underneath his right arm and padded over to the kitchen counter where his Timesaver was plugged in and waiting.

In a moment he had attached the Timesaver to his body. He flexed his metal hand, curling the fingers deftly, turned the arm contraption so it pivoted silently on its elbow joint. "Alright," he said. "Let's get breakfast going."

His silver arm replied with a bleep and blinking light and reached for the pan on the stove while one flesh hand turned the water on and the other got a can of instant coffee. Mornings were all about time. From the moment Sal's alarm clock went off, it was a race for the door. With the extra arm, he figured it was saving him about five minutes. Of course, in a year he hoped to be able to afford another arm, but for now he was happy with one Timesaver.

At 6:21, he walked into the other room and sat on the gloomy sofa. The third arm instinctively reached upwards and clicked on the lamp.

"Thanks," Sal said.

He finished eating his breakfast off the tray on his lap. He still had five minutes before he had to leave. Pleased as he was with the Timesaver, he couldn't suppress a yawn. He added out loud, "I appreciate your help, but I sure wish I could go back to sleep for a long, long time."

The steel arm shot to his neck with such sudden force, the tray flew off his lap into the air. Sal was crushed into the sofa cushion. The silver fingers gripped him tightly. Sal couldn't breathe. The arm was taking his wish literally. It was killing him. Sal's hands clawed numbly at the metallic arm and with his last strength he cleaved the Timesaver out of the socket in his side.

He gave it a skittering kick across the kitchen floor and coughed life back into his lungs.

It was 6:33 when he was able to lift himself off the sofa. He coughed again and muttered wretchedly. The trolley would be rolling by his stop already and clanking up the hill to work.

Sal carefully stood and stepped from the sofa. The air entered his lungs in sawed breaths. He stopped beside the phone, wondered if he should call the automated operator at work. But how could he explain what happened? No, he decided, better not to, he would just have to take the next trolley and get there late.

Back in the kitchen, he looked for the Timesaver. It wasn't on the floor.

He wondered crazily…Where could it have gone? It wasn't like it could move on its own…Or could it?

He remembered when he assembled it—was it Step 19, just before he switched on its power. The directions advised, "You may want to install 4 Double C batteries to ensure the Timesaver's ability in case of unforeseen power outage." Yes, he did install the batteries. He had given the Timesaver a life of its own.

With a hoarse voice, Sal rasped, "I sure wish you would come out and give me a hand…"

A kitchen drawer pushed slowly open, spilling forks, spoons and sharp knives.

A MORNING IN NOVEMBER

He woke up a minute before the alarm clock. Before its shrill garble of music could begin, he reached a clumsy arm out of bed and clicked the button. He lay there for a moment. His wife was a bundled mummy beside him in the dark.

He listened to the rain pelting the window and the sizzle of the cars going by. He knew there were others like him, leaving the hive, going to work, gone all day then coming back.

At 6:03 he moved out of the covers. He stumbled a little then crept around the front of the bed, grabbing his clothes as he went. Two steps from the doorway, he almost fell down the stairs. Half of him stepped off into the air and only instinct was fast enough in the dark to make him grab the railing. He couldn't believe it. It felt like he almost died.

He sat down on the top stair and saw it all happening—his body crumpling and tangled up and falling. After he took a couple deep breaths, he calmly stood and walked down the stairs. A step creaked, his wife mumbled, he continued on.

He went about his morning at home the usual way, making the usual sounds for the twenty minutes before he hurried out the door. It was almost a ten minute walk in the rain and wind to the bus stop.

Behind the cul-de-sac, he followed the wooded path over the creek. There were some puddles he had to avoid. One of his shoes had a hole. He seemed to be all alone in the weather. He came out of the alders and brush and started up the road to 24th Street.

He always got a little nervous when he reached the mailboxes and he caught a glimpse down 24th, expecting to see the bus headlights coming early. Once in a blue moon it would happen and he would have to run. This wasn't one of those mornings though. When the weather was like this, the bus tended to run a little late. It was entropy. He got to the bus stop and stood on the cracked pavement next to the sign post and he waited.

A few minutes went by. A few cars went past, catching him like a moth in their headlights. Down the hill he saw the bus turn off Donovan and paddlewheel towards him. He stood in his usual place, but the bus didn't flick on its orange flashing lights, or slow down. It roared by in a spray of rain.

"Hey!" he shouted and waved. After that, it took him thirty minutes to walk to work. He was late of course and then twenty minutes from the door he realized he didn't have the key in his pocket. It was back at home on the kitchen counter. What could he do? There were forces at work this day.

Still, he took a chance and put his hand to the door, trying it to see if it was unlocked. His hand passed through the silver metal. Without thinking about it, he entered the loading dock, just walking in as if the wall was only a vapor.

IN THE COVER OF CLOUDS

The wind got the better of the robot. It had blown against a balcony and was tangled in the hand railing. Wisteria wrapped around it spindly, kicking legs.

Dwight Chasen glanced at it and kept going. He didn't pay it much mind. After three nights of this weather, the avenue was a littered wind tunnel. He stepped off the curb and crossed.

On the corner of Indian Street, a robot was holding a sign. It said, *Go To The Moon*. When it slowly turned around, Dwight could see the phone number to call for the next rocket flight. He wasn't convinced, in spite of all the work they were putting into getting people to migrate. They go, but aren't heard from again sometimes for years, sometimes never at all. He wondered if it wasn't a lot harder there than the posters let you think.

Sure, life on Earth was supposed to be monotony for people like him. With robots to take care of all their needs, what was there left to do but go looking for something else? So the Moon was getting a lot of attention. It was a Shangri-La. So let other people run off there, he figured. He had things to do to keep him busy. He was on his way to one now.

When he arrived at the Bellweather apartment building, he punched the entry code and entered the musty wooden corridor. Hermes Velcro was upstairs, on the roof, watching the sky, waiting for him.

It was like the future that had been promised. The robots took care of all the menial jobs and the drudgery of the day to day that had been weighing people down for so long. Now the only difficulty was finding things to pass the time.

He had plenty of time to think while he climbed the stairs. He also had plenty to look at. The stairway was plastered with bright posters for the Moon. *See Moon Animals at the Fair!* He actually went to that once but was disappointed, he had seen better ghosts. *And Romance Too!* There was always the promise of that…Romance and adventure. There were posters, robots with signs, billboards and TV spots, but it didn't end there. The dream machines that transmitted at night showed people more. In the middle of one of Dwight's typical hectic dreams of running, he saw a beautiful girl. She waved hello to him. She was waiting for him on the Moon.

Hermes was trying hard to get Dwight interested in clouds—especially in what clouds hid. He tried to make it more interesting and showed him how to find a UFO in the cloud lining. Dwight didn't know about that. Still, he climbed the five floors, then up the ladder to the roof.

When he pushed the trapdoor aside, he saw Hermes right away. He was sitting on a lawn chair like a blister in the middle of the wide, gray tarred roof. When it was summer, your feet would stick to it.

"Hey!" Hermes yelled.

Dwight waved back. He took a look at the sky. He could see the moon up there. It was half green and sparkling blue… the other half was the old gray with craters the old-timers remembered. Beside the well lit moon, a big cloud was sitting. It looked like a good one. Cumulus, he guessed, though to him, a beginner, every cloud was cumulus.

Hermes had resumed his sky watch using binoculars on a spot above the horizon. "Saw a bald eagle earlier," he said when Dwight was near.

"Oh yeah?"

Hermes pointed, "Over there…"

Dwight looked. He saw a crumpled gray twist of clouds above the rooftops to the south.

"You know what I've been thinking?" Hermes put the binoculars down and stared at Dwight over the crooked rims of his glasses. "I think we should try to catch a cloud. There ought to be a way to do it."

Dwight sat in the aluminum chair next to him. "I don't know... That sounds..."

"There," Hermes jabbed his finger at the eastern hills rising off the valley edge of town. "Tomorrow morning. Early." His hand painted and gestured the ragged, forested profile of land. "I'll get there early when the clouds are settled in the treetops. I'll reach out..." He stuck out his mitten and folded it on the air.

Dwight shook his head. "I don't think clouds can be captured like that. Aren't they made of water vapor? What you need is a big jelly jar, with a top on it."

Hermes stared at him. "How's a whole cloud going to fit in a jar?" Now he shook his head, "You have a lot to learn about clouds. Here, try the binoculars. There's a good one above the radio tower."

Dwight took them. His vision swirled across roofs and cars and trees before he focused on the cloud.

"Watch it for a while."

So Dwight watched it for a minute or so. The edges of it were frayed by wind.

It just looked cloudy to him. He started to think, "What am I doing?" He thought of all the other clubs there were. There were thousands of them. Every block or so, there was a telephone booth with the Club Book and numbers to call to become a member. "I should have joined the Dowsing Club," he thought. He had seen them before, digging a hole in a parking lot.

"Stratocumulus Lenticularis."

Dwight said, "Yeah?" with some interest. He guessed clouds were okay. But he didn't want to do this all day.

Something shot through the cloud. It turned for them. Dwight let the binoculars down and stared at the sky. "Look! What is that?" You could see it now, like a rocket. There was a black thread of smoke following it. For a second he thought it was one of those UFOs Hermes told him to look for.

"It's coming this way!" They looked around themselves frantically. The rooftop didn't offer much to hide behind. The trapdoor was too far away. Dwight grabbed his lawn chair and held it in front of himself as a shield. Between the green plastic chair slats, he saw the flying thing dip out of its fall and begin to land.

Ten feet away, it hit the roof. It hissed like a boiling pan of water. Then the sound of it stopped. The rocket motor turned off and in a moment they listened to the silver top of it un-screw. The nose cone toppled off and rang on the tar.

"It's got a message in it," Hermes said. He took a cautious step towards the rocket, slowly approaching it.

"Careful, Velcro."

Hermes reached out as far as he could to pluck the note out from inside it. It was rolled in a tight scroll and tied with a golden string. Hermes took it and stepped backwards quickly. He showed it to Dwight.

"What do you think?"

"I'm opening it," he said, unlooping the string. He flattened the crackling paper across his palm.

He read, "Don't Come to the Moon. It's terrible here."

THEY DON'T LAST LONG

Sometimes they arrive with a flashlight and no idea where they are. That's how it was that winter morning when Darryl Flynn was waiting for the seven o'clock bus.

The sun had not cleared the hill to the west and it was dark. He lived in a valley, the sleeping hills cut out of black. Behind them was the purple sky, a faint gray line spilled where the sun would come up. So with nothing to do but stare around, he noticed the little ball of white light floating on the wall.

It went up the concrete slowly then climbed down. It sat, spotted on the ground, then it started to search again. He could barely see the dim figure holding the flashlight but he knew what it was doing, he had seen them before, he could picture the distress. It might have been hoping for the Taj Mahal, or at least to be landing in the warm neighborhood it had known before.

Instead, look where it landed. He knew that wall. The ruin of what used to be a warehouse from years ago. A cold concrete thing, it was crawled over with the tangled veins of blackberry vines and some graffiti. There wasn't much there to make a person projecting themselves from far away on the Moon happy.

Darryl had to go to the restaurant but today he had another idea. He left the trampled grass by the bus stop sign. He followed the path keeping an eye on that flashlight.

They don't last long. They land on Earth like one bird dropped down from a flock until the first rays of sun make them fade from sight.

His foot slipped on a silver patch of ice that he should have noticed. He wondered if he would get there in time. Was it worth missing his bus just to get close? They weren't that uncommon, you could often run into them around dawn when they sent themselves from the Moon. Their images would linger on Earth, then like phone calls, they would disappear. He hoped he had time.

Or else he hoped that dull looking wall was enough to make a Moon dreamer happy.

THE PEARL COLLECTOR

"I'm meeting a mermaid around here. Somewhere called the Waterfront Café. I don't know why I can't find it."

The man pointed at the sea. That was the way.

It was there on a float, down steps on water, with candles lit along it.

He crossed the plank from land. He looked down. Little fish darted up into the green electric light.

She was waiting for him. Resting against the float, her arms held her up from the water. "There you are," she said. "I was starting to wonder."

"Sorry. I got a little lost getting here. This really is the water-front. I didn't know." He stood there awkward as an aardvark.

She smiled at him and said, "Do you still want the job?"

"Yes. Yes, of course." He still had the bit of newspaper he got that morning. He showed her the scrap of gray print. "Pearl collector…You need someone to gather pearls? Here I am."

"Let me show you where we do our work," she said. He stepped into the rowboat tied to the dock. He steadied himself, grabbed onto the seat and let her pull them by a rope into the deeper harbor water.

"You're not one of those people who might accidentally pocket a pearl or two, are you?" she asked from ahead of the bow.

"Of course not."

"There's a reason this boat doesn't have oars. I wouldn't want you to row it away full of pearls, would I?"

He said, "You sure don't trust people."

"No. I suppose I don't."

"Well, I'm not that kind of person."

"You're not…" she leaned her hand back into the swell of blue so momentarily she submerged. The rope seemed to tug through the water magically. He wondered if she could breathe underwater too. He supposed she could. He didn't know a lot about mermaids. In fact, he was taking chances with her also. He had heard stories about them. Sometimes people would go missing after seeing one. Sometimes people washed ashore.

The rope went slack. He leaned over and looked into his reflection and listened to the lap of the waves hit the hull.

Soon he saw her ghostly form below tying the anchor to the guide line. The rope pulled taught again. He was letting his hand drag in the water when she grabbed.

At first he thought the warning stories were true, she was going to pull him down to drown him. But she broke through the water. Her shoulders were like smooth moon colored stones and she let go. Her other hand held up a basket. Rolling and clicking together in the weave were twenty or so shiny pearls. A little bubble burst off her lips, "Here," she said. "Take these."

He took the basket from her and poured the pearls into the pan at his feet. They hailed into it like rain on a tin roof. He gave her the basket back and watched her roll over, leaving him with a flap of her wide blue tail.

CARS AND RADIOS

Seventy years and he was still there. He couldn't grow any older than high school. He held the hand of his girlfriend from then. She was a grandmother now. Bill Haley and the Comets turned into a slow Moonglows song, that dance that let him lead her across the floor. Bunting ribbons were taped to the dark ceiling, sparked by little shiny dots of revolving light.

There were white vans parked outside the gym. A photo would be taken for the newspaper the next day.

He repeated the grades over and over forever. Every summer vacation, about a month after school ended for the year, he would attend the class reunion looking for her. It was no longer surprising to see how the others had grown older while he stayed the same. And he found it was good for them too, to see him return the way he was, unchanging. He was like a living photograph from their days of cars and radios. He danced with Nan Palette all night and when it was over he led the old woman to her white van, idling by the curb outside.

ICE CREAM EVERY DAY

Big Tony stopped the kid on the corner and held the green Schwinn from moving. It didn't take him long to get to the point. "Give me an ice cream cone every day or I'll break your hand."

The kid on the bike and the girl next to him stared in silence then she nudged her friend. "Say, okay."

"Okay," said her friend.

"Okay, what?" Big Tony asked. He held his hand to his ear.

"Okay, I'll get you an ice cream every day."

"Ice cream *cone*. I want pistachio."

"Okay. Sorry…"

"Good. Good for you. I'll see you every day at…Three o'clock. Will that be alright with you?"

The boy on the bike nodded.

Big Tony let go. His mother dressed him nice. He wore a three piece yellow suit. He took out a white, silk handkerchief and dabbed at his forehead. "It's hot today." Then he left them.

They watched him bob along beside the slatted fence. "At least all he wants is ice cream," the girl said. "It could be worse."

Where the fence turned into a corner, Big Tony went with it and followed it to a tall oak tree. He stopped underneath the big leaves and put his hand on a board nailed to the trunk. With surprising grace, he climbed the wooden rungs and let himself in the door of the treehouse.

There were three kids in the room, reading comic books and he gave them the speech. When he was done, he took a look out the window and added, "It would be awful if you fell out of here and broke your leg…"

"We get it," one of them said. "You'll get your ice cream."

Big Tony tapped his wristwatch. "I'll see you tomorrow. At three thirty." He went out the way he came in. He could hear them whispering, but he laughed. Twenty feet up a tree, he took a deep breath of that summer vacation air, tasting the mint, vanilla, chocolate, cherry flavors that were just waiting for him.

"What the matter?" Bok Devlin sneered, "Can't you control your wabbit?"

"What about *your* wabbit?" the kid answered. His wabbit had tied its leash around him; he was bound up like a cocoon.

"Mine's right here!" Bok yelled. His tan wabbit cowered beside his leg. Bok's wife leaned towards him and whispered. Bok angrily turned his back on the kid and he left, his wabbit skittering beside him.

"Have a good day," the kid called.

Bok chewed on his lip.

His wife was trying to distract him. "Have you ever seen so many flowers this early? It must be—"

"Janet, I can't stand to see people like that! Look at our wabbit! Margie's great. All it takes is a little work. You have to discipline them. You can't let them act up or you'll end up like that kid, all tied up."

Janet shook her head.

"Someone should take that wabbit from him and train it right," said Bok and then he suddenly stopped. He swiveled and went the way they had come.

"No, Bok!"

Bok didn't listen to her. His wabbit trotted beside him. "We're going to get that wabbit, Margie."

He knew it. The kid was just like he left him, still wrapped up, helpless.

"Hey!" Bok poked a finger at him. "I'm taking that wabbit away from you."

"You can't!" the kid said. "It's fresh from the Moon. I just got it."

"Just try and stop me."

Bok grabbed the collar and unsnapped its leash. He dragged

the wabbit into the air and stood it before his face. Looking deeply into its rust colored eyes, he growled, "Listen, wabbit… You behave." He let go of the beast and began to walk. Bok kept one finger curled like iron to its collar.

Janet was coming towards him, wringing her hands like Lillian Gish. What he didn't see was the look his new wabbit gave Margie. Bok would make it another three steps before the two wabbits were fighting.

It happened in slow motion. Bok seemed to be watching an ancient rite on the Moon. All he could do was stare, until something snapped, and he was knocked to the ground.

Of course the news would make the papers the next day. Nobody had known that a wabbit could generate more voltage than an electric eel. Like a dancing cartoon, Bok had been thrown ten feet off the path into the elderberry and thorns.

When he opened his eyes, Janet was leaning over him. There was a blue sky overhead. Bok was deaf and paralyzed and smiling up at her.

DREAM JOB

Ken resembled a water mammal holding his hands limp in front of him. Behind thick glasses, his eyes darted about the kitchen. He had brought back a bin full of dirty dishes, cups and utensils and sat it beside the sink. He also had returned with something else. It was something someone eating in the café had left behind. Ken had dropped it into the big pocket in front of his apron. He took a quick look at it.

It was a taped box with SPY TAPE written on the edge.

In the cramped space of his part of the kitchen, classical music played. It was steamy from the dishwashing machine that would open and close all during his shift as he fed it and emptied it. There was a wetness to the air, a dampness on everything. One light bulb hung from the ceiling. It resembled a beaver's den.

He breathed with his mouth open, his glasses all teary from condensation.

"Hey, Ken!"

Ken quickly opened the dishwasher door. More steam billowed out, hiding him.

"Ken?"

He turned around, mouth open and stared.

"Ken, this gentleman wants to know if you found anything out on the floor?"

Next to the headwaiter stood a guy in a sleek suit. He explained in a gravelly voice, "I think I forgot something important."

Ken took off his glasses and rubbed them across his sleeve.

The man continued, "I was here about ten minutes ago. I left—"

But Ken shook his head no. He busily turned to pile hot clean plates on his arm.

The headwaiter said, "You didn't find anything?"

Ken shook his head no again.

The headwaiter explained to the man with him, "Ken isn't exactly a rocket scientist. He just does the dishes."

The man in the suit gave Ken a long stare.

Ken stacked the plates and began to gather clean silverware from the machine, separating them while the headwaiter and the man muttered. "He can't even talk. All he knows is dishes," the headwaiter repeated. "He doesn't even touch the tips people leave on the tables. I'm sure he didn't take your item."

"Yeah, well if anyone does find it, it's very important."

A second man in a suit filed into the narrow room. "I can't believe it's gone. You had to have that coffee, didn't you?"

"Listen. Here's my card if anything shows up. I'm giving one to him too," the first well dressed man said, jabbing his card into the Ken's hand. "Like I said, it's very important."

Drops of water already stained the card on Ken's palm. There were three letters on it, FBI.

Ken listened to the agents leave, escorted out by the chattering headwaiter. He could feel the weight of the box in his pouch, but they hadn't seen it. Nobody expected him. He spent the rest of his shift hurrying back and forth, clearing tables and restocking the shelves for the cooks, carrying that slight, mysterious weight in front of him.

When he left out the back after five, he let the screen door slam. He was out the in the cold start of evening. He walked with his head down. He crossed the street and chose where the sidewalks were shadowy. Every once in a while he took a quick look over his shoulder to see if he was being followed.

He crossed the last street that bordered the park. He sighed. He listened. It felt safer here. He took his time in the leaves and trees, and in the undergrowth he dropped low on hands and knees, and sort of scurried into the green until he popped up in a little clearing. There was a tree with a hole in its trunk. He reached into the hole and pulled out a canvas bag.

He set it on the loamy ground and untied the clumsy knot on it and spread it open. In the light of the dusk, he could see silverware, keys, a pen, a salt shaker and other little treasures he gathered from the café.

From his coat pocket, Ken took the box and he set it with the other things. His hands were trembling. He wrapped the bag up again and stuffed it back in the trunk.

There was one more thing to do.

A short walk away from his tree in the park, Ken went to a phone booth. He was so tight in the kiosk his breath panted part of the window all foggy, while he reached into his pocket and took out the card. He dropped a coin into the phone and dialed the number.

From across the busy street, he was just someone talking in a phone booth. He didn't have much to say. He hung up, looked around and emerged from the silvery booth.

Cars went past him, the rush hour traffic of people hurrying home, while he faded away like a last note of Chopin.

A POCKET PROBLEM

He was listening to the sound of her voice on the trolley. She had the perfect sound. He even stopped reading to listen. He could listen to her all day. She should be on the radio, talking about weather, or better yet, reading long books while the world carried on. He was in a dream propelled by her.

Then she laughed and said to her friend, "Do you remember when I had a pocket problem?"

His eyes opened up. He stared at the words of his opened book but they were in some other language, they had become Japanese. He actually held his breath while she continued.

"Remember how I used to take the pockets off of clothes?"

He had to close his eyes again. Her beautiful words made a movie. He watched her life of crime, stealing pockets off backyard clotheslines, her silhouette passing across the wet and drying clothes. He was flying with her on a cross-country spree.

When he opened his eyes again, time had gone by. It was just the sound of the trolley. Had he fallen asleep? There was only one other passenger, sitting up front behind the driver. He tried to catch sight out the window of where he was.

Sometimes he did fall asleep on the trolley. He was getting old, it was easy to do. What a dream though! He rubbed his eyes. When he looked out the window again, he recognized the moonlit tower of his apartment building.

He reached up and pulled the cord and a bell alerted the driver. His book was on the floor. With a sigh, he picked it up and put the haiku paperback under his arm where it would be dry from the weather outside. There were silvery marks of rain on the glass.

The trolley slowed to the corner, stopped and the old man shuffled across the aisle, out the door.

The rain did feel good on his face. He thought about the

girl while he walked on Magnolia. Now he could remember her with all those other lifelong wonders. Like time-travel, he could revisit memories of summers and other longtime ago things. She found a place in him small as a packet of garden flower seeds. He carried the sound of her voice beside the feel of hot beach sand in 1975.

When he got to the apartment, he hooked his cane to his bent elbow and reached for his key. His hand slipped across the leg of his pants. The pocket was gone. It had been lifted from the cloth like a wing flown away. His fingers ran over all that was left, only some little frays of broken thread.

DR. BIOCAL STEALS THE SPRING

It's been a long time since Susan Fenton has thought of him. There was no need to be reminded—dark days were just the result of weather, storm clouds naturally formed by ocean air meeting land. For years she worked at the dress shop and lived a quiet life. There was something though, something that crept out of the light springtime rain that peppered the display window. She had been tacking up a green and yellow silk streamer to flow around the ceiling. She lowered her arms and looked outside.

The afternoon street betrayed no slinking dangers: she saw some people walking a dog on the slick pavement, the girl at the flowershop across the street, the traffic light clicking yellow. Still, she held the hammer tightly as she stared at the gray wet city…Dr. Biocal was out there somewhere.

On the edge of town, on the rushing edge of the swollen creek, handfuls of skunk cabbages paw through the mud. Steam drifts catlike around the new plants, vented out of the boggy ground. From a hollow plastic alder stump, a metallic bud rises, a rusted stalk with a cone that blooms an aerial of petals forming a horn. It doesn't take long for all the birds to go quiet.

It was Spring, but it still didn't feel like it. Even with the decorations and the new dresses in the window. It rained for another two days and the cold of winter kept curled in the wind.

Mornings, Susan Fenton wrapped herself right out of bed and went to the thermostat first thing. When would it start to get warm? She poured cold tap water in the pan for tea, set it on the burner, then went to take her shower. By the time she was done, the boiling pan would be ready for her to mix in the tea. Everything in the morning went according to plan, leading to leaving for work, from the alarm clock moment, to the closing of her door.

When she left her place at 6:51, she was right on time. It was only a little sparrow that made her stop. It was looking at her, hopping and flapping wings, but not making a sound.

She took a step towards it, but it flew swooping short bounds that went the way she was going, to the wooded creek. She picked up her pace, she had already lost half a minute, she didn't want to miss the bus. It was raining again, of course, and now the sight of that bird did make her wonder, "Where were the sounds of the other birds?" Especially as she entered the woods under the trees beaded with buds that still hadn't opened, she stopped again to listen. How could it be Spring in here without the morning songs of robins and chickadees or even that woodsaw rasp of jays? Something was wrong, but she had to hurry on.

There were birds though, they weren't hard to miss. They were perched on the branches overhead and on either bramble side of the muddy path. They watched her, it seemed urgently. It must be awfully strange for them to be without their words.

It wasn't until she crossed the footbridge over the creek that her suspicions made her stop again. She knew she would miss the bus. That didn't matter now.

She took a few steps off the path, pushing aside crackling branches as she got closer to the odd contraption. She sunk a little, her shoes oozed over with the mud before she stopped beside it.

It almost looked like one of those ancient museum Victrola pieces, but it was stuck into a tube planted like an alien iron swamp flower.

It made an eerie hissing sound while it sucked at the air, she could feel it breathing in.

A red wing blackbird sat on a limb near her, opening and closing its beak mutely.

She reached into her handbag and pulled out a ball of the wound up green and yellow silk. She softened it in her hand and stuffed it in the horn. With a thup, it sucked in the cloth. It was stuck with an inch or so left flapping out.

The effect was like a switch being thrown: all of a sudden the birds had been turned on.

By the time Susan Fenton arrived at the dress shop, she was a half hour late, she had to hurry before her boss got there, drag the wooden sign out onto the pavement, turn on the lights and do all the other opening chores.

On her walk to work she had discovered two more of the horn contraptions and managed to dismantle them too. It had all the markings of another Dr. Biocal plot, to steal the songs from birds, but why? What would he gain from that?

Carrying the big dress mirror across the room, angled against her, reflecting the backwards world, she caught sight of his name in the looking glass and almost let the whole thing drop. The mirror happened to face into the hall where there was a directory on the wall.

There, in white letters on the black background, amidst reversed names and words, Biocal jumped out at her. She set the mirror down and turned around. She ran into the hallway to make sure.

It had been no trick. On the top floor was listed LaCoib Audio Frequencies. LaCoib was Biocal spelled backwards!

"Oh no," she breathed. She had been past that board every day she worked at the dress shop, but she never really looked at it. The names and businesses would come and go, but this one sent a shiver down her back. *LaCoib Audio Frequencies , Rm. 417*. I could go up there and put an end to this, she thought. All she had to do was lock the dress shop door for a while. She could picture herself on the fourth floor, drawn like a moth to the light of a nightmare.

She jumped when her name was called.

"Susan!" Her boss stood there in the doorway, the rainy street behind her. "What's the matter?"

"I'm—" She had to put everything she might have done away, any thoughts of mystery or adventure, she had to be at work. She would have to wait until 5 PM to go chasing after him.

The Coronet Building was nearly a hundred years old, its floors filled with offices and small businesses like the dress shop. People would flit in and out of it like bees, until 5 PM when the front door was locked. Susan Fenton left her boss counting money and finally stood in that hallway again, staring at that name, LaCoib, 417.

Without hesitating, she started up the rickety stairway climbing through the middle of the building. The stairs creaked horribly under her. She turned on the second floor and kept on going. The entire hallway length of the third floor was dark. She continued, padded on the green light cast down from above.

She paused at the top of the flight. On the wall an arrow pointed to the left, 400-410. She turned right and followed the numbered doors towards 417. She didn't have a plan. She was just letting herself find out what would happen.

The numbers were painted in black on the ordinary frosted glass office door. A business card was taped to the frame at eye level. It didn't look like the lights were on inside. From a room far away music came out a radio, a stale trombone with violins. Susan Fenton took a deep breath and pushed on the door.

It was so easy. No gorillas, no tripwires, no pit or pendulum theatrics.

And she didn't find him in there, lurking behind a console blinking with lights, or pouring the ruby red elixir of Spring

into vials. There was nothing in the room. Like Mother Hub-
bard's cupboard, it was bare. Her footsteps echoed on the
boards over to the open window where the curtains breezed
and let in sun and the whole town sound of birds.

THE AIRPLANE MAN

Casey lifted his tired head and gave a low growl. The window shook with another gust of wind. Someone stood at the glass door with the black of night around him.

Casey barked as the man entered the shop. He held the brim of his yellow straw hat, his crooked arm hid his face. He was dressed in a checkered suit that seemed to blur him as he moved.

"There's quite a breeze out there," the stranger announced.

Don Butler nodded at the odd arrival. He wasn't surprised though, he had been expecting something like this. Those big purple clouds scudding over the bridge, the wind howling around the water tower and pouring off the roofs…Weather like this always seemed to bring out the strange.

So Don just set his book down and waited for the man to speak again.

"M.O.G," the man said and pointed back at those three words painted in gold on the glass door. "Also known as Mystery Opportunity Group?"

"That's right," said Don.

Even though the wind the man let in had settled, Don couldn't help but notice the way the silver model airplane tied from the ceiling strained at an angle, pulling its string towards the visitor who could have been a magnet.

The man moved towards Don. He held a leather briefcase tightly in his hand. The P-38 Lightning pulled its leash in the air, following his footsteps.

"What can I do for you?" Don asked.

"My name's Jersey. I've heard about this place. Don't ask me how…" Jersey had a thin moustache, the kind popular in 1930s movies. He stopped in front of Don's desk. It was covered with papers, magazines, two empty coffee cups, a cardboard box lid filled with scribbled notes, an ivy plant that reached its leaves like an octopus. "I heard you might be able to help me."

Don smiled. "You're trying to get back."

Jersey returned the smile. "Bingo!"

"Well…" Don pushed back his chair and got to his feet. He was so short and wide he was almost round. As if he might roll away, he reached for his cane to steady himself. "I've got a pretty good idea how to get you back."

In the middle of striking a cigarette, Jersey squinted at Don.

Don pointed at the airplane tied to the ceiling.

Jersey stared at it and exhaled. The smoke clouded around the plane. "You want me to get in that little plane?"

"No. That's a clue. Everybody who comes in here looking for help, I figure out what they need. I know it just looks like a bunch of junk and a hopeless mystery to most people, but I look for clues." He had seen his share of time-travelers, pirates, explorers and innocents, and he had helped them all.

Jersey was making a slow circle below the airplane, observing the way it tracked him, puffing his smoke like a steam engine on a loop.

Don explained, "You see how that plane follows you around."

Jersey stopped. The plane stopped. Jersey said, "Well, it's true I am a pilot. Do you think I'm supposed to fly back?"

Don raised his cane and smiled. "Like you said: Bingo!" He shuffled around his desk. He was wearing slippers. They looked like bark wrapped around his wide feet. "Let's take a ride to the airport and see if we can find you a plane." Don could see it happening that way.

They got in Don's car. It wasn't far. Out to the airfield, there were cows in the fog. Though Casey would usually bark at them, he lay low on the floor in back.

It was dark nighttime at the airport. A string of neon pearls ran along either side of the runway.

Don parked in the grass next to a hanger. They got out. There was an airplane glowing as brightly as the moon. It moved softly as a moth towards them.

OUT OF ONE WORLD INTO ANOTHER

The double doors closed and with a wheeze the elevator began to pull itself upwards. Jakob Kale could relate. He was 89, a papery old man in a blue cotton suit clutching an equally worn clarinet case. He breathed with a faint whistle. Through the gap in the door, the floors could be seen as a yellow light going by like someone lowering candles. The pit of the elevator shaft could be glowing with them like a Viking tomb. Jakob waited. He looked forward to these late Sunday mornings when he would go to the rooftop and play music beside the pool with his friend Benny Ruel.

The elevator began to slow. Jakob held the rail on the wall. There was always a slight bump, still enough to shake him. After that jolt, the doors cracked and slid open in to a short hallway leading to the last door. Jakob's whistle had turned into a hum, a ragged song in his head. There was no way of telling what the weather would be on the other side of the metal door. It was out of one world into another. He was glad when it was sunshine waiting.

Jakob gave the door a steady push and stepped into gray. It was as if a cloud had settled down on the roof of the Lombard Apartments. He almost called out for Benny when two dark shapes became men walking towards him. Strange as it was up here, unrecognizable, he wasn't afraid of them, only a bit astonished.

They wore uniforms, epaulets and visor caps like Prussian counts, or, as they came closer, he decided they resembled the doormen of some palatial big city luxury hotel. In the fog they seemed to glide up to him.

"Mr. Kale," the one on the right said. "You don't have much time."

"Your friend needs your help," the one on the left said with a chirr. They seemed mechanically controlled.

Before Jakob could speak, he heard a yell and a splash. It sounded like Benny really was in danger. Jakob hurried around the two hotel generals. He ran in a sort of tottering way through the fog. "Benny!" he cried.

Something crashed into pieces. Jakob arrived, his shoes crunching on pottery, broken shards of clay and flowers.

Benny's hands flashed at him from the swimming pool, then sank like terrible birds. Jakob moved dreamily, grabbing a long aluminum pole with a net at the end, pushing it into the water until his drowning friend seized it. Jakob pulled him over to the tiled edge of the pool where Benny held on to life again, coughing and a gasp of a word, "Jakob…"

The old man though had taken an unsteady step backwards. It was too much for Jakob. He held a hand over his heart. The fog swirled around him, dragging him like thick ivy. He stopped at the balcony. The city, everything, was hidden from view, it was only this cloudy scene.

"You did it," said the uniformed guard next to him.

"It wasn't his time," the other continued.

Jakob couldn't speak. He clutched a knot of blue suit cloth. The pain had turned into a music, it was like a deep bell tone had been struck in him.

From a deep pocket, a guard took out a little booklet, a gold stamped cover, the size of a passport. He turned the pages of it, flip, flip, flip, and stopped on the last page. There was no room left. He held it towards the old man for him to see.

There was a sigh in the air. A step away from the building, ten stories above the street, another elevator was waiting for him.

ABANDONED TELEVISION STARS

In 2007, Edward John Smith, the captain of the Titanic was thawed out on a live television broadcast. The host of *The Sylvan Moore Show* reported each slow movement as the ice melted. Technicians buzzed around the captain, plugging in the wires, connecting him to a monitor.

"This is it, folks!" Sylvan Moore grinned.

He directed a close-up of his hand pressing the flashing button that would Frankenstein the frozen man back to life.

All that fanfare and it didn't work so well...

The captain wasn't ready for the thrill of television.

His time had come and gone. He walked offstage; he just wanted to get back to the water so he could go down.

Looking for the way, wearing his Titanic uniform around the city streets, he stands on bridges, sees reflections, goes to the aquarium, sits in the middle of Green Lake on a rented red rowboat, walks through carwashes, goes wading in creeks after a heavy rain.

When it snowed that night, he took off walking in it. His footprints led off into the trees.

He walked in a dream this time. Nothing around him made much sense after Sylvan Moore woke him up. As usual, he looked for water.

Along the white trail came a man familiar to him, though he could scarcely believe his eyes.

Edgar Allan Poe looked like the charcoal illustration in his *Tales of Mystery and Imagination*. He had been on Sylvan's show another week ago, also left and wandered through America's future just as lost as the captain.

Edward called out to him.

Edgar turned to see the man standing in the fountain. Running water kept it from freezing. After a grating pause, Poe nodded and approached the soaking captain, asked him if he needed help.

"Mr. Edgar Allan Poe, I presume?"

The dark man nodded.

"I left my copy of your book back on the Titanic." He stepped out of the fountain, his boots landed on the cement and water pooled. "I enjoyed it very much."

Before the next hour, the two men discovered *The Sylvan Moore Show* had unleashed more lost souls. They found presidents, Frederick Douglass, inventors, and plenty more abandoned television stars by the end of the day. In the evening they all gathered in front of the studio skyscraper. Emily Dickinson wrote a note for delivery to Sylvan Moore. Wild Bill, Annie Oakley and Sitting Bull kept an eye on the studio guards. It was getting tense. It looked like a mob gathering, demanding their return to another century.

DELORY MARTEL'S HISTORY OF MONSTERS

Above him he heard the thud of the shutting trapdoor in the attic and after a moment the clicking of her footsteps descending the stairs. Delory Martel glanced at his ticking alarm clock. It was after 1 A.M. Now it was Saturday, he thought. He listened to the witch in the hallway. It was a quiet house at night, until she showed up.

He imagined she would be hanging up her broom, maybe on a rack on the wall. He thought of her sitting on the edge of her bed, the springs creaking, and swore he could hear first one boot hit the floor, then the other one. He bet she wore red and white striped socks and she was wriggling her toes. Then he left her alone. It was time for him to go to sleep too. But he was working on his book. He didn't want to stop yet.

He didn't stop writing until after dawn. Some crows were cawing in the tree outside his window. He was tired but he wanted to stay awake a little longer. He was waiting for the newspaper delivery.

A branch shook in the pale morning light. One of the crows had loosened a chestnut. Delory listened to it clip through the big green leaves and hit the sidewalk.

It was another twenty minutes later and he was almost asleep in his chair when he heard the creaking, squeaky bicycle approach. Delory scooted his chair closer to the window and leaned on the ledge.

The girl on the bicycle was down there, steering with one hand and holding the newspaper with her other hand. She pitched the rolled paper at the house and pedaled past. She caught her balance and was gone.

Delory smiled. He could see the newspaper at rest in the grass. He waited, watching, and it didn't take long.

A blurry human shape smeared across the lawn from the

porch. It almost looked like a heat wave bending the air.

Delory watched the ghost pick up the newspaper and carry it back to the porch. He knew the ghost would sit on the rocker chair to read it until the full light of daylight would cause it to fade from sight. The paper would be left there on the porch rolled up and left for Delory.

He went back to his chair and sat down. He didn't use his bed anymore, not since his wife had disappeared. After eight years of marriage his wife started to shrink. Not by much; at first her clothes weren't fitting on her right. She thought she was losing weight. She tried vitamins and powders mixed with hot water, but she was going fast. Delory would go to work and come home and find her three inches shorter. By then she wouldn't leave their apartment. She didn't want to be seen, she was half the size she had been. She would stand at the window like a candle looking out.

It was apple season when he lost her. When he got up that September afternoon, careful not to press into her, he got ready for work and they said their goodbyes. She was wearing the smallest doll clothes he could find. It was a bright yellow dress with a flower painted on. He had to lean so close to hear her. He left a note folded next to her. For her it would be as big as a billboard. See you soon. I love you. She waved at him.

He couldn't see her as he stopped at the door. He was sure his voice would roll thundering to her, so he only waved back. He would be gone for over nine hours. When he finally re-turned that night she was nowhere to be seen. Of course he combed the room looking everywhere hoping for any sort of sign, a little written message on the floor, but she had gone microscopic.

Even all this time later, he was careful walking in the room. She could be somewhere floating on the dust.

The White Moth of Morning fluttered at his window while Delory slept in his chair. The moth brushed at the glass then it settled down onto the ledge and fanned its moonish wings.

This happened every fair morning it wasn't raining or windy. From the soft forest of the moth's back stepped Delory's wife. The bedroom was purple and blue with dawn. Beside her, the moth took off with a giant flapping of wings and wind, leaving her to watch her sleeping husband. He didn't know. He slept on until afternoon.

When he got up and left the house, Delory happened to be outside at the right time.

He waited by the flowers along the fence for the post office jeep to drive up to his mailbox. The windshield didn't reveal anyone driving it. Delory waved at him anyway. An envelope seemed to levitate out the open door.

"Got a letter for you," said the invisible postman.

"Great. Thanks." Delory took it out of the air. The envelope was addressed to him in his own handwriting. "Ahhh," he groaned. He knew what it was—a rejection letter.

"You get drafted?"

"No," Delory told him. "It's from an agent. Listen…" He cleared his throat. "Thank you very much for recent query regarding your novels. After carefully reviewing your proposal, I have decided not to pursue matters."

"Jeeze, that's awful polite."

Delory held the letter by the corner like the wing of a moth. There was always so much hope he put into these things that would bang into the night. It was starting to get to him. Then he remembered who he was talking to.

The poor postman used to be visible. He had been out walking his dog before work. It was a blue sky October morning and he looked up and saw a white cloud, shaped like a hawk above him. The edges roiled and transformed as it dropped at him. It was a spinning ball of cloud that hit him like a meteor.

Last summer the postman told Delory that story. He'd been invisible ever since. So Delory, holding the rejection letter, wasn't the end of the world.

"Well…" said the voice behind the wheel, "I have to push

on. Sorry about your letter. I always feel a little responsible for the letters I bring."

"Don't worry about it. I'll just send it out again. Maybe…" He waved as the jeep pulled away, seemingly driving itself. The steering wheel turned, the gas pedal went down and it left.

Delory stuffed the letter in his coat pocket and walked to work.

He thought about it though. He tried to make believe it was okay. The telephone poles stood along the sidewalk in rows. It was another day.

Food Giant's huge letters sat on the rooftop. They were lined with red neon and yellow bulbs that he would turn on at dusk. The ornamental trees lining the parking lot were starting to turn orange. Some of the leaves were falling off already. He kicked at a half green crumple and stepped over the curb.

A photo booth was planted on the edge of the parking lot. There was a silhouette in the window. He walked that way to go say hello.

If you weren't ready for the sight of her, it was quite a surprise he supposed. Brasilia Jones had been facelifted and surgically altered to exactly resemble the painting of the Mona Lisa. No, it had not been her choice—as a model, looking like that certainly narrowed the possibilities of her work. Her doctor had done that to her while she was unconscious, never dreaming what her simple nose-job would become.

Delory came around the side of her booth and then faced the open window. She had her back to him. She wore her black work robe, filling an envelope with vacation photos. When she turned around she was lit by the overhead lamps, a faded mountain landscape poster behind her, with that look of haunted ages.

"Hello, Delory," she said.

"Hi, Mona. How are things in picture land?"

"Fine."

She seemed a little glum but he couldn't tell. "How's Nat?"

"He's fine." She murmured, "He's over there." She nodded her head almost imperceptibly in the direction of the Food Giant entrance.

Delory turned. "Oh, yeah." Nat was arranging the flowers by the doors. "I'll go say hello. Good to see you, Mona."

"Likewise." A flat, almost smile crossed her pale face.

Delory walked between the parked cars until he got to where Nat bent arranging long stem roses. The back of his green uniform was adorned with a flower, stitched with Cole's Flowers logo.

"Hi, Nat."

"Delory!" Nat stood up and flashed him a smile. "You ready for work?"

"That's why I'm here."

"Well, I won't stop you," Nat said. "What do you think? Do you need a rose for someone special?" He flourished a hand at the flower display."

"No. I'm pretty much alone."

"Well, if something happens," Nat grinned, "You tell me."

"You'll know," Delory said.

Nat laughed.

Delory left him and went in the whooshing electric doors of Food Giant.

There were Halloween decorations on the windows and orange and black streamers running like rigging down the aisles. Everything was familiar to him though—the smells, the light, the aisle past the dog food that led to the time clock and the freezer where the yeti lived.

Delory stamped his card in the time-clock and fit his time-card back on the wall. The clock was old enough to have seen hundreds of people come and go. He opened an orange locker door and took off his jacket.

There wasn't much room inside. His apron was on a hook. A paperback was on the top shelf. There was a photo of his wife taped to the metal wall. He remembered the day she had been the size of that photograph—it was the last time they had gone outside together. He carried her like a doll. He had to put her in his pocket when they were followed by a crow. Just to be safe.

He put on his green apron. He noticed again that it needed to be washed. There were flour stains and some jelly. He straightened his nametag. Most of his shift was pretty simple—straightening shelves, restocking, sweeping, relieve the cashiers during their dinner breaks—it would all be done and time would go by. But first he had to wake the yeti.

The freezer had a latched heavy wooden door with a round porthole. The window was frosted with white cold.

Delory read a note taped to the window before he took a hold of the silver handle and heaved the door open. A sighing blast of frozen air puffed out. There were boxes on pallets, big bags and piles of frozen food wrapped up.

The cold blew from a hole in the floor. He rubbed his arms and stood next to the sturdy wooden ladder. A faint pour of Classical music on the radio drifted up. The radio cord was plugged into the wall and it snaked down to the sound below. Delory gripped the cold plug and pulled it from the outlet. The music stopped. He waited in the quiet. It wouldn't be long.

"Hey!" Delory said.

In the ice cave under Food Giant, the yeti stirred. It sounded like a piano being dragged across gravel. The ladder next to Delory shook as the yeti climbed up out of the deep sea colors.

Delory said, "Hi, pal." He stepped backward to make room for the creature.

With hands like oven mitts, the yeti pulled himself up to the freezer room.

Delory glanced at the big furry face, the red eyes and steaming nostrils. "Looks like three pallets came in with that other stuff." He pointed. "Also, they want that block of ice turned into a swan." He stomped his feet, "I'm getting cold in here!" he grinned. "I guess that's it for now. Oh—and we need a wheelbarrow of chipped ice when you can get to it. Thanks." He patted the yeti's thick yak fur arm. "I'll see you later, amigo." The yeti had his work to do, Delory had his.

The day at Food Giant passed into evening.

The neon rooftop sign had been on for a while and Delory stood just outside the back door amid the slag of broken down, wet cardboard boxes. Nighttime had crept over the neighborhood and lied down to sleep. Blocks away, the lights on the playing field fuzzed at the dark sky. Rain hissed under the passing car tires and tapped and beaded on the milky car parked on the shiny, slick asphalt.

Delory liked to take his fifteen minute break out here. This was his time to be in the air, away. He stood in the spilled green light from the store and let his thoughts go out over the rooftops until he was emptied out. Who was he, standing there, so motionless? He was there for fifteen minutes then if you blinked he was gone.

That was the nature of time.

Two hours later, he took his supper break. He left Food Giant again.

This time he went through the whooshing front doors and looked back only to revel in the sight of the burning and twinkling sign on the roof. Mona's photo booth was closed and he crossed the street in a light rain that only furred on his skin.

There was a late night noodle shop where he could have a hot bowl and read his book, the paperback he had tucked under his arm.

Painted on the window of the shop was the word *Goulash*. From the ceiling inside, a dim chandelier was suspended. The tables were lit by candles. It looked like an eighteenth century room.

Delory entered and clearly heard the music that had only been a trembling murmur from outside. It was a gypsy song, a crackling recording played out the brass horn of a Victrola.

Two elderly women sat at a table with bowls of soup and

the Count peered around the corner from the kitchen to see who had entered his shop. A long black shadow fled from him across the floor.

"Aaah," the Count sighed. "Delory...How are you this evening?" A small white towel was wrapped over his wrist. His other arm held a dish he had been drying off. The Count bowed towards Delory; a dipping gesture that creaked with five hundred years of manners. He was an elegant old man. The candles flickered whenever he neared.

"I'm good, Count. I just stopped in for some noodles."

The Count nodded and turned on his heels, causing his black cape to swerve on his shoulders like a pair of wings.

Delory chose his usual table, a round wooden circle not much bigger than a steering wheel. He sat with his back to the wall and set his book before him. It was a used paperback he got called *A Big Book of Yellow Paint*. The bookmark showed he was almost done with it. He would probably finish it by the time his meal was gone.

While Delory sat there, the Count returned from the kitchen carrying a plate. A dark thick slice of pumpernickel roosted on it like a crow. So silently had the old man appeared, the click of the plate on the table made Delory jump.

"Excuse me. I won't be joining you, Delory. I have already eaten."

As the Count returned to the glowing orange light of the kitchen, he paused beside the Victrola. His long fingered hands deftly flipped the record over and he bit the needle into its shiny groove. Another song began. He billowed, quiet as a ghost, past the two women who sat staring at their soup.

When Delory returned to work, there were only a few cars parked in the lot. The Food Giant sign was now a blooming field of bright lights. The night could have been an August day and it reminded him of an afternoon two months ago when he was walking to work.

A red car was parked in the corner beside a wilting ash tree.

Delory stopped nearby to watch because something was going on. There was a woman next to the car hood writing furiously. She spotted Delory and sputtered, "Can you believe it?! Someone left their dog in this hot car with the window barely rolled down! I'm leaving them a note. People like that shouldn't be allowed to have dogs." She lifted the windshield wiper and slid her note underneath. "It's animal abuse!" she continued. "Just look at the poor thing," she bent closer to the window as the wooly creature inside shifted and neared the glass. When a shiny black nose pushed at the crack in the window, the woman groaned tragically, "Poor thing…"

"What's the note for?" came a voice from inside the car. The window rolled down a foot or so. Delory could plainly see the furry face.

The woman gasped, fish-like.

Delory could tell it wasn't a dog—he was a boy, maybe a teenager.

"I said, what's that note of yours all about?" He held out his thickly haired hand and snapped his fingers, "Lemme see it."

"What?" she clucked.

"Is it a love note?" the Dogboy asked slyly. He showed his sharp white teeth. "You wanna ask me out on a date?"

"You—"

"What's the matter with you, lady?" He reached a long, hairy arm outside and tried to grab the note off the windshield but she was suddenly aware, snapping her hand at the note before him and ripping it free. She clutched it in her fist.

The Dogboy chuckled. "That's alright…You can tell me what it says."

The woman's horror had passed a little. She was able to speak, "I thought you needed me. I hate people who leave their dogs in cars. I thought you—"

The Dogboy was still chuckling. Then he stuck his tongue out and let it loll. "Oh, I like it hot, lady."

She let out a shriek and fast as that turned and sprinted

towards the street.

The Dogboy stuck his head all the way out the window and howled after her.

Delory passed the spot where that happened.

The rain reminded him of another day.

When Delory was a boy, his family had a black telephone that sat on a shelf by the stairs. It was a rotary dial. The numbers were all on a wheel and it was there for a game he liked to play once in a while when nobody was home. He would randomly dig a finger into the little plastic circles and hopefully those seven numbers would connect with a ring.

"Hello?"

Whether it was a man or a woman he would tailor his question accordingly. He might say, "Are you the man who picks up the garbage?"

There would be that pause on the phone line, like a flower bud when you wondered what the color would be when it opened. And come to think of it, maybe that was why he made those calls when the weird mood struck him and he was only ten and alone.

"No, that's not me, Sonny."

"Well, your house must be a mess!" Then, heart pounding, he would thump the phone back into its cradle and glare at it like a toreador. That was certainly part of the thrill of making those calls too. Usually, he would stop there. He had been successful. He had crossed the trapeze wire without falling down. He could go outside, climb a tree, or ride his bicycle, or a hundred other things. But that rainy day he put his hand back on the phone.

It was raining cats and dogs. Even after all those years, he remembered how he felt looking out. The window was a movie screen of a day too wet to play. He picked up the receiver and tried dialing again.

"Hello?"

"Are you the woman who washes?" he asked her.

All he heard in the phone was water. At first he thought it was the rain outside, the runoff from the roof peaks and leaky spouts, tapping gutters, shrubbery and leaves. But there was more. There was all kinds of water and he swore there was the ocean too. He could hear waves. Could he even smell the sea right through the phone?

"Yes…" she answered.

His cheek was wet where the phone rested against his skin.

He pulled the slippery black plastic from his face. Water streamed down his arm, soaking the green carpet. There was seaweed clinging to him. It took all his strength to use his other hand to press the telephone buttons and break the connection.

The water stopped pouring out of the receiver. It was over, but it was like a wave crashed through the window.

As Delory sat down on the stairs, miles away, she put the shell back on the rock. It was dappled by the sunlight on the waves above her. A school of minnows made a wide turn around her.

Not much else happened at work until Delory got done.

He was leaving it behind, crossing 46th and cutting down Woodlawn Ave.

That's when he spotted the glow-in-the-dark family, half a block away, making a halo of light in the shadows of the chestnut tree. You could have mistaken them for ghosts if you didn't know who they were. These late nights, or very early mornings, he would often see them on his walk home, doing something as ordinary as this—standing there like a string of light bulbs attracting moths.

He supposed this was their time, what they looked forward to all day when the sunlight made them like everyone else. Now, this was their world.

Delory stood on the curb in a dark splash of shadow and watched them.

Delory was too far away to tell what they were doing. They looked like sunflowers. There were five in the family. He couldn't remember their names but he would wave when they passed.

It was raining a little. He could see a few stars in the one patch of sky open in the cloud layer. The other night he saw an owl bouncing along the rooftops.

When he got close enough to them, Delory waved. It looked like they held violins, their arms were up and sawing, and once he got closer he could hear them playing. It wasn't Mozart. They were making the sound of crickets. It was such a perfect imitation that Delory had to tuck himself in to a shadow so he could listen. He loved that summer night sound. He wished their serenade would travel to his house. It was only a block away. He hoped they would follow him there.

The lamp on the corner lit the bumpy rainy streets. He walked on the smell of wet fallen leaves, then he was there, ascending the cement stairs to his house.

A glance up at the roof peak and he saw the seagull standing on the chimney. It had its head tucked beneath its wing, sleeping. It would be dawn in a while, the east side of the steep roof waited to catch the first soft touch of sun. Below the gull on the west side, the roof would stay cool with the blue silver night painted on.

Delory went inside thinking about that seagull and feeling like he too was perched between day and night. Who else was up at this weird hour?

The glowing family was…The Witch might still be soaring around the wet sky…Come to think of, it was mostly the monsters of one kind or another.

The carpeted stairs creaked to the hall on the second floor. He found his door and entered his room. The house was quiet. Even the ghost must have been sleeping in the eaves, waiting for the morning news to arrive.

WHEN I'M A DEER

I don't have much time before it happens. Already I have a headache and reaching up to my temples I can feel the beginning of horns as my fingers ball in my hands. I only have a minute or so before the transformation is complete so I get out of bed quickly. Standing makes the room spin. It's best to crouch.

My fists slip clumsily pushing the door open. Our trailer has two bedrooms, attached to this slightly bigger room. My son sleeps in the other bedroom. He's probably awake now though, worrying. Our dog gives a whine too.

I put my hands on the floor and I'm walking on all fours to get to the front door. This has happened enough times now that we've got all the kinks worked out. I use my mouth to grab the cord and the door swings open and I'm free. I give one of those leaps a deer can do so easily and I'm flying. I think of my son for a second and then, as I land, everything that is human about me is gone.

I'm in another world. Off the bank of the driveway, I'm in the woods. When I move, I listen and wait, still as can be. I am with every cool flower blossom and sweet stalk of tall grass, breathing all the stirring underfoot and up above, the moon is humming and pushing shadows down through the trees. Eyes glowing, ducking back into the leaves, every sound is attached to something.

That's where the time went, between leaving our trailer and coming to, in this cold wet morning in the weeds behind 7-11. It isn't a good way to wake up, shivering, hugging my icy bare legs. I would hate to be discovered this way. Fortunately, when I'm a deer I always know where to cling out of sight and all I have to do is wait…My son is on the way. Soon I will hear the baying of our dog as they track my path from last night.

THANKSGIVING STREET

When Richard arrived in town he was homeless for a while. He stayed at The Lighthouse. He observed the people there and found a couple he could trust, who he could leave the shelter with in the morning. Every city has its nearly hidden homeless world, alleys, corners, shadows, and every city works differently, functioning unique to the circuitry of its streets. Richard would learn how to spend those days in all kinds of weather until nightfall brought them back to The Lighthouse.

One thing he noticed everyday—there was a woman in a wheelchair stopped along the wall of Rite-Aid. She had a can full of pencils, a bowl for money and she was always smiling. That's what got Richard's attention. How could she smile like that day after day, in the rain, in the cold, in that wheelchair with her pencils? Richard asked his two companions about her. He said he wanted to go over and give her some coins and maybe a miracle would happen.

But they stopped him. They weren't even laughing. There was nothing smiling about her, they told him. They were serious. They said it happened every day at three o'clock. Come back here then and you'll see.

So Richard spent the day with them haunting the town, on the move, stopping where it was safe. Richard broke from them when it was getting close to three and made his way back to Rite-Aid. He stood just off the sidewalk between a tree and a wall and watched her. Living on the street you come to believe just about anything. There really are monsters and cold horrors, but also shining moments where something amazing could happen. Your luck could flip and land suddenly as a coin, heads or tails, good or bad.

She was checking the watch on her wrist under that rugged thick coat. Pretty soon her secret would be out. Richard watched her gather her pencils and pull up her money onto her lap. She leaned and watched the street to the left. Every day it happened this way, his companions had said.

A limousine pulled out of the traffic and stopped beside the Rite-Aid curb next to her. Then that smiling, crippled woman stood up and folded her chair.

The limo driver opened the door for her and she stashed her wheelchair and her money and pencils and got into that long luxury car and was driven away.

Richard asked me if he told me that story before.

I said no.

I was waiting for my bus to show after a long day at work.

It was cold sitting on that stone bench, watching crows, listening to him. Thanksgiving was the next day and he told me his plan.

All week he had let his beard grow. He still wore the same clothes, that homeless uniform. Once you've been there you never really leave. Even with a room in a boarding house and warm places and enough money to buy what he needed each day.

Tomorrow he was going to the Old Town café for a free Thanksgiving dinner. Sometimes they didn't give you very much. He would get his plate and eat his spoonful of potato, turkey with cranberry sauce. Then he would go back to his room. He would shave and put on different clothes. Once he looked like a new person, he would go back out into the cold November street and return for another plate of free food.

THE THREE HEARTED SAINT

The Three Hearted Saint from India or Tibet lived in a yellow house, sitting like a statue, surrounded by chanting and the clicking of little chimes. If you walked the neighborhood you could hear it going night and day like machinery until one morning, before the dawn bell, the white painted door opened and out he went.

Not in his bright robes, he walked along wearing clothes from the donation box. There was no reason to think he was anyone although his footprints left diamonds of dew on the pavement.

He followed the street slanting to the sea. All the trees pointed the way. Cars parked by the curb or some rolled past him, wheels crackling on cement.

He seemed to know where he was going. When the street turned into a bridge he stepped off the sidewalk, ducked beneath the bare branches onto the steep hillside crumbling cold earth, weeds and trash.

On the sides of his shoes, he slid down the embankment. The bridge vaulted overhead making a wide dark slash across the gray sky. He stopped with the loose stones and a rolling bottlecap at the edge of the dirt. A flat stone was there, waiting for him. He sat beside the hurried river, took a deep breath and shut his eyes.

While The Three Hearted Saint reflected on the water, a salmon rippled in the shallows next to him. It stopped and stayed in place just out of reach. Its body moved slightly, enough to keep it there, nibbling on the edge of concrete.

The Saint was so used to the sound of cars overhead, rumble and thump, the salmon was something new and he opened his eyes. The fish dallied at the cement, as if tasting it, testing it to see how many salmon it would take to pull the city down, bridge by bridge, filling the streets with streams. It could all begin with this one fish. But that didn't happen. It gave a quick splash and returned to the river flow.

Like the salmon, he let the world go around him. He was only one more being. Still, when the man at the store asked, The Saint almost told him his name. That would have been a mistake. There were people looking for him, maybe the storekeeper was one of them. So he kept quiet and opened his hand paying coins for a can of peaches.

The store with its own little temple bell closed behind him, ringing as he left. Truthfully, he must have been known. Every day he bought peaches there, he was leaving a trail.

And a trail can be followed. It has beginning and end. His is one that goes back along the wet sidewalk, to the river's edge, under the bridge where a shrine of empty peach cans grow.

JACK'S COW

What do I know? I've never been past the fence. The field has been my home. When I say field, believe me, picture the ground packed hard like clay and here and there pockets of muddy water. That's where I used to be. For some reason, I'm walking outside on the road. Jack is taking me somewhere.

I pretend it's okay. What do I look at? Fence posts, hedges, the clouds. I've never gone this far before. I never wonder. There's a rope around me. It doesn't hurt. Jack just pulls me along. I guess he wants me to see something.

I didn't know I could walk this far. Oh, there's a farm I never saw before. Look at that meadow. I didn't know the land could grow like that. I imagine myself there…Each day in the grass tall enough to brush me. Buttercups!

Back where we live, Jack, his mother and I, we have a clapboard house sitting on dirt. I spend all day looking for something green or with petals, dreaming about a field like that… But Jack won't stop to let me in there. He pulls on my rope. We must be going somewhere very important. And Jack is so serious too, like the time he tried to fix my fence. I wish Jack would just let me look at those clovers. I guess he wants to go with this road and follow it all the way to the distant steeple and roofs of town.

If it wasn't for this rope, I'd be across that ditch in one leap. I could live in there and die of happiness.

A splash from the direction I wasn't watching made both of us jump.

Someone said something, "You selling your cow?" and Jack pulled me to a stop.

"I am," said Jack. "For a good price."

I didn't like the man who stood there leaning on a fence post all wrapped with barbed wire. I didn't like him but there was nothing I could say to Jack.

The man took a wet footstep out of the irrigation ditch. "I'll give you five magic beans," he said. He reached in his long coat and found a flowered handkerchief. From it he poured the magic beans into his open palm.

Jack took a step closer. The shiny beans watched him like owl eyes.

I mooed. I pulled on the rope. I didn't like this at all. I know Jack. I know what's going to happen next.

ED STOREY, THE 2 STORY MAN

Every summer the circus came from the train station down Ohio Street, right past their house. Every year they set up chairs on the lawn. You could hear the band and then for the next five minutes the circus would march past.

This time, in back of the chairs, Ed Storey walked back and forth, from their driveway to the lilac tree. He was ten feet tall, moving with the smooth grace of a giraffe. This year Ed was ready for the circus. He wore a suit with a sign board that said *For Hire* on one side, and *The 2 Story Man* when he turned around.

The milk truck flashed its lights at Ed and the driver waved.

Below, in front of Ed, his family waved back at the driver.

By the time the circus began to near, the Storey's yard looked like a circus too. Everyone in the chairs held sparklers, a girl had her dog jumping through a hoop, and the boy on stilts went back and forth. He was tall as the corner of the roof. He could reach out and touch the TV antenna.

"When the circus sees me," he told everyone, "I'll be on my way." All his life he wanted to ride on those buses and trains with the circus. Everyone was here to wish him the best.

"I see them, Ed!" his sister called up to him.

Ed had some juggling pins but he would hold onto them until he saw the ringmaster. Juggling on stilts wasn't as easy as it sounds.

The band echoed up the street as it approached, block by block, then it was loud and there before them. Like a record running out of steam, the band staggered and stopped in front of their house. Clowns and dancers and ponies were piling up. They all stared as Ed Storey began to juggle.

As the circus ran into itself and dammed up the street, it overflowed the sidewalks into yards and gardens. A zebra got loose and ran down an alley. There were tightrope walkers climbing the telephone poles. A lion cage parked in a driveway. The ringmaster had to push his way to Ed's yard. Before he could say anything or notice Ed on his stilts, everyone in the crowd gave a sigh like a pigeon coop. The ringmaster turned around to stare at the decorated yard—the dog, the sparklers, then he caught sight of Ed Storey on stilts, holding his arms out like wings.

The boy pressed a button or turned a lever and all of a sudden, a rocket launched him off the stilts. Gray smoke frayed beside the house into a steep contrail curving out of sight over the town.

The people parked in the chairs on the grass were the first to react. "Eddy!" his mother screamed. That started others and the people in the circus too had never seen anything like it. But with the bigtop performers all stopped and overflowing, the ringmaster had to act quickly.

"Great!" he shouted. "Great finish, Ed! Now, everyone get moving!" He shouted and pushed until the circus began to untangle and move forward. He did sneak a glance at the sky but there was nothing to see, the smoke had drifted and the trees covered the distance. Of course he hoped the kid would be okay, but he had to get the circus to the fairground. Time was money—that's what they said—and the show must go on. He tipped his hat towards the Storeys. He helped push the lion cage back into traffic. The circus parade continued.

The Storey's ran for their cars. They left their yard with overturned chairs and the stilts dropped like chopsticks. They drove off in the direction Ed had flown.

As far as tricks go, it was a pretty good one and though it was genuinely dangerous, Ed felt sure he could pull it off. He wore a rocket pack. He pressed a button or turned a lever and the rocket took off while he dropped through the smoke to the ground and hid. Everyone would be watching the rocket. When everyone gave up hope, he would reappear.

That was his plan anyway, as the rocket motor fired. He forgot to unlatch the rocket pack. He was attached as it arced over the wires and trees, fast as a cannonball.

The circus show did go on. The ringmaster tried to forget the incident and he tried his best with the audience as he brought on act after act.

Around the tents the night blazed with bright strings of light bulbs and searchlights further off by the growling generators. Nobody seemed to be looking for a flying boy.

About a half mile away, the poplar trees sighed beside the drive-in. Outer space filled the long wide screen, dots of stars and a rocket. Cars were parked in rows pointed towards the movie.

The movie was one of those typical stories, someone was all alone or so they thought until they were running for their lives.

The people who went to see the circus missed what happened at the drive-in.

Ed Storey stirred to life. He discovered where he was…Laying along the top edge of the theater screen. He turned himself and unlatched the spent rocket pack. It fell off and landed with a clang in the rose garden below.

Very carefully, Ed sat up, holding onto the bolted metal. He rubbed a bump on his forehead. He must have been knocked unconscious. He could see all the cars, his audience.

As he crawled along the top of the screen, one by one the cars noticed him. They flashed their headlights and the horns drowned out the movie. Hands stuck out windows and clapped.

Ed found the ladder that climbed down the back of the screen. He had to take his time, holding tight sometimes. He didn't want to fall this close to the circus. He could see the glow of their tent in the lights spilling out of hundred watt bulbs.

BATTLESHIP

It was a beautiful day. The blue sky was a sea with only a few clouds floating white islands a long way from the golden sun. Randall was on a date. He pulled the oars and they tucked into the sparkling lake with barely a whisper. Swallows whirred low. Balloons were stacked around the lake like flowers.

It would have been a lot prettier if his date had shown up. No such luck. He had waited forty minutes by the entrance to Enchanted World and she never appeared. Plenty of other couples and families came and went. It was a popular spot to be, especially so on a day like today…Such a warm and soft summer afternoon.

Randall stopped rowing. It only made him hot. He loosened his tie, took his suit coat off and tossed it where his date would have sat. She should have been smiling there, instead of a rumpled pile of his best blue cloth. The music from the merry-go-round drifted across the smooth dance floor of water. For just a moment, Randall considered throwing himself overboard. But dark as the still water was, he knew it was a manmade lagoon and probably no deeper than three feet.

He let the oar blades dip back into the shallow black pond. He gave a halfhearted pull towards shore.

"A-7…" A strange voice echoed from the speakers mounted on tall lampposts circling the lake. The air whistled and not more than fifty feet away, a great splash broke the lake.

Randall was so surprised his right hand slipped on the oar and nearly let it go. The water roiled as if a shark thrashed its way back to the depths. Randall took another stronger draw on the oars.

The speakers buzzed again. "H-9…" This time the high pitched whistle shrieked and an explosion of water nearly threw Randall from the boat.

Soaked, ears ringing, Randall yelled, "Hey!" at the shoreline. Some people were stopped by the other parked rowboats. They waved to him.

"C-3…" A splash of water occurred near the land and Randall could see more people stopping and cheering as the geyser deflated. Randall was only vaguely aware of the clapping for him as he bent his back and rowed fiercely. The shore wasn't far. The explosions were random. There was no reason to think he couldn't make it.

SMILE REPAIR

As he drove, hurrying through each yellow traffic light, taking corners with a screech, making a wild plunge into the other lane to pass a bus, he worried he might already be too late. He couldn't remember the last time he smiled. He may have used it at work, passing someone in the hall on a Friday afternoon, but the last time that smile had come out of the blue...It must have been years.

"Hurry, hurry, hurry!" he told the delivery truck in front of him. He was close to Smile Repair, just a few more blocks to go, when suddenly he felt his mouth shift. "No!" he screamed as the smile fell off. It drifted from his face like a dry leaf off a tree, tumbling lightly to land on the seat next to him.

Pulling out of the traffic to the curb, Gil Harris parked the car and leaned over the passenger seat. The edges of his smile crinkled up slightly off the cover of a book resting on a pile of other strewn things. He hadn't cleaned his car for weeks. Gil carefully tapped the smile onto the flat of his hand. It felt no more than a feather. Before it could float any further, he opened the book and slid the smile onto the page. He carefully closed the covers, trapping it safe in there, pressed like a flower. It could stay flat between the pages until he got to the clinic. Of course he couldn't smile, but he was greatly relieved as he steered back onto the road.

At the next corner, Gil turned and there, towering over the asphalt was the big neon sign, Smile Repair. It grinned in the air, turning slowly on its pedestal. Gil would have smiled. As it was, he pulled into the lot and grimly parked in a spot near the door.

He leaped from the car with the engine still knocking and gasping, rattling itself off.

The double glass doors of Smile Repair hissed open and he

dashed across the plush carpeting to the reception desk.

Right away, he noticed the pretty secretary smiling at him, and right away he felt like a prize fool, unable to return the smile. He stopped at her desk and muttered, "I lost my smile." He rubbed his taut mouth.

"Oh dear," she sympathized. She opened a folder and her painted fingernails flickered through some paper, searching for a form. "Here we are…" she said and there was that startling smile again.

Gil touched his mouth. It felt like a broken wing.

She held a pen poised over the page. "When did you lose your smile?"

"I just did. On the way here. It's still in my car. I put it inside a book."

"That's wonderful," she said. "Why don't we go get it and see if we can reattach it?" She stood. The flowers printed on her red dress swerved and realigned all around her. "Where's your car?"

He couldn't talk. He pointed.

She laughed. It wasn't cruel, it was smooth and sparkling a sound as poured water.

Gil was almost certain he was blushing. He quickly turned toward the entrance to lead the way. Regaining his voice, he told her, "My car's right there." Through the glass doors, his Pontiac grill gave them a lopsided grin. The bumper was held up by a shock chord, looped and hooked around it. As he fished for his key, the glass doors whooshed open.

"It's a lovely day," she said. For her, he was sure it was.

Gil stuck his key in the lock on the passenger side and re-acted. "Oh! It's already unlocked!" For a second, he worried someone may have opened the door and stolen his smile. A good one could fetch quite a price.

He gave the door a heave. A plastic water bottle and a crumpled section of newspaper fell at his feet. He quickly tossed them back at the seat. Gil turned, wishing he could make a joke. Her tanned legs stood next to him, close, tapering into a pair of shoes the color of buttercups.

Taking a breath, Gil searched the chair. "I put the smile in a book…" What a mess his car was! It looked like he'd been living in that front seat. "It should be right here…" He ran his hand under the seat and felt among the wrappers, a map, what felt like a bat, and then he found it. It must have slid off to the floor when he parked. His fingers folded around the book. "Here!"

Gil stood up outside the car and showed her the book.

"Wonderful!"

He caught her smile again. The worry had left him, she could do so much with that smile.

Gil opened the book and flipped through. A lot of words went by and he saw something else flash past. "One second…" He dug a thumb back into the pages and started over. "This is it."

She leaned closer. He could smell her long hair. The book got heavy and tipped ever so slightly. His smile floated free and curled on itself like a campfire ash rising on the air.

Gil gave a startled yelp and reached for it, but the smile had caught some unseen breeze. It was so soft and light and on its way, gone.

Gil's arm dropped with the book like a pendulum.

If there was any hope left in him, it seemed to have flown too until he felt her hand touch his shoulder. She spun him round to her and pulled him in for a hug.

Gil stood there warmed by her. He reached his hands up and touched her shoulders too. When she loosed her hold and took a step back, he opened his eyes. It could have been the nicest smile he had ever seen.

MOONCALF PRESS

It was over. The light in the world was turned off. There were still some lights on in the building below but the globe that slowly turned and glowed blue on the rooftop of the Post-Intelligencer was dark and Parker Weems and everyone else who worked for that newspaper would have to find new jobs.

Parker's old van almost seemed to limp out of the parking lot. It sputtered and shook across the wet asphalt and turned to join the stream of traffic on Elliott Avenue. The windshield wipers smeared the rain. A helicopter stayed stuck on the glass like a firefly.

Around the south end of Lake Union, past the marinas, the billboards, the flower stand, and over an iron humming bridge, Parked steered the way home. He shifted into third gear as he went uphill, through the park. Trees bunched up to the road and reached overhead touching branches. The radio reception, the orchestra he was listening to, burred into static, got lost in the big wet garden.

Parker rolled his window down to listen to the engine churn echo back from the maples and firs. You had to know where to look in the shadows to see the tiled roof of the pagoda go by.

As the park turned into his neighborhood, the radio sputtered back to life. The news was on. It would have been headlines if there was still a paper—it was the second night of rioting downtown. "None of the violence is expected to stop the president from addressing the world leaders." Parker turned the radio off and braked.

The van stopped beside his house. It was dark and quiet. He could hear the rain patter on the rhododendron leaves before he rolled the window back up. Pocketing the key, he got outside.

He clanged the door shut and walked the mossy stones to

the garage. This was the sort of thing he did for years, coming home from work, going in the garage. A painted sign on the wall read Mooncalf Press. He liked to think this was his real job.

Parker tapped the light switch and went back to his Volkswagen.

The van was filled with cardboard boxes, things the P.I wouldn't need anymore. There were type trays filled with letter blocks, rollers and reglets, tympan papers, ink and oil cans, quoins and gage pins, all that had rattled away with every bounce in the road. Parker twisted the handle and opened the side door and saw there was something more.

Someone had been hiding in back of the van for all that ride in from the city. The figure moved awkwardly on his knees out of the stacked boxes into the light spilled from the garage doorway.

Even though he couldn't believe it, Parker stammered, "Mr. President?"

"Yes," said the familiar tall man, crouched against the ceiling. He glanced at the windows, "Is it safe to come outside?"

Parker took a step backwards. "Of course. It's just my driveway."

The president stepped out and gave a quick nervous look around. "Is that your house?"

"Yes, would you like—"

But the president passed right through Parker's words in his hurry to the garage. Shutting the door of the van, Parker followed him.

"I'm sorry to impose on you. I can explain." The president stood near the printing press. "Would you mind closing the door?"

Parker did so, but he stood there staring. It was like watching the man on television.

"Thank you. I said I could explain," he sighed. "I'm not so sure I can." The room was silent.

"Well, I don't blame you for running away," Parker said. "If that's what you're doing."

The president gave a short laugh.

Parker continued, his words becoming almost giddy, "I don't know how you lasted this long. It must be crazy. Everything you've been through. I remember when you were elected, we were so happy. We had such faith in you. It felt like you were going to change everything—stop all the wars and lies and the corruption that has been killing our planet. I had so much hope in you. I believed you were a revolutionary. I considered you one of those rare people who come along at just the right moment in history when they are needed the most… Then I don't know what happened. It got so I couldn't even read my own paper, the news was too upsetting. I can't even tell what you want anymore."

The president just stood there and listened.

After he said it, Parker felt like a heel. He was a bad host for talking to his guest that way. Politics seemed to bring out the worst in everyone.

"Is this a printing press?"

Parker nodded, "Yes."

The president gave the big metal spindle wheel a small push. "Does it still work?"

"Yes, of course. I make books, folios, I typeset broadsides." Parker held up a sheet of parchment, "Like this one." It was filled with the words of a poem. "You can put it up on a wall."

"How long would it take to make something like that?"

Parker shrugged. "Not long. I'm pretty good at this job. I've been doing it for years."

"We don't have much time. They'll be here pretty soon and I'll have to go back." The president picked up a tray full of letters and gave it a shake. "And there is something I want to say."

THE SLEEPING CONTEST

Janson Wares and his wife Barbara parked on the street in front of the big house perched on the hill. Barbara held a glass salad bowl on her lap and breezed out the door. She was excited about the party. Janson was not. He had been a work all day and all he wanted to do was sit at home and watch a movie, or listen to some calm record. He was tired. When he shut his eyes and let his head relax against the rest, he felt like he could fall right to sleep.

The next moment there was a rapping on the window and his wife barked, "Janson! What are you doing? It's cold, let's go!"

He saw her standing out there on the sidewalk, the breath of her words hung in the air. He said, "Okay, okay." It would have been so easy to be asleep.

She was right though. It was cold, too cold to be standing around outside.

"Come on," she said.

"Here," he said, holding out a hand, "Let me take the salad."

"No, I've got it." Her shoes clicked on the icy pavement, staying a few steps ahead of him. "Don't you love those lights?"

There were colored Christmas lights strung up the steep driveway. It looked like the runway for an alpine gondola. Janson mumbled. He remembered there was still a cord of lights wrapped around the fir tree back home, waiting to be reconnected to this year's electricity.

The house above them glowed amid the bare branches of lilacs and other dormant flowering trees. Barbara puffed the way.

"Look how lovely!" she said. There was a big wreath on the door with a red ribbon and more bright lights climbing the wall like ivy. "We have to get our lights back on," she said.

"I know. I was just thinking that."

Barbara cradled the glass bowl and knocked on the door. While they waited, they could hear people in there, the murmur and buzz of talking and laughter and a Christmas song, Bing Crosby laying it on thick.

The door made a snapping sound as it swung open into the cold night. Warm air bellowed into Barbara and Janson along with the smell of cinnamon and a wood fire.

"Hello!" Sonya Perez waved her arms and beamed at them. "Come in, come in!" She hugged them each as they entered the room. "Let me take that delicious salad, Barbara."

Janson followed them as the hallway turned into a big room bunched with people. Janson wandered over to the table and gave it a look. He took a cracker. He took a bite and crunched it woodenly. Barbara's salad had been added to the rest of the platters and servings.

The cracker had not done much for Janson's appetite. With the beginning of interest, he watched a small fly that had just landed on the rim of a bowl of jello. It rubbed its hands, readying itself like a diver to hit that green shimmering pool.

"Janson."

He left the world of the fly. Sonya stood beside him.

"You look mesmerized," she said.

"No. I'm just tired."

She smiled. "Me too."

"If I closed my eyes, I could fall right asleep."

"Me too."

"I bet I could fall asleep before you," he said suddenly.

"I doubt it."

Now that he looked her in the eyes, he could tell. Despite all the flurried energy of throwing a party and entertaining everyone, he could see that she was really tired. It was written on her, dug into the lines around her face.

She said, "It would only take me a minute." There was no hesitation in her voice. She was absolutely sure.

Despite that and the sudden fact that the challenge had actually made him more awake, Janson said, "Forty five seconds."

She wasn't backing down. "Thirty five."

The party was just a sound in the background.

"You can't beat me," he said.

"Oh yes I can. Thirty seconds." And just like that, she sunk to the floor and was under the long flap of tablecloth. Her face reappeared in a moment, "Well, come on. Let's find out who can fall asleep first."

"It won't be you," Janson said as he lowered himself. On all fours, he pushed aside the patterned cloth and found there was quite a bit of room underneath. It was easily as wide as a double bed.

Sonya lay there opposite him with her hands knitted across her stomach. "Alright," she said. "Get comfortable."

He did. He chose to lie on his side, his legs curled slightly, his left arm tucked below his head. He shut his eyes. He smiled. Yes, he thought, this was good. He could win. "I'm ready."

"Alright," she yawned. She whispered, "Begin."

Begin, Janson thought, I'm beginning. It was as simple as letting go of a big heavy balloon, letting go of dry land. The distance between him and what had been grew further and further apart.

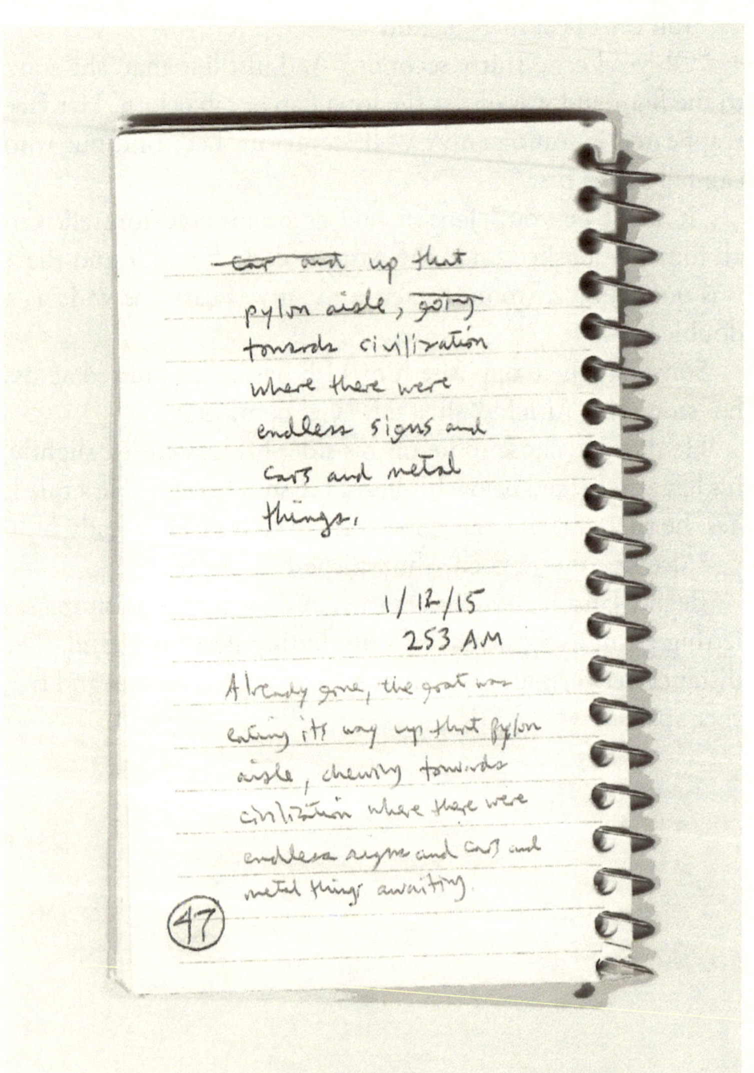

Original notbook with ending of "The Cartoon Goat."

THE CARTOON GOAT

"I've got the pig trained. I put a few kernels of corn under the stump and they root around it, loosening the earth so I can pull it out." Dion paused to take a sip of coffee. "Lately I've got them taking down the old barn. They pull down the rotten boards along the foundation and I come by afterwards with a magnet and pick the nails they left behind."

"Why don't you just get a goat?" I asked. "To eat the nails."

He scoffed. "Actually, goats don't eat metal. That's a commonly held fallacy."

"Really?"

"Do you know how that began? Back in the day when people had trash piles in their yard, they would observe goats apparently eating tin cans. But that's not what was happening. The goats were eating the glue off the wrapper."

"Really?" I repeated.

He nodded and folded his hands behind his head.

"Well, in cartoons goats don't have any trouble eating metal. I think what you need is a cartoon goat."

"I'll tell you what," Dion said. He stood up and with a grand gesture took out his wallet. "You find me a goat that can eat nails and I'll give you fifty dollars."

And that's how I ended up at Animation Rentals.

It's not the kind of place you would expect. I would find out. But it would work.

I turned off Lakeway into the tight little lot next to the post office. Right beside it is Animation Rentals, a low building with moss growing on the loose gutter. I parked my pickup truck in front of the scratchy looking bansai pine tree and stared at the storefront window.

What a sight.

A poster of a cartoon rabbit filled half of the glass. He wore a top hat, a tuxedo and a monocle that twinkled with a star of light. There were other smaller posters of cartoon characters forming a sort of quilt that covered the window and hid what was inside. The door had a big yellow card, a smiling alarm clock and the word OPEN.

I've never been to Animation Rentals before. I've only seen their commercials on TV and it was that smug look on Dion's face that made me drive there, open the door and enter in search of a cartoon goat.

If the window display was meant to convey a place of bright, bustling cheeriness, the truth couldn't be further off. Animation Rentals was crowded with cardboard boxes piled haphazardly on shelves along the walls and in the middle of the room. The air in there smelled of cigarette smoke. The source stood about ten feet from me—a white rabbit well over six feet tall, wearing overalls and a straw hat, with a cigarette pinched in his yellow teeth.

"What can I do you for?" he drawled.

The thought of bringing this eight foot rabbit to Dion's farm crossed my mind. It would be worth it to see the look on Dion's face.

The tall white ears shifted towards me to catch my reply. The hat had been cut with two slits to allow them through.

"Actually," I said, "I came here looking for a specific character."

The rabbit gave me a sour look. "We prefer to be called creations." The colors in him seemed to ripple like a provoked cuttlefish.

"Right. Sorry. I'm looking for a specific creation. I'd like to rent a goat."

"Hmmm." He hooked his thumbs beneath the straps of his overalls. "Seems like there's one in stock. Follow me."

A cartoon chicken scurried out of his way. I watched its brightly colored feathers shimmer under a low shelf.

The rabbit took me down a steep set of creaking stairs. It

smelled even dustier down in the basement. He flicked a light but it just seemed to make the room gloomier. Tall shadows loomed, thrown from pallets full of more cardboard boxes. He slowed at one pallet bed. It was strewn with straw. He jabbed a white thumb at it as we passed. "That's where I sleep," he told me.

Just beyond, we stopped at a big metal door. It was constructed of metal patches like an iron blanket hung up to dry. I read the painted letters on it. Absolutely No Admittance. Below was an asterisk shaped like a snowflake and, This Means You. The door was padlocked to the wall by an absurdly thick short length of chain.

"What's in there?" I asked. My guess was a gorilla. And it must have been an angry one.

The rabbit turned and gave me a withering look. "Not a goat."

Then his shuffling gait continued with me walking in his acrid wake. There was another door. This one was less ferocious looking. Tacked to its ragged wood was a cardboard shingle. The rabbit gave a hoary resemblance of a laugh and read the scrawled word on the sign, "Goat." He wrapped his mitten sized paw on the handle and turned it open.

The room, no bigger than a broom closet, was lit by a light bulb suspended from the ceiling on a black wire.

The cartoon goat regarded us and gave a bleat. It didn't look like much. It was painted a dull shade of purple. There was an orange handkerchief tied around its neck.

The rabbit reached out a long arm and grabbed the goat by the handkerchief, lifting it from the room like a suitcase. Its legs hung down straight, its yellowy eyes darted from the rabbit to me. "Will this do?" the rabbit asked me.

"I guess so. Does it eat metal?"

The light bulb shine glinted on the big rabbit's bifocals as he tipped his head back to laugh. After that sawing ragged outburst he rasped, "This goat isn't particular about food." Shutting the door he said, "Here," and passed the goat to me.

I took it by the handkerchief handle the way he had done. It was light as newspaper. "Mind
your shirt sleeve."

The goat's teeth clacked together, missing me by an inch. "He is hungry, isn't he?"

The rabbit shrugged. That rabbit had seen it all.

Carrying my strange cargo, we retraced our path in the gloom and then up the stairs to the room we started in. The rabbit led me to a desk in the corner. He sat in a whicker chair that shrieked under his weight. He tapped some numbers on a calculator key pad and said, "That's thirty seven dollars, ninety cents for the day. The price goes down to thirty five for each additional day."

"What a deal," I said.

"Cash or credit?"

I set the goat down to dig out my wallet. I was counting out bills when I felt a tug at the hem of my trouser leg. Sure enough, that little devil had taken a bite from the cloth. My white sock showed like a bone.

The rabbit snickered as I scooped the cartoon goat airborne again and held it out at arm's length.

"He might eat you clean out of house and home."

"Yeah," I said, "Well, I hope not," as I struggled to leaf out forty dollars.

"Shoot," the rabbit chuffed. He scooped my money and placed it in a tin box. He took his time looking for change. The cartoon goat was really giving me a struggle. His back legs caught me with a sudden kick that stung my thigh.

Of course the rabbit loved that. Everybody loves a rube. He gave me a crumpled dollar and some loose change and pulled at his chin thoughtfully, "Looks like you got your hands full now."

"Yeah, thanks." I shoved the money in my pocket. I had to hold the dervishing goat with both hands.

"See you soon," the rabbit told me with what I think was a wink.

As I limped for the door, he called out, "You sure you don't want to buy insurance?"

"What for?" Of course I should have, but right then I just wanted out of Animation Rentals. I could barely hang onto the cartoon goat and I surely didn't want to give that hayseed rabbit any more of my money. I did wonder what cartoon he dropped out of. He had probably been drawn just for that job.

I left the store and hobbled around to the back of my covered pickup truck. With the squirming animation in one hand, I dropped the tailgate and pushed the goat into the canopy. There was plenty of room in there for him to sulk and cast moody looks out the little oval window. I was glad I had taken the time before coming here to clean everything out. If I'd even left a wrench in there, I'm sure he would have eaten it.

I shut the gate and locked it, leaving him in that near darkness. I rubbed my leg where a welt was already forming. When I got home I'd have to put ice on it. Stupid goat…I wondered if this was a bad idea. But I had already paid for a day's use of the goat. Also, I didn't want to see that rabbit's reaction if I tried to return it so soon.

So I got behind the wheel and started the engine. All the happy, colorful posters danced across the window of Animation Rentals but I knew what was really inside.

While I reversed, I did the math. The goat rental was $37.90. Dion would give me $50 when he saw the cartoon goat in action. I drummed my fingers on the steering wheel. That meant I'd make a profit of $12.10. It hardly seemed worth it.

As I turned sharply back onto Lakeway, I heard a clatter of hooves from the cab hidden behind me. I didn't exactly feel sorry for the goat slipping around back there.

The traffic on Lakeway was bad, bumper to bumper. I couldn't even see the lake so many buildings had crowded up to the shore. It would be nice to get out to Dion's farm. He had a few acres out in the county. He had gardens, a big pond stocked with koi, and of course those pigs he was so proud of. Only another half hour and I would be there.

I turned on the radio. I listened to a baseball game. It was raining there. In the most dejected dialogue, the announcer described the harrowing view out his press box window…The sheets of rain, the shallow lake that was forming in right field. He went into such detail I almost turned the windshield wipers on, though here it was just an ordinary day.

I found another station and decided I preferred music as the road carried me out of the city.

Trees took the place of telephone poles and in a wide swatch of open field I could see the mountain surrounded by clouds. I opened the window to let in some of that clean air.

Dion lived down a gravel road. I had been there a few other times. He had a party once a year where he would serve one of his beloved pigs, baked and crisp with an apple in its mouth.

The truck hit a pothole and my leg struck the gear shift lever. For a second I dropped the wheel to grab my poor leg. The truck veered crazily towards the irrigation ditch cut deeply into the shoulder. I stomped on the brake with a few choice words echoing about me. The gravel slid beneath the wheels.

What kind of maniac lets a hole like that grow in a road? I cursed Dion and his pigs and his stupid road and stepped outside to cool off. Also, I wanted to make sure I hadn't broken the axle or blown the tire.

I checked the right side for damage. I got low enough to smell the manure roiling in the ditch. The suspension looked fine though, as far as I could see, and there was still air in the tire. It had just been a wicked hole in the road.

When I walked to the back of the truck though, I discovered an even bigger hole. Half the tailgate had been gnawed clean away in a pattern just big enough for a goat to leap out. I felt a few drops of rain prick my skin.

Why had it not crossed my mind that a cartoon goat would

eat the metal of my truck? What an idiot I had been!

Of course there was no sign of it on the gravel road behind me and the fields on either side were like paintings. Who knew where it hopped out? I would have to retrace my steps.

There was no room to turn the truck around. I had to put it in reverse and drive with the engine whining, window rolled down, scanning the brush and nearby woodland, watching in the mirror to stay on the road.

I braked when I got back out to the paved road. I looked both ways and pulled out. The truck clunked into forward gear and sounded relieved to do so. I knew the cartoon goat would stand out in those paddies or hard scrabbled fields—it was such a blur of color it would be hard to miss.

The radio was no help. The stations had turned to static. We were either too far from the city or this bleak farmland just didn't attract the music and chatter of radio waves. I turned the dial off.

It seemed like a lost cause. With all the land around me and all the time it had taken me to get this far, the goat could be anywhere.

Then as the road bent around a crop of stones, I had a clear view.

On a river, miles away from here, a dam had been built and out of that boiling water came the power of electricity, which was conveyed to the city across the land on tall pylons. I'm sure you've seen these before. The towers walk through forest, over hills and valleys, making a path that's clear on either side as if that humming electricity is its own invisible raging river, pushing through land. I slowed the truck to a stop on the shoulder and stared.

From the side of the road, off into the gulley and into the weeds where it escaped, that cartoon goat made a beeline for those tasty metal works. With nothing holding them up, the wires lay unspooled and tangled on the ground. Some were sparking and had started the fuzzy glow of brushfires. Already gone, the goat was eating its way up that pylon aisle, chewing towards civilization where there were endless signs and cars and metal things awaiting.

THE BEAUTIFUL DAYS

They were going through boxes in the garage, sorting out things into piles they wouldn't need anymore, when he reached into cardboard and found something he hadn't seen in years.

"Would you look at this?" he said and pulled the black cloak out to show his wife. He chuckled. The cloth of the tuxedo was wrinkled and musty, like a moth found locked in a drawer. Embroidered on the silky black lapel was a gold light bulb. He held it out to her and announced, "Mr. Know It All!"

She sighed. Her hands were full of old clothes. She tossed them to the floor and pointed, "Throw it on with the rest."

"Are you kidding?"

He folded the coat over the edge of the box and dug back in for more. "Here's the pants. Good as new…And the hat!"

"Oh, no," he heard his wife mumble as he fit the plastic light bulb shape onto his head.

"Ask me something," he grinned at her.

"Not this again. I thought we were done with this long ago."

But it was plain to see he wasn't done.

He gathered the old uniform and drove to the drycleaners downtown.

He sat in a red chair by the counter and watched the machinery, waiting for that moment when it would reappear on the overhead track, wrapped in clear plastic.

He tried reading a magazine but he was too excited. He paced the linoleum floor, stared out the window, and jumped whenever the conveyer started to move.

There were other tuxedos too. A couple times he hurried up to the counter, only to be disappointed. It would be different when he was Mr. Know It All again—he wouldn't ever be wrong.

When his uniform finally did arrive, he paid in a fumbling

hurry and he was so eager to put it on he rushed to the bathroom to change. Didn't Superman used to do that? he wondered. Or did he use a telephone booth? In any case, the small wooden paneled room would work just fine for his transformation. He was done with his old self and threw what he wore before into the trash.

With his tuxedo and light bulb hat on, he gave himself a grin in the mirror. "If you've got a question," he said, "I've got the answer."

There was something about the design of the hat—no, not something—it was scientifically constructed to make use of brainwave activity, and as he left the drycleaner, his mind felt like a windmill, spinning with thoughts. He was almost lifted off his feet, propelled down the sidewalk in his new tuxedo.

The first person to stop him was a postman. "Hey, Mr. Know It All!" he called. "Long time no see! Hey, what's the zip code in Albuquerque?"

"87048," he instantly replied.

That was only the start. As he continued on his way he was like a squeaking wheel, chirping out answers.

"Andalusia…That would be the #105 bus you want…The Keystone Cops…" He was like a light, attracting moths. He forgot how exhilarating it was—also exhausting, answering questions as he roamed the town. It had been a while but the answers came easily, he hadn't forgotten anything.

After an hour, he began to tire. It was too much work, he couldn't handle it alone. He sat on a park bench, but they sought him there.

"The Pythagorean Theorem…Two cups of flour…Daylight savings…"

There didn't seem to be anywhere people wouldn't find him.

So many facts rattled about in his mind he could almost feel the gears gnashing in, catching and overheating his brain.

"Mozart," he told a young woman holding a fussy baby, "Try the clarinet concerto." And as he rubbed his temples, it dawned on him. Short of hiding out in some subterranean branch of the sewers, or on the roof of an abandoned building, the only place he could go was home.

He reached his arm out into the traffic and hailed a cab. He was lucky he didn't have to wait long. He only answered three questions before he opened the yellow checkered door and got in the back.

He gave the address on Maple Street and shut the door. He waved goodbye out the window and sat back in relief.

It was getting late. Somewhere along the way the sun had set. The cab was warm and the radio played.

The driver cleared his throat and spoke. "You're that guy everyone's talking about. Mr. Right Answer?"

He sighed. "Mr. Know It All."

The driver laughed. "Quick—what's two million times 17,000?"

"Thirty four million."

The driver shook his head. His eyes looked back from the mirror. "That's some talent." They slowed for a red traffic light and the driver raised a hand off the wheel. "Okay, here's what I really want to know." His hand held a folded newspaper. "Will Steady-Go take the first race tomorrow?"

"What? I'm not a fortune teller."

"Come on! I'm asking you a yes or no question. So will my horse win?" He took the cab wheel again and drove them through the intersection. "Well…What'll it be?"

Mr. Know It All sighed. "Yes," he whispered.

"Hah!" The driver took a punch at the ceiling. "That's great!" He looked over his shoulder for a moment with a toothy smile. "Now we're getting somewhere. What about Polaroid? Should I put some money on them?"

"I have to get out here." The cab was slowing behind a car at another light. Mr. Know It All opened the door. With one foot outside, he turned to throw some money over the seat. "This is my stop."

"Come on!" the driver yelled.

He began to run. The sidewalk was a row of stores closed for the night. Every once in a while someone would call out to him, but he made it to Maple Street without being stopped.

He was glad their house was unlocked. All the smarts in the world and he had thrown his key out with his old clothes. He shut the door and locked the latch. Nobody could follow him inside. That was fine with him—he was done being Mr. Know It All. Right there in the hallway, he took off that tuxedo and plastic light bulb hat and dropped them on the carpeting.

"I'm back!" he called.

He heard his wife say his name.

"You were right!" He started down the hall. "That was an awful experience. I'm never wearing that uniform again." He pushed the bedroom door open.

She said, "I knew you'd say that."

The sight of her in her red satin Smarty Pants suit stopped him in his tracks. He hadn't seen her like this since that long ago time when they were going out. Seeing her standing there in the light of their room, time just seemed to have fallen back. The sight took returned him to the beautiful days, when he would wear his uniform and she wore hers, and they would walk out together, arm in arm, to take on the whole wide world.

These stories are collected from spiral notebooks and these little hand-sewn books that appeared in editions of only three or four:

LAWN VETERANS (1989)
THE SHRINKERS (1990)
PAYING FOR WATER (1990)
GOOD DEED RAIN (1991)
TREE FROG (1991)
THE END OF BERYLLIUM (1997)
YOUR FAVORITE WORLD (1998)
BRAND NEW GHOST (1998/1999)
UNIVERSAL THIRTEEN (1999)
CHAMPION DREAMERS OF THE WORLD (2003)
TRELAWNY CABLE CAR (2003)
THE LAST OHIO MORNING (2004)
THE NEW BOOK OF ENDANGERED BIRDS (2004)
A PARENT'S GUIDE TO RAISING PIRANHA (2005)
SINKING CELESTIAL (2006)
WITH THE UTMOST KINDESS AND CALM (2006)
THE PEACEFUL ISLAND (2012)

I also include stories from my self-published magazines:

PIE IN THE SKY (1992-1994)
UP (1995)
WAVE (1997-1998)
SUCH & SUCH (2007-2008)

Other Books by the Author

Ohio Trio (Bottom Dog Press 2001)

Bowl of Water (Bottom Dog Press 2003)

Another Life (Bird Dog Publishing 2007)

Home Recordings (Bird Dog Publishing 2009)

The Mermaid Translation (Bird Dog Publishing 2010)

The Selected Correspondence of Kenneth Patchen
    edited by Allen Frost (Bottom Dog Press 2012)

The Wonderful Stupid Man (Bird Dog Publishing 2012)

Saint Lemonade (Good Deed Rain 2014)

Playground (Good Deed Rain 2014)

Roosevelt (Good Deed Rain, 2015)

5 Novels (Good Deed Rain, 2015)

Opposite page:
My best story review, from my 9th grade teacher, Mrs. Weber,
in 1980

A

I walked up to the massive steel hull of the moored passenger ship. Printed in bold white letters on the stern was written "Titanic II." The four smoke stacks bellowed out a light black mixture which curled through the air and disappeared. The ticket I was holding stated that this was a one way trip to Mexico. On the way back I would fly. As I shuffled into the line leading into the ship, I was unaware of a dark cloaked figure following close behind me.

Part of my assignment for my newspaper had been to report on the cruise of the Titanic II. Large as this huge liner was, it was quite crowded and it took several minutes to get to my cabin. When I finally arrived, I set my baggage on the bed and walked out the door into the densely crowded hallway. I pushed my way through more people and made my way towards the bow. I dropped down a flight of stairs and stared out over the wooden railing. The waves curling around the bow and the gulls screaming at each other mingled together to form a sort of pandemonium. Suddenly I heard a

www.ingramcontent.com/pod-product-compliance
Lightning Source LLC
Chambersburg PA
CBHW050949210726
48287CB00004B/1196